Elizabeth Beacon h[illegible] [illegible]rytelling and, with the West [illegible] [illegible]s a glorious setting for her b[illegible] [illegible]er education as a mature stuc[illegible] [illegible] in an office, before finally tu[illegible] [illegible]atical heroes and their stubbc[illegible] [illegible] dream job; writing Regency [illegible]

Regency Surrender

August 2018

September 2018

October 2018

November 2018

December 2018

January 2019

February 2019

March 2019

April 2019

May 2019

June 2019

July 2019

Regency Surrender: Forbidden Pasts

ELIZABETH BEACON

MILLS & BOON

First Published in Great Britain 2018
By Mills & Boon, an imprint of HarperCollinsPublishers
1 London Bridge Street, London, SE1 9GF

ISBN: 978-0-263-26790-7

52-1118

MIX
Paper from
responsible sources
FSC™ C007454

This book is produced from independently certified FSC™ paper to ensure responsible forest management.

For more information visit: www.harpercollins.co.uk/green

Printed and bound in Great Britain
by CPI Group (UK) Ltd. Croydon, CRO 4YY

LORD LAUGHRAINE'S SUMMER PROMISE

Chapter One

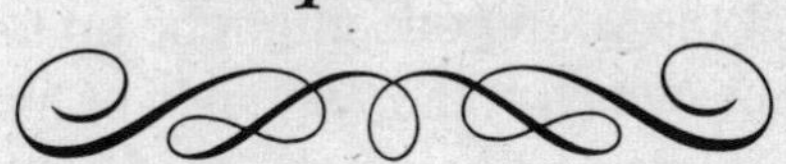

'So where is this Cataret House School you might recall if you weren't feeling "quite so mazed" by the heat?' Sir Gideon Laughraine, otherwise known as Mr Frederick Peters, asked the pretend idiot he'd hailed for directions.

The idler scratched his grizzled head and shrugged as Gideon bit back a curse and wondered if anyone else would be about on such a sweltering afternoon. Unless he found a field being worked close to the road, there was probably nobody who wasn't at work or staying inside out of the sun within hailing distance, so he dug in his waistcoat pocket for a small coin and held it up to encourage the man's memory.

'That's it over yonder,' the man finally admitted with a nod towards a farmhouse on the opposite side of the valley that looked as if it had delusions of grandeur. 'Likely you'll find the old girl in, but young miss went down the track to Manydown a half hour ago.'

Gideon bit back a curse and flipped the coin to the knowing rogue before turning his weary horse and following in young miss's footsteps.

'I wouldn't want to find the old besom in a hurry either, mister,' the knowing idiot told him before slouching off to spend his windfall in the local ale house.

'Needs must when the devil drives,' Gideon muttered grimly, not much looking forward to that encounter either, then he forgot the 'old girl' by wondering what the young one might be up to.

Would she blench at the very sight of him and look as if the devil was on her heels, or give him that delightful smile he still remembered with a gasp of the heart all these years on? Who knew? Lady Virginia Winterley was right though; he had to find out if his wife would ever smile at him again outside his favourite dreams.

Dear Boy, his late patroness and friend began the letter that heralded the third quest on her list, left in her will to chime with every new season of the year after her death. He'd had no inkling he was one of the unfortunates she'd decided to do good to until that demand he do as he was bid for the next three months was put in his hand by the new Lady Farenze.

I am quite sure it will come as a great surprise to you when dear Chloe tells you that you have the next quest on my list.

Well, yes, you're quite right there, my lady, he thought with a shake of his dark head to admit she'd outfoxed him once again.

It should not be, she continued, as if she were standing at his shoulder and could see the sceptical expression on his face when he finally realised why

Luke Winterley's new wife had sought him out to hand him the letter from Lady Virginia.

You are my beloved Virgil's secret grandson, and it is only out of consideration for your cousin, Lord Laughraine, that we have not been able to claim you openly. If we did so it would take away the only legal heir he has left to carry on his titles and estates and we both love and respect Charlie Laughraine far too much to do that to him or you. I know the true facts of your birth have been a trial to you ever since you were old enough to realise what the gossips had to say about your father's true parentage, but they are a great comfort to me.

I shall always be glad I had time to watch you grow from the haunted, unhappy boy I first encountered into the fine man you are today, even though I've had to do so without my darling Virgil at my side. It has been such a pleasure to see you make your own way in life, much as I know Virgil would have done if he wasn't born the heir to vast estates and the Farenze titles.

I don't have words to say how much I loved my husband, and finding a way to drag you into my life was a selfish act, since you resemble him so closely in ways that go beyond a purely physical likeness. You do have that, of course, although I think James favours him more in outward details than you do, dear Gideon. You also have a true heart and a kind nature to balance that sharp mind of yours and it has been a de-

light for me to come to know you so much better these last few years than Virgil ever could while he was alive, for all his pleading with your father to let him at least know his grandson.

I think Esmond would have done anything to hurt his true father and withholding you from him was a way to show he had the power to hurt the man he blamed for ruining his life.

Gideon stopped and stared into the middle distance. He refused to think about his vexed relationship with his father and both Virgil and Esmond were beyond his intervention now, so he could worry about his wife instead. Callie had gone a determined distance from her aunt's house on this devilishly hot day. He managed a rueful smile at the thought of what she would have to say about his heart and even the faith in his kindness Lady Virginia made so much of in her letter, not much to his credit he suspected. Once again he wondered what was so urgent Callie needed to walk out to find it on such a sweltering afternoon. Was she meeting a lover? A jag of hot jealousy made him gasp and a shaft of pain clutched at his gut.

After her last arctic-cold letter telling him never to contact her again, then nine years of silence, she wasn't going to welcome him, but Lady Virginia was quite right, drat her. He checked the inner pocket of his coat where it lay across his saddle brow and heard the reassuring crackle of hot pressed paper against silk lining. An unconventional lawyer like him often needed a safe place to keep important letters, but this one was a very mixed blessing and its contents were already imprinted on his mind.

I know what I am going to ask of you is more than I demanded of dear Luke and my beloved godson, Tom Banburgh. I hope you have come to know them as a true kinsman and a stalwart friend these last six months, by the way, for you have lived without either for far too long.

So, your quest is to find your wife, my darling boy, and ask her for your heart's desire. I can't tell you if she will listen or be generous enough to give it to you, but you have to find out if there is any chance for your marriage, or between you make an end to it with dignity. If you go on as you are, you will be a haunted and lonely man for the rest of your life and I do so want you to be happy.

I was lucky enough to find the man I could love with everything I am, even luckier to live with him as long as I did, but you two children managed to love and lose one another before you should have been out of your schoolrooms.

Seek out that unlucky girl of yours with an open heart and discover if you can live together, Gideon. If you cannot, then agree on a separation and make some sort of life apart. I believe two such stubborn and contrary people were made for one another, but there's no need to prove me wrong for the sake of it.

What you choose to do about Raigne and the splendid inheritance you are legally entitled to, as the last official Laughraine heir, is up to you. My advice is to stop being a stiff-necked idiot and listen to your cousin. Charles Laughraine has never been in the least bit like your supposed grandfather and his uncle, and I thought Sir Wendover Laughraine one of the most soulless and heartless men I ever came across, but his nephew is a very different man. As you have called him your Uncle Charles ever since you were old enough to talk I have to suppose you realise he is very happy to consider you part of his family, whatever the true facts of the case may be.

No doubt your wife will go her own way, but as you and I both know her to be Lord Laughraine's natural granddaughter, she owes him a hearing even if she won't listen to you. The future of such a large estate and all the people who depend on it must be decided before many more years go by. I wish it could be otherwise and please believe Virgil would have been delighted to openly claim you as his grandson, even though your father hated any reference to his own irregular birth and would never hear of it.

Charlie Laughraine is nigh as old as I am now and time will outrun you three stiff-necked idiots if you are not careful. All I have to add is a warning never to take anything that aunt of hers says at face value and look deeper into why that young romance of yours went so badly awry.

Don't you shake your head at me again, Gideon Laughraine, I know you long for the love of your young life with everything you have in you a decade on from losing her. Admit it to yourself, then all you need do is find out if your wife suffers the same burden and do something about it.

Gideon almost wished he could forget the last letter from his friend and one-time mentor and ride back to London as fast as this unlucky beast would go. He could carry on with the nearly good enough life he'd made without his wife and the family they might have rejoiced in by now. What a fool he was to have agreed so readily to act as an extra pair of ears and eyes during Lady Virginia's year of discovery for her four victims, though.

How had he thought he could stay uninvolved, even without this latest bombshell? No, a strong sense of justice made him corrected himself; they weren't victims. The first two quests made Luke Winterley and Tom Banburgh the proud husbands of much-loved new wives. Two triumphs chalked up on the slate for the Lady then and, if he knew anything about himself and James Winterley, the score would be levelled by two lone wolves beyond redemption. Would Lady Virginia had wasted her energy on a more worthy cause and let him and Winterley go to the devil in their own way.

When she set out so determinedly this afternoon Callie intended to get to Manydown as fast as possible, so she could get back before anyone noticed she'd gone, but this clammy heat was defeating her. She slowed down but carried on, despite the nagging suspicion she should go back to Cataret House and give up on her dream for today. The sad truth was she couldn't face another afternoon of idle boredom now her pupils were with their family or friends for the summer. After a week of this heat and being at the beck and call of her aunt with no excuse to be busy elsewhere, she felt she must leave the house before they livened up a dull summer with an argument that ended in tears and days of stony silence.

It was quite wrong of her to feel like a virtual prisoner at Cataret House when the school wasn't keeping her too busy to notice. Aunt Seraphina had been quite right—they'd both needed to start their lives anew nine years ago. They were let down and betrayed by two very different husbands at the time, so why not pool their limited resources and hire a house big enough to start a school? It had seemed a wonderful idea back then; they could live modestly on the profits and she could help fifteen young girls of mixed ability and middling birth learn about the world, or as much of it as young ladies were permitted to know. Her life had felt blank and hopeless at the time and Aunt Seraphina's idea was inspired, but now a little voice kept whispering *is this all*?

No, she wouldn't listen. She had experienced the storm and lightning of her great love affair and all it turned out to be was a mistake that hurt everyone she had ever cared for. The school made enough and their pupils were happy. If future wives and mothers were better informed people for having passed through their hands, maybe in time the world would change and ladies would be more highly valued by a society that regarded them as the legal chattels of their husbands, fathers or brothers. Here she was busy and useful and known as spinsterish Miss Sommers, and that was enough, most of the time. Nine years ago it had been impossible to drag the failure of her marriage about like a badge of stupidity so she reminded herself why she had wanted to leave youthful folly behind and shivered even in this heat.

Living in genteel poverty as her true self somewhere out of her husband's orbit would have been worse than waiting on her aunt when the girls were away and feeling shut into this narrow life. Most of the time she enjoyed helping other people's daughters learn about the world; and they employed a visiting dancing teacher and music mistress to add to Callie's more academic teaching. Knowing her niece had absorbed the late Reverend Sommers's scholarship far more eagerly than his daughters had, Aunt Seraphina let Callie teach the girls some of the lessons their brothers could expect to learn as a matter of course and where else could she do that? She reminded herself she was always a stranger to herself during the summer when there was little to distract her from the life she'd chosen. At this time of year she must fend off memories of passion and grief that were best forgotten; the secret was to occupy herself and this was as good a way as any.

Her mind was racing about like a mad March hare this afternoon, so even tramping the hills on a blazing hot day obviously wasn't distraction enough. Perhaps it was time to escape into daydreams then. They gave her a way to ignore all but the worst of Aunt Seraphina's scolds even as a small child and now they took her to places she hadn't even thought of back then.

The hope of living a different life firmed her resolution to find out if her writing could lead to more than she dared hope when she first put pen to paper.

It was probably best not to speculate on the reply she might find waiting for Mrs Muse at the receiving office in answer to her latest correspondence with a maybe publisher. She had to distract herself from this wild seesaw of hope and dread. So she gave up looking for wildlife to identify on a day when it was asleep and wondered idly how ladies lived in more exotic countries where it was like this much of the time. She was sure high-born women rested during the burning heat of the day and did not walk alone when barely a breath stirred grass grown lifeless as straw against her bare ankles. Right now she could be lying on a silk-cushioned divan, saving her strength for the cooler night to come and dreaming of her lover. The contrast between such an idle and slumberous afternoon and this one snatched her back into the present. She sighed and wished she could ignore questions about where she was going on such a sultry day, so she could order the gig and drive herself to Manydown.

At least her ancient straw bonnet kept the full force of the sun off and Aunt Seraphina couldn't accuse her of ruining her complexion, but she dreamt wistfully of airy silks, made to whisper against her limbs as she strolled about her fantasy palace. It would feel sensual and pleasantly wicked to go barefoot on a satin-smooth marble floor and for a moment she felt as if silky stone was under her feet and wriggled her toes in sensual appreciation, which made her jolt back to reality again to hot, sweaty and gritty English feet tramping through a baking landscape.

It was nearly nine years now since Grandfather Sommers had caught the fever that killed him from Aunt Seraphina's late and unlamented husband. When Reverend Sommers followed his unworthy son-in-law to the grave there was nothing to keep either of them in King's Raigne, and leaving the village where she grew up meant Callie could be herself again. It was a common enough name and nobody was going to look for her, so she went back to being Miss Sommers, spinster, and Aunt Seraphina became Mrs Grisham with an imaginary husband to mourn when their new neighbours came to gossip. They were less than twenty miles away from Raigne and it felt a world away from that famously grand house and the tightly knit Raigne villages.

Better not to think about her old life, she decided, dreading the hurt and sorrow those memories threatened even after nine years away. Where was she? Ah, yes—going without stockings, partly for economy and partly because it was too hot to endure them. Perhaps the old, impulsive Callie was alive under the schoolmistress, after all, so she concentrated on walking and her quest, but it was too hot and familiar a walk to distract her for long.

Anyway, it was impossible to feel bold and sensuous and longing to be shameless with a handsome lover when you were weighed down by chemises and corsets, petticoats and a sternly respectable cambric gown. Somehow she couldn't force the fantasy of that longed-for lover back into the dark corner where she kept her deepest secrets today, but nine years on he wasn't the man she had fallen in love with, anyway. If her husband stood in front of her now she probably wouldn't recognise him, and the thought of the painful arguments and angry silences before they parted made her happy to dive back into the life of a fantasy Callie, who longed for a very different lover from her one-time one, so where had she got to with that?

Ah, yes, she was languorous with longing to see him again after spending mere hours apart. There would be cooling fans waved by unseen hands to stir the heavy air and cleverly devised cross-draughts in that marble palace under a merciless sun. She drifted away from the court ladies idling away the scorching afternoon with gossip as they waited for the world to stir again. When it did the scent of exotic flowers and rare spices, the flare of bright colours and wild beat of music and dancing would light up the night with an urgent promise of excitement and passion and longing fully sated at long last. It was too exciting to allow her to worry about who was in and who was out at court. Of course, they would all be weary again the next day and doze through the hot afternoon, so they could dance when night fell, but it would be worth sore feet and all day waiting for the thrill of being totally alive again in her lover's arms when darkness fell.

Something told the real Callie if she had to live such a life she'd rage against rules that forbade a lady contact with the world beyond the palace walls, but flights of fancy weren't meant to be realistic. She sighed and knew she was hot and sticky and unpleasantly dirty once again, so what would the eager Callie Sommers of seventeen make of her older and wiser self? Not much, she decided, wishing she could go back and warn the headlong idiot not to dream so hard or passionately so that her today could be different.

Shrugging off memories that wouldn't change for all the wishing in the world, she resisted the urge to throw her bonnet into the nearest hedge and be less suffocated by the life of a confirmed spinster. She untied the shabby ribbons instead and felt the faintest trace of a breeze on her damp skin. It was the gritty unpleasantness of grey dust changing to mud between her sweaty toes that made her escape into a dream of walking naked into a wide pool full of rose-petal-scented water this time. Imaginary Callie felt coolness and luxury surround her and knew she was loved and valued above riches by the prince of this splendour.

Now that was the most dangerous fantasy of all. She shook her head to refuse it and felt a brief thunder of blood in her ears. Aunt Seraphina's dire warnings about females who recklessly strode about the countryside with no regard for the conventions might come true if she was overtaken by dragging heat on a public highway. Wondering if her aunt ever looked at her, Callie tried to be amused by the idea plain Miss Sommers could excite ungovernable passion in any male who found her sprawled on the road.

She needed to keep her wits about her if she was going to walk to the receiving office and be home before she was missed, so no more daydreams until she was back in her bedchamber, where she could work on her next book in peace. Today even her aunt had succumbed to the heat and left Callie free to do as she pleased for once. So she couldn't let another day go by without finding out if the novel she had laboured over so hard in secret might be published. So, yes, it was worth being hot and sticky to get word Mr Redell might agree to publish it at last.

Despite the heat she managed an excited hop and skip at his opinion her work showed promise. He had suggested changes and refinements, of course, but it wasn't a flat refusal. Perhaps she could earn enough to rent a little cottage one day and mix with friends she chose, get ink on her fingers whenever the fancy took her, then dig her garden and cook whatever she wanted to eat out of it. It was such a heady daydream she didn't hear a hot and weary horse coming up behind her until the animal was close enough to shy at her modest bonnet.

His rider cursed him for a jingle-brained donkey and consigned him to the devil even as Callie's thoughts span back with a sickening jolt. Shocked to her toes by the sound of that particular male voice, she froze as if an enchanter had put a spell on her. No, she wouldn't look round, but he was taking in her unfashionable bonnet and faded gown as he fought to control the skittish beast, because he realised he was blaspheming in front of a lady. Callie was far too busy coping with absolute shock to take note of his apology. She was wrong; she must be. Gideon was miles away, probably in London, and this was a stranger. Turning to reassure herself she was imagining a nightmare, Callie found out exactly how wrong she could be.

'Oh, the devil,' she said flatly.

All the blood in her body seemed to have drained from her head into her hot, dusty feet and taken her panic-stricken heart with it. Black spots danced in front of her eyes and now her fickle heart was thundering a tattoo so loudly her head was full of the relentless beat. Panic raced over her skin in shudders of cold on the hottest day of summer so far.

'How missish of me,' she managed in a fading murmur, but neither willpower nor vanity could stop her reeling—the truth of him beating against her hastily shut eyelids, as if he was stamped on them like a brand. This *was* Gideon.

After all the years of wanting him night after night—so much useless longing—then wishing they had never met, he was back and there was only so much abuse a woman's body could take. Callie let the darkness suck her in so he didn't matter any more.

Chapter Two

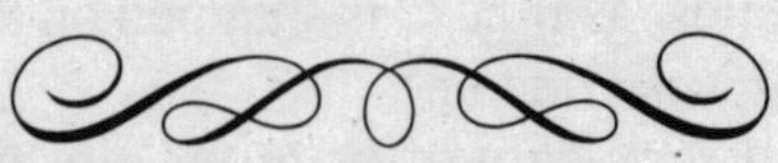

Gideon fought to hold his much-tried horse back from bolting. The woman Lady Virginia ordered him to seek out and come to terms with had wilted like a faded lily at the sight of him and made the wretched beast panic even more as she fell to the ground. As he tried to soothe the beast his heart thudded to the beat of iron-shod hooves too close to her contrary head.

'To think I was afraid I wouldn't find you here,' he murmured between curses as he finally fought the animal to a weary standstill.

Nobody could accuse the Calliope Sommers he knew of being vapourish and his heart ached. Sir Gideon Laughraine must be a worse rogue than he thought if his wife fainted at her first sight of him in nine years, so what hope was there for his sooty soul?

'And a very good afternoon to you, too, Lady Laughraine,' he muttered, wondering what his noble clients would think of 'Mr Frederick Peters' under his real identity.

He almost laughed at the idea; this name was hardly a true one, but it *was* the one he had to call himself when all aliases were stripped away. Too late to gallop back to town and save her from confronting her worst nightmare now, so he quietened his hack and avoided looking at his wife until his breathing calmed as much as it was going to today. The bitter knowledge that she once told him not to bother her again as long as he lived made him gasp as if she had written it a moment ago. She hadn't replied to a single letter he sent since so she still thought their woes were his fault. Still, he'd be damned if he'd ride off and leave his wife sprawled in the road for any fool to trip over, so he couldn't leave again yet.

Gideon jumped from the saddle of his weary horse to crouch over his wife with a fast beating heart and a gut-deep fear for her safety that told him he still cared. He frowned at the shadows under her eyes, then his gaze lingered on the dusky curve of her eyelashes as he recalled how they felt blinking sleepily against his own skin. No, that wasn't a road he could travel and stay sane. Compared to the skinny girl she was her face was softer and yet more defined; his coltish Callie had grown up and he hadn't been here to watch it happen.

Of course, the old Callie was vital and lovely, her glossy dark hair always tumbling out of whatever style she tried to tame it with. Her dark brown eyes were full of life and often brilliant with mischief, or passion, as she urged him recklessly to match her, as if he needed urging. Of course, the young man he was must be flattered, but he'd truly loved her. No other woman could rival her even now. He'd met accredited beauties and numbered one or two as true friends, but they didn't hold a candle to the Callie he first fell in love with. His young love was as lively and adventurous as she was lovely and it tore at his heart to see so little of her in the contained and outwardly staid woman lying in his path.

He watched her slavishly for signs of returning consciousness, or was that a story he told himself so he could gaze at her? Her lush curves were accentuated by the tiny waist he used to span when he lifted her off her grandfather's steady grey horse when they met secretly. He could only see it because gravity defeated her high-waisted gown and was it foolish or wise of fashion to conceal such a figure from the gaze of hungry male predators like him? he wondered. Considering the allowance he'd struggled to make her in his days as a clerk, then an unconventional lawyer, and the increases he'd made since, he wondered what she spent his blunt on, though, because it sure as Hades hadn't gone on clothes.

Her gown had been washed so many times the white of the base cotton was yellowed and a simple print of gold rosebuds faded. It was hard to pick out pattern from background and he doubted it was in the first kick of fashion when it made its debut far too long ago for her to be wearing it now. Shock at the sight of her dropping to the ground in a dead faint might be making his attention swerve to unimportant things, but it was a puzzle he intended to solve as soon as she felt well enough. It *was* infernally hot, though, so maybe she didn't want to mire a good gown on a tramp through a sweltering countryside.

'What the devil are you up to, Callie?' he murmured as he settled his hack by a nearby tree and frowned as if he might read answers on her pallid face.

She looked heartbreakingly vulnerable lying in the dust as he strode back to her. The rise and fall of her bosom told him she was breathing steadily, but she had been unconscious far too long. He wanted to pluck her up off the dusty road and guard her from any threat life could throw at her, even if he was the worst one she could think of. For a breath-stealing moment he wondered if she had a terrible illness. No, he could see no sign of prolonged ill health in her smooth skin and unwrinkled brow, so she hated him so much she lost her senses rather than meet him face to face.

He checked her breathing, then stood over her so his shadow would shield her from the sun. He watched her achingly familiar heart-shaped face for a long moment, then averted his gaze. He was too much of a coward to watch her wake up and see revulsion tighten her features when she realised he wasn't a bad dream. His wife lay unconscious at his feet and now he was lusting after her like a green boy as well and it shamed him. He also felt fully alive for the first time since he left her, despair biting harder with every step he took. She was smiling faintly in her sleep next time he looked, as if drifting happily in a world that didn't have him in it. He suppressed the urge to howl like a dog at her latest rejection and went back to brooding over a past that couldn't be altered.

Callie was drifting on a thick cloud of feathers while angels whispered benedictions in her ear. For a moment she really believed Gideon had come back for her, so it was perfectly rational to hear angels, but why did this one sound so angry? And did they really carry tall ebony canes and have masses of snow-white hair and piercing dark-brown eyes? Her grumpy angel frowned and remarked it was little wonder she was bad-tempered with two idiots like her and Gideon to worry about when she had better things to do.

Acting like a die-away miss never solved anything, young lady. A fortnight of Gideon's three months has already been used up with his shilly-shallying. Best to let sleeping dogs lie indeed—whatever is the boy thinking of? It doesn't make sense to do anything of the sort when they're only sleeping their lives away as if that's all there is for them to worry about. Just you wake up this minute, my girl, and stop being such a ninnyhammer. You haven't been happy without him since you sent him away, so get up and face him and a few facts at the same time, the spectre ordered her with a stern look and Callie frowned as waking up suddenly seemed a good idea.

Her airy cloud deflated and she felt far less comfortable avoiding Gideon than she had when she welcomed unconsciousness with a sigh of relief. She wrinkled her nose as a bit more reality crept in; this was a hard resting place with too many stones for a lady to lie about on as if she had nothing better to do.

'Go away,' she croaked, hoping to reclaim her quiet cushion of feathery peace instinct warned her not to relinquish as the dragon-angel ordered. She might be lying on a dusty road dreaming impossible things, but she didn't want to face real ones right now.

'Would that I could,' Gideon's voice replied and a heavy thump of her heart reminded her why she'd welcomed an attack of the vapours in the first place.

At last she gave in and blinked her eyes open, because she didn't want to dwell on the regret in Gideon's voice. He sounded absolutely here and far away all at the same time and wasn't that trick typical of him?

'What *are* you doing here?' she murmured with an unwary shake of her head. Dark spots wavered in front of her eyes and warned her some shocks weren't to be got over lightly and she lay down again until they went away.

'Straight to the nub of the issue, as usual,' her husband said wearily.

She glanced up at him looming over her and saw worry and frustration in his grey-green eyes, but still couldn't stand up and face him. Maybe in a moment or two she'd find the right blend of courage and calmness, *and maybe never*, a sceptical voice whispered and she wasn't sure if it was hers or belonged to the forceful spectre she dreamt up just now.

'If you can endure me carrying you, you'll recover far better in the shade.'

'Be quick then,' she ordered, waving her dusty hand imperiously as a defeated queen.

'Your wish is my command, Highness,' he joked as he lifted her up as if she were made of fairy dust.

Callie knew perfectly well that wasn't so and felt the power of him when he plucked her from the ground without a hitch in his breathing. Was it right to be insulted by his rock-like composure? The Gideon she remembered was slender as a lath and she could read him as easily as a child's primer, yet this man was a closed book to her. Her body responded to his as if it recognised him and that would never do. Callie the lover—the wife, came alive again in a hot flash of fiery need. Horrified to feel so aware of him, she squirmed and he told her testily to keep still lest he drop her.

Once upon a time he was the sun to her moon; the reason she got up in the morning and slept at night, if they could spare time for sleeping. Surely she had more sense than to fall under his spell twice? Of course she had. The moment she could set one foot in front of the other without falling over, she'd march away and prove he meant nothing to her.

'Put me down, Gideon,' she demanded in a breathy voice she hardly recognised.

'You'll fall over if I do.'

'Nonsense, I'm perfectly well.'

'Of course you aren't.'

'I wish you'd let me walk, I'm not a child,' she complained, even though she sounded like a pettish one to her own ears right now.

'Stop behaving like one then,' he said in a preoccupied tone, as if he had more important things to do than tidy his inconvenient wife off the King's Highway.

'I'm not. I feel sick,' she said querulously, wondering what had come over her. Gideon had, of course, and he was as calm as a rock while she felt as if her whole world had been turned upside down.

'Then I'm definitely not putting you down.'

'It's a lie,' she confessed with a blush she hoped he couldn't see under the liberal coating of dust miring her cheeks. 'I thought such a neat gentleman as you wouldn't want that fine silk waistcoat spoilt and you'd put me down.'

'You really can't wait to get out of my arms, can

you, Wife?' he said with a quirk of his mouth that might pass for a smile in a dark room.

'No more than you can to ride off and forget me for another nine years,' she retaliated childishly, unable to stop her tongue saying things she'd rather it kept quiet about.

'You do me an injustice, Calliope. How could I ever forget you?'

She distrusted his words, took them as mockery. Tears stung her eyes for a perilous second, but the thought of tear tracks in the dirt made her wince. She blinked hard and stared into the little wood he was carrying her towards until they dispersed. She should dismiss him from her life as lightly as an old gown, but perhaps she could lie about a lover to disgrace him with and persuade him to go away. Except she'd never met a man who made her feel the way he did. If she wasn't careful she'd become the sort of female who lay about on sofas half the day and wafted about like a low-lying cloud for the rest of it. Or hoped for impossible things, and wouldn't that be a waste of time?

'I *can* still walk, you know,' she said crossly.

'Of course you can,' he replied, a hint of laughter in grey eyes that had an inner ray of green round the pupil only a lover would know about.

The thought of long-ago intimacy with this man caught at her heart. Now he looked and sounded almost familiar it made her recall times when they looked and looked at each other for what felt like hours, or simply lay close marvelling at one another until desire was too hot for peace and they peaked into the sort of earth-shattering climax that made her shiver even over such a chasm of time. That wasn't the way to be cool and armoured while they agreed terms. It was good for him to hide his true self now; it would make life easier while she waited for him to go again.

'And I wish to do so right now,' she told him emphatically.

'I may not be much of a husband, but I'm not going to watch my wife stagger about the countryside half faint in this heat like a drunkard.'

'Nonsense, I can cope with the sun perfectly well.'

'Of course you can,' he said indulgently.

How come she could hear him smile as he soothed her like a fractious infant again? 'The shock of seeing you made me faint, but I would be perfectly well if you hadn't taken me by surprise,' she claimed with a frown that was clearly wasted on the barbarian.

'You were so overcome with delight at the sight of me you lost your senses then?'

'That wasn't delight,' she snapped.

'I know.'

'And what the devil are you doing here, Gideon?'

'Now *that* sounds more like the outspoken Callie Sommers I know. I thought I'd mistaken you for someone else for a moment back there.'

'I *am* someone else,' she told him gruffly, doing her best to believe that was good.

'Not from here you're not,' he teased as he shifted her slightly in his arms and they finally reached the little wood that ran alongside the road. 'You feel exactly like her to me.'

'Well, I'm not,' she said crossly. She hadn't been since Gideon put his ring on her finger and the blacksmith at Gretna pronounced them man and wife.

'No, you're Callie Laughraine,' he said blankly and she told herself that was a good thing. One of them should have their feelings under control and hers were anything but.

'I spent a long time forgetting her and manage perfectly well without a husband to tell me what to do and how to do it nowadays,' she insisted.

'As if I ever could awe, persuade or bully you into doing a thing you didn't want to. You were always your own person and even as a silly stripling I never wanted you any other way, Calliope.'

'I have no idea why my mother gave me that ridiculous name,' she said to divert them from the memory of how much he'd loved her when they eloped to Gretna Green. It hurt to linger on the past and wonder if they could have built a wonderful marriage together, if life was a little less cruel. 'She might as well have put a millstone round my neck as named me for one of the Muses.'

'Lucky you have a beautiful voice and a love of poetry like your namesake then, isn't it? Perhaps she simply liked it. I always did.'

'Yet how you used to taunt me with it when you were a repellent boy. If I had the gift of epic poetry, would you stop carrying me about like an infant?'

'Because you're named after a goddess?'

'No, because I asked you to, although I should like to be a bard, if we lived in better times and women were taken seriously as such, but I never wanted to be a goddess with so many unpronounceable sisters to quarrel with.'

He wasn't to know how serious she was, so she supposed it was unfair to stiffen in his arms when he chuckled. At least now she felt icy and remote again and he'd almost done it—he'd nearly disarmed her with flattery and wasn't that another warning to be wary? Best to remember he was a professional advocate now, a pleader for apparently lost causes, and that they could never be friends. At least then she would hurt less when he walked away again.

'You can put me down over there,' she ordered, pointing at a convenient tree stump.

'I'll drop you in the stream if you're not careful, Your Majesty,' he muttered darkly.

She shot him a glare as he set her down as if she was made of bone china, then stepped back with a mocking bow. 'Now go away,' she said sternly.

'I wouldn't leave your aunt stranded in the middle of nowhere ill and prey to any rogue who happened along and I never liked her, so how can you imagine I'd leave you, Callie?'

'I'm not my aunt,' she defended herself absently.

'Something I thank God for on a daily basis, my dear.'

'Don't call me your dear and don't blaspheme.'

'But I'd hate to be wed to your narrow-minded and joyless relative, my dear.'

'She stood by me when nobody else would and I told you I'm not your dear,' she told him shortly and wondered if it was worth standing so she could stamp her foot and show him she hated that false endearment on his lips. Deciding it wasn't a good idea to stand up and wilt, then sit down again before she proved anything, she tried to look serenely indifferent instead. Clearly it didn't work; he was having a job to conceal a grin at her expense.

'Perhaps you'll allow me the one freedom a married man can safely claim, which is the privacy of his own thoughts?' he said with a pantomime of the henpecked husband that made her heart ache for all they'd lost.

'And perhaps I won't,' she snapped.

'Afraid you won't like them, Calliope?'

Terrified if he did but know it. She sniffed and tossed her head to let him know she was completely indifferent, then regretted it immediately as the wild thundering in her ears told her she hadn't recovered enough to flounce off and leave him standing like a forlorn knight spurned by the damsel he'd got off his horse to rescue.

'If I was I'd have no wish to know, would I?'

'As well if you don't, perhaps,' he told her gruffly as he turned from rummaging in the pack of his weary horse and removing a flask.

'Please don't try and force brandy down my throat, Gideon,' she protested.

'I don't indulge in alcohol now,' he said as he handed her a flask of clear water lukewarm from its journey.

He drank too much wine during the latter days of their marriage and the memory of him drunk and bitter as gall made her shudder. Not that he'd laid violent hands on her, but the thought of all that darkness and despair chilled her to the bone.

'Never?' she was startled into asking as his words sank in.

'Only when a cook puts it in a sauce or some fanciful dessert when I dine away from home, but not otherwise. I drank too much and made things much worse between us. So you see, I've managed to put one of my baser impulses behind me,' he said with a rueful smile that did unfair things to her insides.

'Abstain from alcohol for your own good, but don't pretend it's got anything to do with me. If you set any store by what I wanted, you wouldn't have come here and cut up my peace like this,' she told him disagreeably to disguise it.

'I can't leave yet, but the drunken, headlong boy I was back then was repellent and I promise you I've done my best to kill him off. I doubt anyone mourned him.'

I did, argued an inner Callie who refused to be silenced. *I wept myself to sleep for the lack of him by my side every night for far too long. Until I realised he was never coming back and I was the one who told him to go, in fact.*

'Devil take it, but I'm a rogue to plague you when you're as unwell as a person can be without being carted about on a hurdle,' Gideon exclaimed and she couldn't stop a wobbly smile at the sight and sound of him as familiar to her as her own face in the mirror at last.

There—he was her Gideon again; a quick-tempered and passionate young man who could turn her knees to water at the very flicker of that self-deprecating smile or a sudden urge to wild action that made living with him such a clash of surprise, dread and delight. 'Come, Wife, let's get you home before you drop unconscious at my feet for the second time today,' he added masterfully and she frowned at him again, wondering if she could ever bring herself to live with a gentleman who was so used to getting his own way, then shocking herself with the idea she might like to try, if things were different.

'If you arrive on her doorstep, Aunt Seraphina will have the vapours even if I don't,' she warned him, and he actually paled at the thought of her aunt, who hadn't liked him even before he ran off to Gretna with her niece.

'She has plenty of experience,' he said darkly and turned towards his hitched horse.

'You could simply ride away again, nobody would know,' Callie suggested desperately. Being lonely and a little unhappy was a state she knew so well that the idea of changing it in any way looked strange and frightening from here.

'We would, wouldn't we?' he said as if that decided the issue.

'Yes,' she admitted with a sigh, 'so we would.'

Chapter Three

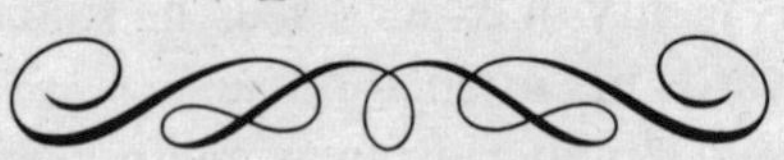

Simply getting Callie to ride his horse while he led it caused an argument. Gideon wondered if they could stop carping long enough to put the fragments of their marriage together and called up all the patience he'd learnt during his years without her. He should have remembered that aspect of marriage better and the magical glee of loving her less, he supposed grimly. Still, they were talking, even if it was in snaps of irritation. The odd moment of rediscovery made this all seem heartbreakingly familiar then strange by turns and he almost wished he'd slung his unconscious wife across his saddle brow and ridden off with her like a pirate with a princess.

'Comfortable?' he asked after the silence had stretched so thin he couldn't endure it any longer.

'What do you think?' she challenged. 'You should have let me ride astride as I asked instead of perching me up here like a doll.'

'And have half the yokels in Wiltshire looking at your legs? I think not,' he managed to say as even the idea of it made him rampantly jealous.

'I doubt they would bother when they saw the rest of me,' she said with a sweep of her hand at her dusty person that set his steed dancing and set Gideon's overstretched nerves on edge. He tried hard to rein himself in at the same time as he clamped a firm grip on the bit and forced the idiot horse to stop wasting its energy, as well.

'They would. You look magnificent,' he told her tersely and surely that wasn't a pleased little smile she was doing her best to hide behind that hideous bonnet? 'As a girl you were lovely, now you're beautiful, Callie,' he added and heard her snort of disbelief with mixed feelings.

If she thought herself an antidote, would it make his task as her jealous and fiercely protective husband easier? If he ever managed to win her back, of course. Yet if she was blind to her own attractions she would draw in wolves the moment she set foot in a ballroom at his side. So, on second thoughts, his life would be hell if she had no idea how potently her lovely face and fine figure and that firm disbelief in her own charms could affect a man. He groaned aloud at the idea of following her about like a possessive stallion for the rest of his life in order to make it very clear she was his mate and he didn't share. No, that really was putting the cart before the horses and he had to hold back all this hope in case it crashed to the ground around him again.

'Are you hurting in some way, Gideon?' she asked innocently, and what was he to do with such an odd mix of *naïveté* and sophistication as his estranged wife?

'It's been a long day,' he said with a shrug.

'It's probably about to get a lot worse,' she warned as Cataret House came into view again and she was quite right, just not in the sense she thought.

'Aye, your aunt never could abide me, could she?' he replied as if that was all that troubled him right now when even the thought of her as his true wife again was rendering him unfit for any company at all, let alone hers.

'No, she's deeply distrustful of all men and, considering the one she was wed to for so long, I'm not at all surprised.'

'So why *did* she marry Bonhomie Bartle, Callie? They never had children, so I doubt they were forced to wed for the sake of a child as my parents were. It always puzzled me what those two saw in one another as they seemed to hate each other every bit as much as my mother and father did.'

'Grandfather told me she insisted on marrying him, although he begged her not to go through with it, so I suppose she must have loved him once upon a time. Nobody forced her to wed the man and I never knew what she saw in him, but why do any two people wed each other when they don't have to?'

'Because they want to spend the rest of their lives together, I suppose,' he said and cursed his clumsy tongue when she refused to meet his eyes. Finally they had reached the sloping drive and he and his weary mount slowed in deference to the day and the incline and at least despair was having a dampening effect on his foolish manhood.

'Mr Bartle was heir to a wealthy baronetcy, before his great-uncle took a young wife and began producing heirs in his old age.'

'So they ended up poor and disappointed?'

'Yes, but I don't think either of them ever thought the world well lost for love.'

'Perhaps not,' he agreed and refused to make the challenge her averted gaze and tight fists on the reins told him she expected. *But we did once,* his inner idiot argued all the same and he told it to be quiet before it drove the rest of him mad.

'Nobody will answer the front door, you might as well lead this unlucky animal to the stable.'

'Where are your outdoor staff?' he said with a frown at the sheep-cropped turf and the faintly down-at-heel air of the whole place.

'Aunt Seraphina says the war has made everything so expensive it's impossible to keep a handyman and a groom. We have maids and a good cook she insists we employ to keep our young ladies healthy.'

'And her liking for fine dining has nothing to do with that, I suppose? What have you been doing with the allowance I make you, Callie? You certainly haven't spent it on yourself, so I hope you haven't been learning your aunt's nip-farthing ways.'

'As senior schoolmistress I take a small stipend out of the fees, but it's not enough to turn myself out in the sort of style you seem to expect, Gideon,' she said as if he was being deliberately obtuse and the notion of who gained most from their estrangement took firm root in his mind as Virginia's warning about Callie's aunt rang true yet again.

'At first I could only send enough to clothe you decently and live in modest comfort, but now the money I pay into an account in your name every month could easily run a house twice this size and still allow you to dress in style without penny pinching.'

'It would? Why don't I seem to be receiving any of it then?'

'An interesting question, don't you think?'

Callie looked thoughtful as they rounded the corner into a modest stableyard and he saw two good carriage horses and a trio of fat ponies looking curiously back at them from a nearby paddock.

'You keep a pair of carriage horses, yet I see no riding horse? How do you endure it, Callie?' he asked as the memory of her riding like the wind at his side slipped into his mind and made him wonder what other privations she suffered while he had been coward enough to take her at her word and stop away all these years.

'I'm not a wild young girl now, I grew up.'

'Did you? Have you ever taken a good look at what you prefer to a life with me, Callie? By heavens, you have a very effective way of making me humble for all the sacrifices here seem to be yours and the luxuries your aunt's.'

'She stood by me. She made a home for us both and at least we had each other—there was precious little else to be glad about at the time.'

'A far more comfortable home than she could afford without you.'

'No, Gideon, you don't understand. The school produces a reasonable income, but I have no desire to cut a figure in local society. My aunt likes to pay calls and it keeps our school in the minds of potential clients. She sees to the business side of our enterprise while I tend to the girls in our care. We do well enough without you.'

'So you must always believe her before me?'

'No, of course not,' she argued half-heartedly.

Gideon had to bite his lip as he helped her out of the saddle, then steadied her, because she had endured a great shock today and, if his suspicions were right, there were plenty more of those to come.

'The household has been at sixes and sevens since we found you gone,' Aunt Seraphina scolded benignly as she bustled towards them as soon as she and Gideon walked out of the baking stableyard and into the cool of the stone-flagged hall of Cataret House by the garden door. 'How could you wander off on an afternoon like this, Calliope? You should be resting or keeping yourself occupied indoors during the heat of the day if you really must be busy.'

'I felt restless and miss the girls, Aunt, but you must see we have a visitor. I'm sure you don't mean to scold me in front of him,' Callie said.

Gideon was right here and Aunt Seraphina knew her niece had come home on a hired horse led by a stranger in shirt sleeves, because the maids were on pins at the sight of any man in this out-of-the-way place. One as handsome as Gideon would set their hearts aflutter and their tongues wagging nineteen to the dozen, but Aunt Seraphina was stalling while she took stock of the situation. Callie knew her aunt a lot better than she had when Aunt Seraphina was a rather aloof figure during her childhood and she had seen that look before. The sight of Gideon had unnerved her and she was turning over ways to turn the situation to her advantage in her mind before she acknowledged his presence. A little while ago Callie would have blamed him for the unease between him and her aunt, but now she wasn't quite so sure all the faults lay on his side, after all, as she sensed a mighty fury kept under iron control in her apparently calm relative.

'I considered it best to pretend you are not here, young man. You have more cheek than I thought you possessed to walk in here and expect to be welcomed after what you did,' Aunt Seraphina said as if he was a naughty schoolboy.

'My husband has a right to be here, Aunt Seraphina,' Callie surprised all three of them by asserting.

One of the maids listening on the stairs let out a gasp and another nudged her to be silent so they could keep listening, but Callie knew they were shocked Miss Sommers was claiming a husband at all, let alone one like this.

'The man isn't fit to black your boots, let alone saunter in here as if he has a right.'

'Since I'm not one to wash my dirty linen in public, I suggest we adjourn to a less public space for the rest of this discussion, Mrs Bartle,' Gideon said smoothly, and it said much for his new air of authority that all three were inside the drawing room with the door shut before her aunt protested his use of her true name when she was known as Mrs Grisham here.

'Now, how do you explain yourself, young man? As if that's possible,' Aunt Seraphina said in a voice that made schoolgirls tremble, but didn't affect Gideon at all.

'Later. Now your niece needs peace and a cool bath after her exertions and if you had half the real concern for her welfare that you managed to fake all these years you would stop arguing with me and see she is cared for.'

For a moment there was such tension in the carefully gentrified parlour that Callie fancifully wondered if it might become visible as a lowering mist in the overheated air. She blamed this odd sense of detachment on her faint. Her aunt's gaze fell under the chilly challenge in Gideon's and she waved a long-fingered hand to concede a skirmish, but not an entire war.

'Calliope is very pale, but you insisted we come in here to argue over the matter whilst she could have been resting before her bath, so you can ring for the maids and see if you can get them to do anything sensible now your arrival has set them atwitter,' her aunt said as if recovering from the sight of Gideon walking in through her garden door as if he had every right to be here.

'You're giving me carte blanche to reorganise your household then, ma'am? Rather reckless of you, don't you think?'

'What does a man know of domestic economy?' Aunt Seraphina scoffed and Callie reminded herself they always brought out the worst in each other.

'Enough,' Gideon said wearily and surprised Callie into staring at him again.

Once upon a time he would no more have dreamed of running a household than he would of swimming to the Americas. Now he rang the bell, ordered tea and a bath for her and approved a light menu for dinner in an hour's time before Aunt Seraphina could regret her dare and take back the reins of her household. Callie had made him into this self-sufficient man by refusing to be any sort of wife to him, so why was she feeling nostalgic for days when he would look helpless and wait for her to correct his feckless bachelor ways?

'Well, I'm ready to admit you have changed in that aspect at least. It proves nothing about the rest of your life,' Aunt Seraphina told him severely.

'I have no need to prove anything to *you*, madam,' he replied shortly and they waited in stiff silence for news that Callie's very necessary bath and tea were ready for her.

'There we are, miss. No, I mean madam, don't I?' Kitty the upstairs maid told Callie as if she might not be able to see the bathtub and waiting tea tray herself.

'Thank you, Kitty. I can manage very well by myself now,' she said quietly and refused the silent invitation to confide her secrets. 'You may go,' she added as the inquisitive young woman stood as if expecting to outwit her mistress's unassuming niece by sheer persistence.

'Don't you want your back soaped, ma'am? Oh, no, of course you don't. You've a fine husband to do that for you, don't you?' the girl said impudently.

'If you don't want to be turned off without your wages, I suggest you think about that and do as you're bid, Kitty,' Callie said and met the girl's bold gaze serenely.

'I dare say the mistress would have something to say about that,' the brassy piece said as if she hadn't a worry in the world about being dismissed.

'I doubt it. She didn't want to take you on in the first place and I suggest you consider which of us is the teacher and Mrs Grisham's niece and which one the maid,' Callie said so quietly the pert creature looked away as if there was a lot she could say but she didn't choose to right now.

The girl managed an insultingly small curtsy as she left to prove she wasn't cowed. Kitty had turned up here all but destitute and begging for work, then managed to go from maid of all work to head housemaid in a matter of months. Callie wondered if she had a hold over her aunt to manage such a rapid rise at the same time as it occurred to her she should have been more aware of what was going on around her. Lately a few of the schoolgirls had come to her with tearful claims that Kitty took their secrets to Mrs Grisham after she snooped to find them. Aunt Seraphina claimed Kitty was doing her duty and punished the girls, not the maid. Absorbed in writing her book at nights and teaching the girls all day, had she been making herself too busy to miss Gideon? And had she let her pupils down by being so preoccupied?

It had hurt to even breathe without him near her in the early days when she began to come alive again and had to live without him. As she undressed and slipped into the unheard-of luxury of a bath before dinner, Callie let her thoughts drift. How were Gideon and her aunt to coexist under the same roof even for one night? They had always loathed each other and it disturbed her that Aunt Seraphina made no effort to hide her dislike. She'd better hurry down before they came to blows. Of course, then her thoughts must veer back to Gideon and the power he seemed to exude now as she sighed blissfully at the kiss of cool clean water on her overheated skin.

Her cheeks flushed ridiculously as the idea he

would once have insisted on climbing into this tub with her and done all sorts of sensuous things to persuade her it didn't matter if they slopped bath water on the floor. Had he been tortured by such wanton longings all this time, as well? No stern lectures from her sensible side could kill off the little sensualist who recalled how hot and passionate a bath with the man you loved could be, but he had all the skilled beauties of the *demi-monde* to choose from whenever he wanted to slake his lust, hadn't he? The idea of such a virile young man enduring nine years of tortured celibacy, because he'd wed in haste and repented at leisure, was laughable. That blush of hers went places he would have followed with hotly fascinated eyes in the old days as her whole body overheated with remembering what a passionate and driven lover he was.

She shook her head at the very idea he'd burned and cursed the lack of a wife in his bed all this time as she had the loss of her one and only lover in hers. No, it was simply impossible for him to have lived like a monk for the sake of a woman who'd told him to leave and now she shivered and told herself not to be a fool. He would keep his mistress in comfort and lavish all the fiercely focused passion he'd once saved for his wife on a beauty who couldn't demand a joint share in his life. Her hands clawed at the vengeful thought of how she'd like to use them on his mistress and it took more force of will than she liked to make them straighten again at the idea of another woman in thrall to her husband, her lover, and hadn't she needed him far more than some beauty who could take her pick of keepers and chose Gideon?

Yet if he made love to the confounded woman half

as ardently as he had to her, the wretch must simply live for the next time he felt in need of a woman. Even when he must have hated her more than he loved her after their first flush of wild infatuation, he'd still wanted her very urgently indeed, she recalled with a feral shiver of heat that reminded her how much she had longed for him all these years all over again. And wasn't it ridiculous that here she was, lying in her bath, dreaming of her one and only lover, when she should be busy arming herself against his lies.

She couldn't pretend he'd ever forced her. Most of the reason she made him go was her endless need of him and his passionate lovemaking. It was destroying her self-respect and making her hate her dependency on a physical act that no longer bonded them like twin souls. Instead, it made the chill between them when they were not making love more arctic. Squeezing her eyes tight shut, she forced herself to remember all the reasons why Callie Laughraine couldn't need her husband and let out a stuttering sigh. There, she was rational again now. It was folly never to dare risk carrying his child again, but it was what kept her tightly hemmed inside the closed world her aunt decreed since the day Gideon rode away, in return for pretending her niece never married him in the first place.

'I'm not a silly little girl in thrall to a lone wolf any more, Gideon Laughraine,' she muttered into the sultry air. 'Don't you dare dream of pulling the wool over my foolish eyes and enchanting me into thinking the sun rises and sets in your eyes ever again.

'Of course not, Callie, why would he think you a passion-led fool when you're sitting here dreaming of him, as if every moment he's not close to you is wasted as far as you're concerned?' she chided herself. 'And I refuse to be that girl again. She hurt too much to dare it twice.'

Galvanised into action by the dread of dreaming her evening away like a besotted girl, until someone came to find out why she was still sitting in her bath like a very odd exhibit in a museum, she washed the dust out of her hair, then soaped herself vigorously until even the memory of her sweat-streaked face and mired feet was gone. She stood up and used the rosemary-and-cider vinegar rinse she made to tame some of the wild curls her dark hair sprang into if she let it. It would soon dry in the heavy warmth of this July evening and she sat on her bed to comb it out, reluctant to put the practical petticoats of Miss Sommers on over her cool, clean skin.

The weight of her long hair as it began to dry against her bare back felt sensual and a little bit decadent now Gideon was in the house. Yesterday it would have been a damp nuisance against a workaday body she did her best to ignore; today Callie Laughraine was alive again and waking up after her long hibernation felt almost painful. A wary inner voice whispered it was better for her darkest secrets if she slept on, but her lover was nearby and she squirmed against the plain bedcover in a rush of hot anticipation she hadn't let herself feel so powerfully in years.

Even before she knew what love was she'd felt that forbidden flash of excitement at the very sight of Gideon Laughraine, she recalled guiltily. She and Bella from the Grange and Lottie from the Home Farm used to run wild over the Raigne estate as girls. She recalled with a wistful smile the chance of meeting Gideon busy with some boyish mischief was the highlight of her day back then. As a girl she secretly adored that gangling half-wild boy and when she began to grow to what she'd thought a woman, her feelings ran much deeper. She loved him; no point pretending it was a girlish obsession she would have grown out of.

That girl thought she'd been put on earth to love Gideon Laughraine and there didn't seem much point pretending she had never done so. It didn't matter—she didn't love him now and hadn't done for years, had she? Idealistic, dreamy Callie Sommers put an angry boy on a pedestal. It was as much her fault as his that he wasn't the hero she thought him. She stopped combing her hair and stared at nothing in particular as if it might tell her why she committed all she was to him at seventeen to his eighteen.

The truth was that lonely, uncertain girl was ripe to fall headlong at the feet of an unsuitable young man. Perhaps that was why her grandfathers connived at the union they wanted and Gideon's father did everything he could to stop it. Of course, the legal heir and the last real heir's bastard child marrying each other would set the succession right and secure the future of Raigne once and for all, but she and Gideon were real people with hearts and souls who deserved to make such life-changing decisions for themselves.

Except they conveniently fell in love with one another and what would it have taken for them *not* to back then? More than they were capable of, she decided, as the huge power of that feeling threatened to remind her how little this life away from him was. The enormity of it, as if a pent-up dam of emotion was about to wash her along in a great flood, echoed down the years. Instead of wild passion it threatened huge sadness now, though, so she built the dam back up and pretended it wasn't there as best she could.

Even so she donned her lightest muslin gown and pinned her hair up loosely, because it was still damp and she couldn't bring herself to screw it into the tight knot her aunt thought proper tonight. She wasn't a spinster schoolteacher, she was Lady Laughraine, and what was the point pretending now Gideon was here? Feeling a little more like a baronet's lady, she went downstairs and could tell her husband approved of the small changes in her appearance from the glint of admiration and something more personal in his grey-green gaze as he rose to greet her.

Chapter Four

'Hmm, I'm not sure about that hairstyle, my dear, and white has never suited you, but I'm glad to see you look better than when you came in this afternoon,' Aunt Seraphina said as soon as Callie joined her and Gideon in the sitting room that evening. She caught a glimpse of Gideon's quick frown and it made her think about her aunt's words a little more deeply.

'I prefer my hair like this,' she said calmly. 'It feels cooler and all those pins were making my head ache.'

'And I hardly recognised you in that governess's bonnet and tightly bound hair this afternoon,' Gideon said, as if they had been parted only a few weeks and he was marking a few subtle changes in his wife's appearance.

'I suppose a married woman is permitted a few liberties that would be folly in a single lady of your advancing years, Callie, my dear,' Aunt Seraphina conceded doubtfully.

'I will never aspire to the extremes of fashion that lead fast young matrons to damp their muslins and crop their hair, Aunt, but Sir Gideon Laughraine's wife cannot dress like a schoolteacher.'

'You were content to dress modestly until he arrived.'

'I should have found the line between modest and frumpish sooner then,' Callie said, feeling rebellious when she thought of all those long nights inventing characters and living her life vicariously so she could pretend it was enough.

'You do seem to be longing tonight for the very life you begged me to take you away from the day he left you alone and bereft, don't you?' Aunt Seraphina asked, the thought of all her niece was risking by doing so clearly paining her.

'I'm not sure,' Callie said, but for a moment she thought her aunt's gaze was hard when it met hers this time. She was wrong, of course she was. They couldn't have lived and worked together all these years if her aunt secretly hated her, even though her aunt was so distant and disapproving when Callie was a child. 'I shall always be grateful to you for standing by me when I needed you to so badly, Aunt Seraphina, but I'm a relatively young woman and can be permitted a little vanity on occasions like this,' she teased, but Aunt Seraphina's lips tightened and her hands clenched before she managed a polite titter and an airy gesture to deny she was a killjoy.

'Of course, my dear, you will have to excuse an anxious old woman who wonders if you're playing with fire.'

'I'm hardly flaunting myself like a houri because I left a few hairpins out of my toilette tonight,' Callie protested because she couldn't imagine how anyone could see her plain gown and simple hairstyle as provocative.

'I'm glad to see you looking more like yourself, but Mrs Bartle obviously takes her duties as chaperon and mentor seriously, my dear,' Gideon said silkily.

Her lamentable wardrobe and lack of a riding horse might be behind his suspicion her aunt had not been acting in Callie's best interests all these years. She thought of his assertion that he had sent large sums of money to her over the years and noted a bead of sweat on her aunt's upper lip. It was very hot, perhaps even she couldn't stay cool and composed in such weather.

'Of course, Calliope is my niece,' the lady said stoutly. Once it would have been a huge concession to call Callie *niece*, as she was the by-blow of Mrs Bartle's younger sister. The fact she owned up to her now persuaded Callie this was all a misunderstanding.

'Thank you, Aunt,' she said sincerely.

'And therefore you must want her to be happy,' Gideon said so smoothly that Callie really didn't know why her aunt shifted under his steady gaze, 'must you not?'

'Of course, which is why I never encouraged Calliope to get in touch with you,' Aunt Seraphina countered as if it were war.

'Or to reply to any of my letters, perhaps?'

Callie had difficulty not gasping out loud at the implication he had written more than once. A single letter would have soothed some of the jagged places in her heart, but more than one? That would have been like a bridge between the old Callie and Gideon and the new world she had no map for after he left. She eyed them both warily and wondered who was lying now.

'I have no idea what you mean,' Aunt Seraphina said smoothly, but Callie saw a few giveaway signs under her front of unruffled confidence that her aunt was less sure of herself than she pretended.

'What a convenient memory you do have, ma'am,' Gideon countered.

'A very *inconvenient* one as far as you are concerned, young man. Time has not wiped out any of your past sins for me even if my niece seems to have lost her memory of them tonight. I might have kept one or two letters from Callie when we came here, but she was in no state to read your self-serving excuses for what you did at the time.'

Memory of exactly how painful that period of her life had been made Callie glare at her husband and wonder why she doubted the one person who stood by her. 'Thank you, Aunt Seraphina. I don't think there was any excuse for what you did either, do you, Gideon?'

He held her gaze as if he had nothing to be ashamed of and suddenly Callie felt weary half to death and wished he would simply state his business with her then go.

'Of course there isn't,' her aunt answered for him.

He was about to deny it, but Kitty came in to say dinner was ready before either of them could say another word and then they only exchanged small talk. The maids were in and out with this and that and Kitty's busy ears were always on the alert for gossip. Tonight they must be aching with the need to know more about the handsome husband Miss Sommers had brazenly owned up to as if she had never lied about him in the first place.

Somehow Callie got through the meal without blurting out something indiscreet through sheer tiredness. She felt horribly confused every time she glanced at Gideon and wondered if he was right to jolt her out of the settled life she had made without him. Maybe Aunt Seraphina had got carried away by a desire to protect Callie. If she had to walk the line between protecting a close relative or telling the strict truth, how would *she* cope with the dilemma her aunt faced?

The idea she would have preferred to make her own choice slipped into her mind. She had a right to know Gideon had tried to contact her or even win her back. At first she would not have listened, of course, but what about later? Maybe, she let herself know. She wasn't quite sure if she should despise herself for being weak or add another reason not to trust Aunt Seraphina as unquestioningly as she had for too long to the list.

'I believe we may have a thunderstorm tonight,' her aunt announced once it was clear none of them could take another bite of whatever it was Cook had served them.

Callie had no idea what she ate while she struggled with her confusion in silence. Grandfather would be appalled by her lack of manners tonight and she wondered if either of her dining companions had noticed. The other two were probably too busy eyeing each other suspiciously to note that conversation wasn't flowing merrily tonight.

'Your stableman assures me the weather won't break for another day or two. I agree it feels clammy enough to whip up a storm at any moment, though,'

Gideon said, as if trying to pretend there wasn't an atmosphere of sticky tension in the room that was nothing to do with the summer heat. He shot a concerned look at Callie and she realised he was doing his best to stop more worries adding to her growing pile of them tonight.

'I don't fear thunder and lightning as I used to, Gideon,' she said calmly enough, for if she had gone pale it was out of weariness and not her old terror of storms. After their baby, Grace, died at birth the weather was the least of her worries and since then she'd comforted so many terrified schoolgirls she could endure the worst storms without flinching.

'I'm glad to hear it, but you do look weary, my dear. Perhaps we should all retire early to try and sleep as best we can, despite this ridiculous heat?' he suggested.

'Where will you sleep?' she asked unwarily, then blushed at the impossible notion a husband might expect to share his wife's bed.

'Apparently there are plenty of rooms that lie empty here over the summer,' he said as if the idea had never occurred to him.

'I will ask Kitty to have a bed made up for you then,' she said stiffly. She wouldn't have welcomed him if he'd made a move to share her bed, but it felt a little bit unforgivable that he hadn't bothered to try.

'No need, the kitchen maid found me bed linen and we sorted it out between us. I shall be sleeping in one of the pupil-teacher's beds tonight, since none of the younger ladies' accommodation is big enough for a full-grown male,' he said with a shrug that told her he understood her inner conflict about his sleeping arrangements and wondered why she thought he was so insensitive as to demand his marital rights when she was so pleased to see him she lost her senses this afternoon.

'Then can I be rude and retire betimes, Aunt? I am very tired.'

'Of course you must do so, my love. Little wonder you feel exhausted after such a shock as you suffered today, although I still have no idea what you were doing wandering about the countryside alone?'

It seemed a good idea to pretend she hadn't noticed it was a question, not a statement of exasperation. Callie placed a dutiful kiss on her aunt's expectantly raised cheek and gave Gideon a look that challenged him to demand the same. Surely he couldn't expect her to take up marriage where they left off, even if he was willing to sleep elsewhere tonight?

'I can't do right for being wrong, can I?' he whispered when he opened the door for her, then lit her a candle from the store in the hall, despite the fact it only ever seemed to get half-dark at midsummer.

'No,' she said as she went past him with as much dignity as she could manage. 'Goodnight, Gideon.'

'Goodnight, Wife,' he murmured and the shiver that softly spoken challenge sent down her spine sped her upstairs more swiftly than her weary feet wanted to go.

Gideon wished his reluctant hostess goodnight and retired to the narrow room a girl who wasn't rich enough to continue her education without acting as an unpaid teacher to the littlest members of this school warranted in this household. He was sure Callie tried to prepare her for life as a governess or schoolteacher as best she could, but all her aunt would care about was that she cost next to nothing.

He shivered at the thought of any daughter of his enduring such a regime at this school without Callie here to soften its hard edges. He must be very weary, because the idea of his lost child made tears stand in his eyes. They lost so much when their little Grace died before she was born. His little girl wouldn't be so little now. Nine years old, he thought, as he stripped off the stifling correctness of summer coat, neck-cloth and waistcoat. He could almost hear her furtive giggle as she peeked into her father's room to see if he was asleep yet and might not notice if she crept downstairs now the house was settled for the night.

Perhaps she would be leading the rest of her parents' brood astray by now, as well. Encouraging the little ones to join her illicit feast of whatever left-overs sat in the larder from dinner, or daring them to join her in the gardens by moonlight to pick straw-berries and peer at a nest of kittens in the gardener's bothy. He missed her so much tonight. Now he and her mother were under the same roof for the first time in years he felt she should be here, too. Even the slight chance of being properly married again made their daughter seem so alive he could almost hear and touch her. The one ghost he desperately wanted to see was never quite there to be marvelled at; his little girl was always just outside his field of vision, hinted at in the odd little whisper and gleeful laugh his imagination allowed him to know of her.

'Ah, Callie, we would have loved our little angel-devil so much, wouldn't we?' he whispered to the still hot air and called himself a fool.

Hope was almost as bad as despair in the still silence of this sultry night. Yes, there was a slim chance he and Callie could try again, but it wouldn't work if she carried on relying on her aunt to tell her what to think. He *could* force himself on his wife; take her away from here and show her how skewed her aunt's view of him and the rest of the world was. Legally he could make her take him back into her life. It wouldn't feel much better than enduring life without her if she didn't want to be with him, though, and he sighed bitterly at the very idea of such a hostile and empty marriage.

Impatient with himself for wanting the whole loaf when half a one might be all he could have, he opened the window as softly as he could on to a listening sort of night. He'd learnt years ago there were far worse terrors lurking in the darkness than the suggestion of a breeze. Too on edge to undress fully, he heeled his evening shoes off and pulled back the covers on the pallet-like bed, so he could let his body rest while his mind went round in circles like a spit dog on a wheel.

'Good morning,' Callie greeted Gideon the next day.

She wasn't fully awake yet, after swearing to herself she wouldn't sleep a wink, then dropping straight into it as if she hadn't done so for a week. Still she felt her heart flutter at the sight of him so vital and handsome as he strode into the breakfast room. Part of her had missed him every hour of every day since they parted. That Callie saw the world in richer colours now the love of her life was back in it; the rest was deeply sceptical about his return and eyed him warily.

'Is it? I thought we might have slipped into afternoon while I was waiting for my lady to leave her chamber,' he teased and she made a face, then took a closer look under her lashes.

'Where on earth did you get that bruise?' she asked, suddenly more wide-awake and able to stare right at him.

'You might well ask.'

'I am doing so,' she said with a stern frown that told him she wasn't going to be fobbed off with a rueful shrug this time.

'I'm staying in a house I don't know,' he said as if that explained everything.

'And…?'

'And I walked into a door in the dark?' he offered, as if he didn't think it was a very likely story, either.

'A door with a fist?'

'It wasn't a fist, it was a ewer. I suppose I should be grateful your upstairs maid didn't have a chamber pot in her hand at the time.'

'What on earth were you doing chasing the maids round the house in the dark?'

'I'd as soon pursue the Gorgon with lustful intent as that sly minx, even if I was given to preying on servants,' he said quietly and stepped over the close the door, clearly aware Kitty would listen if given the slightest excuse.

'I heard someone creeping about the house in the small hours of the morning,' he admitted as if he hadn't wanted her to know.

'Kitty might be sly and untrustworthy, but she has

access to any room in the house by daylight, why would she steal about in the dark?'

'Apparently she heard whoever was tiptoeing about and decided a housebreaker was searching the attics. I admire her courage, even if I abhor her curiosity.'

'She left her room in the middle of the night to pursue a burglar with only a water jug? I'm not sure if that's brave or reckless.'

'Neither am I,' he said with a preoccupied frown. 'But she was a damned nuisance either way. Whoever was creeping about the house heard us and got away while Kitty was using her weapon on me.'

'Yet it was a bright moonlit night and almost too hot to sleep, surely someone would notice a felon running from the house into the countryside?'

'So you would think.'

'And if they didn't, the prowler you were both chasing must have come from inside the house,' she said it for him, so he couldn't pretend not to know.

'Possibly.'

'You have a suspect?'

'Maybe,' he answered even more cautiously.

She wondered if it was possible to box your husband's ear at the same time you were making it clear he meant nothing to you. Probably not, she decided, and plumped down in her accustomed seat at the breakfast table after gathering up her breakfast more or less at random. It was an occupation and she had to eat if she wasn't to risk another attack of the vapours.

Chapter Five

'How odd that nobody bothered with us before you came here,' Callie said once she had chewed a corner off a piece of toast and sipped a little of her tea to force it down.

'Hmm, or that my arrival caused it to happen,' he countered.

'Why are you really here, Gideon?' Callie asked, weary of dancing round such an urgent topic and eager to get back to real life. This whole situation felt far too dangerous to her peace of mind and she simply wanted him to go, didn't she? 'If you have met another woman and wish to marry her, I must disappoint you, I fear. I won't take a lover so you can sue him for criminal conversation, then divorce me.'

'Well, I certainly didn't come here for that,' he said fastidiously, as if the very idea was unthinkable and a bit offensive.

'Then why *are* you here? There's nothing to interest a man like you here.'

'Of course there is, there's you.'

'No, there isn't. I won't be used because you suddenly find yourself in need of a wife and I'm the one you have.'

'That's never how it was between us and you know it, Callie.'

'Oh, really?' she asked scornfully. 'So our silly little love story wasn't a plot to put the broken parts of our families back together, after all, then? I must have imagined those furious accusations you threw at me after we got back to Raigne from our hasty flight to the Border. Miss Calliope Sommers dreamt a fine young buck carried her off to Gretna so they could wed for love. His father forbade it and her grandfathers schemed to help them elope, oh, yes, it's obvious now—you must have been right all along, Gideon. That naive seventeen-year-old girl obviously planned every step of the journey with your furious father pursuing us to spur you on. What better way to be my Lady Laughraine one day and rule the place my illegitimate birth cut me off from? Wasn't that how your neat story to absolve you of guilt and pile it on me went? Such a shame I didn't know who I really was until you told me, don't you think? Or are you still convinced I'm lying about that and wed you because Lord Laughraine's son died without legitimate issue and he wanted his great-grandchildren to inherit everything I couldn't lay claim to without you?'

'No, although I don't doubt Lord Laughraine and your other grandfather schemed to marry us to each other and tidy up two mistakes at one go. I still can't believe they thought it a good idea,' he said with a bitter grimace. 'No need to remind you I'm the son of Virgil Winterley's bastard and have no right to

Raigne, but I wonder your grandfathers didn't see what a poor bargain they were offering you.'

'And I was such a good one? The by-blow of a sixteen-year-old schoolgirl and the artful young rake who refused to marry her? Don't make me into someone I'm not, Gideon.'

'You bear no responsibility for them, Callie. You're a fine person in your own right and I was as deeply honoured you agreed to marry me back then as I am now,' he said as if he didn't regret their hasty marriage over the anvil, but how could he not?

'Thank you, but if that's true you should stop blaming yourself for your father's and grandfather's sins,' she said with a wry smile at his false view of her as some sort of paragon she shouldn't find flattering. 'I've been told your real grandfather was nothing like his son in temper, even if your father was his spit in looks, so you must follow him. I deplored your hasty temper and love of danger, but I was never afraid of you. Even when you were in your cups I knew you would never hurt me or our child.'

She saw him flinch at the mention of their lost baby and wished she'd minded her tongue. It was too soon to revisit that sore place again, so Callie remembered Esmond Laughraine raging how he'd kill Gideon before he let them wed instead and wondered how a good man was fathered by an angry bully. Had Esmond suspected who she really was and hated the idea a future grandson of his might truly inherit Raigne? Such a bitter man might do everything he could to prevent the marriage for that very reason.

She was as puzzled by his furious opposition as Gideon at the time, but she supposed selfish jealousy could explain it. At the time she knew she wasn't a brilliant match for the grandson of a baronet and a peer of the realm's great-grandson, but even she knew Gideon wasn't quite that. She recalled the love in Lady Virginia's eyes when she talked of her late husband and knew a lady of such character and spirit could never love a man who was anything like Esmond Laughraine at heart. Her Gideon must be like his grandfather in more than looks then and shouldn't that possessive worry a wife who expected him to leave as soon as he'd told her what he'd come for?

'I would cut my own arm off rather than hurt you, but I managed it, didn't I?' Gideon said at last. He watched her lower her eyes, then stare out of the window to avoid his gaze and sighed as if he had the weight of the world on his shoulders. 'Sooner or later we must talk about it, Callie. If either of us are ever to be father or mother we can only be so together with any honour, unless you'd rather stick the carving knife in me and risk the next assizes?'

'Don't joke about murder,' she snapped, shaken to her core by the very idea.

'I think I must, Wife, or sit and howl for what you don't want us to have.'

'Now you're being ridiculous and where were we with this sorry tale of loss and betrayal, and why you're bothering me with it now?'

He sighed and poured himself a cup of coffee to wash down the breakfast he seemed to enjoy about as much as she did. 'I admit when your maternal grandfather told me the true tale of your birth, I only saw concern for your future and the Raigne inheritance behind his plot with Lord Laughraine to set the succession straight again. I never stopped to see you had no idea who your father really was until I told you. Little wonder you didn't defend yourself against my wild accusations when you must have been shocked to your core by the news and never mind the interpretation I put on it. Hasty boy that I was then, I felt more like a stallion put out to stud than your proud husband and lover all of a sudden and I came home and accused you of ridiculous things in the heat of temper, then made things worse by refusing to back down after I'd cooled off, even though I knew I was wrong to suspect you of being in on their plans. I never really considered how you must have felt when you found out who your father really was from a furious young idiot. It was that crack in our marriage that finally opened up and ruined everything we had wasn't it? I ruined it all simply because I was too proud and arrogant to admit to being wrong,' he said bleakly.

'You were very young,' she heard herself excuse him.

At the time it seemed inexcusable, yet it must have been agonising for the boy he had been to wonder if his wife married him to get the heir Raigne needed so badly. Sir Wendover Laughraine's three legitimate sons were dead from fever, accident and battle by then and the current Lord Laughraine's only child, her father, had died before she could even remember him. So why on earth had Sir Wendover still refused to admit his wife had imposed another man's bastard on him as his youngest son? Because that bitter old man was too proud to publically admit the truth, Gideon was heir to a huge fortune and vast old house he didn't want or believe he deserved and she was the last true Laughraine. Except she wasn't a true one at all, was she?

'You were even younger,' he replied, 'and already carrying my child so it was unforgivable to storm and rage at you like that, even if there was any truth in that tale I made up to make myself feel better. I was so afraid you didn't love me at all, you see?'

'Why wouldn't I?' she said with a reminiscent smile for the handsome, brooding boy he was at eighteen she hoped didn't look as tender as if felt.

'Because I'm not a lovable man. All my life my father cursed me as the reason he had to marry my mother. He'd call her a sanctimonious prig one moment and whore the next because she let him seduce her. Heaven knows he could be charming when he wanted to and she had a reputation for being far too proper for her own good, but she was a naive and sheltered young woman who believed him when he said he loved her. She said a lot less than him about how much she hated being trapped in a marriage neither of them wanted because I was on the way, but I doubt she could put her hand on her heart and swear she loves me even today. We meet once or twice a year now my grandfather has taken her back into the fold, but so far we haven't managed to like each other very much.'

That confession of how bleak his childhood really was almost broke her heart. How could they not have blamed themselves when he was the innocent party? That disgusting bet Esmond Laughraine had made to seduce a bishop's daughter no other man would dream of even trying to get into bed without a very public ceremony and a wedding ring was appalling, but the bishop's daughter had succumbed of her own free will and Gideon had no choice about the matter at all. He wouldn't quite believe her if she championed him now, because she had turned away his love, as well. Despite all the good reasons she thought she had at the time for doing so, how much damage she had done by taking the easy option? Yes, it was simpler to cut out the despair and hurt from her life and go on without him, rather than patch up some sort of marriage between them. But none of that would put things right between them now and make him believe he was a deeply lovable and honourable man, despite his shocking betrayal of her when she was at her most vulnerable.

'You make me sound so meek and mild, Gideon—as if I sat and softly wept all the time you were accusing me of luring you in with my witchy wiles,' she chided lightly, because it was better than weeping and letting him see she pitied the boy who grew up with parents who didn't deserve him.

'You gave as good as you got, didn't you, spitfire?' he said with a wry smile, as if he remembered those furious rows and their making up afterwards with affection.

'And will again if you're not careful,' she said, chin raised to warn him she was no doormat nowadays, despite her nun-like existence since they parted.

'Good, because I wouldn't have you any other way,' he said with a boyish grin that did something unfair to her insides.

'It's just as well I have no intention of changing then,' she said.

Was she secretly conceding that, for the right incentive, she might be tempted to try again? No, she didn't want to be a convenient wife, primped and perfumed and ready to oblige her lord in the marriage bed as part of a cynical bargain. If they resumed their stormy marriage it must be as equal partners. Yet he was so self-sufficient he looked as if he didn't need anyone nowadays, let alone a wife who would demand a place in every aspect of his life she could get a toehold into.

'What will happen to Raigne if we remain apart?' she asked abruptly, the thought of being with him for the sake of a huge inheritance sour in her mouth as she tried to swallow it down with cold tea. 'I dare say you would be accepted as the heir without me.'

'I might be the legal heir, but you're the true one.'

'Yet you love Raigne and nobody else will keep the place as you will.'

'You could if you wanted to.'

'I'd be laughed out of court. I'm your wife, so everything I own is yours.'

'And what if Prinny decided to challenge me on the strength of some old gossip and the wrong family resemblance? You can see why they were so keen for us to wed, can't you? Still, at least when we eloped we simply wanted to be wed and never mind anything else.'

'We should have known better,' she said sadly.

Her husband stared out of the window at another cloudless morning as if he was unable to feel the warmth and she tried not to care. 'Indeed we should,' he said at last in that clipped, carefully controlled voice she was learning to hate.

'I'm sure Grandfather Sommers wanted us to be happy,' she said as if that made the gulf between those young lovers and now a little less.

'I wish you'd believe Lord Laughraine does, as well, Callie. It's not his fault we looked for reasons to hate each other when our baby died. I wish you could find it in your heart to forgive me for that, even if everything else I did and didn't do is beyond it.'

He looked as if memory of the quarrels and furious silences that marred their marriage had been a hair shirt to him ever since. Memories of long, hot nights of driven passion after they found out what her grandfathers were up to slipped into her mind and whispered they couldn't have felt such endless need for each other if all they had was lust. Then she thought of their baby and shivered. Nothing had mattered to her but the terrible space their little girl left behind her in the dark days after that terrible journey from London to King's Raigne to bury their child in Grandfather Sommers's recently dug grave.

She simply hadn't any emotion left over for Gideon or anyone else after that. Even the irony of hearing her real mother invite Gideon, Callie and Mrs Willoughby's sister, Aunt Seraphina, to stay with her whilst they considered what to do next, since they had nowhere else to go at the time, was wasted on her. For the first time her true mother opened her life to her secret child and they might as well have been on the moon for all the difference it made to Callie. Her withdrawal from the world was a way out of heartbreak and she'd dived into that grey nothing as if not feeling anything was all that mattered. No doubt

Gideon felt desperate for comfort, painfully young and bereft as he was, as well. It wasn't an excuse for what he did, but she wasn't as blameless as she liked to believe at the time.

'First I'd have to forgive myself,' she said with a sigh, and half-heartedly pushed a slice of cold bacon round her plate so she wouldn't have to meet his intent gaze.

'You must, Callie, there won't be a pinch of happiness for either of us until you do.'

'I'd have to look past a lot more than petty quarrels and grief for there to be an "us" again, wouldn't I?' she challenged him.

'Ah, and there's the rub. You don't want to see past that farce, do you?'

'No,' she admitted bleakly. 'There's no excuse for what you did that day.'

'Yet even in a court of law a person is innocent until proven guilty. You didn't bother to wait for niceties like that before you condemned me, did you?'

'I expect that's why you like them. I prefer to believe my own eyes,' she said bitterly.

'You still want to think I was unfaithful, don't you? Whatever I said fell on deaf ears because you had already given up on us. It was a good excuse to finally push me out of your life and you've certainly done your best to forget I exist ever since.'

'How could I? We had a child,' she said with the sadness of losing her daughter still raw in her throat after all these years, and her absence seemed all the more savage now they were in the same room and she wasn't here.

'Yes,' he said bleakly, '*we* did.'

* * *

'Ah, there you both are,' Aunt Seraphina said as if she had been looking everywhere for them before she breezed into the room.

Anyone else would feel the tension and leave them in peace. Callie caught herself out being disloyal and managed to smile a half-hearted welcome.

'I thought you two had broken your fast and gone out long ago,' Aunt Seraphina remarked blandly, although the door would hardly have been shut in that case, so why lie?

'I had a disturbed night,' Gideon said, reverting to unreadable again.

Callie felt as if some golden opportunity to understand all they'd lost and gained had been brushed out of the room like house dust.

'Poor Kitty is mortified she mistook you for a burglar in the dark last night, Sir Gideon,' her aunt went blithely on. 'We can't sleep safe in our own beds of a night any more. I really don't know what the world is coming to,' she added, shaking her head as she poured herself coffee and refused anything more substantial as if it might choke her.

Her aunt did look careworn this morning, as if she hardly slept last night. So why didn't she admit hearing noises in the night if she was sleepless for most of it?

'Whoever it was knows there is a man in the house and a very alert housemaid now, so I doubt they will ever come back,' Gideon said, as if he'd never discussed the likelihood of the disturber of the peace coming from inside the house with Callie.

'Well, I admit now that I should have listened to

you, Calliope, and found another handyman when we found out the last one was more often drunk than sober, instead of trying to manage without as best we could,' Aunt Seraphina said, and why did Callie feel as if every word she said had a ring of falseness this morning?

'We could get a dog,' Callie suggested with a half-hearted smile to admit they had had this conversation many times and her aunt still couldn't abide dogs.

'I think another man of all work would be less trouble,' Aunt Seraphina replied with the polite titter even her niece was beginning to find irritating.

'There are plenty of dogs at Raigne. Lord Laughraine has a pack of assorted ones that follow him about the place,' Gideon reminded his wife as if it might be a carrot to get Callie there, if his own desire to have her home wasn't enough.

She felt little and petty for making him feel he had to tempt her, but couldn't he see what a huge undertaking it was for her to go there with him? It would mean trusting all she was to him and, without the headlong, driven love between them ten years ago, how could she do that when even mutual obsession hadn't kept them together before? Her heart raced at the very idea and she searched her morning for an excuse to avoid him and work out what she really wanted to do.

'I dare say the servants hate the work such hairy animals cause,' Aunt Seraphina said sourly and Callie felt guiltily irritated by her naysaying ways.

'They are as happy to see them as he is every morning,' Gideon said with a fond smile for the man he had no right to call uncle, but Callie never doubted the affection between two men who had every reason to dislike and distrust one another, yet did not. She wriggled in her seat against a pang of guilt because she had cut herself off from her grandfather as well as her husband and that too seemed petty and rather little this morning.

'I'm glad to hear the creatures don't sleep in his lordship's room,' her aunt went on with her subject like a bulldog worrying at a bone.

'Only two or three at a time,' Gideon said, as if enjoying Aunt Seraphina's reluctance to call a peer of the realm's habits distasteful. 'But I doubt anyone could get into the house without them raising the roof.'

'Oh, but I couldn't endure all that mess to keep a chance felon away,' she said with a shudder. 'I shall trust employing an extra man will put the housebreakers off trying again.'

'I should like to have a dog about the place,' Callie said wistfully.

'His lordship would be very happy to find you one,' Gideon said.

'There you are, you see, my dear? Your husband has found the perfect way to lure his wife back to Raigne and keep her happy, has he not?' her aunt said with false brightness, as if he was offering Callie a childish bribe to resume their marriage and she might not be clever enough to spot it.

'If you will excuse us, Aunt, Gideon and I have a great deal more to talk about than our pets or lack of them,' Callie said and rose from her seat before the lady could argue.

'You mistake my concern, Calliope. I know you

are a woman now and not a silly girl taken in by bribes and promises,' her aunt said with such dignity Callie knew she was offended.

'Then why make such belittling comments in the first place, Aunt?'

'Because he always set us against each other and now he's doing it again,' Aunt Seraphina said with an accusing gesture at Gideon, who looked impassive and made Seraphina seem shrill and begrudging by contrast. 'It's my duty to point out you always were a fool for this man and don't show many signs of learning from past mistakes.'

'I have run the academic side of this enterprise and proved myself a woman of ability and character. You cannot trust me with all that, then accuse me of being an empty-headed idiot the first time I show any sign of questioning your wisdom, Aunt.'

Aunt Seraphina looked unconvinced for a tense moment, then sighed heavily and nodded as if to affirm Callie was a different creature from the heartbroken girl of nine years ago. 'Very well, my dear, I must trust you have learnt judgement, I suppose. You will remember what happened last time, though, won't you?' she said with what looked like such genuine anxiety for Callie's well-being that Callie branded herself an ingrate and reassured her aunt she could hardly forget.

The insidious thought slipped into her mind that, if Aunt Seraphina was truly as devious as she must be to have hidden hers and Gideon's letters for so long, she would know arguing against her niece and Gideon having time alone would make them more suspicious. No, that had to be unjust and unkind of her, she really didn't think her aunt could have kept so much of her essential self hidden for so long when they lived in the same house.

'I don't know why I'm letting you drag me out here when I need to get ready for the new term,' Callie protested half-heartedly ten minutes later. 'But why did you refuse my aunt's offer of the gig so we could take a drive before it gets too hot to move, Husband? Are you ashamed to be seen with me in such a drab getup?' she added.

Gideon saw self-doubt was tripping her up again and how could she not know she was one of the most beautiful creatures he'd ever laid eyes on?

'Don't put words into my mouth, Wife,' he teased and got a half-hearted smile out of her. He resolved to make sure she never had to worry about being less than perfectly turned out ever again and promised himself yesterday's gown would go into the ragbag as soon as she had even one new gown to eke out her meagre supply.

'Then why don't you want to leave the house or gardens?' she asked suspiciously.

Did she think he was lying to disguise his distaste for her plain round gown and old-maid-like cap? In fairness his first impulse was to rip that monstrosity from her head so her glossy dark curls framed her enchanting face again, but he had to tread on egg-shells around his love if the hope he couldn't quite keep bricked up in his mind wasn't to crash and die, and he would never do that to her, anyway. She had endured enough slights and humiliations at the hands of her sly aunt over the years. So he would go on treading carefully round the snags that had been put in her self-confidence for as long as it took him to reassure her she was his lady and his love and beautiful to him whatever she wore. Best if he didn't think about what she might not wear and look even more superb and delicious if they ever got close enough to be man and wife again right now.

Meanwhile they had set out on a sedate stroll towards the orchard. Callie must have noticed how closely he was watching the house and was looking suspicious about his motives for staying within sight of it until he was proved right or wrong about her aunt's motives for keeping her so close all these years and him so far away.

'You were ill yesterday and today you need to rest. Anyway, perhaps I'm curious about this house and the people you have lived with all these years?'

'Why? We are a simple people living a quiet life.'

'I doubt there's any such thing as simple people with straightforward lives.'

Gideon had half an eye open for the signal the little downstairs maid agreed to make if the Missus or Kitty-Cat, as she called Mrs Bartle and Kitty, went up to the attics. The rest of his attention was caught by his wife flushing as if he'd smoked out her darkest mystery and he almost forgot to watch for a duster being shaken out of the window three times, after all.

'What guilty secrets are you keeping, Callie? Besides me, of course, and I think we can say that cat is already well and truly out of the bag.'

'I am a simple schoolmistress, I don't have time for secrets,' she said, but didn't quite manage to meet his eyes. Gideon felt a terrible, heart-plunging fear she might have a furtive admirer or even a lover, after all.

'Am I going to have to kill some besotted country swain, Wife?' he managed coolly.

'What's sauce for the goose, Gideon dear…' she said and let her voice tail off so sweetly he felt his old wild fury stir under the goad of hot jealousy.

'Don't play with fire,' he warned her austerely.

'I told you yesterday that I have no lover.'

'So you did. What's this mysterious secret you feel so guilty about then, Wife?'

'I don't feel guilty exactly,' she prevaricated, clearly wondering if she trusted him enough to let him know what it was and that didn't hurt him, of course it didn't. It wasn't as if he needed to know the inner secrets of her very soul. Such intimacy was for true lovers and she didn't have one of those any more—not even him.

'Then what do you feel?'

'Disloyal, I suppose,' she admitted at last.

'To me?'

'Of course not.'

'Oh, no, of course not,' he echoed rather hollowly and told himself not to be a fool. He hadn't expected to be welcomed back into her life with open arms, so he couldn't complain she didn't think he deserved her loyalty.

'You weren't here to be disloyal to,' she explained as if that covered everything.

'So I wasn't. What is this dark secret you don't feel guilty about then?' he asked grumpily, wondering if he was wrong about her aunt, after all. Maybe Mrs Bartle didn't have a secret cache of his and Callie's letters hidden somewhere. Perhaps she received his and found them so distasteful and embarrassing it was easier to pretend she did not.

'I write books,' she confessed as if it were a sin on a par with poisoning ambassadors or defending guilty criminals against the might of the law.

'You do?' he asked, startled to hear it, but instantly proud of her all the same. 'Should I have heard of you?'

'Not yet, I am trying to correspond with a gentleman who says my work is nearly ready for publication, but my aunt and my husband seem determined to get in the way.'

'So *that* was what you were up to yesterday?'

'Yes, I use another name to exchange letters with him, since Aunt Seraphina disapproves of lady novelists. I have a dream of living on my own and teaching only one or two days a week and Aunt Seraphina certainly won't approve if I succeed. So I pick up his letters and send mine off to him without my aunt's knowledge.'

'What a dark horse you are, my Callie,' he said, thinking that at least those letters stood a better chance of reaching their destination than any she entrusted to her aunt ever had.

He had always known where she was, of course—what sort of an investigator would he be if he hadn't?—but she made no secret of her identity when she reverted to her maiden name. He should have sent his letters by courier and insisted he put them into her hands only, but he had been as taken in by Mrs Bartle's air of refined integrity as everyone else. After that letter setting out Callie's hatred of him and fervent wish never to set eyes on him again, he lost heart and his letters were desperate pleas for a hearing and protests of innocence she didn't want to believe in.

Except Callie hadn't written it, had she? It occurred to him Reverend Sommers had made a far better job of raising his granddaughter than either of his daughters. Was that why he taught Callie as if she were a boy rather than a girl? Maybe that good and clever man saw the mistakes in his daughters' upbringing and devoted himself to teaching Callie his moral code and fine principles instead of leaving it to a governess to instil a set of ladylike accomplishments that had little practical value or interest to a girl with a fine mind like hers.

'You really don't mind?' she asked as if she had been expecting doubt or fury.

'No, why on earth would I? And after you informed me I have no right to be offended about anything you do, I'm surprised my feelings matter so much to you, anyway.'

'Of course they do, but you know perfectly well that if I had admitted to a secret admirer you would have torn him limb from limb and locked me up in the highest turret of your castle,' she teased back, and didn't that feel wonderful?

Gideon stamped down hard on a fierce need to kiss his wife senseless. It was best not to run before they learnt to walk again as man and wife and he didn't want to let his raging need of her stampede through the fragile relationship they seemed to be building brick by careful brick. He wondered how he could convince her he was perfectly happy for his wife to write, as long as she did it while she was living with him instead of alone or with her aunt.

'Why is Biddy waving her duster so wildly from the landing window, Gideon? It really looks most peculiar.'

'She is?' he exclaimed and turned to see the tail-end of the signal he and Biddy had agreed on. 'The devil, that's even sooner than I expected. Excuse me, I must hurry or I'll be too late,' he said absently, then loped off, hoping she understood he'd far rather stay and talk to her, but time was a-wasting.

Chapter Six

For a startled moment Callie watched her husband dash back towards the house as if it were on fire. She could stay out here and wait for him to come back and tell her what he was up to, she supposed, but he had a poor record for sharing secrets, so she hurried after him. It wasn't because she couldn't stand being parted from him now they were within touching distance of each other once again—it was curiosity, plain and simple. Her heartbeat quickened, anyway, but she was running to catch up now and that was perfectly understandable.

'Stay here,' he ordered when they reached the hall and he realised she was on his tail, then stopped so abruptly she cannoned into him.

'No,' she murmured and gave him a push towards the stairs to let him know there was no point arguing.

'Exasperating woman,' he mumbled under his breath. She glared when he half turned to glower at her and bade him watch his step. 'Keep quiet then and don't give us away,' he told her softly and they went up the stairs while she was trying to think up something pithy enough to demolish his arrogant certainty he was in command.

Tight lipped, she did her best to tread as stealthily as he did, but that was impossible. She managed to avoid the stair that creaked after he did the same without seeming to think about it. He must have explored the house with this sort of stealthy pursuit in mind. It looked as if the dangerous adventures Lady Virginia hinted at when she visited were very real and not a cunning scheme to soften her heart as she thought at the time. She was glad she hadn't known what he was really up to at the time and terrified he knew too much about the darker side of life to be her idealistic and loving Gideon again. Now where had that come from? She didn't want this man to be anything of the sort to her again, did she?

Never mind that now, they were on the half-landing and heading for the attic stairs. That seemed so absurd she stopped wondering how she felt and kept as close as she could to him. Her world felt right and safe when she was near him and that should worry her. The door opened without a sound and why were the hinges so well-oiled when these rooms were full of lumber? The maids slept on the other side of the house and the stableman lived over the stables, so what had once been the male farm-servants' quarters were now empty.

Why was Gideon creeping towards a lot of dusty rubbish as if on the track of lost state secrets? Callie noted footprints in the dust on the twisting staircase and held her breath for a moment, then shook her head in disbelief. There was nothing much up here and it was already uncomfortably hot. His tension still made her listen for the slightest noise and she recalled a few Gothic touches in her own novel then wished she hadn't. It was absurd to let her imagination run riot, but she felt a flutter of superstitious fear before she told herself sternly this was no time for spectral visitations. They were a few steps up the twisting stairway when Gideon waved his hand to stop and she forgot imagined horrors for real life.

Frozen in her tracks, she was cross with herself for obeying orders like a soldier on parade. From the soft murmurs ahead it sounded as if there were two people in the little storeroom furthest from the stairs. Impatient at him for being a step closer to danger than he was prepared to let her go, she pushed the small of his back to urge him on. He resisted, as if he had to stand between her and hurt like a wall. He must have felt her impatience with such overprotective nonsense, because he reluctantly went up a step so she could hear, as well. First there was her aunt's voice saying something impatient and a lighter voice in reply. Why was Kitty arguing with her aunt here when they could do it downstairs in comfort? It didn't sound as if they were discussing using the rolls of dimity and calico stored here to make new gowns and aprons for the maids. Her aunt economised on them until threadbare, but surely that wasn't an important enough to linger over in a stuffy attic on a day like today.

'You are impudent,' her aunt raised her voice to say regally, as if trying to overawe Kitty with her importance as head of a school and Kitty's employer. 'Nobody will believe a vagrant maid over a lady of means and standing in the neighbourhood.'

'They won't have to. I'll have my money *and* keep my place till it suits me to leave. You won't want me to tell the constables what I know, will you, Mrs Bartle?'

'I changed my name to avoid being known as the widow of a depraved fool. That will earn me more sympathy than censure.'

'You can say you're the queen of the fairies if you want to. It's what you did to him that'll make them prick up their ears. I can read, you see? I wonder you never bothered to find out I was hired to keep an old woman out of mischief in my last place. She taught me to use my talents, then I learnt how stupid it was to trust anyone when she turned on me.'

'I expect she saw you for the cunning little ferret you really are.'

'I'd be careful what you say, Mrs Bartle. When the world knows what you did to keep your niece here and her husband's money flowing into your pockets, nobody will believe you. Such a sweet story for the scandal sheets, I dare say I'll make a fortune if you're too stupid to pay up.'

Now Callie knew why Gideon warned her to stay silent. Kitty's words seemed to echo like a clap of thunder and fell into her mind so surely she knew they were true. She managed to stifle a gasp of horror, but her senses were intent as Gideon's as she realised everything she and her aunt had built here was a sham. With him here—the real Gideon next to her—the truth of him somehow cancelled out her aunt's lies.

How had she believed every word Aunt Seraphina said against him until yesterday? Was he right; did part of her want to believe him guilty? Maybe it had been easier to blame their ills on her husband, but didn't that make her a coward as well as a fool? She had hardened her heart against him and believed her aunt must love her because she was there after everyone else fell away. Every artlessly accidental comment about her appearance, Aunt Seraphina's clever slights and well-placed reminders of all Callie had lost at the hands of a careless husband kept her locked down and hurting, but she hadn't seen the truth because it was easier not to.

'No one will believe *you*,' Aunt Seraphina was sneering and how hadn't Callie seen through her until today?

'The stableman is coming to take this lumber down so the boxes are empty for my niece's luggage and he certainly can't read, so it will all be ashes in a few minutes.'

'No, they stay here and I keep the keys.'

'You couldn't stop a fly doing what it wanted, let alone me, now could you? A fall down those awkward stairs will remind you who is mistress here and who is the servant.'

If Kitty didn't have the sense to shiver at the casual malice behind that question Callie did it for her. 'If aught happens to me, the landlord of the Crown in Manydown has a letter saying who to look for. Do you want him and half the county on to you for attempted murder?' the girl said boldly and she was evidently a more subtle opponent than Aunt Seraphina thought.

'So that's where you've been sneaking off to. I should never have let my niece persuade me to give a trollop like you a chance when your last employer turned you off for chasing her sons. She never mentioned blackmail, though, curse her for a soft fool when you should clearly be in the local bridewell.'

'We're both bad, but you could've been better if you wanted. As for that milksop I worked for, I knew far too much about her spindle-shanked sons for her to risk it and they weren't worth it, anyway. Miss Sommers is a better woman than either of us and took me in despite that woman's spiteful tales, but you betrayed her long before I got here, didn't you? So who will the world judge the worst rogue of us two, Madam Bartle?'

'You spied on her for me, despite owing her a roof over your head, and blackmail is a serious crime. If you survive the little accident you're about to have, you will regret relying on that weak sot from the Crown for aught but a roll in the hay, you know that, don't you?'

'He has me to put steel in him, Mrs Bartle, and I have this,' the little maid said triumphantly and Callie heard her aunt gasp. 'An account written by your husband of times he was ill after he ate with you and accidents he had on his way *out* to get drunk and not coming back as you claimed. He even knew a man you paid to murder him. They had a fine spree with the money, then you decided to do the job yourself and he went in fear of his life. He should have run instead of staying, but what a fool you were to keep his evidence.'

'How did you get your grubby hands on such drunken nonsense?' Aunt Seraphina whispered as if she dared not admit it existed out loud. Through the heavy stillness of the hot attic Callie could hear fear in her voice and knew this was true, as well.

'I found the secret panel in your desk drawer I bet you wish was big enough for all the letters you stole over the years. Being bedridden herself, the old lady I was meant to keep quiet in my last position thought it a fine joke to teach me the tricks of such places and find things her son-in-law hid from his wife so she could make him do as she said.'

'That's where you learnt your disgraceful trade?'

'Of course, and a cunning old besom she is, too,' Kitty said admiringly. 'Why else would he pay a maid to keep her happy when he hates her like poison?'

'He still managed to dismiss you.'

'That's when I learnt never to trust sly witches like you and make sure I know more than they do. The old woman moved her treasures, then told her daughter I was warming her precious sons' beds.'

'You were lucky not to be whipped at the cart-tail,' Aunt Seraphina scorned.

'I knew too much, but then the old lady gossiped and I couldn't get work. Don't you look down your long nose at me, Mrs Bartle, I was born with nothing and make my way as best I can. You were born a lady and only took me on because I'm cheap and you thought I'd be so grateful I'd do whatever you bade me.'

'And you would be on the parish now if not for me.'

'Not I,' Kitty said confidently and somehow Callie believed her. 'I wouldn't be set up for life neither, though, so I'm happy to tell your niece what you did if you don't pay up. If this paper gets to the magistrates, stealing from your family and keeping a man and his wife apart all these years will be small beer next to wilful murder.'

It went so quiet in the chamber under the roof Callie could hear the crackle of paper as the girl held that damning account out of the Aunt Seraphina's way as she did her best to grab it from her.

'Enough,' she whispered to Gideon, convinced the two people in that room were so absorbed in their struggle they wouldn't notice if a town crier was standing on the stairs.

'Indeed,' he agreed, and somehow managed to launch himself up the last few stairs and past the partition wall as swiftly and silently as a hunting wolf.

He easily topped Kitty and Aunt Seraphina and snatched the letter from Kitty before she even took in the fact he was behind her, throwing it back to Callie. Catching by instinct, she laid it on the stair and got ready to join in if he was too gentlemanly to ward off two biting, spitting furies.

Gideon must have learnt the folly of being a gentleman with she-cats since they parted. He grabbed Kitty by the waist and lifted her off her feet so he could aim her at Aunt Seraphina like a weapon. Her wildly kicking feet landed a good few blows on Aunt Seraphina's substantial person as the girl tried to turn in his arms to scratch and bite him. Luckily both women were soon winded and Gideon stepped back.

'How enlightening,' he said casually. 'See if Biddy's friend the groom has returned with the magistrate yet, will you, love?' he asked Callie without turning round.

'Of course,' she said, carrying Bonhomie Bartle's statement at arm's length as if it were as noxious as the man who wrote it.

She ran downstairs, unsure Gideon's gentlemanly instincts would let him hold those two at bay much longer. The memory of the deadly pistols he pulled out of his pocket as if he used them to hold felons up every day reassured her. For all she knew he ran such risks on a daily basis. She could see him doing exactly that when she turned her back on him. Occupied with her own thoughts, she watched Squire Evans ride up to the house as fast as his fat old cob would carry him and remembered the evidence in her hand. She darted into her term-time office and locked it in the box where she kept the girls' pocket money. If Gideon chose to show it to the authorities she would hand him the key, but somehow she didn't want her aunt's downfall to be caused by a man she had despised and feared herself.

'I still can't take it in,' the magistrate said after a spitting and furious Kitty was escorted off the premises with her bundle of belongings and Mrs Bartle locked in her room. 'Mrs Grisham seems such an upstanding woman.'

'I suspected nothing, Mr Evans,' Callie said with a rueful shrug.

'So why were you suspicious, Sir Gideon?' the squire asked.

'I just knew something was amiss,' he said with that closed expression Callie hated. 'I would rather our gullibility went no further, if you take my meaning, sir?'

'Ah, yes, well I don't see how that can be, Sir Gideon. If we prosecute the woman, we'll need a good case and yours is by far the strongest.'

'I intend to keep all the evidence pertinent to it in a safe place and if you return the letters Mrs Bartle used to blackmail her neighbours anonymously she will have nothing left to live on but her wits.'

'No doubt she'd thrive, since "the wicked flourish like the green bay tree" as it says in our prayer books. Inconvenient to have all that linen washed in public, is it?' The squire tapped his red nose with a beefy forefinger and reached for the glass of excellent brandy Aunt Seraphina kept for wealthier visitors.

'Lady Laughraine and I will be living not fifteen miles away and I don't want the whole world to know what fools we've been,' Gideon agreed confidentially.

Apparently her husband had become a fine actor over the years they were apart. Callie suspected he didn't care a straw what their neighbours thought, given the gossip it had been enjoying at his expense since before he was born. He was doing it for her. She shook her head to show him she could weather being thought a fool to tell the world her aunt was a thief and a liar. He pretended not to see, so she gave up and made an excuse about needing to steady the household and left the room. They would have to stay here another night at least now and, although Cataret House had been her home for nine years and she'd thought herself content here, she couldn't wait to be quit of the place.

'My aunt will spread all sorts of wicked gossip about us if you let her go, Gideon,' Callie warned as they went upstairs later to assess what to take with them and what she was happy to leave behind.

'If she tries it, I'll find her and stop her,' he said so coolly she shivered and believed him. 'Never mind her, how many of your belongings do you want to take with us, Callie? I'd prefer to travel as light as we can.'

'Exactly when did I agree to go to Raigne, Gideon?' she challenged half-heartedly. Somehow the thought of going home was very tempting, even if she would be going to the 'Big House' rather than comfortable King's Raigne Vicarage.

'Would you rather we went to London, or somewhere else altogether then? I don't much care where we go as long as you come with me.'

'Raigne is your home.'

'One you have a great deal more right to call so than I have.'

Callie shook her head, because that huge old barn of a house would never seem like home to her, but nine years of loneliness and longing told her pride would make a very poor bedfellow if she insisted on staying apart and aloof from her husband and refused to admit they might manage to remake their marriage if they both tried hard enough.

'If I come with you, it can only be a maybe to resuming our marriage, not a fait accompli, Gideon,' she warned, but both of them knew it was a huge concession. Callie wondered if he felt as if he hardly dared even breathe deeply lest this hope for the future shattered in their faces all over again, as well.

'It's far more than I dared hope when I came here, so that will do me for now. In the meantime, how much of this do you really want to take now, and what can be sent on later, my not-quite wife?' he said with a smile that invited her to find their not-quite anything status almost comfortable.

'I don't have many possessions that really matter,'

she said, gazing round the shabby room as if through a stranger's eyes. 'One or two books are from Grandfather Sommers's library and then there's my grandmother's pearl necklet and a miniature of them when they were young. Apart from my writing box, I can leave the rest without a qualm.'

'Then pack those and any essentials and we'll leave as soon as you're awake in the morning. I'd like to get to Raigne before my honorary uncle is out on the estate and it will be cooler and less trying to travel early in the day.'

'How can I stay at Raigne, Gideon? I hardly ever set foot in the place when I lived at King's Raigne Vicarage,' she protested, the thought of bowling up to the Tudor mansion as if she had a right suddenly felt impossible again.

'It's your home and heaven knows you've more right to call it so than I have.'

'No, you love the place and belong there as I never will.'

'That's nonsense and I know Lord Laughraine wants you home nearly as much as I do. You're his only grandchild, Callie, and he's a good man who truly only wants the best for you. He might have seemed remote and uncaring when you were a child, but apparently your other grandfather begged him to let you grow up without the stigma of your birth shadowing your childhood. No, don't grimace like that, love, Reverend Sommers was quite right. I might have been born within wedlock by the skin of my teeth, but it's bad enough for a boy to be mocked and derided for what the gossips say his parents did. I would never wish it on a girl who might end up being tarred with her mother's supposed sins before she was old enough to know what they even meant.'

'We can't know now, can we?' she managed to say past the torn feelings that were threatening to clog up her throat and make her weep, not for herself but for him and all the slights and sly whispers he'd been left to cope with as best he could since he was old enough to take notice.

'I can, but it's quite safe to love him, Callie. Don't turn him into a conniving monster because your aunt was one and you don't trust your family now. It was wrong of me to drag you to London when we got back from Scotland. I should have left you at Raigne to learn to know Lord Laughraine. You were carrying our child. He and his household could have fussed over you while I was in town learning my trade. I was selfish to insist on having you near all the time. I can't tell you how much I wish you'd known him as the fine man he is before you went through hell, Callie. You might have turned to him for love and support when I failed you then, instead of your stony-hearted aunt.'

'If wishes were horse, beggars would ride,' she replied tightly as she began opening drawers and pulling out books so she wouldn't have to look him in the eye. 'And I wouldn't have stayed behind, anyway. I loved you far too much to be parted from you while we waited for our child to be born,' she finally admitted gruffly.

'You would have put up with it for her sake,' he said and bent to pull a little trunk out of the cupboard she was staring into without seeing the old clothes and winter boots that just wouldn't do for Sir Gideon Laughraine's lady.

'We don't know that it would have made any difference if I was anywhere else. Don't second-guess fate, Gideon. It does no good and will drive you insane if you let it,' she said, her own struggles with that particular demon haunting her.

'No dear,' he said with mock humility she knew was meant to lighten her thoughts. He went out to retrieve some of the boxes the stableman had emptied ready for her departure, those that really were full of worn-out clothes and ancient account books. 'Do you need anything else?' he asked, seeming to accept it was best to deal with details right now.

'I think not. Where do you intend to sleep tonight, Gideon?'

'I could insist on sharing this room, but I'm not a fool,' he said with a sceptical glance at the narrow bed and ancient furniture, as if he wasn't sure it was up to the weight of a fully adult male if he stayed.

'No, and it's best if I do this alone,' she said mildly, refusing to hint at her feelings about sharing a bed with him again, mainly because she wasn't sure what they were herself.

'Don't forget I'm here now,' he told her mildly, even if there was an intensity in his complex grey eyes that made her long for things she wasn't even ready to admit to herself she wanted yet.

'I learnt to walk my own paths while you were away,' she warned.

'Part of being married is learning to walk together without stamping too hard on one another's toes, isn't it? I've been without you for a very long time, Wife,' he reminded her so softly it felt more significant than if he were to shout his frustration from the rooftops.

'I still lived a very different life from you and it will take a while to accustom myself to yours if we find a way past the pitfalls. My aunt isn't the sole reason we were apart these last nine years,' she reminded him with a severe look to remind him that war wasn't won.

And I need to work out if I can endure living with a husband who only wants to share my bed because he has no alternative without making our marriage vows a lie, she added an unspoken aside. He sighed and seemed to resign himself to her mistrust for a little longer. Then he smiled wryly to say he was tame again and there was no need to worry he was going to beg.

Chapter Seven

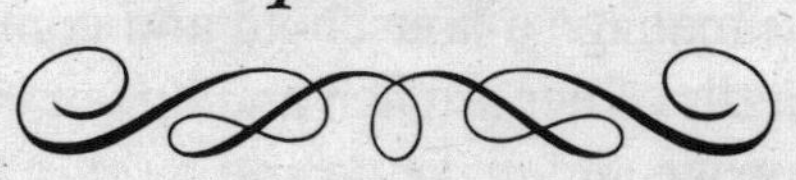

'What has it been like, Callie, this life you made without me? Not being a girl, I don't know what they're taught or how they are before they appear in society as if sprung fully formed from the egg.'

How could she refuse to try to breach the gaps between them? It was a start if they understood each other better, she supposed, but some of the old rebellious Callie whispered, when was he going to tell her the adventures he'd had without her?

'Much depends on the family she comes from and the one she might make one day. Grandfather Sommers's classical education didn't prepare me to instruct young women about the niceties of life and I left that to my aunt. I do know aristocratic young ladies have very different ambitions to genteel ones, though, and our teaching was always aimed at the latter.'

'So what does a genteel young lady need to know?'

He surprised her by meekly handing her any items she nodded at and putting ones she rejected in neat piles as they worked in an easy harmony she would have found incredible only yesterday. It felt oddly intimate having him share the room that was her sanctuary for so long, yet he made it seem normal to silently debate over her most intimate garments and possessions in front of the man who should have shared her life, so how could she tell him to leave her alone and go back to being the outsider in this otherwise all-female household?

'How to manage a household and control a budget, the details of her kitchen and how it is supplied. how to contrive and make do and be sure her family are in credit with the world in every way possible,' she said as she tested that question in her head and tried it out on what she had done her best to teach her young ladies. 'She needs to know enough of the world to keep certain parts of it out of her house and encourage other ones in with the right degree of hospitality. To record and examine accounts, visit her neighbours and be a useful part of her local community, and value truth over show, as well. I don't know if I can really describe an ideal wife since I doubt such a paragon exists. The closest I can get is to say she should be well informed and able to care for her family, ready to love her children and support her husband's endeavours as best she can, yet still be a woman of character in her own right.'

'And for all that they need algebra and natural philosophy and a smattering of Greek and Latin?' he asked, looking at the pile of books she was thumbing through to find which ones she could leave behind and which must go with her.

'I only teach those if a girl shows an aptitude for learning and a lively curiosity about the world. Their potential husbands are taught them as a matter of course, so I see no reason to rob a girl of a chance to explore them before she has to be busy with a family.'

'It's a wonder you restrict yourself to a few extra lessons with your brighter pupils. Your late grandfather seems to have treated you like a student at Balliol.'

'All that learning didn't do me much good, did it?' she asked, avoiding his gaze as she tried not to look back on the idealistic, impulsive girl she was when she fell in love with him. 'I was so full of wondrous myths and legends and tales of wild adventure I couldn't see real things as they were.'

'What were they then?' he asked quietly.

'Impossible,' she said bleakly, the gaps and betrayals of her young life piling up to remind her what a fiction her dream of perfect contentment with her hero-lover was.

'No, it was possible. We only needed time to grow up and cope with such hot passions in the everyday world. Left to ourselves we would have found a way, Callie. You have to believe that or we might as well set up a nice little school for you in Bath and hire a law office for me on the moon.'

'Perhaps we should,' she said with a half-smile at the thought of him negotiating with the ancient gods of Olympus for the rights of a celestial body.

'Don't. It's unthinkable to turn our backs on a last chance at love,' he said hoarsely and there he was again, the true Gideon under all that gentlemanly self-control.

'If we can't laugh together, we'll never be anything but strangers at heart,' she warned him. 'Half of what went wrong between us was because the intensity of our love felt so fierce. If we're going to try again, our marriage must be rooted in real life.'

'I expect you're right, but could we agree not to laugh about parting again, if you want me to stay sane while we work our way round the thorns?'

'I'll agree to that, Gideon, but I refuse to be rushed into anything else.'

'What do I have to do then, Callie? I warn you I'll go down on my knees and beg if I have to sooner or later and you'll find it embarrassing and ridiculous. Just agreeing to come to Raigne with me is hope enough for now, though, so I'll excuse you that ordeal for as long as I can endure the temptation of you so close and not abase myself,' he said, and how much of what he said was serious and how much a joke? She eyed his careful smile and unreadable gaze and decided it would take longer than a day to read the true Gideon under all that armour nowadays.

'The world will still believe we're together again,' she said flatly and wondered if she had been stupid to agree to go to Raigne with him, after all. 'You only came back yesterday, Gideon, we haven't had time to get used to each other as we are now, let alone as man and wife.'

'At least at Raigne we can be the people we really were all along.'

'Without my aunt trying to wreck us all the time.'

'Yes, a new start, Callie, that's all. At least this time I won't have to spend hours at my law books and you won't be living in a strange city with people you have little chance to know.'

'I see the logic of it, but what if we fail publicly this time?'

'Would that be so much worse than not trying at all?' He strode over to the window and back again, looking as if this cramped little room was closing in on him. It felt too small to her now; a cell built with Aunt Seraphina's lies, and she bit back a reckless urge to go tonight, dark and dangerous thought it might be to risk travelling at night. 'Tell me truly you only want to find another school to teach in. That you can forget the chance of a family and I will smother my hopes and promise not to trouble you again,' he finally said as if it hurt.

He stood still and met her eyes, let the guard he kept round himself drop. Did she really want this man she once loved to beg? No, it couldn't have been love in the first place if she did. So here she was up against words she didn't want to say.

'Yes…' she breathed at last, then saw pain and bleak loneliness in his gaze before he blanked it and realised he thought she meant yes to him going away. 'I mean yes to Raigne and us, you idiot,' she told him brusquely. 'But that's all for now,' she reasserted even if she had seen the truth of his longing behind his wary eyes.

'It's enough,' he said shortly and she could see from the way his shoulders relaxed that the hard control he'd kept his mouth and those dear, familiar green-shot grey eyes under was lifted.

Feeling a little ashamed of herself for making him reveal more than he wanted to in order to combat her attack of the dithers, she still felt as if she were walking the edge of a precipice.

'Well, that's finally settled then,' she said briskly

and began packing as few boxes as she could to take away tomorrow.

'Good, I'd hate to have come after you if you change your mind, because I warn you, Callie, I won't go away quietly this time. I'll follow you and make a nuisance of myself even if you travel the length of the land to avoid me. You have given me hope, Lady Laughraine, and I can't give up on it now.'

'I won't go back on my word now. I admit when I thought about it again the whole idea of being at Raigne together frightened me, but I'm steady now and only want to be quit of this place, so you'd best let me finish packing before I go to sleep on my feet.'

'Very well, concentrate then and stop trying to distract me, Wife,' he said with a cocky grin that reminded her again of her young love. Who would have thought she'd be so glad to see that young scapegrace under all the frost the years had put into Gideon's gaze?

It was done, her life for the past nine years packed and ready to go. The small pile of luggage by her bedroom door seemed a poor showing for twenty-seven years of life. Callie concluded travelling light taught her people matter more than things, but had she been weak to agree to go to Raigne with Gideon? Instinct said no, here was a chance for a bigger life than the one she had here, yet her imagination reeled at the very idea of being a wife again. Torn between hope and fear, she knew any chance for their marriage must be grasped, but it felt so huge to let go of the past and seize it.

She tossed and turned on the narrow bed that had

seemed perfectly adequate for so long, but now felt restrictive and hard. The real trouble was she couldn't put all the wild hope Gideon's arrival had rekindled in her heart back in its box and lock it away again. There had been such passion, such love, under their youthful infatuation with each other, that her most hopeful self whispered those huge forces couldn't simply be dead between them now. Yet their dreams of mutual love and need and a future together were smashed all those years ago. What if Gideon didn't share her fantasy? She squirmed against the sheets and told herself it was so humid tonight it was no wonder she couldn't drop off to sleep as if nothing much had happened.

Her whole world had changed, so what was the point of lying here fooling herself she was about to drop off as contentedly as if it was just another day? Unable to endure even the added heat of a thin and patched sheet over her as the heat seemed relentless and sticky all around her, she knew she must face the biggest fear of all about her new life some time. What if she still loved Gideon under all the bitterness and pain and loneliness? And what if he didn't love her? Impossible, she would never have been able to go on with her restricted and very single life for the past few years if she was secretly panting with passion for a lover who it turned out had not really existed.

Except maybe she had been secretly, deep down where she didn't let herself think too much but just feel, maybe there she had been waiting for him to ride up and carry her off. Despite all the pain and bitterness and tears and wild arguments of that brief year of marriage when they were both so young, looking back that was the part that felt like her real life and this one some sort of wicked enchantment that kept them apart and only almost alive. An image of her aunt as the wicked sorceress with legendary power to keep two lovers lost in a dream world and obedient to her commands almost made her laugh for a moment, until she reminded herself how serious Aunt Seraphina's sins were.

Unable to stay still and contain the fury that wanted to howl and weep at all the chances she and Gideon lost to live and love together because of Seraphina Bartle, she got out of bed to pull the curtains wide and very gently inch up the sash to let more air into this stuffy room. Never mind the dangerous night air Aunt Seraphina insisted on keeping out of the house like demons from hell, or the bright moonlight that shone in and might even keep a less wakeful person from their slumbers. It felt good to connect with the greater world, to feel the air and see the moonlight she shared with the rest of this vast racing world of theirs and Gideon in particular. Maybe he was doing just as she was, sitting in the uncushioned seat of his window and breathing in air still heavy with heat as he stared at the miracle of a night almost bright as day? Close on the heels of that thought came the idea of one day sitting with him dreamy, well loved and content as they shared everything she now had to sense alone.

No, that was going too far. If she was to stay sane she must learn to be practical and a lot less idealistic. For now she would learn to be as happy as she could be with what seemed graspable instead of aiming for the moon. If it all went wrong for them at Raigne, at least she and Gideon knew they could live by their own efforts now and perhaps be happier doing it. There, now she was thinking their reconciliation was inevitable and it couldn't be. How could she trust her inner self to a man who had betrayed her at least once already?

It was a dour thought to try and go to sleep on, so she pushed it aside as best she could for another day. It was time to stop looking back and go into the future as best they could, but she wished she was a wild girl again just for tonight, so she could be free to do as she pleased and walk into the hills one last time by the light of the July moon. She had come to love both the remoteness of this sturdy old house and the half-tamed emptiness of the wide hills all around it and she would miss that and the girls she had done her best to equip for lives that would not always be as easy as they might seem to anyone less fortunate.

So was Gideon struggling to sleep alone as well tonight, or already lost in weary slumber after his demanding wife-hunting trip and last night's excitements? No, thinking of him asleep without her was never going to lull her into dreamland; it felt too wrong for them to lie apart like enemies in different camps dreading the next battle. She sighed heavily, then went back to bed to try counting sheep. No, they looked too much like Aunt Seraphina, and wasn't that an uncomfortable thought? Sheep wearing unlikely flaxen wigs and a superior expression would put her off the silly creatures for life and there were far too many of them in this part of the world to risk that calamity.

In the distance she thought she heard a soft thud

and a murmur, but it was over almost as soon as it began and she turned over when she heard a vixen bark a warning at cubs big enough to know better by now and blocked her ears to the normal noises of the night. It wasn't term time, so she didn't need to worry about nightmares or wakeful girls away from home for the first time and longing for their parents. She felt herself retreating from this little world that seemed so safe for so long, Miss Sommers's days were numbered, but could she really be Calliope Laughraine again? She had married Gideon ten years ago, but it would feel like living with a man she didn't know if they took up where they left off. Whatever happened between them, she was about to live in a house beyond most women's wildest dreams.

The very thought of trying to make some sort of life in the mansion she visited on sufferance as a child felt so alien she might lose an essential part of herself if she tried to see herself as wife of the next Lord Laughraine. Deciding she preferred a world she had some control over, she set about plotting the knottiest bits of her next book in her head. The intricacies of it soothed her and she was halfway to dreamland when she realised her latest hero looked exactly like Gideon. Already drifting, her mind was too wrapped up in a sleepy fantasy of finding a happy ending in her husband hero's arms to reject the notion he might still be her hero, after all, and she fell asleep with a welcoming smile on her face.

'So where *did* you end up sleeping last night, Gideon?' Callie asked the next morning when they were on their way from Cataret House so early this might be a dream, as well.

'On a chair in your office, lest your aunt can pick locks as well as escape from upstairs windows,' he replied gruffly.

'I knew I should have woken up properly and investigated the noise I heard in the night,' she said with a grimace for the empty room and improvised rope of bedsheets they had discovered this morning. 'At least Kitty wasn't here to give you a matching pair of black eyes, but I'm surprised you didn't hear my aunt escape as you seem to have the senses of a cat.'

'I knew she would go, why else do you think I was dozing in that uncomfortable chair? I had to make sure she took nothing of ours with her this time,' he said and shifted his shoulders as if they were still stiff from holding such an unnatural position for so long.

'You have had a difficult time since you arrived, haven't you?' she said with a wry smile for his poor bruised face and the shadows even under his good eye from lack of proper sleep. 'Poor Gideon,' she added and surely it wasn't quite right to feel such a rush of joy at the mere sight of the boyish smile she remembered from the old days in response?

'Lucky Gideon,' he corrected softly and the look he slanted her made it clear she was the reason he thought it was worth it.

She smiled back and let herself enjoy this odd journey through a luminous dawn. They were sitting on the box of what she still thought of as her aunt's carriage. As he was driving the sturdy pair she refused to be shut inside a stuffy, swaying box on wheels on such a perfect morning. So the little kitchen maid was inside the coach in her stead, dressed in her Sunday best and feeling like a Queen of England, she assured Callie, and shook her head at an offer to sit in the fresh air, as well.

'I've never rode in a real coach before, miss, I mean, my lady, and the missus would scold me something wicked if she caught me getting that wrong again, wouldn't she?' the girl said with a happy grin.

Callie smiled back in silent glee neither of them need tiptoe round her aunt's notions of propriety ever again. Now she let herself feel the thrill of a new start life in the shape of Sir Gideon Laughraine as well as the fears she struggled with last night. His stray lady was about to be reborn as a potential aristocrat and apparently Biddy was going to scale the dizzy heights of lady's maid without going through any of the stages in between.

'She's never going to fit anyone's idea of a proper lady's maid,' Gideon warned softly as they moved on to the main road to Manydown and Biddy waved regally at a startled farm labourer about to go off to the fields for the day.

'That's why I engaged her,' Callie admitted, the thought of a silently critical dresser who would sniff and disapprove of her new mistress making Biddy's pleas not to leave her behind a good excuse not to engage one. 'I couldn't let her be turned into the world with nothing, now could I?'

'Perhaps not, but we could still find her a place more fitted to her skills when we get to Raigne. Your personal maid will have to cope with a large collection of gowns and can the girl sew? She won't know how to clean a riding habit or wash the ostrich plume fashionable females festoon their bonnets with. If all Biddy can do is wash pots and pare vegetables, she'll be in the suds the first time she's called on to do something less than straightforward to my lady's wardrobe.'

'No, she won't, suds are what she's escaping from. For one thing, I'm not a fashionable female. For another, she can sew perfectly well, because my aunt insisted all the maids she employed could do so to save a sewing woman's wages. I'm sure someone at Raigne will be glad to show her how to keep my habits clean and what to do about anything I manage to spill on my favourite gown and she might as well learn to be a lady's maid at the same time I find out how to be a lady.'

'You are already a lady. Let's not have that old argument again.'

'Very well, we'll leave it for another day,' Callie conceded with a look about her at the early morning sunshine and another fine day. 'Where do you think my aunt has gone?' she asked after they had driven through Manydown to startled faces as the early risers saw Mrs Grisham's niece on the box and Biddy waving regally at them from inside the carriage as if practising for her coronation.

'How would I know?' Gideon said as he got the feel of the pair and set them bowling along the better road to the main highway that would lead them to the other side of the county and Raigne, hopefully before the sun could climb too high and make the journey wearisome.

'You seem to find out what makes a person tick a little too easily nowadays,' she replied, feeling the tug of intimacy as she adapted to the movements of his strong body brushing hers as he expertly flicked his whip or softly reassured the more skittish of the two glossy chestnut horses he was driving to an inch.

'I don't much care where she is or want to understand her,' he said shortly.

She sensed something held back and turned to give him a very wifely look. 'Now I'm wondering why I don't believe you,' she said as he tried to be inscrutable again.

'So am I.'

'Maybe I know you too well?' She paused and took another look at the blank expression he was trying to fix as he concentrated on his horses as if they were far more restless than they appeared on a fine morning with a smooth road ahead. 'You let her go, didn't you?' she said as the unlikelihood of such a daring escape dawned at last.

'Oh, yes,' he said with a smile that would have looked just right on a fox picking hens' feathers out of his strong white teeth of a morning. 'First we had a little talk and then I suggested she leave before I called the Runners.'

'I hope you're not going to tell me my aunt has taken to highway robbery?'

'No, but your unlikely maid is probably resting her feet on an extra box I slipped into the carriage before we set out.'

'She had my parents' letters as well as ours, didn't she?' she said, and it was as much a statement as a question. He'd seen the echo of their own tale in her parents' ill-fated love affair and known exactly what to look for. Apparently the wild young man she married had grown up to be a clever and subtle man.

'Yes. It's all about power, Callie, a need to control those around her without them realising she's doing it,' he said wearily and she felt cold even on this sunny July morning at the idea she'd been dancing to Seraphina Bartle's tune all her life without realising it.

'Why extort money from anyone else, though? She already had what I earned for her with our pupils as well as what you sent me to live well on while you struggled.'

'Only at first, I do very well now.'

'Stop trying to divert me with your tale of rags to riches, Husband, and kindly answer my questions, you're not in a courtroom now.'

'I feel as if I might be,' he teased her, then sobered. 'Last night she confessed Bartle ran through any money they had and left her a mountain of debts. Whatever the details of his death might be, she didn't deserve that.'

'Now who's making excuses for her?'

'I'm trying to understand. She always knew right from wrong, your grandfather would see to that, so why lie and cheat and take such pleasure in making her family unhappy?'

'Because she married Mr Bartle, perhaps? Maybe a cow looked at my grandmother the wrong way when she was carrying her and that did it? Who knows? She lied and stole and did her best to ruin our marriage and nearly wrecked my mother's life beforehand.'

'She didn't need to do much to part us, did she? I did most of it for her before you even got back to

King's Raigne and fell into her clutches again,' he argued bleakly.

'Don't, Gideon,' she protested, fighting tears at the desolation in his voice.

'Very well then, let's talk of the weather, shall we?' he said bitterly. 'I'm heartily sick of your aunt as a subject of conversation and we might as well find something neutral to while away the tedium of our journey.'

'Of course, it seems set fair to last out the week, don't you think?' she said stiffly; she could hardly complain that he'd lapsed into brittle social chit-chat when she was the one who didn't want to talk about her aunt.

'The harvest will be ready long before its time if it continues thus, don't you think?' he went on relentlessly. 'Lord Laughraine must be fretting about the chances of sudden downpours and thunderous tempests ruining the crops as we speak.'

'If he happens to be awake so early in the morning, of course.'

'There is that,' he agreed as they reached the next village and he was so preoccupied holding back his pair to let a herd of sheep cross the road there was no need to talk at all.

Callie fixed her gaze on the horizon, but saw little of it. He was right to shut himself off from her in a way. Towards the end of their marriage he did all he could to keep them together, although they were so young they scarcely knew how to go about the daily business of life as man and wife, until that last day when she must have decided it wasn't worth it. She couldn't think about that right now, but wasn't she the one who never quite believed she deserved to find true love? Miles slipped by and they pretended interest in the passing scene and she tried to let the subject slip out of her mind, because they were too shocked and weary to talk of the past without making things worse right now.

She managed her usual escape from too much reality by considering how this scene or that chance encounter with a group of travellers, a market day, or a drove of cattle might change or bend the plot of her next book. Nothing more noteworthy happened until she was holding the horses while Gideon went to buy the next set of tickets from the toll keeper.

'You don't look like any coachman I ever encountered,' a deep and amused male voice drawled from behind her.

A gentleman she'd never seen before in her life halted his dancing mount beside the carriage very much against that fine animal's wishes. He bowed from his saddle with such elegance she felt dowdy and windswept and fervently wished he'd go away. 'Good day, sir,' she said with distant politeness.

'It is now,' he said with a rogue's grin. 'And a good day to you, as well, Miss Whoever-You-Are,' he said, with a wary glance at her gloveless left hand that made her blush and wish she hadn't thrown Gideon's rings back at him when they parted all those years ago.

'Sommers,' she said impatiently, more out of habit than a wish to deny her husband and then it seemed foolish to correct herself to a stranger she would never see again.

'I can see that,' he murmured with a grin that made

her realise what was meant by wolfish and she wished Gideon would hurry back.

'I am called Sommers,' she explained shortly, doing her best to ignore Biddy's cough of disagreement and her fine imitation of a disapproving chaperon.

'And every bit as lovely as a summer's day you are, too, Miss Sommers. What a fortuitous coincidence that I happened on you today whilst we're in the midst of that fine season, as well,' the wolf told her with such admiration in his oddly familiar green-and-grey eyes she might have been all of a flutter, if Gideon hadn't already dazzled her for good.

'Nonsense, I'm not lovely and neither is being too hot for comfort day after day,' she snapped with a glare at the heat haze on the horizon. 'I do wish people would stop comparing me to a summer's day, it really is most unoriginal.'

'Shakespeare? I feel I ought to know, but I never did mind my books at school.'

'It is from one of the sonnets and I was flattered to have it quoted at me once,' she said, recalling the heart-racing sound of it on Gideon's lips, but then, if he'd recited a list of linens when they were young and in love it would have taken her breath away. 'It grates sadly upon repetition.'

'I shall obtain a book of sonnets and learn them off by heart for future use,' the stranger said with what looked like real admiration in his eyes and Callie wished she hadn't forgotten her married status in a moment of absent-minded annoyance.

'I'm not interested in an idle flirtation, or any other sort of idleness for that matter. I wish you good day, sir,' she said firmly.

'It might not be so idle as you think,' the man said and made her wonder if all the gentlemen in so-called polite society required eye-glasses and were too vain to admit it.

'It had better be,' Gideon's darker voice said from behind them.

Chapter Eight

'Peters, what the devil are you doing here?' The stranger greeted him as if they knew each other. Plainly they didn't, or the rake would know her husband's real name.

'Winterley,' Gideon replied coldly and it made her think again about his other life and how many secrets it held. Apparently he had another name altogether and what else had he failed to tell her about his existence since they parted?

'You know each other then, gentlemen?' she asked as brightly as she could when they looked about to challenge each other to a bout of fisticuffs, if she was lucky.

'Not as well as we think,' Gideon said tightly and wasn't that the truth, Callie thought cynically, wondering if anyone knew Sir Gideon Laughraine but Gideon himself.

'But perhaps better than you would like us to?' the man challenged him. If they were friends at all, it was clearly a prickly sort of friendship.

'Perhaps,' Gideon said, and addled Callie's brain

by climbing back into his seat and holding her hand as they faced his dashing acquaintance together. 'We certainly don't know each other well enough for you to have met my wife, Winterley, and that makes me wonder why you felt free to accost her on a public highway.'

'Now here's a dilemma,' Mr Winterley drawled with a hard glance in Callie's direction to tell her what he thought of her lapse of memory. 'To give the lie to a lady, or admit you and I know each other not at all?'

'Well, my dear?' Gideon said with a frown as he dared her to deny him again.

'I am indeed Lady Laughraine, but tend to forget it now and again. I beg your pardon, Husband, Mr Winterley,' she said with a nod of curt apology towards each of them.

'Lady Laughraine?' Mr Winterley asked blankly. He shot another shocked glare at Gideon that said there was indeed more to her husband's other life than she knew. 'What a truly dark horse you are, Mr Frederick Peters.'

'My husband's full name is Gideon Frederick Peter Dante Laughraine, sir, but I shouldn't take it as a slight you didn't know him as such until today because he only lets the world see as much, or as little, of his true self as he thinks it needs to know,' Callie told him with that alias of Gideon's going round and round in her thoughts as she wondered what he had been up to in order to need it.

The tall stranger seemed to pause on the edge of giving at least one of them a blistering set down before he took in Gideon's ponderous string of names, then a look of unholy glee lit his face instead and he sent Gideon a mocking grin, as if he now knew far more about him than such a private man could want him to.

'You appear to be an even darker horse than I thought you, Laughraine,' he said slowly. 'Oh, well met, Sir Gideon, and how d'you do?' he added mockingly.

'Well enough, but I'll never understand you if I live to be a hundred, Winterley,' Gideon said with a manly shrug. 'Ours has never been a conventional marriage,' he added casually, as if he and Callie kept it to themselves out of a perverse delight in secrets. Since she was the one to demand it came to an end nine years ago, she could hardly complain if he was making weak excuses for that deception now.

'Then perhaps you should consult with your wife and match up your stories better in future. I wish you both a good morning and hope to see you at dinner. If you dine together as man and wife and not under your chosen aliases in different counties, of course?'

'Then you are staying at Raigne?' Gideon asked as if it confirmed his worst fears.

'Lord Laughraine will invite me, d'you see? This time I rashly agreed to stay for a week or two to escape the husband hunters, since the little darlings will go to Brighton on Prinny's coattails to carry on their craft out of season. Like a gullible innocent up from the country I agreed to his latest invitation to enjoy some bucolic tranquillity at his expense and quite forgot he was a great friend of Virgil and Virginia's. Although given what has happened so far this year, I should feel less of a fool now I'm looking at the very good reason he wants me there, shouldn't I?' Mr Winterley said mysteriously.

Callie supposed Gideon knew what the man meant, since she felt him flinch and heard a bitten-back curse. The only Virgil and Virginia she knew of were the last Lord and Lady Farenze; Gideon's late grandfather and his wife. Still with that look of unholy amusement in his eyes, Mr Winterley blithely gave them both a seated bow before wishing them a genial farewell. Then he rode off as if he'd happened on an amusing sideshow at precisely the right moment to enliven a tedious moment.

'Who on earth is that?' she asked.

'A friend, although you wouldn't think so at times,' Gideon replied tersely.

'A friend you were about to call to account for simply exchanging greetings with me?' she reminded him recklessly.

'I have no patience with Winterley's sort of politeness. You should be wary of him, too, Callie. He's slippery as an eel and about as trustworthy as a fox.'

'Maybe it takes a rogue to know one.'

She tied the trailing strings of her bonnet into a militant bow she regretted as soon as the close-woven straw closed the heat in and threatened to make her head ache. Refusing to undo it after making such a grand gesture, she silently dared him to comment.

'There's no maybe about it,' he said with an unrepentant grin and they resumed their journey in what she hoped was a dignified silence.

'I have no wish to know what you have been doing while my back was turned,' she managed to lie after they had continued for half a mile with her staring everywhere but at his face. An internal picture of a parade of his lovers kept plaguing her, as if a grey mist had settled on her shoulders in the most unlikely cloud and was blighting a glorious morning.

He sighed as if she were proving to be the most exasperating of travelling companions and answered the question she had been trying so hard not to ask ever since he came back into her life. 'No, Callie, I don't have a mistress, nor a discreet married lover bored with her husband after filling his nursery with heirs. I've been celibate as a monk for lack of you, but you'd be sensible to wish I was busy chasing every strumpet in town right now. You're right to watch me as if I'm a starving wolf about to swallow you down in one hungry bite, so maybe you'd best avoid provoking me with the likes of James Winterley again. I want you so badly every inch of me is on fire and at least now you can't say you haven't had fair warning.'

'No man who loves as passionately as you could go nigh on a decade without a woman,' she said sceptically, the image coming into her head of him in the arms of some sensual charmer purring with pleasure at his splendid body and skilful lovemaking.

'I am a married man, in case you had forgotten,' he said shortly.

She tried to shrug off the doubts that made her want to smack the smile off that smug imaginary siren's face, but he was a fully adult man and she couldn't seem to get reason to overcome jealousy now they were side by side and she had felt the flex and steel of his body next to hers for mile after mile. Perhaps she should have agreed to travel in the stuffy carriage away from him, after all.

'You revelled in being my lover, then my wife, before you decided I was a villain and you hated me. Don't pretend you don't want me nigh as much as I want you.'

'You taught me not to trust my one and only lover, Gideon,' she said as images of them locked in the wilder excesses of passion threatened to leave her certainty she never wanted to risk loving him again in the dust.

'This isn't the time or place for picking at old wounds,' he warned with a significant nod back at the carriage where Biddy was fanning herself in the growing heat and beginning to look as if she regretted choosing that seat over this one. 'I won't admit to something I didn't do, though,' he added in a low, driven voice.

'I don't want to love you again, Gideon,' she warned. She was breathless and on the edge of something dangerous and had to protect herself from being so vulnerable again.

'Maybe I won't ask you to,' he replied flatly, before halting the carriage and insisting Biddy squeeze into the space atop the graceful little vehicle between them.

They were close to the end of their journey at last and Callie spotted familiar landmarks and the outlying parts of her grandfather's former parish. She distracted herself from her galling and petty jealousy of Biddy for her place next to Gideon on the narrow coachman's seat by wondering who still lived where they were when she left and who had moved on. Inevitably some of the parishioners would have joined her grandfather in the peaceful churchyard of King's Raigne Church. She winced at the very thought of that grave and knew she had to visit it before very many days had gone by in her temporary home to make peace with the past.

It seemed best to tell herself this was temporary. The very idea of being mistress of such a huge and venerable house one day might terrify her half to death if she dwelt on it. She glanced at her husband over the top of Biddy's head and knew she would be more open to his persuasion if he wasn't Lord Laughraine's heir. Then they could simply return to London when the heat of midsummer died down and live a humdrum life. A sense of justice her grandfather instilled in her argued she must put her dread of the Laughraine inheritance aside and see Gideon as he was, rather than one day lord and master of Raigne.

There, now they were almost through Great Raigne and a particularly strait-laced widow she recognised as an incurable gossip was waiting to cross the road. The lady took a second look at the modest carriage and exactly who was driving it and her mouth fell open like a cod fish.

'Oh, dear,' she muttered to Gideon, then summoned up a cheery smile as they swept past as if a Laughraine always drove his own carriage with his wife at his side and a maidservant for company. 'Our eccentric method of travel will be all round the Raigne villages by the time she's walked the length of the high street.'

'I have no intention of keeping our arrival quiet so they might as well get used to us,' he said, a challenge in his voice she hoped Biddy wouldn't notice.

'If your uncle really wants you to stay here and begin to learn the management of the estate we must live here for at least part of the year, though, and Mrs Prosser never did like me,' Callie said with a sigh.

'She doesn't like anybody much, but she does love a title. We should do well on that front.'

Callie stayed silent in deference to Biddy's eager interest and watched for Raigne's elaborately carved and twisted Tudor chimney stacks. There they were, as familiar and strange as ever. The sight of the mellow nobleman's mansion in the distance made her think of her childhood. She had thought it a palace full of exotic things and fairy-tale people. Later she was allowed inside the side door of the giant's castle at Christmas, when the Sunday School children had tea in the housekeeper's room and were given a present to take home. Aprons for the girls and shirts for the boys, she recalled with a grimace. If she had any say here she'd make sure children received something more interesting in future.

She wasn't even through the gates and she was rearranging cherished traditions. It wouldn't go down well in the servants' halls if she seemed ready to take over before she had her feet through the door, and she must step carefully if she was to be accepted as a proper wife for an heir to Raigne. The real question being did she want such a role in the first place? Gideon was Lord Laughraine's acknowledged heir, so she supposed she had no choice as she was Gideon's wife. She sighed gloomily and wondered how many girls in the Mayfair ballrooms she suspected Gideon was familiar with would give their eye teeth for the position she had no desire for.

Yet King's Raigne was home in a way Manydown never had been and this was Gideon at her side, as familiar and strange as the world she had left behind when she married him. It felt right to be back in some ways and so wrong in others she could hardly endure to think about it. Under the reproaches he hadn't made and the sore places in her heart, could they come to love each other in a less overheated and dangerous way than when they were so ridiculously young? They would be fools not to try, so she really had to stop being a fool and step into the future with a little resolution and more hope they would somehow find each other again.

Trying not to dwell on the challenges ahead, lest she jump down from the carriage and run away before they even got to Raigne, she eyed the shady groups of ancient oaks and elms in the parkland they were passing through instead. The sun was high in the sky and cattle were sheltering from it under the wide-spreading trees, lowing to their calves and lazily swishing flies away with their tails. They looked timeless and indifferent to the comings and goings of men and that made her feel better somehow.

'Welcome to Raigne House, Biddy,' Gideon said as he drew the horses to a halt on the neatly raked carriage sweep and jumped down to help them down to solid ground.

'Coo, it's big, ain't it, Mr Gideon?' she said as she stood looking at the place as if it might develop a voice of its own and tell her to go away immediately.

'True, but it's also a home.'

'Not for the likes of me, though, is it?' she replied,

and Callie wondered if it had been fair to bring the girl with her, after all.

'Come now, Biddy,' she said bracingly, 'would you rather have stayed at Cataret House and waited for the next tenant to take over?'

'Oh, no, miss. I want to stay with you, but people who live in a place like this will know I'm no lady's maid. You'd better send me round to the kitchens.'

'No, you took the job I offered and I need you,' Callie said. 'You will soon grow into your new tasks, as I must into mine.'

'If you say so, miss, I mean, my lady,' Biddy said with a harassed look at the boxes strapped to the back of the coach and another at the great front door as it opened and a very solemn butler came out. 'Shall I have to unpack for you, my lady?' she asked before he was close enough to hear.

'If you please, I don't want some smart housemaid looking down her nose at my humble wardrobe.'

'No, of course you don't, my lady. I suppose there's books and things about looking after a proper lady's clothes and whatnots, ain't there? Someone in this great place will be able to help me with the long words, won't they? You'll be far too busy to help me now, but I'm that glad you taught me to read, Miss Sommers because there's a book about most things, ain't there?'

'Of course and that's a very good notion of yours. I shall send for an appropriate one as soon as I can,' Callie said soothingly and turned to meet the butler's stern gaze with nearly as much trepidation as Biddy.

'I'd love to know what a lady's whatnots are,' Gideon whispered, and Callie laughed, then relaxed a little. 'You were quite right to insist on bringing your protégée with us,' he added, then turned to meet the ancient retainer as a long-lost friend.

They were conducted upstairs to a vast suite of rooms Callie concluded was the finest guest accommodation in the house. His lordship must have known they were coming because there wasn't a holland cover to be seen, or a speck of dust on the highly polished furniture and gleaming treasures in this glorious old state room. Gideon seemed to have taken a lot for granted in sending word they were coming before she agreed and she must point that out to him when they were alone again if she wasn't to develop into a mouse-like woman. Now she had to hide an impulse to follow Gideon into his splendid bedchamber instead of meekly heading for her own, because at least he was familiar in all this stateliness. The loss of him at her side brought back all her fears of losing herself in this vast old barn of a place in more ways than one.

'There's a bath being got ready for you in the dressing room yonder, Lady Laughraine,' Biddy informed her. 'You ain't half going to be clean, ain't you, miss?' she added, then realised she'd forgotten herself again. 'Blessed if I'll ever remember, my lady,'

'Blessed if I will either, Biddy, now please shake out my best muslin and find a clean chemise and petticoat for me.'

'Yes, miss. I mean, my lady.'

'Don't leave me alone, will you, Gideon?' Callie asked an hour later as they met up in their vast sitting room ready to go downstairs and meet her grandfather in his own lair.

'What, never?'

'Idiot, I mean until I learn the way of the house, but on the other hand please don't leave me alone with his lordship, ever.'

'Difficult, he's been living for the moment you would agree to see him and make peace.'

'I can't see why. I'm a reminder of what should have been if I was born to his daughter-in-law instead of the Vicar's unwed daughter. He has to be ashamed of me.'

'No, but he is ashamed of what his son did to you and your mother.'

'How do you know?'

'Because I asked him about what happened back then and he told me. We have stayed in contact, since I saw no reason to cut myself off from him and he wanted to stay close to you by proxy. Not that I was close to you in any way or could tell him anything about you, since you told me I sickened you and you loathed me with every fibre of your being and never to contact you again.'

'I didn't, you know that now, but we must forget what my aunt did before it drives us mad.'

'I can't, Callie, any more than I can forgive what she's done, so please don't ask that of me next. Suffice it to say, Lord Laughraine and I thought you must be throwing his letters on the fire as well as mine and he's been too afraid of stirring up a past you found intolerable to ride over and demand you speak to him. He says he and his did enough damage to you and yours, but your aunt must bear a great deal of the blame for all of it, though, don't you think?'

'Yes, but does he truly think that?'

'Which bit are you wondering about being untrue this time?'

'I deeply regret not suspecting my aunt was destroying my letters and challenging her version of the truth, Gideon, but does his lordship really want to know me?'

'Of course he does, he's not the sort of man who judges a child for something they are completely innocent of. I'm a far greater obstacle to Christian forgiveness than you will ever be—he would have every excuse to hate me, given how the succession stands, but he can't even manage that, so just give him a chance, Callie. I promise you he's nothing like the ogre you seem to have made of him in your imagination.'

'I'm beginning to see that. For years I thought he was happy to leave me in ignorance of who I truly was so he didn't have to admit his son was a rake. I know we weren't going to talk about Aunt Seraphina, but she does intrude into our lives even now, doesn't she? Until we understand exactly what she did we can't forget her. She said my paternal grandfather is as proud as the devil and would never openly acknowledge me, but everything she told me was a lie. Yet the poor man's heart must sink at the prospect of me as the only source of Laughraine blood left, unless he's prepared to make an April-and-December marriage and that doesn't seem likely as he's been a widower for over twenty years, does it?'

'No, he was devoted to his wife and seems genuinely happy for us to inherit Raigne one day between us.'

'Who says there can be an us? I'm not sure I can do it again, Gideon,' she asked, panicked by the certainty if she was left alone with him too long she would make a fool of herself and beg to be his true wife again.

'Not yet, maybe, but one day I hope to change your mind. Meanwhile I'm not made of stone, despite your obvious belief to the contrary.'

'You must be, if you really haven't had a mistress all the years we've been apart.'

'We're back to that again, are we? Very well, if it makes you feel better I'll swear on anything you ask me to that I'm telling the truth. I've been on the rack for you, Callie. In the early days I often couldn't sleep for the lack of you in my bed and at my side. I daydreamed about making love to you when I should have been slaving at my books and stayed working at my first and mostly hopeless cases late into the night because I hated going back to a place I couldn't call a home without you in it. I can't count the number of times I set out to find you because I couldn't stand being alone any longer. Then I'd remember the last weeks when you wouldn't even share a room with me and that infernal letter you say now that you never sent and it would strip me of any hopes or dreams and I'd go back to my law books and do my best to pretend living without you wasn't hell on earth. All I had left of you was those vows to be faithful only unto you and I kept them,' he ended defiantly and no doubt he had, after they parted, since he looked as if the emptiness of those years had been punishment enough for any man's sins.

'I'm sorry for all those wicked, wicked lies she told using my name,' Callie said lamely, reeling at a sight of her wild and passionate young lover fully alive under the cool facade he used to keep the world at bay. 'We were good friends, once upon a time, though, weren't we, Gideon? Perhaps we could be so again,' she added clumsily.

Chapter Nine

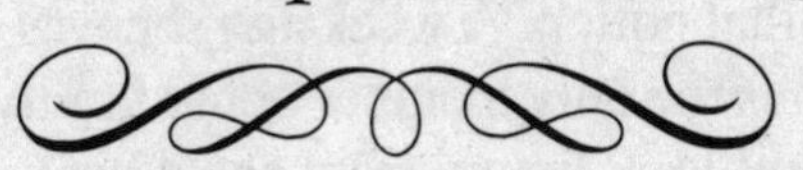

'Are you two coming down, or do you intend to camp out at the top of the stairs for the rest of the day?' Lord Laughraine asked from the great hall below them. Callie was touched to see he couldn't wait in some stately room for them to come to him and glad he had interrupted an awkward conversation with Gideon.

'My wife really needs a rest,' he told his honorary uncle, as if her welfare was far more important than protocol. It warmed a chilly corner of her heart to think she was his first concern, even now he was back with his family and clearly very welcome.

She tugged at Gideon's hand and led him towards the stairs to silently show him she had a mind of her own, even if she didn't want to challenge him for fussing over her in public right now. Who would have thought she'd ever be so anxious to meet her other grandfather again, after all her doubts and scruples about her origins? This tug of mixed emotions was pulling her first one way and then another and if she looked pale it was more an indication of her inner turmoil than some physical frailty Gideon had convinced himself she suffered from. She must find a way to prove otherwise soon, but now she was about to meet his lordship as her true self for the first time in her life and she needed all her energy for that.

Could Lord Laughraine really own her as his kin as well as Gideon's wife? She was unsure how she felt about that notion. A week ago she was convinced her aunt was the only member of her family she could rely on, and look how wrong she'd been about her. Now she was torn between wanting to love and trust her paternal grandfather and distrusting his motive for wanting her and Gideon here. Grandfather Sommers had brought her up to see the good in people and this wily old aristocrat was as lonely as she had been in his own way. If she locked up her heart and threw away the key because it was easier than trusting anyone, she would be no better than Seraphina Bartle. She raised her chin as she walked down the grand staircase at Gideon's side, doing her best to look serene and much calmer than she felt.

'If you have had as big a shock as I have today I'm not the least bit surprised you feel exhausted,' his lordship said genially when they were face-to-face. 'Welcome home, my dear. I'm so glad to see you back in King's Raigne with this young rogue again.'

Callie held out her hand, since she wasn't quite sure how to answer him, and Lord Laughraine surprised her by shaking it solemnly, then bowing to her like an old-fashioned gallant. He embraced Gideon as if he'd accomplished something wonderful by bringing her here and all her aunt's assertions a bastard grandchild would never be welcome at Raigne rang hollow. How much damage the wretched woman had done by playing on Callie's insecurities, a goodly few of them caused by her in the first place.

'Thank you for bringing her home, my boy,' he said gruffly as he stood back and seemed to recollect they were standing in a lofty hallway where anyone might chance on them. 'But you should have sent word you were coming sooner so we could receive you in a much more suitable style for my heir and his lovely lady.'

'I agree about Lady Laughraine's beauty, of course, but bad pennies like me don't turn up every day, do they, my dear?' Gideon said with a sardonic smile that hinted it still hurt him that she had fainted at first sight of him after all those years.

'It is to be hoped not,' she replied tartly. 'One husband is quite enough for me.'

'You asked for that one, my boy,' his lordship interrupted.

'I did, and now we're keeping my lady standing in the hallway, Uncle Charles, whatever can we be thinking of?' Gideon joked with none of the defensive fury he would have shown after being wrongfooted in the old days.

'And here's Mrs Craddock with her bevy of chicks. It's a bit late to line up and make Lady Laughraine run the gauntlet now,' Lord Laughraine greeted his stately-looking housekeeper and a phalanx of maidservants. 'Where's Craddock with his cohort then?' he barked and made Callie feel better about the ritual of the heir's bride having to greet the household ten years after she and Gideon got back from their scandalous wedding.

'He's late as usual, my lord,' Mrs Craddock said repressively, but with a decided twinkle in her acute blue eyes that made Callie think she might be able to live with the formidable woman, after all.

'Here's my great-nephew's lady parched for some of that tea you all seem to set such store by nowadays and we're keeping her standing about in a draught.'

'Even if you were, I would be glad of any breeze on such a hot day, Craddock,' Callie told the now not-quite-so-stately butler as he puffed in at the head of his line of footmen and all the other male servants such a huge old house needed to keep it running smoothly.

'It's gracious of you to say so, Lady Laughraine,' he said with a harassed glance to where the smallest members of his troop were jostling each other as they got into line.

'What a splendid picture you all make,' Callie said in a louder voice and managed to place only her fingertips on Gideon's offered arm instead of hanging on to it with both hands as the enormity of the changes in her life sank in. 'Shall we begin at the beginning and work our way up, Sir Gideon?' she managed to suggest steadily enough as the ranks lined up in opposing lines from youngest up to Mr and Mrs Craddock.

'It's often the best way, Lady Laughraine,' he answered, as if rather amused by this peculiar situation and perhaps that was the only way to deal with being feted as the heir and his wife, considering they didn't really belong here at all.

Callie almost quailed when Mr and Mrs Craddock turned, ready to head down the serried ranks of servants and introduce them one by one. All those years ago when she used to come here with the Sunday School at Christmas she remembered being sure Craddock was more important than the owner of this vast, echoing house and Mrs Craddock must be on a par with the Queen. Now she knew they were slightly less important than that her knees were still wobbling and so much seemed to depend on making a good impression on this huge staff when she must look more like a governess than the possible lady of Raigne, but luckily Lord Laughraine waved them away.

'I hope I know everyone who works for me by now,' he told them and listed them with such accuracy Callie knew she had more to learn than she'd thought.

She was all too conscious of Gideon's presence as they made their way along the lines, feeling guilty about that interrupted conversation. He'd bared a young man's agony and in return she limply offered to be friends? She blushed for her own awkwardness as they reached the end of the line and solemnly shook hands with the butler and housekeeper.

'Perhaps now we could have that tea?' Gideon asked with a glance at her hot cheeks.

'Of course, Sir Gideon,' Mrs Craddock said as if she was worried Callie might not be up to the heat, as well, and the household hastily dispersed. 'Would you like it served in the Little Sitting Room or the Library, my lady?'

Callie tried not to look blank.

'As the Library is on the west side of the house it might be cooler at this time of day,' the woman suggested helpfully.

Callie meekly agreed, then had to rely on Gideon

to guide her in the right direction. He belonged here as she never would, but if he had to live here then so must she, she decided stoutly. When he tried to tell her how much he'd missed her she'd panicked and fobbed him off with an offer of friendship. She almost wished she hadn't caught another woman leaving his bedchamber that awful day at Willoughby Manor. Her breath snatched at the remembered horror of seeing Cecily Willoughby all sleepy eyed and ruffled as she closed the door on him with a cat-like smile of satisfaction. Callie knew her mother's stepdaughter wanted her out of the house, but to seduce her husband in order to achieve that end seemed a little extreme now, didn't it? The very thought of them together made her feel sick even now and it was high time she got control of herself again. Gideon and his lordship were watching her as if they weren't quite sure how to cope with whatever ailed her.

'I'm a nodcock to let all that happen after our journey and everything else you have had to endure lately,' Gideon said. 'We will leave you to drink your tea in peace.'

'There's no need. You know I've never been given to wafting about like an invalid, Gideon,' she told him more impatiently than she meant to, because she was so confused by her new life and her feelings for him. 'I taught a bevy of girls their lessons day after day for nearly a decade, so I can assure you I'm more than capable of a journey of less than twenty miles, then meeting his lordship's staff. I shall contrive to stay on my feet for the rest of the day without too much difficulty, as well.'

'I'll leave you two to talk about whatever you have

to talk about and find my pack then,' Lord Laughraine said. 'Do you object to dogs, m'dear?' he asked as if she had a right to say yay or nay to them.

'My aunt would never have one in the house, but I always wanted one, my lord.'

'Glad to hear it,' he said, and went off to resume his interrupted morning.

'I didn't mean to snap, Gideon,' she explained before he could use his lordship's exit as an excuse to make his own, 'and I'm not going to faint again, so there's no need to look at me as if I might explode at any moment, you know.'

'Was I doing that?' he asked, and relaxed when Craddock ushered in two footmen and a maid with the tea tray and enough little bits of nothing to feed a small army.

'You're right,' she said as soon as the butler shut the door behind him after a gesture from Gideon to signal they wanted to be left in peace.

'I am?'

'Yes, I wish you'd stop being so exasperating about it.'

'It happens so seldom,' he said with a grin that did those unfair things as she was trying to pour the tea.

'Now look what you've made me do.'

'See?'

'Oh, Gideon, now we're acting like an old married couple, aren't we?' she asked, and why on earth did her tongue insist on tying her in knots at the most inappropriate moments?

'It's what we are, or rather what we should be,' he said with a shake of his dark head as his smile faded and a brooding look took its place when he stared at the shabby boxes he had ordered carried in here.

In truth, she had very little experience of how old married couples were together. Her grandmothers were both dead by the time she was old enough to really remember them and nobody could call her aunt's marriage happy or harmonious. She felt a poignant sadness for the marriage she and Gideon should have learnt to live together these past ten years and for nine of them they had only been apart.

'We have to look at them some time, don't we?' she asked as she followed his gaze with a frown for the missed chances and lonely years the loss of those letters represented.

'Not now,' he said at last. 'I don't think either of us is quite ready yet.'

'We can't ignore them for ever or she will have won,' she cautioned.

'Leave it a day or two for us to settle into who we are now. It won't make much difference, Callie, and I'm not ready to be rational about the betrayal they represent yet.'

Here she was thinking he was almost too rational and yet there was fury and a terrible weariness in his eyes that made her heart thunder because she could see her beloved Gideon there, for all Mr Peters thought he had him so firmly under control. Surely it wouldn't be difficult to love that Gideon and the new one, as well? *No,* her inner wanton whispered, *it could even be delightfully easy. That one was a boy, this is a fully grown man.*

Gideon fought the need to crash his fist into the nearest wall and straightened his fingers before he did serious damage to the fine plasterwork and his wife's serenity. Such a hot blaze of fury roiled inside him that he paced over to glare out of the window until he could speak calmly again. No, calmness was too much to ask, he decided, as the magnitude of what that woman had done washed over him again and a red mist wanted to snuff out the self-control he'd learnt over the past, lonely years apart from his wife and what passed for his family, for a Laughraine who wasn't really a Laughraine at all.

'I should have come to find out why you didn't answer myself, but I was too much of a coward,' he said as his anger turned inward and mocked him for that oversight. 'There's no fool like a painfully young one, is there?'

'I don't know. I was being one myself at the time.'

'That's both of us blaming ourselves then, but going over the past isn't going to help you adjust to your true role in life now, is it, my lady?'

'I admit I don't feel I shall ever be a fit mistress for a great house like this. I'm not equal to your future peers and their aristocratic wives, either.'

'Neither am I, don't forget. I don't much care for all that pomp and social chatter, either,' he said truthfully. 'I want my wife back, Callie. If you decide you can be my lady all well and good and your grandfather will be delighted, but I never expected to inherit Raigne. We can live under any roof you like so long as we do it together.' His whole life hinged on her decision, he decided, with a sick feeling in his stomach she might still find the idea of being married to him again too awful to consider.

'I don't think we can refuse an inheritance like this, can we?' she asked, and at least she hadn't snapped an emphatic *no* back and him and flounced out of the room in disgust.

'I have no right to any of it except through you. I almost wish I could prove my father was the late Viscount Farenze's son and not Sir Wendover Laughraine's, but if there was evidence Wendover would have used it years ago. All that talk about not lowering his pride to legally disown Virgil Winterley's bastard, once he realised who the boy really was, was made up to save face. He'd have done it in the blink of an eye if there was even a sniff of proof he was cuckolded so neatly he never suspected until it was too late.'

'I always thought your grandmother quite wicked to seduce a schoolboy like that. Lord Farenze was much too young to seek an affair with a woman old enough to be his mother,' Callie pointed out.

'True, but Sir Wendover was a harsh and sometimes violent man. I dare say he gave his wife every cause to stray, but no opportunity. Watching a young Adonis run tame about Raigne that summer must have tempted her to take a lover even her husband didn't suspect, don't you think? According to my uncle she was still a celebrated beauty well into middle age and I doubt my grandfather had the poise or maturity to resist her if she set out to seduce him.' The detail of his father's birth was something he did his best not to dwell on, but she was quite right. 'I don't know why I'm trying to defend her, though, because you're quite right. It was unforgivable to use a boy to take revenge on her husband, but how could she care so little for her son? She left my father to find out who he really was when he was not quite a man. Little wonder that he never recovered.'

The constant tension and bitterness of his childhood reminded him how far the shadows of that long-ago sin reached, but he wasn't the angry young man with parents who hated each other now. Being a churlish and rootless young cub lost him everything nine years ago and she had a right to know all he did about his father's birth. Not talking about such things had cost them too much last time. 'Lady Virginia believed in her husband, so I shall have to, as well. My grandfather told her of his first affair before they married since he was ashamed of it, but he swore he only realised my father was his get at the same moment everyone else did.'

'Did you know that she came to see me, your Lady Virginia? I don't think she had it in her to beg, but she did order me to relent and forgive your sins, both real and imaginary, and I refused to listen. Now I see that she must have been speaking from bitter experience, although I was so sure such a legendary beauty never had a real rival for her husband's affections. Lady Virginia would have had some very sharp questions for him to answer before she let him adore her again when they found out he had a son, though, wouldn't she? Especially considering they were not blessed with children of their own.'

'I didn't know anything about her finding you and giving one of her infernal lectures, Callie. She never said she'd met you face-to-face. I suppose even if you had written me a scorching rebuke for sending her, I wouldn't have received it, would I?' he managed to joke bleakly.

That chance his patron and step-grandparent tried to make for them felt like a new burden of grief. Lady

Virginia loved him, despite all his attempts to cut himself off from any of the softer emotions by the time they got to know each other. She had regally ignored every barrier he put in the way of letting anyone love him after he lost Callie.

'People call me a clever lawyer behind my back, but I was an idiot not to suspect your aunt was stealing our letters until I arrived at Cataret House to find things so very different to how they should have been. I thought a stony silence was your reply to my pleas for any sort of reconciliation you cared to ask for, under any terms you wanted to name. It seemed like your way of making me understand you hadn't the slightest intention of listening to anything I had to say and, after that letter you sent to me through my then employer, Mr Poulson, telling him to make me understand I must never even try to contact you again, I was sure there was no hope for us.'

'I didn't send you any such letter, Gideon, I swear it. I felt raw and betrayed for a long time after we parted, but I would have read your letters anyway and certainly not have closed myself off from you so frigidly as that. I thought your refusal to send any sort of reply to *my* letters meant you were very happy living without me in London with some delighted young woman to make you very comfortable indeed when I had only made you sad and heartsick. I really should have listened to your Lady Virginia, shouldn't I?' Callie said, and it seemed so foolish of his young self to believe she had such cold hatred in her heart for her worst enemy as she had written to him. 'If I had received any of your letters I wouldn't have let you suffer unnecessarily, I would have answered you at the very least.'

'So if everything was as you thought it that day and I really was unfaithful to you with your mother's stepdaughter, you'd have forgiven me for it in the end, would you?' he asked recklessly, tension twisting at his gut as he waited for her answer. Silence stretched. 'I'm a yahoo to even ask such a question,' he concluded when it went on too long for it to be a yes.

'I can try,' she finally managed and there was that half a loaf again. Why should she forgive him something so unforgivable? And why couldn't he settle for that half loaf and be grateful to have any bread at all after all that happened in the past?

'Drink your tea, Callie, and I'll go and see if your grandfather has found a puppy to chew up those deplorable shoes you were wearing the other day yet. We can talk of impossible things another time,' he managed to say as if his wildest hopes hadn't just fallen round his feet again.

'Gideon, no, you can't leave me sipping tea and wondering what happened,' she protested as he strode hastily away before he said something else he regretted.

'Yes, I can,' he said before he loped out of one of the full-length windows, then escaped from the terrace before she had time to put her cup aside and run after him. 'Oh, hell and the devil confound it, I have to, Callie,' he muttered as he strode towards the lake and launched into a pounding swim through the spring-fed water to wear his hurt and temper and sense of loss out against the indifferent elements. He wasn't a machine; he couldn't cut himself off from his feelings, at least he couldn't now she was here to tug them to life every time he laid eyes on her. 'You failed again, Gideon,' he murmured once he was finally exhausted, and still the hurt of wanting her, needing her in his life and never having her want and need him back pounded in his head like Odin's hammer.

A truly genteel lady left staring into space by her furious husband would take to her bed and remain elegantly exhausted until he grovelled for mercy. Callie dashed after hers, but soon got lost in the maze of ancient knot gardens and elegant parterres and realised she would never find him when he didn't want her to, at least until she knew this place better. Luckily the house was a landmark impossible to ignore, so she found her way back to the terrace and stumbled breathlessly towards the still-warm tea to slump in her chair with all the finesse of a half-empty flour sack. Now her previous soul searching was wasted she had it to do again. Why couldn't she settle for what she could have? Why chase the dream her passionate young lover was truly her perfect knight, faithful to her for life?

He was the man she longed for with every frustrated inch of touch-deprived skin. She wanted him so badly it hurt *not* to say all the yeses she'd had no chance to give him for years, but she couldn't get one past her lips at the right moment, despite longing for him with every fibre of her being. If only Lady Virginia was still here she would have the benefit of a female viewpoint on their situation, whether she wanted it or not. It would be skewed in Gideon's direction, of course, but Callie could see why the unpredictable old lady loved Gideon so much she couldn't admit he would even think about betraying a wife he loved as much as he had her back then. The fact she caught Cecily Willoughby leaving his bedroom in a state of dishabille was damning, though. What reason had the little cat got to lie that he was her lover?

Her gaze shifted to the battered boxes of papers from Cataret House he must have left here for safe keeping. His letters to her must be in there with hers to him. Why not read them and find out what excuse he had for wanting her stepsister when he couldn't get attention from his wife? Whatever they had to say on the subject they should have been in her hand years ago, hoarded under her pillow and carried about with her until they were illegible, even if she didn't act on them and go to London to seek him out as every instinct she had told her she would have done, if he could only persuade her that he still loved her.

She put down the teacup she had only picked up again for the sake of holding something a little bit warmer than she was. She felt cold to her finger-tips, but surely that was impossible with the sun at its zenith and the heat unrelenting? Still, she shivered at the thought of that last day at Willoughby Manor and what felt like the end of everything that truly mattered. It would only take a few steps and a little more curiosity to find out what his letters had to say about it.

The leather covering and iron-edged corners of the boxes were battered and worn so the wood underneath showed through here and there. She suspected they once belonged to Grandfather or Grandmama Sommers before her aunt took them over. The Reverend

Sommers had been a curate to her grandmother's governess when they met, so either of them could have owned such sturdy but unpretentious items as they moved from place to place until they could finally afford to marry. The fact their travelling boxes were so well used told her it was an agonising wait. No wonder Grandfather didn't want the same for her and Gideon. When they fell in love so young it must have reminded him of his beloved wife and the years they had had to wait to marry.

She was distracting herself from the rights and wrongs of doing this without Gideon. Callie recognised a scuff mark on the lid of the one from the attic where she finally found out what her aunt had been up to all these years. Was that really only yesterday? She flinched from what she was doing when she realised it was two days since she set out for Manydown with no idea Gideon was coming to change everything.

She stepped back from the little trunk that seemed too much like Pandora's box with all the sad secrets of the world inside it. This wasn't right. If they were ever to trust one another with all their secret hopes and passions, she and Gideon must read the letters together. If they never did trust enough for that, what was the point of looking at all? Inside a polite marriage of near strangers it didn't matter if his words had been a plea or a blame to her eighteen-year-old self. Wondering how she could hold back her very self if Gideon demanded his marital rights as a means to pass Raigne on to another generation, she shoved a clenched fist into her mouth to force back a sob.

Lady Laughraine did not sit and weep over tattered boxes full of old letters, or let the world know she was married to a man she couldn't stop loving and nothing would induce her to tell him so. Callie might, in private, but in company she would be my lady, as self-contained and miserly with her emotions as Sir Gideon Laughraine had learnt to be with his.

Chapter Ten

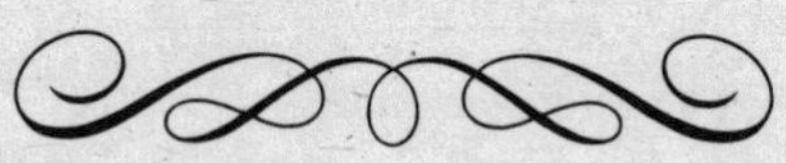

'Well, my boy?' Lord Laughraine greeted Gideon when he was finally fit for company and found the library occupied by its rightful owner again.

'Very well, thank you, Uncle Charles.'

'Hmm, well, you're here. I suppose that will do for now,' his lordship said with a shrewd glance at Gideon's damp dark hair and the bruise by his eye everyone else was pretending not to notice.

'The wonder is I'm not alone. I'm content with that small miracle.'

'Don't be a fool, of course you're not. You can pretend to the rest of the world you're as passionless as an iceberg if you like, but you won't take me in. Wouldn't think half as much of you if you were. The last thing this family needs is a cold fish like my Uncle Wendover, just look at the mess he made of everything if you don't believe me.'

'I try not to,' Gideon said with a genuine smile.

How come he had always felt so close to this particular Laughraine when they shared not a single drop of blood? He supposed it was kinship of the spirit—

rather like the one Tom Banburgh, Marquis of Mantaigne, had had with Virgil and Virginia. Gideon had tried hard not to envy his new friend that bond when he had this adoptive uncle of his to thank for all the lighter moments of his own early life. He wasn't quite sure he had always succeeded. Virgil was his true grandfather and part of him had been jealous to begin with. In the end Tom's love for Virgil had opened his eyes to the real man. Gideon's father had reviled his true father so often during his childhood that Gideon grew up thinking he must be a monster. As he matured logic told him Esmond Laughraine wasn't exactly a son to be proud of. Finding out what a fine job Virgil Winterley had made of the deprived and abused orphan boy Virginia rescued from his guardian as a ragged and barefoot orphan had fully opened Gideon's eyes to his own grandfather's strength and kindness and banished the spectre of a venal and neglectful beast who had his fun with another man's wife then walked away whistling a merry little ditty. Esmond had built up that myth in his own head to obsess over in his drunken rages and it said a lot more about him that it did about Virgil Winterley.

'I wonder how different our lives would have been if my father took after his mother instead of his sire,' he mused now.

'I doubt Wendover would have noticed if it wasn't so obvious the boy and Virgil could have been struck from the same mould. Most of us Laughraines are dark haired like the Winterleys and Wendover never could see much beyond the end of his nose,' Lord Laughraine observed with a shake of the head for an uncle he clearly hadn't liked. 'He was a hard man, but you know that. I suppose he had good reason to be furious his late wife foisted her love child on him as if she had nothing to be ashamed of.'

'Yet my father didn't deserve to be hated for something that wasn't his doing.'

'Ay, it was a sad mess and Esmond always refused to have anything to do with Virgil, however he had tried to do his duty by the boy and your father did his best to keep you from your real grandfather, as well. Heaven forbid you should love one another and leave Esmond to his bitterness and the brandy bottle. Virginia kept a close eye on you after Virgil died, though. Dashed clever woman, Virginia, bit of a challenge as a wife, I imagine, but Virgil always loved one of those.'

'I must have inherited something from him then, but did Lady Virginia really open doors for me, then make sure they stayed open when I refused to use your family name to further my career? To think I believed I'd made my own way in life all these years.'

Gideon wasn't quite sure why it seemed so important to be independent of every part of his family when he left Raigne now. For that to work they would have to feel the same anyway and for some reason the man he had always called Uncle Charles, although he was officially his father's cousin, had always been ready to own him as the heir. Perhaps Esmond had worn out all the hatred between Laughraine and Winterley? Or maybe none of it mattered if his granddaughter ended up Lady of Raigne?

'All Virginia did was remove an obstacle or two, the rest was up to you.'

'And I'm not sure I want to know what they were.'

'Never mind that now, what matters is what you

plan to do next. I'm past my three score years and ten, Gideon, and you two need to learn about the house and estate if Raigne is to flourish when you inherit.'

'I know very little about farming and less about estate management.'

'You do all that juggling with the truth and finding ways round an argument you lawyers use to get round the facts, don't you? A few surly farmers and the odd land dispute won't flummox a man who can hold his own with such slippery rogues as you're accustomed to. You won't be able to slip in and out of the dangerous places you frequent more or less unnoticed now, though, so perhaps it's as well if you put that part of your life behind you now you have a wife again. I need you to stay whole and hale and hearty if you're to keep my granddaughter happy for the next fifty years or so, my boy,' he added with a look that said his lordship kept a far closer eye on him than he had any idea of. 'Can you promise to stop getting yourself stabbed, shot or bludgeoned?'

'You make me sound so inept,' Gideon said lightly.

'Anyone would think you wanted to get yourself killed,' his lordship said with a challenging stare Gideon found hard to meet as he looked back on the hurt and angry boy he'd been nine years ago.

'At one time it seemed an acceptable hazard,' he admitted with a shrug.

'Not to me it wasn't and not to my granddaughter either, whatever the true reason you quarrelled, then sulked about it for so long. Don't you dare rake up all this business between you again and win her back, then go adventuring and risk yourself to some wild fool's bullet or knife. If she doesn't either shoot you or abandon you again for putting her through hell every time you're off on some mad start, I will do it for her.'

'After a threat like that one, I promise to leave Frederick Peters behind as soon as I can, as long as Callie doesn't throw me out of her life again. If I can't have her, I shall need an occupation desperate enough to stop me putting a bullet in myself.'

'Have you told her so?'

'Not yet. We only met again two days ago and she still doesn't trust me, although she may now trust her aunt even less.'

'So unless she trusts you and believes your side of whatever story that woman cooked up all those years ago, you won't admit you love my granddaughter every bit as madly as you did then?'

'I don't know yet, but please leave us be, Uncle Charles. Think what damage you and Sommers did between you with well-meaning interference last time and let us find our own path through the mess this time.'

'As long as you don't take too long about it and risk her thinking you don't care.'

'Untangling the misunderstandings of a decade takes time and I have learnt patience these last nine years since Callie and I parted, my lord. I suggest you do the same while we find out if we can endure being married again.'

'Oh, very well, but kindly remember I'm not getting younger and marriage is for more than the year you managed last time,' Lord Laughraine said with a resigned sigh. 'None of this matters tuppence ha'penny if you two can't happily run in harness together.'

'No, nothing matters then,' Gideon confessed.

'You weren't a slow-top ten years ago.'

'Ten years ago I thought she loved me.'

'Of course she did, the girl would never have taken such a risk on you if she didn't. You were a damned fool then and you're still one now, but for some reason she wanted you anyway so I dare say the rest of us can learn to put up with you.'

'Now I feel so much better about myself. Thank you, my lord.'

'Don't mention it, my boy. Now pass me another glass of that claret, then go and find out how that girl of mine is doing. I dare say she needs rescuing from one of Mrs Craddock's grand tours of every linen cupboard in the house by now.'

'Yes, my lord. Is there anything else I can do for you, my lord?'

'Can't think of it right now,' Lord Laughraine said as regally as the Prince of Wales. He raised the refilled glass to his lips to hide a smug smile and nodded in mock dismissal as Gideon went off to do as he was bid for once.

A soft knock on the door between one vast bedchamber and the next made Callie jump as if she'd just been prodded with a sharp stick. Surely Gideon wasn't going to demand his marital rights so soon after getting her to share this lovely, lofty and yet somehow intimate old suite of rooms with him? Her heart had done that familiar thump then race the moment Mrs Craddock told her there was no need to feel alone in such a vast space since her husband's room was just next door.

'Come in,' she managed to call as steadily as if she wasn't tempted to leave by the other door before he could open the one his side.

'Don't worry, I only want to know if you're feeling better,' he said softly as he entered on such silent feet she wondered again how he'd learnt to move so stealthily and, more importantly, why. 'Mrs Craddock suspects you have a headache.'

'I just wanted a little peace,' she admitted truthfully. 'Raigne is very beautiful and full of history and treasures beyond my wildest dreams, but I'm not in the frame of mind to appreciate it somehow.'

'I really have turned your world upside down, haven't I?'

'Well, of course you have, Gideon, isn't that what you intended?'

'Who knows?' he said, playing that infuriating trick of retreating into his thoughts. Since he was looking about as blank as a man could without actually being asleep, he must be fighting feelings he didn't want her to know about again. 'Nobody could say you were delighted to be my Lady Laughraine, could they?'

'No,' she confirmed shortly. 'Mr Winterley called you Peters at the toll gate this morning, Gideon, so I must be Mrs Peters, as well, mustn't I? Has that been your alias all these years?'

'One of them,' he said cautiously, but he must have seen her mouth tighten at the thought of more secrets and he held up a hand to admit he was being defensive. 'Yes, then, but I use others to go places even Peters can't go. I have lived as Frederick Peters since we parted and Sir Gideon Laughraine would be torn apart in some parts of the underworld where Sir Wendover Laughraine made his name. My supposed grandfather was a ruthless, corruptible man, Callie. I should be glad that I stand very little chance of taking after him.'

'Is that why you stopped using his name?'

Gideon shrugged, then seemed to recall she had a right to know more than anyone else. 'I'm not entitled to it and I was tired of the lie. You didn't want me under any name, so it hardly mattered what I called myself.'

'Yet here you must endure the name you were born with, must you not?'

'Yes, since it's the one you took when you married me.'

'If I was born on the right side of the blanket it would have been mine by right,' she reminded him clumsily, but perhaps it was as well to get this tired old subject over and done with and hope they could move past it to something better.

'Well, I certainly didn't get it that way. Does that mean you resent me for bearing the name you ought to have had if your parents had married each other?'

'Of course I don't. Neither of us could help things that happened before we were born and I'm female, anyway. You would be the heir even if my parents had made me legitimate.'

'Not if they had had more children and one was a boy,' he pointed out with a mocking smile.

'Well, of course not, but they didn't and you are Lord Laughraine's heir whether you like it or not,' she told him, with a militant nod. 'My grandfathers went to great lengths to make sure the succession was wrapped up right and tight,' she reminded him, then wished she hadn't as that blank look came between them again.

'The estate could still end up in Chancery if the Prince chooses to challenge me,' he said, as if talking about an abstruse legal problem that had nothing to do with him.

'But you're the heir and I'm the last heir's only child, even if I am a bastard, so he can't do anything.'

'Not if we are reunited,' he said, looking at the naked ring finger of her left hand.

'I gave my rings back to you. Produce them and I'll wear them again,' she challenged.

'When you're my wife again, I will,' he parried.

'We both know there's more to marriage than four legs in a bed, Gideon,' she reminded him even as hot colour bloomed in her cheeks and her most intimate memories reminded her how satisfying it was to share a bed with her lover.

'Don't be vulgar, Lady Laughraine,' he cautioned with a cynical smile that told her he'd spent too much time with the likes of Mr Winterley over the past few years.

'And don't pretend you're a prude, Sir Gideon,' she snapped back.

'This really is the most unlikely conversation, Callie,' he said with a real smile that threatened to leave her spellbound all over again. 'Two days ago I was a stuffy lawyer and you were a very proper schoolmistress, and now look at us.'

'I'm still dressed like a governess and you are a fine gentleman,' she pointed out.

'Tomorrow I will send a messenger to the finest

dressmaker in London with your measurements and a slavish description of your colouring and all the other perfections a besotted husband can boast about,' he promised, 'but you still don't look like any governess I ever came across,' he added huskily.

'Lady Laughraine is a married woman, so at least she can go about looking a little less buttoned up than Miss Sommers could in this heat,' she admitted as she fought a silly compulsion to do them up again, in case he didn't like what he could see of her.

'We're alone in Lady Laughraine's rather splendid bedchamber, Callie, you can go about it in nothing at all if you so desire,' he replied hoarsely.

'Would you desire me so?' she heard herself say, as if a siren had taken over her mouth and was determined to get her into trouble she wasn't ready for quite yet.

'I would desire you if you were dressed in armour from head to toe and fenced about with a hostile army, but you should be very wary of playing with fire, my lady.'

'I should,' she murmured so softly he bent his head to hear, or at least that was the story she told herself. 'I am,' she added even more quietly, and felt his breath on her lips as she slicked them nervously with her tongue and his gaze went molten.

'Quite right, too,' he affirmed so softly that they needed to be closer still. There, his mouth on hers. Firm and yet so gentle it almost brought tears to her eyes. She felt warm right into places that had been frozen ever since he left. Her breath gasped in and then stuttered out. This was her lover, her young love.

Gideon was kissing her again and how had she lived without him for nine long years?

'You're right about the fire,' she managed to say as he raised his teasing mouth the sliver of an inch so they could breathe. Desire was simple enough, yet complex as the deepest labyrinth. This, though? This was far more than desire and she hardly dared find a name for it so she stopped trying as her senses searched for all that was her Gideon and unchanged and everything that was a new one and even more intriguing.

'How unexpected of me,' he joked, and this time she could feel the smile against her mouth before he took that kiss deep again and her very toes tingled. She could have sworn lightning flashed right through her and into him, or was it the other way round?

She gasped as another jag of heavy longing heated her beyond anything as simple as plain fire. Breathing in the scent of him, the sharp combination of shaving soap, clean linen and unique essence of pure Gideon she had deprived herself of for so long, she hummed with pleasure. So she forgot how it felt to say no to either of them, welcomed the heady thrust of his tongue with a moan to say it had been too long since they feasted on each other.

Now his fingers shook as he ran touch along her jaw, played with a stray curl of her raven-dark hair. Then he found the silken skin just behind her ear where he knew she was most seducible and used it to drive her even wilder. Her lover. Here was her lover and he knew every inch of her. Exhilaration coursed through her because he was back with her, kissing her, seducing her with all he was and all they could be on his lips and in her heart. The feel of his racing heartbeat under her hand said he was as caught up in the wonder of it as she was. Raising her hands to loop them round his neck and demand more and deeper, she heard bells ring and shook her head in puzzled denial. Thunder might crash through their veins, hot lightning was definitely trying to sheet through her as she shook with years of pent-up need and anticipation, but what had bells to do with their lovemaking?

'They tells me that's the dressing bell, miss, I mean m-my lady…' Biddy stuttered to a halt as she realised exactly what she was interrupting. Her face was a picture of such horror Callie had a hard time biting back a hysterical giggle. 'Oh, lawks, miss, that's just why I should be in the kitchen and not up here,' she said, and went to dash off and ask for something more like her old job back.

'Don't go, Biddy, your lady has need of you if we're to be ready in time for dinner,' Gideon said sharply.

After one huge gasp of protest he sounded as if he was used to being caught making love to his wife every day of the week and Callie jumped back as if she'd been stung instead of kissed within an inch of ecstasy.

'Indeed,' she managed, a little less smoothly, but if she refused to look at either of them she could push all that glory into the back of her mind, as well. 'Order some hot water brought up as soon as you can and lay out the good soap if you please, Biddy,' she said quite in the grand manner. Maybe she could be her ladyship, after all.

As Gideon stepped back with a shrug that said

goodness knew what, she wondered if she could be his lady, though. She didn't have it in her to cut off her emotions and parcel them up for the odd moment of sensuality before they set about the business of making heirs for Raigne House and its attendant acres. Still the inner heat and her heart racing and that rush of delirium in every part of her argued otherwise.

'After I have changed I will wait for you in our sitting room,' he said with that unreadable expression back on his face.

He refused to meet her eyes and let her see what he was thinking, so what else did she have to work with but the miserly part of himself he was granting her? 'No, please go down and join your uncle. I will be as quick as I can.'

'Very well, my dear,' he said, and gave her the sort of nod he might give any lady of his acquaintance, then he left before she could lose her own much less steady self-control and throw something heavy and breakable at the door as it closed after him.

'Oh, well done, Gideon,' he murmured to himself once he was safely through that devilish connecting door and safely on the other side. 'Your wife will feel so much better about being alone with you now,' he added and only had to picture her dishevelled and delicious and blushing like a schoolgirl to know he was a crass and lusty fool.

Idiot boy, she's a woman, not some Gothic heroine, he almost heard Lady Virginia's voice say, as if she might be sitting atop the cornucopia over the great canopied state bed when she was clearly busy enjoying her heavenly rest and being reunited with her adored husband at long last.

'Much you know,' he told a woman who wasn't there. If a mad doctor was about he might as well commit himself to his care and save himself weeks of torture while Callie decided whether or not she wanted a husband again or not.

Said you were an idiot, didn't I? Ought to know by now that her pride will keep her from admitting anything of the sort after you bungled that so badly.

'Oh, be quiet, woman, as if I need a ghost to tell me I'm a fool now when I know it perfectly well,' he told thin air as he strode about the room in a desperate effort to get his ridiculous body under control. The fact of his wife a room away and that reach halfway to heaven in her arms had him in such a state he was currently an embarrassment to both of them. He had a whole evening of frustration to get through without Winterley's knowing grin telling him what a lust-driven fool he was for Calliope, Lady Laughraine, all the time and a blush of embarrassed consciousness heating her cheeks every time she dared look his way.

If I didn't love your grandfather so much I might give up on you, Gideon Laughraine, that unreal echo of Lady Virginia informed him crossly. *With your share of Virgil's looks and a pinch of his charm it shouldn't be totally beyond you to win your wife back before it's too late.*

'What do you mean too late?' he gasped, a catch of fear in his gut for Callie's safety.

He glared about him as if he might still manage to surprise her late ladyship's shade perched on a window seat or lurking in a dark corner, but the room was serene and quiet and all he could hear now was his own quickened breathing. Any sense he wasn't completely alone had gone and he quartered the room like a dog chasing shadows before he chided himself for listening to a wild part of his own imagination. He breathed in deeply and made the effort to calm himself down all over again.

'Dratted contrary female,' he muttered darkly about a ghost he couldn't let himself believe in. 'Loving me didn't do Callie much good last time, so why on earth would she risk doing it again?' he said like a child whistling in the dark to convince himself.

A marriage of convenience was all he could expect now, he supposed. He was certainly done with chasing impossible dreams, and from her reaction to his arrival at Cataret House she wasn't exactly enamoured of him, but years of bitter regret made the dream he could have seem rosy enough, if it ever came true. A shaft of evening sunlight fell on the tapestry of a long-ago lady holding court and looking none too pleased with her adoring knights, 'Know how you feel,' he informed one dejected and lovelorn example and shook his head at his own folly. Then he went to his dressing room to wash and shave once more, then hurry into his evening attire so he could go and find some company to distract himself from his ills until his wife was free to disapprove of him again.

Chapter Eleven

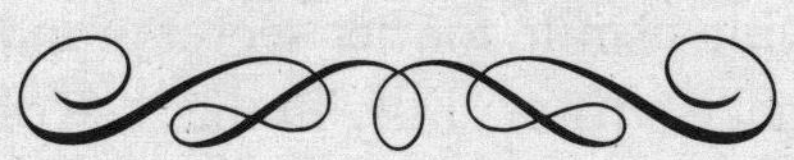

'Lady Laughraine, what a pleasure it is to see you again,' Mr Winterley exclaimed the instant Callie stepped inside the small drawing room after a hasty wash and changing into yet another plain muslin gown Biddy had managed to iron creditably under Mrs Craddock's patient instruction.

'It would certainly be one for Lady Laughraine's husband if he could see past the prattling rogue standing between him and his lady right now,' Gideon said grumpily, and Callie's fickle heart raced again at the very sound of him. At least jealousy had jolted him out of his chilly lawyer's persona and made him sound like a husband again, so she smiled at the rogue graciously because that certainly felt like a favour.

'Good evening, my lord, Gideon and it is Mr Winterley, isn't it?'

'A very good evening to you, my dear, this old place seems brighter now you're back here with this scapegrace nephew of mine at last,' Lord Laughraine greeted her, and she was touched by his attempts to fit her into his household as his heir's wife, instead of a scandal waiting to happen. 'You appear to be blooming again after your rest, despite my staff and this restless nephew of mine doing their best to wear you to a frazzle. I told them to leave you to settle in at your own pace, but I might as well have saved my breath.'

'Thank you anyway, my lord, you are very kind,' she said with a smile for her secret grandfather she couldn't make stiff or chilly in the face of his genuine welcome.

He seemed happy to let her set the pace of their relationship, or maybe he didn't want to acknowledge her and rake up the past and who could blame him? Except without the facts of her birth coming out, Gideon's claim to Raigne was weak. She wished the whole business was pared down to a husband and wife finding out if they could live as that, but years of loneliness had taught her to take life as it was rather than longing for an elusive ideal.

'Lord Laughraine might be, but I'm not,' Mr Winterley interrupted her thoughts with an extravagant bow she suspected was meant to infuriate Gideon. 'You look more enchanting tonight than you did this morning, Lady Laughraine.'

'And I suspect you of being a flatterer, Mr Winterley,' she said coolly.

'Would that I was, my lady, but since you're wed to this unworthy and secretive fellow, I must learn to live with the sad fact he found you first,' he said with a wicked smile she ought to distrust.

'Are these what are commonly called town manners, Mr Winterley?' she asked with a wry smile, because it was heady to be lied to extravagantly by such a dashing gentleman.

'No, my lady, a sign I have good eyesight and the sense to know a diamond of the first water when I see one.'

'Speaking as the man who recognised my wife's unique qualities many years before you set eyes on her, Winterley, I'll thank you to stop flirting with my lady. I'd hate to have to break that arrogant nose of yours, although I really can't imagine why some public-spirited husband hasn't done so already.'

'From the look of you, Laughraine, you resort to pugilism more readily than I do as a matter of course, but perhaps you could persuade Lady Laughraine to own up to you a little more often so fellows like me might not be quite so awed by her beauty before they realise she has an attendant dragon?'

Seeing the underlying challenge between them was only half in jest, Callie moved to stand next to Gideon. 'I believe it's considered polite to overlook a fellow guest's eccentricities in the best circles, isn't it, Mr Winterley?'

'As I rarely move in them, Lady Laughraine, you're talking to the wrong black sheep.'

'Ah, d'you hear a noise outside? Expect that's Finch and his lady arriving for dinner,' Lord Laughraine intervened hastily. 'I trust you don't mind such company so soon after your arrival, m'dear?'

'Of course not, Gra…my lord,' Callie said and almost let the cat out of the bag in front of the far-too-acute Mr Winterley. 'I shall be delighted to see them again.'

Outside company at dinner suddenly seemed a

wonderful idea, especially when it was her other grandfather's successor as vicar of King's Raigne and his gentle wife. The living was given to him as he was Grandfather Sommer's curate when Grandfather died. Callie suspected Lord Laughraine had persuaded the bishop to encourage them to stay in the Raigne villages to take some of the burden of a widespread parish off the Reverend Sommers's ageing shoulders when Mr Finch should have been going on to a parish of his own. Whatever the reason they stayed and, when Mr Finch got the living through circumstances he would never have wanted, it proved a popular promotion. It would be hard for even the most cantankerous villagers to dislike him, but it still felt odd for Callie to think of anyone but her grandfather as vicar of King's Raigne.

'My dear, I'm so glad to see you and Sir Gideon back at last. We all missed you sadly and his lordship has been longing to welcome you home again,' Mrs Finch said, and refused to shake hands politely as she gave Callie a motherly hug.

'Thank you, Mrs Finch. It's lovely to see you both and it feels so good to be back,' she replied, not quite ready to add 'where we belong' until she was sure of it herself. 'And, dear Mr Finch, how are you, sir?'

'All the better for seeing you, my dear, although I suppose we must learn to call you "my lady" now Sir Gideon is a baronet, must we not, my love?'

'I don't know about my husband, but I refuse to be called by a mere title when you mended my clothes and skinned knees when I was a child. You saved me many a beating from my aunt for getting into mischief when her back was turned, you must call me

Callie and never mind such pomp between such old friends as we all are.'

'Only in private then, Callie,' Mrs Finch allowed with a look that said she considered Mr Winterley family for some odd reason.

'Aye, you're right as usual, my dear. We don't want to be encroaching,' her husband agreed, and Callie smiled and shook her head because she couldn't think of any two people less likely to step over the line.

The arrival of the now middle-aged couple broke the tension in the fine room full of mellow evening light and they chatted about hot weather and storms and the prospects for a good harvest. Even Mr Winterley forgot he was a sophisticated town beau and joined in the talk of a far smaller world than the one he was used to. Then Craddock came to tell them dinner was ready and they filed into the small dining room to an impromptu feast instead of the small family dinner they expected.

'I couldn't stop them, m'lord,' Craddock said dolefully as every luxury Raigne could command at short notice was brought in. 'You know how it is when a bevy of females get an idea in their heads.'

'Aye, well, I suppose our widows and pensioners will eat well tomorrow and for the rest of the week. Tell them they were quite right to make sure everyone can celebrate the return of my heir and his wife, but perhaps you might remind them Sir Gideon and Lady Laughraine are but two slender people when it comes to making preparations for feeding them in future,' Lord Laughraine said with a rueful look at the groaning board.

'I'm sure I can rein them in tomorrow, but they

would insist on a feast to welcome Sir Gideon and his lady home.'

'Have you been dining on husks like the Prodigal Son for the last few years then, Laughraine?' Mr Winterley asked Gideon mockingly.

That trick he had of quirking one dark eyebrow made him look more cynical than usual, but who did it remind her of? Callie leapt to what should have been an obvious conclusion the moment she first set eyes on the man and almost gasped out loud. He was an inch or so taller than her husband and a year or two older, but standing side by side they could be brothers. Of course, the family name of Viscount Farenze was Winterley, wasn't it? This stranger was Gideon's cousin on the wrong side of the blanket, so what on earth was he doing here?

Mr Winterley didn't seem like a man swayed by family feeling, or altruism towards his fellow beings. Whatever his motives, why had it taken so long for her to realise he was Gideon's kinsman? Now she did she could see they were as dark as one another. They shared a natural elegance and grey eyes set under strongly marked dark brows. Their noses were Roman enough to look haughty at times, but that was where the likeness ended. Gideon's eyes were kinder and he seemed less severe than his secret cousin.

Wasn't that an odd word to choose for a man with the manner of a care-for-nobody? She tested it against what little she knew of him and, yes, it still seemed to fit. The real Mr Winterley was austere and a little fierce under that careless charm, and a far more dangerous man than he'd have you believe. That conclusion told her two things—first to be wary; second that Gideon was her touchstone and she judged the inner life of other men by her husband. She met Mr Winterley's bland gaze with a challenging look and he smiled, as if acknowledging he had his own reasons to be here when Gideon came home, but what they were was a mystery he intended to keep to himself.

'You know very well I haven't, Winterley, I'm surprised you need to ask,' Gideon answered his cousin's double-edged remark. He sounded careless, but the slight trace of a frown he smoothed away before anyone but Callie could see it said he was uneasy about Mr Winterley's unlikely visit to Raigne.

'You might have done before this January for all I know,' Mr Winterley said blandly.

'You may not have acknowledged my existence before then, but you know we lawyers rarely starve in garrets as poets and Jacobins are supposed to,' Gideon replied.

'I usually take care to avoid lawyers whenever possible, but at least they're not as annoying as brooding mountebanks and unwashed revolutionaries. I'm quite prepared to do the polite to either, if you have one concealed about the house of course, my lord, but please don't ask me to join the ladies at lionising either breed.'

'Do you really think us females so easily taken in by dramatic poses or a distracted manner, Mr Winterley?' Mrs Finch replied in her quiet way. 'I doubt Lady Laughraine or I will swoon with delight, even if we come across a real hero whilst in your company.'

'So a hero is like a prophet without honour in his own country, Sir Gideon. You appear not to be very good at crowing from your own dunghill,' Mr Winterley said, as if impatient with his cousin's secrets when he clearly had plenty of his own.

'I'm no hero,' Gideon replied as if it was close to an insult, but Callie saw a faint flush of colour tint his surprisingly tanned cheeks and wondered what he'd really been up to.

'Rich Seaborne and his Lady Freya would disagree with you, and Lord Forthin and his countess, oh, and most of the Seaborne interest, as well, don't you think? They would be a lot less happy today if not for Mr Frederick Peters,' Mr Winterley said as if he was a small boy dropping stones into a still pond simply for the love of making a disturbance.

Callie thought his reference to Gideon in association with the illustrious Seaborne clan and their web of aristocratic connections could be pure mischief, or a warning to her husband that he couldn't keep one side of his life away from the other any longer.

'None of that called for any great heroics on my part. Mine was mainly a supporting role and came about by chance,' Gideon said repressively, as if he didn't care to talk about it.

Callie made no attempt to set up a polite buzz of small talk with Mr and Mrs Finch to oblige him, because the slightest hint of what he'd been up to all this time felt precious.

'Come now, Winterley, you've told us enough of a tale to make us curious and now we're intrigued. First we'll dine, then I think we could eschew our brandy, gentlemen, or take it into the drawing room if the ladies permit? You can tell us the whole tale over our teacups,' Lord Laughraine said jovially and neatly spiked Mr Winterley's guns.

Callie tried to do justice to Cook's feast, but her attention wasn't on her dinner. Her husband was good friends with the grandson of a duke and maybe the current Duke of Dettingham, as well, was he? Gideon belonged to a powerful family, was heir to another and had been hobnobbing with the great and the good. Now he encouraged a light flow of polite conversation, did his best to coax her into eating more than she wanted to and all she really wanted from him was a hint of who was really behind all those shifting personas of his and what that passionate kiss had meant to both of them.

'No more,' she said, shaking her head at the peach he was about to slip on to her plate piece by piece. 'I couldn't eat another thing.'

'You're too pale,' he murmured as if he had been far more conscious of her every mood during this rather odd dinner than she had any idea of.

'Not from lack of food and it's just been that sort of a day somehow,' she told him clumsily, and his expression froze as if he thought that kiss part of the reason she had found it a little too much. 'You must admit it was eventful,' she added and somehow made bad worse.

He gave her a faint, polite nod, as if listening to a stranger he hadn't taken to and turned away to speak to Mrs Finch on his other side. Their tentative accord felt fragile as gossamer all of a sudden and why did she have to be so inept at expressing her feelings to the person they mattered to most? Wasn't a convenient arrangement a better future than the one she had woken up to every morning before he came? She flinched at the idea of going back to loneliness, then felt Mr Winterley's cool, assessing glance on her. Shocked by the perception in his hard green-grey eyes she tried to blank her own. If he wasn't such a detached and uncaring gentleman, she might almost believe he was challenging her not to hurt his secret cousin.

Could it be he cared about Gideon under that cynical detachment? It warmed her heart a little to think one member of his family was prepared to stand at his back if he needed it, but she took a second look and decided she wasn't quite sure she would want this dark knight behind her in any fight—in front where she could see him perhaps, but not with the most vulnerable part of her trustingly unguarded. Maybe she imagined that moment of brotherhood, maybe she was wronging a man who did his best to be unknowable. One thing was for certain, though: she felt nothing for this man who was so like Gideon, yet so different under those dark good looks. She raised her chin in a silent challenge to mind his own business and let them work out their futures without his interference.

'My nephew has eschewed the bottle, Finch, and you don't indulge, so I'm happy to restrict myself to tea tonight,' Lord Laughraine said genially when it was obvious nobody could eat another thing. 'I'll get Craddock to bring the decanters to the drawing room if you'd like to join us, Winterley, or you can stay here in peace and quiet with your port.'

'I'll give my luckless head a night off from dissipation, my lord,' Mr Winterley said, and Callie thought he was laughing at himself this time.

A casual observer might think Mr Winterley the

perfect gentleman, but shouldn't a cynical beau like him be paying court to the beauty of the moment, attending mills, racing curricles or leading young cubs astray, instead of dining with two soberly married couples and a lord old enough to be his grandfather in the country?

'Well then, my boy, what have you really been up to whilst trying to fool me you were busy out-prosing old Poulson on the lawyer circuit?' Lord Laughraine asked as soon as they were settled in the vast small drawing room again.

'Nothing very momentous,' Gideon said as if saying it with enough conviction might make them forget Mr Winterley's hints to the contrary.

'If you don't let those closest to you into your confidence, Laughraine, the truth will come back and bite you,' that gentleman informed him with a frown that confirmed Callie's suspicions his was a deeper and darker character than he liked to pretend, and one who knew a great deal more about her husband than Gideon liked known.

'And if I do I will be betraying the personal affairs of some fine people who have since become my good friends,' he protested with a very straight look for his cousin that said this was all his fault, which it was, she supposed, as she listened eagerly for the story Mr Winterley was about to force out of him.

'As they are your friends they must trust you. Tell your family and your good friends here, man, or you might lose everything you hold most dear all over again. I am quite sure anything you may confide in them will go no further and I already know it so you can't hide your adventures from me and I haven't broadcast them in the streets so far, have I?'

Before Mr and Mrs Finch could get up and declare themselves beyond the scope of family, Gideon seemed to decide these particular cats couldn't be put back into the bag now he was more likely to mix with the *haut ton*. He waved them back into the seats they were already half out of and on the point of calling for their gig.

'Winterley is right for once. You are the least likely people to betray a confidence and I should like you to know what I was about so you are as wary of strangers in the Raigne parishes as I shall have to be if we remain here for long periods of time.'

Callie shivered at his implication dangerous characters might want to pursue Gideon for revenge and listened intently to the tale of Mr Peters's adventures her husband told with a determined counterpoint from Mr Winterley when he did his best to belittle his own part in them. It seemed Mr Richard Seaborne had disappeared to protect his first wife and her child by her first husband and his unlucky family, then they spent six years not sure if the man was alive or dead. The adventures the Seaborne family embarked on to try and find their black sheep; Rich Seaborne's adventures and tragedies as he lost his wife in childbirth and three years later chanced upon a fine lady lost in his forest hideaway, then fell in love with her, seemed a wilder story than any Callie had managed to come up with for her books. She was spellbound by the tale and eager to hear the rest of it from one of the Seabornes and sure Gideon had underplayed his part in the happy endings they all seemed to have enjoyed since.

'Oh, my dear Gideon, what an extraordinary tale you have to tell, but what risks you have taken with yourself,' Mrs Finch said as if stronger words might be excusable, but she couldn't come up with them.

Gideon looked sheepish, as if he'd been caught out in something reprehensible, and Callie ached to walk into his arms and tell him otherwise. He had been her hero at eighteen, but it seemed he'd been rashly determined to rescue a good few people from their dragons since then and she wasn't there to try to stop him taking such risks.

'My boy, I'm glad I didn't know the half of it whilst it was going on, or I'd have had you kidnapped and brought back here myself years ago,' Lord Laughraine added in a low, shocked voice that sounded as shaken by the dangers Gideon had faced as Callie felt.

Gideon was staring at her, as if her reaction was the only one he really wanted to hear and she simply didn't have words to let him know. She shook her head numbly and held his gaze with fear and pride in his reckless bravery in her eyes as she did her best not to shake or cry out at the chances he'd taken and how often he could have got himself killed. How many injuries had he suffered that even Mr Winterley hadn't managed to find out about? And then there was the awful suspicion it was her fault he had so little regard for his own skin; that he thought she meant all that nonsense she had spouted on their last day together. She recalled a hysterical rant about it being better for her if he was dead or had never been born rather than see him betray her with her mother's stepdaughter.

'I...I... Oh, Gideon, how could you think such a thing? I didn't mean a word of it,' she blurted out in the weak voice she recognised with horror from the day he came back to her and she fainted at his feet. She must be about to do something equally foolish to have said that in front of her grandfather and Mr Winterley.

Gideon looked blank for a moment, which was a good sign, wasn't it? If he had listened to her half-crazed ravings that day, and carried them into every one of those quixotic adventures with him, he would have known what she meant straight away. Then he seemed to cast his mind back to that awful day, as well, and shook his dark head as if she should never have thought up such a silly notion.

'No, it wasn't that. One thing just led to another and I could help, you see? That was all it was, I promise you.'

He understood. Thank heavens for that. She looked up to find her grandfather's eyes on them and realised he did, as well. Goodness knew how, when they might as well be speaking in code. Luckily the Finches and Mr Winterley were making themselves tactfully busy, talking of reforms that needed to be made to the law and better enforcement of it, to notice the byplay between her and Gideon, or they had decided it was none of their business. Lord Laughraine went to join them and stoke the fire as best he could until the two of them had finished washing their dirty linen almost in public.

'Never mind the past,' she managed with a shrug that said it did matter, but she was determined to concentrate on now. 'Promise you'll stop now?'

'That depends on you, don't you think?' he asked bleakly.

'Oh, unfair,' she protested, the tear and fire of her own hot temper threatening to break through her terror at what he had been doing with that whipcord strong body and stubborn, brilliant mind these past few years, when he ought to have been with her. 'And unworthy of you, Sir Gideon,' she added with as much dignity as she could muster when the shock of him risking so much was still making it impossible for her to stand and face him on shaky legs that were sure to let her down.

His gaze was sombre, as if to tell her if they failed at marriage again he couldn't make a promise to stay at home and mope. 'Yes. I'll stay here,' he said with a heavy sigh, as if it was a vow he made very reluctantly indeed. 'Lord Laughraine needs me even if you don't,' he added quietly.

'I'm here, aren't I?' she challenged, because she wouldn't be if she didn't intend to try.

Nine years of letting herself drift without him said trust wasn't one of her strongest suits, so how could she sit here and blame him for lack of faith in her? There had to be a way of keeping her passions under control and loving him from a distance, as a polite couple who agreed to be together for the sake of Raigne and all those who depended on it. Yet it was a poor little shadow of what might have been if the early promise of their marriage hadn't withered away. Didn't a hero deserve someone better than a coward as his mate?

'Why are we arguing about something neither of us wants to happen as if it already has, Gideon?' she asked, still avoiding meeting his acute grey and green gaze because she couldn't let herself admit she still loved him and risk his eyes growing cold and a look of distaste flitting across his handsome face.

'Because we're overtired and intent on running before we can walk?' he offered as if he knew that wasn't it.

'I apologise, my lord, I must be more weary from the road and all these festivities than a self-respecting Corinthian ought to admit to,' Mr Winterley said after an artistic yawn he might be trying to disguise, if he was tired at all, which Callie doubted

'I keep country hours nowadays,' Lord Laughraine interrupted with an intent look that told Callie she looked as wan as she felt. 'Now Finch and his lady have called for their gig and Winterley has been overcome by a rare attack of tact, I shall seek my bed if you two lovebirds will excuse me,' he added with a strong dose of irony Callie tried not to hear.

'I never truly kept anything other than country hours, my lord,' she replied with her best attempt at a smile after a demanding day.

'Once I could dance all night long, then happily come home with the dawn and still be about the estate of a morning as if I'd slept the sleep of the good all night long, but my own Lady Laughraine did love a party, God rest her soul. Consider my house your own and stay awake all night long if you choose to, Gideon, but I'm for my bed. Glad to see you home, my boy, and happy to welcome Lady Virginia's favourite relation under my roof, Winterley, even if you are a resty young devil and I'm not quite sure how she put up with you.'

'Thank you, my lord, but I have a very noble elder brother who takes most of the accolades in my family, including the position of Virginia's most favoured relative,' Mr Winterley said with his face impassive as a statue's. Callie saw a little way into his true character at last and felt sorry so much bitterness lay between this man and his half-brother, the current Viscount Farenze, for she supposed he had been trying to help Gideon back into his real life with that intervention tonight, hadn't he?

'It strikes me that you two, as Virgil's great-nephew and Gideon as my cousin, are like two peas shucked out of the same pod, Winterley. You both refuse to see where you're valued most,' his lordship said with a direct look at Gideon.

'How ungracious of us,' Mr Winterley said with a would-be careless shrug, but Callie noticed the hot slash of colour across his cheeks and knew those words had hit home.

'It's more important than a little social gaucheness none of us quite believe in, my boy,' Lord Laughraine told Mr Winterley, then offered his arm to Callie as if he knew her legs still felt uncertain after Gideon's latest revelations.

Gideon looked as if he was about to claim the right to escort her upstairs, but she shook her head, so he turned away looking self-contained as ever and she had to bite back an invitation to accompany him wherever he would like her to go.

'Don't suppose they'll come to blows if we leave them to it, m'dear,' his lordship confided when they were out of earshot.

'I dare say not,' she managed to say calmly enough.

'Might have done so a decade ago, of course, but Gideon's not an impulsive young idiot any more.'

'I never meant to hurt him,' she told him impulsively, glad they were between one floor of possible listeners and another.

'We never mean to hurt those we love, Callie, but being frail human beings we manage it, anyway,' he said as if he spoke from experience. 'There's a corner down here where nobody can hear and I think you need to talk to someone who will try to be impartial.'

'Why must we talk about it now?'

'I don't want my granddaughter under my roof at last and feeling as if she's only here because I can't avoid it. Spare me a few minutes and a hearing for your other grandsire's sake, if not for my own.'

'After the plotting you two got up to all those years ago, I'm not sure I want to.'

'So you let that business fester, did you? I never thought you a coward, my dear, not even when you turned the boy away, then punished yourself as well as him by living with your aunt instead.'

Callie flinched at the idea she had been doing just that. Had she been sleepwalking all these years not to realise what she was doing? 'I didn't care where I lived at first and then I stayed because I wanted to be busy,' she admitted.

Chapter Twelve

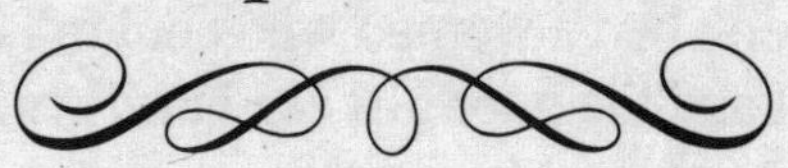

His lordship lit a branch of candles from his night-stick as if this might take some time. They were in an odd-shaped sitting area over the imposing Tudor porch. Callie could imagine the ladies of the house sitting here to read and embroider in the good light from the huge leaded windows, or waiting with over-stretched nerves for their chosen lover to race up the avenue and beg for their hand.

'Habit can be as destructive as active malice,' her grandfather said with a sad sigh that spoke of one or two of his own he regretted.

'Maybe, but if you disliked the situation so much, why did you never make a move to intervene between myself and Gideon years ago?' she asked curiously.

'I may be a bit of a slow-top, but in the end I learn not to make bad worse. If only I had let your father work out his own destiny, we might have been openly related all this time and he could still be alive. I wouldn't listen to his scruples about marrying the good girl his mother and I picked out as ideal for him when they were in their nurseries. Lady Richenda

Brierly was and still is a fine girl and I'm fond of her, but she'd have been happier in a convent if she lived in a Catholic country rather than wedding my boy out of duty to her parents and her maker. We thought we were doing our best for them both and served them a backhanded turn instead. It's my belief they were never truly man and wife, because my Will wouldn't bed a woman who couldn't endure the marital act and the poor girl can hardly bring herself to share a room with a member of my sex under the age of seventy even now.'

'It doesn't excuse what he did to my mother,' Callie argued.

'Nothing could, but he was young and weak and must have had doubts about the marriage they sleepwalked their way into, thanks to their bungling parents. I let his mother spoil him when he turned out to be our only child to survive infancy and lacked the will to deny him very much myself, except a free choice of lifetime partner and bedmate—the one choice he should have made by right. My Will never had to fight for anything, so he buckled at the first sign of opposition and did as he was bid. He might have left your mother to starve if Sommers wasn't a good man who wouldn't turn his back on the girl or her babe. I can't excuse Will for that, but I bear much of the blame.'

'I suppose my mother was ineligible,' Callie conceded, feeling disloyal to her very young mother although Mrs Willoughby seemed to have little feeling for the daughter who must be a constant reminder of her folly. 'Grandfather Sommers was the truest gentleman I ever met, but his family struggled to send him to school, then keep him at college long enough to get his degree. The same with my grandmother, I suppose. No wonder you and Lady Laughraine were not delighted when your son declared his intention to wed the vicar's youngest daughter instead of the titled lady you picked for him.'

'Trouble is he never did. The boy muttered a lot of half-formed excuses about a girl who made him feel a better man instead of a monster. He grew up too late to hold on to what he could have had, d'you see? Regretted it to his dying day, but he hadn't the courage to run off with the girl and risk ending up cast off without a penny to bless himself with. Told me later she insisted she wanted to marry a man with his own income and a tidy estate, but if you ask me your aunt had more to do with that statement than your mother. Seraphina Sommers always had a sly look about her, even as a girl, and she used to pinch the other girls black and blue if they were prettier or better natured than she was. Every girl in the parish was one or the other, so I'm not at all surprised she grew up to be a shrew. Should have realised at the time she was up to something.'

'You could hardly do that if my father didn't tell you who he wanted to marry.'

'Maybe not, but upbringing is a curious business, isn't it? You and your mother had the same home and education as Seraphina Bartle and turned out like chalk and cheese. Gideon's father treated him worse than a mongrel dog, yet he grew up a good and honourable man. Can you honestly see him being weak and spineless enough to desert the woman he loved and their unborn child so he could wed a woman who could hardly endure to touch a man simply because someone told him to?'

'No,' she agreed, feeling she'd been trapped by a very cunning opponent. 'He would have made a dash for the border before anyone had time to realise they were gone.'

'So why do you still blame him for your wrongs, Callie?'

'Because I'm weak like my father,' she said as she got up to pace to the now sightless windows and stare out into the twilight of high summer. 'When my world fell apart I sent Gideon away,' she admitted to the night as she couldn't seem to do so face-to-face. 'He pleaded with me to stay close by, even if I wouldn't live with him any more, but I said no and wanted a new start where I could pretend none of it had ever happened.' Callie thought she heard him move, but couldn't turn round and see reproach in those dark eyes so similar to her own. 'Anything that made me feel better was my concern and I wanted him to suffer and grieve and feel dead inside like me, and I succeeded. So, I don't deserve to be happy, you see? I haven't been so for the last nine years and I don't know if I ever will be now.'

'We could be undeservingly happy together,' Gideon's husky voice suggested from behind her and Callie gasped in horror that he'd heard her.

'After all I've done and said to make you turn away from me?' she asked steadily, eyeing his reflection in the dark glass as he moved closer. Her skin prickled with goosebumps and her nerves shivered in that old familiar dance of sensual awareness, despite the fact she was holding her breath for his reply.

'If I had been stronger back then I would have camped out in the hills when you refused to have me in the house,' he told her as he came to stand beside her. 'We had a lot of growing up to do, though, didn't we, Callie?'

'You appear to have done yours,' she said, and found the courage to turn round and face him again. Lord Laughraine looked almost as shocked as she felt that Gideon had managed to appear without making a sound. She acquitted him of getting her to speak about feelings she would probably have kept hidden if she knew Gideon was there and her grandfather shifted and cleared his throat as if speaking came hard when such raw emotions felt almost tangible in this gracious old corner of the house.

'Time I was in bed,' he said gruffly, and waved away Gideon's offer of help. 'We can talk another day, my dear, but Gideon has waited too long to have his say. Remember that nephew of Virgil's will hear more than you want him to if he can, though, won't you?'

'Goodnight, Grandfather,' Callie said with a shrug and a wry smile to admit it wasn't the best time to call him so with that warning in the air.

'Goodnight, child,' he said huskily and went to his rooms looking as if he thought something momentous had happened today and he was very happy about it.

'I was wrong about him,' she admitted for Gideon's ears only.

'He's pleased as a dog with two tails to have you here, but you're weary half to death and we don't need to talk now if you don't want to. Will you trust me to escort you to your room and help you as best I can, since I heard you tell Biddy not to wait up?'

'Yes, I've been lonely, too,' she agreed with a heartfelt sigh. 'And I do trust you.'

'For now,' he added for her. 'You certainly didn't at Willoughby Manor.'

'Why did you have to remind me of that? I had almost forgotten the real reason we parted all those years ago in my shock at Aunt Seraphina's scheming.'

'All these little, locked places in our lives will wreck us again if we let them, Callie,' he said flatly, and, of course, he didn't relish dragging such a painful subject back out into the open, either.

'Perhaps you're right,' she said with a sigh as he finally ushered her safely into the lovely sitting room that led off theirs and she wondered if she would ever find her way round this huge old house without a map.

'This suite proves to me how delighted his lordship is to have his grandchild under his roof at long last, Callie, for I certainly never warranted such gracious rooms on visits to Raigne in the past,' he said to lighten the atmosphere between them.

She frowned as she realised he was taking another step back from those who cared about him and refused to let him. 'He loves you, Gideon,' she said.

'Lord Laughraine is a realist. He makes the best of a bad hand.'

'And you think *I'm* blind?'

'What I think is I was too young to make a good fist of what we had and we let it die between us. Your grandfather knows what a poor husband he inflicted on you.'

Callie watched the guarded shine of his eyes in the mellow shadows of the candlelight. She wanted to be aware of every beat of his heart and was curious about each thought in his handsome head, but did she dare let herself care so much for a man who didn't seem to want to love anyone these days? Untrue, he obviously loved Lord Laughraine and she suspected he could be a steadfast and loyal friend, but when she looked back at the wild and passionate boy he had been she longed to find a trace of that pent-up yearning in the man she had helped make him.

'We were painfully immature, weren't we?' she asked as she considered his headlong loving of once upon a time.

'Aye,' he said heavily.

'And now we have grown up apart,' she said sadly.

'Maybe, but I never gave another woman more than a passing look from the moment we two first kissed, Callie. You have to believe me about that, even if you think everything else I have to say is a lie.'

'How can I?' Callie held up a hand to stop him. She recalled the horrifying sight of Cecily Willoughby scuttling away from a half-naked Gideon, all ruffled loveliness and almost guilty, as if it happened only a moment ago. 'I knew it was my own fault even when it happened, you know? I refused to let you share my bed and even my mother warned me a man can't resist temptation for ever. I had to keep you at arm's length because I felt as if I'd break in half if I let you back in. I couldn't tell you that back then, but I have the words to say I wasn't strong enough to let your grief in, Gideon, and I'm sorry.'

'Don't be, I deserved for you to shut me out. You were right not to listen to my abject apologies for saying you manipulated me into marriage at your grandfathers' behest. I was a damned fool to let my wretched father drive that particular wedge between us. He gloated that I'd been used as a stud to put a real Laughraine heir in the nurseries at Raigne.'

'Was that why you listened to me when I insisted on living in London with you?' she asked, feeling a new level of betrayal threaten and wishing it didn't sting so sharply. 'So our child couldn't lie in the Laughraines' cradle and make his twisted tale come true?'

'No, I couldn't endure parting with you, even when it would have been far better for you and the baby to stay in the fresh air and live at Raigne while I continued my education so I could support you properly one day.'

'I wish you'd told me so at the time.'

'You see what I mean about all those petty little secrets that kept us estranged?'

'Some weren't quite so little,' she said bleakly.

'You mean the silly chit who wrecked our marriage?' he said with a grimace of distaste she still refused to find convincing.

'Maybe we were already floundering, but we would have come about if not for her.'

'Would we, Callie? I would have fought a pack of hungry wolves for you, walked a continent if you had asked me to prove how wrong I knew that tale of my father's was, but you refused to share a meal or a room with me. Then that lying little doxy pretended to be caught in my bed and you believed her. I never laid a hand on her but to push her away, I promise.'

'Her blonde ringlets and wide blue eyes could have taken in a far cannier gentleman than you were then,' she objected weakly, because she couldn't quite let herself see that she had allowed so much time gape between them for the sake of a lie.

Cecily Willoughby had been as lovely as a spring morning back then. Callie had felt so dull and uncaring of anything but missing her baby at the time that she could hardly endure looking at her own face in the mirror. Of course, her husband preferred a lovely and forbidden bedmate to the one the law and the church sanctioned. To believe otherwise would make Gideon's love greater than hers and she couldn't let herself admit responsibility for nine years of empty loneliness.

'Not for me, she was easily as heartless as your aunt and I wouldn't touch her with a nine-foot pole even if I wasn't married to you. If you won't grant me faithfulness, at least credit me with some taste, Callie,' he said coolly, and watched her with that lawyer's gaze of his—guarded, wary and unreadable.

'You blame me for everything, don't you?'

'No, I curse myself for pushing you to let me share that visit to your mother's home with you. I wanted to take some of the hurt and grief and rage off your shoulders, but I'd caused most of it to begin with.'

'No, but I didn't want to share it. I would have to admit you hurt as much as I did and grief was all I had left to give our child, you see? I was a miser with it.'

There, she'd said it at last. She expected his grey gaze to harden and for him to walk away in disgust. He shocked her by nodding as if he understood and staying.

'You were eighteen years old, Calliope. You had lost your grandfather one week and our baby the next and all I could do was drink and damn the devil, then ride out in a temper because I couldn't seem to find the right words to comfort you. If not for that selfish little harpy getting between us, I would probably have broken my neck on one of those midnight rides, or forced my way into your bedchamber to beg to share it and you would have hated me even more.'

'I might not have and I didn't hate you, anyway. I needed to realise you hurt, too—even if I cursed you for being such a reckless idiot in the same breath.'

'I still miss little Grace, you know,' he admitted as if he was embarrassed about it and wasn't that her fault?

He had every right to mourn their daughter and he thought she would resent him for doing just that. How could she have doubted he'd loved their baby, after what they did when she died? He was her fellow conspirator against the laws of church and state that said an unbaptised child couldn't be buried in a Christian burial ground. By the time they took in the idea of burying their little girl in unhallowed ground, Callie was struggling against the pall of indifference that seemed to wrap her up against the world, but Gideon was right when he said Reverend Sommers would welcome his great-grandchild into heaven, happy to embrace her in death as he couldn't in life. They put a bundle of rags and stones wrapped in a tiny shroud into that dank hole on the wrong side of the churchyard wall and set off to furtively bury Grace in King's Raigne churchyard with her great-grandfather.

'Neither of us will ever forget her,' she admitted as she recalled how stalwart and kind he was throughout that nightmare journey.

Why could she only admit that now, so long after

the event? Then the world seemed to be going on as if nothing momentous had happened and it felt like an insult to Grace's unlived years, but why had she blamed Gideon?

'What do you think she would make of the way we are now?' he asked.

'We would be different if she was still here. I failed you both.'

'No, Callie, her death was an act of God. Go on blaming yourself, or the fates, or the time of day, or month, or year and you will never escape the past, or be the woman our girl would want her mother to be.'

'How could she want me to be anything?' she burst out with a flash of her old, impotent anger with him and the world. 'She's dead, Gideon. Gone, blank, absent and any other definition of the word you can add. I try to feel her near and she's just gone. Like you for the last nine years, she simply isn't there.'

She blinked away a tear and got her temper and grief back under control just in time to see him flinch as if she'd hit him. Sensitive, passionate Gideon was there under all that frost and she'd hurt him again. 'I know you went at my bidding, Gideon, and I'm sorry. I took an easy way out because it was less trouble than fighting for our marriage and everything else we should have been able to have together, even without our little girl.'

'Cecily Willoughby couldn't have driven us apart if I hadn't already blamed you for your grandfathers' schemes to throw us together,' he said bleakly.

She couldn't deny it because he was right. Mistrust had already been too strong for comfort between them and Cecily's spite had done the rest. 'I suppose not,' she said wearily and felt as if they were half a continent from each other rather than a few yards.

'You're tired half to death and I'm a villain for promising you peace, then dragging all this up again. This clearly isn't the right time to talk about any of this and I'll bid you goodnight now, as I clearly can't be rational around you right now. You can rest easy in that splendid bed knowing I won't trouble you unless you actively invite me to, by the way,' he said stiffly, all his defences firmly back in place.

'Goodnight then, Gideon,' she said softly, because she couldn't bring herself to brazenly say she didn't want to sleep alone any more. She watched him walk away in the reflection of a beautifully wrought mirror and all the hopes and dreams that kiss had started up in her secret wanton whispered she was a fool.

'Goodnight,' he murmured and left her, the complicated great idiot.

Had she believed anything he said? Gideon shook his head and realised he had no idea if his wife still thought he'd taken her stepsister to his bed or not, so he wasn't the only one who had learnt to guard his thoughts during their years apart. Little wonder after what they had to do to bury Grace with the whispered rites of the church Callie managed to recall even through her haze of grief. What a fool he was for expecting her to take him back as easily as if she'd never suspected him of adultery. She had been broken-hearted over their child when it happened, so no wonder, after endless miles of holding their precious, perfect baby in her arms so they could bury her in secret, she almost lost her reason for a while.

Gideon rubbed a weary hand through his severely styled dark hair and felt impatient of the tight self-control he'd learnt to live with as Frederick Peters. It was the best he could do with the life he had then. But now it felt as if Peters's shell was too small and his essential self was locked inside a hard prison he had to break out of or be crushed. He paced the lovely old room adjoining his wife's; the stark emptiness of the opulent bed about as tempting as a hollow under a hedge. She had kissed him back, though; he recalled the feel of her lips, familiar and eager under his, and moaned. The grind of endless need tightened and had to be reminded more than that hot, sweet kiss was a fantasy it was best not to dwell on right now.

He ignored the feather softness and clean luxury of the heir's bed and stripped off in an attempt to fight his body's ridiculous state with cold water from the pitcher he'd ordered earlier against the trial he knew was coming. As well to be prepared for this familiar demon, yet this time it felt as if the devil himself sat on his shoulders and whispered temptations he had to find a way to ignore, somehow. He eyed the fact of his sex, rampant and stubbornly ready for action the instant he thought of his wife a mere few inches of carved oak away, and wondered how it could be so blindly stupid.

He groaned again and hoped that oak was thick enough for her not to hear. If she came in to find out if he really was in mortal agony, he wasn't sure he could restrain the beast inside him any longer. He reminded himself it was an agony he'd pay over time and again to get his wife back, then redressed and took himself and his sex off to a hard bed in a forgotten attic where they might find an hour or two of forgetfulness of this old, familiar torture. He had something he hadn't enjoyed for years tonight, though, for all the gnawing frustration and fever of dreams and nightmares he was about to endure. Hope. Even the slenderest form of that was pure gold to a man who lived without it for so long.

Chapter Thirteen

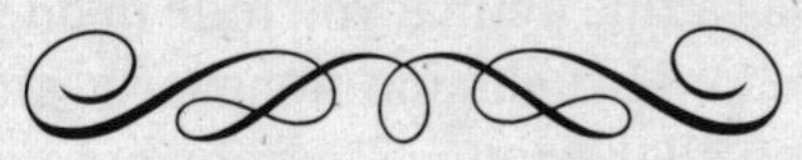

'Good morning, Lady Laughraine,' Mr Winterley greeted Callie the next morning.

'Good morning, sir. It promises to be a lovely day,' she said, and slipped into a chair by her grandfather with an ease she would never have dreamt of feeling yesterday morning. 'We have been most fortunate in the weather, have we not?' she said, absently looking for a sign Gideon had been here, or was yet to emerge from his bedchamber.

'Good morning, my dear. We need rain.' Lord Laughraine objected to her topic as if he was wondering why they hadn't arrived together. She blushed as the wish they had slipped into her head and refused to go away. 'Your husband has been and gone,' he finally informed her gruffly.

Did he know she and Gideon had not slept in the same bed? After all, she *was* his only hope of a great-grandchild and was that all this grand family reconciliation was about? The Laughraine succession was the rock that had wrecked her marriage the first time and she refused to let it destroy any second chance she and Gideon had of remaking their marriage. No, she had to stop this and learn to trust again. Aunt Seraphina had proved herself a stony-hearted villainess, but that didn't mean every person she was related to by blood was cast in Mrs Bartle's image. Maybe her grandfather was simply a man of few words before he had broken his fast and was ready to face the day.

'That was a fine animal you rode in on yesterday, Winterley,' Lord Laughraine pronounced after a while as if to divert all their attention from that empty place. 'Must be some Arabian in him.'

'The rogue who sold him to me swore a sultan's favourite stallion got him on his pack horse. He was a French deserter, though, and I'm not sure he'd know the truth if it stood in front of him with a cannon aimed towards his vitals.'

'Sounds plausible enough. Looks as if there's plenty of strength in the animal's hocks as well as show and good looks. Deceptive beast, but the real thing at bottom,' his lordship concluded with a straight look at the animal's owner to say like master like horse.

'He suits me well enough, anyway. I'd like to breed him if we ever find a place to build a fine stable block to house him and his harem,' Mr Winterley said casually, as if not quite able to admit it was a dream he'd had since he first found the animal and realised his promise.

Callie was almost shocked at his casual reference to setting up a stud and using that fine stallion he'd been controlling with such casual ease yesterday to found it on, before she remembered a married woman could safely hear such plans, even if her aunt might try to hustle her out of the room if she was here, and wasn't that a dreadful thought?

'Are you visiting the area to search for a suitable home for your horse then, Mr Winterley?' she asked, reminding herself it was high time she cast her aunt's narrow morality aside and became her own woman.

'That's an odd way to put it, Lady Laughraine, but you could be right,' he admitted as if it had only just occurred to him he could have a home, as well.

'You could found a fine stud with that beast and I can point you to a few promising mares if you seriously want to settle down and breed from him, Winterley. Virginia used to fret over your restlessness whenever you were off on one of your adventures.'

'She certainly didn't let it show. I always thought she was glad to see the back of me. Before he wed again and found other ways of putting all that tiresome energy to good use it was as well to make myself scarce before my brother and I argued so hotly we managed to kill one another.'

'I doubt it would have come to that, but Virginia worried whenever you disappeared to one of those outlandish countries you kept running off to when her back was turned. She cared about you, boy, whatever you've convinced yourself to the contrary.'

'So it would seem,' Mr Winterley said, and did his best to pretend he was too absorbed in his breakfast to find that revelation surprising.

Callie felt a moment of camaraderie with the man. She had half-sisters and a half-brother she could never be close to, as well, mainly because she was a mistake it was better they didn't know about, but a respectably born aristocrat must have a different reason to be estranged from his kin, and something told her he was as far adrift from them as she was from hers.

'Might be worth you taking a look at the Saltash place,' her grandfather suggested, seeming determined to get his guest out of the house while Gideon was away from it.

There was no need to do so on her behalf. All Mr Winterley's dark good looks and raffish charm couldn't distract her from her husband, but she supposed her grandfather didn't know that, since she did her best to disguise her obsession. Her heartbeat scurried even at the thought of Gideon, though, and she felt almost as breathless and silly as a young miss gasping for love. And where the deuce had he got off to this morning? At this rate she'd only see Gideon at the odd meal and for some reason urgency drove her this morning, as if this chance for them was fragile and elusive as a bubble and needed to be caught before it burst.

'Where and what is this Saltash place of yours, my lord?' Mr Winterley asked with the resigned look of a man who had his morning mapped out for him, whether he wanted to inspect a potential stable or not.

'Must be about ten miles across the other side of the Raigne valley and further into the hills, but my stableman will tell you more if you ask him. Dare say he has a groom he can spare to show you the way at this time of year, as well. Most of the house needs rebuilding or knocking down, but the land is good and there's a fine spread of woodland and arable and pasture to keep the estate right, if only someone would see under all the neglect and take it in hand. Might suit a restless fellow like you, a challenge like that.' Lord Laughraine trailed the task like a huntsman laying a tricky scent to keep his hounds busy.

'I'm no farmer.'

'Afraid you might fail, Winterley?'

'Not sure I even want to try,' the gentleman returned as if his good manners and patience were both near the end of their tether.

'Think of it as a good ride on a fine day then,' his lordship said ruthlessly, as if he had no idea he was being a managing host. He then ordered the butler to convey his orders to the stables that the best hack in it should be made ready for Mr Winterley while his own rested and young Bradley could take the second-best one in order to keep up with it.

'Sir Gideon took the tempest out hours ago, my lord,' the man said so at least Callie now knew her husband had gone out before she was up, let alone at the breakfast table, and she wondered uneasily if he'd slept at all.

'Mr Winterley must make do with the Dancer and Bradley can have that new gelding and tell him to let me know how he goes.'

Mr Winterley made an elegant bow to his host, planted a brazen kiss on Callie's hand and bid them both good morning as if he hadn't a care in the world.

'Impudent young rascal,' Lord Laughraine observed mildly and Callie concluded he liked the late Lady Farenze's problem nephew, despite his ruthless determination to keep him out of her orbit as often as he could manage it.

'I'm quite capable of seeing through a rake nowadays,' she told him, in the hope it might stop him fighting dragons that didn't exist.

'Maybe so, but I'd avoid giving Gideon an excuse to lose his temper over that young rascal if I were you.'

'Has he still got one?' she asked a little wearily.

'Aye, and take the advice of one who's had to watch that boy brought up by a pair of idiots who didn't deserve him and avoid giving him an excuse to lose it. Gideon doesn't think he's worthy of being loved, d'you see? Might admit he's well enough looking if you catch him at the right moment. Can hardly deny it when the rest of your sex seems to find him very presentable indeed, but he's not confident of his own attractions with someone who matters to him like you do. I've done my best to show him I prefer Virgil's grandson to any my uncle could have had if his true sons lived, but the boy thinks of himself as a cuckoo in my nest and that's that as far as he's concerned.'

'He's still a stubborn idiot then?' she asked with a wobbly smile.

'More or less, for all he thinks he's such a cold-blooded man of the law. I suspect he's got that wily senior partner of his to thank for making sure he doesn't give away more than he makes at that lawyering he's insisted on doing, although I told him there was no need and he should stay here and learn to manage the estate. Of course, he'd sooner starve himself than see you want for anything, as well.'

'Truly?' she asked wistfully.

'What fools love does make of us, Callie girl,' her grandfather said with a wry smile and tried not to look smug about it.

'I never said that I still love him,' she argued.

'I dare say Gideon's the only one ignorant of that particular fact. You hardly know the rest of us are in a room the moment he steps into it.'

'How ill mannered of me,' she managed weakly and wondered how to cope with the idea everyone except her husband knowing how she felt about the great dunce. 'It sounds as if he could be a rich man, though, if he exploited those connections you and Mr Winterley claim he's made in the last few years,' she added, because she might as well find out what she could about Gideon's new life and she couldn't give herself away twice, could she?

'I dare say he does well enough for himself, but I doubt the great and the good would trust him if he trumpeted his dealings with them like a cock in his own hen yard.'

'How would I know? I'm as ignorant of the *ton* as they are of me, thank heavens.'

'If you're willing to admit you're married to Gideon at last you won't be able to remain so for long, child. It's the world his friends belong to, whatever stable they come from, and they'll stand by him just as he stood fast for them when they needed him to.'

Callie heard the note of warning in his voice and shivered. 'My mother and her family will suffer if the tale of my beginnings ever gets about, though, won't they?'

'Then we must find a way to include her sad tale in our plans for the future. No, my dear, don't shake your head and try to deny it. Now your aunt has no reason to keep silent about it that tale will soon get out.'

'Gideon threatened to pursue her with every resource available if she so much as whispered it,' Callie protested.

'And how would he prove she was the source of any gossip? That's the beauty of scandalmongering—it only takes a few judicious words dropped in the right ears for it to spread like the wind and who is to say who began it, let alone prove it? Sooner or later we will have to tell that tale first, so she can't blackmail anyone else with her nasty little half-truths embroidered with lies. Anyway the real choice is for us to leave things as they are to avoid a scandal now and risk a never-ending lawsuit over the Laughraine succession after I'm gone, or tell the truth and dare the devil. If I make you my heiress, no court in the land could deny me the right to pass Raigne on to my only grandchild, whichever side of the blanket you happen to have been born on.'

Callie would have spoken, but he seemed determined to have his say so she let him; she owed him that much and perhaps a lot more if this second-chance marriage of hers and Gideon's actually worked out as she was beginning to hope it might.

'I know you loathe the idea of your true birth coming out and I dare say you consider that scheme your other grandfather and I dreamed up when you were a mere babe ruined your happiness with Gideon, but think, Callie, how much it will save him going through one day if we tell the truth now. He might have to face a court and admit he's the progeny of my aunt's by-blow and not the legitimate heir to the Laughraine estates and titles as the bare facts seem to declare him one day, if you don't let the truth come out.'

She shuddered at the idea of Gideon's legal adversaries publicly humiliating him. However hardened he thought he was, however little he believed he cared for the good opinion of his fellow aristocrats, he'd be hurt and ashamed as he told a truth he didn't have it in him to lie about. How could she let him go through that ordeal if there was an alternative?

'What about entails and legal caveats?' she asked warily.

'My father and grandfather trusted me to leave what they passed on to whoever would care for it best. For all its age and splendour it's only a parcel of land and chattels, Callie. When you reach my age you realise it's not the things you have accumulated that make a life, but those we managed to love along the way.'

'So now you're telling me not to put a high value on names and acres and accusing me of being taken in by them? I thought I was doing the exact opposite and you really are very like Gideon in some ways, my lord, or perhaps he's like you?'

'I truly hope so, he's a fine man.'

'Yes, he is, and a far better person than I deserve. But how am I to discuss all this with him? We can hardly talk about our future when we don't have a present.'

'I suppose you must come to terms with one another then. I suspect his absence this morning has more to do with too much avoidance in the past than any desire to avoid you now. He is a man, after all, my dear. I'd be a fool not to have noticed how slavishly he follows your every step and gesture when you're together and draw my own conclusions about how much and how urgently he wants you as a lucky man always wants his wife. Perhaps it's time you let yourself see how surely you could drive him mad waiting for you to admit you want him back, since the rest of us have already noted it. Even young Winterley knows you are an impossible cause now he's spent an evening in your joint company, but he's a wild one, is Master James. You'd do well not to give him an inch of rope to tangle you and Gideon up in. It might save us all a lot of trouble if you admit to feeling something powerful for Gideon before he can try it.'

'Even though you sent Mr Winterley off for the day as if you didn't trust me to repulse his half-hearted attentions?'

'He has a dangerous reputation and a reckless spirit. If he thought he could stir up trouble between you and Gideon, he'd do it for the fun of seeing what happened next.'

'And you invited this man to stay under your roof, even though you knew your friend Lady Virginia was about to interfere in all our lives and try to throw Gideon and myself together again?'

'How did you know about that?' he said unwarily, then looked very conscious he'd confirmed what was only her suspicion about this business.

'I wasn't sure I did, until now.'

'Ah, well, it was fairly obvious, I suppose. Virginia loved Gideon and only wanted him to be happy, so don't make her interference another reason not to be reconciled with him, girl. I know you're a Laughraine and can't help being contrary, but it really would be cutting off your nose to spite your face if you let Virginia's notions of doing good to both of you send you running in the opposite direction out of sheer stubbornness.'

'Is that what we do?' she asked, thinking if Laughraines were stubborn then the Winterleys took the palm for sheer perversity, if Gideon and his cousin were any indication of the breed.

'Who does what?' Lord Laughraine asked rather absently.

'Laughraines,' she explained patiently. 'Is that what they do? I really have no idea. Until the day before yesterday I thought I knew how the Sommers family worked, but it turns out that I was wrong, so I should like to know which of my virtues and vices I get from the other side of my family,'

'According to my late wife we're born stubborn to a fault and about as easy to lead as an army of farmyard cats, but she could hardly be considered an unbiased observer as she was easily the most determined woman I ever had the good fortune to encounter,' he said with a fond smile at the portrait of his late lady in her prime over the mantelpiece.

'I don't have much hope of turning into a meek and mild lady of leisure then, do I?'

'None at all, I should imagine, and I doubt Gideon would want you to if you did. I should think it's about as boring as day-old rice pudding to live with such a milk-and-water creature for life.'

'But you wouldn't know, would you?' she said, eyeing the stunningly beautiful girl in that picture. Despite the comical effect of powdered hair and skirts as wide as she was tall, the vivid face under the towering hairstyle of the day was unforgettable and she suspected the lady herself was every bit as fiery and full of character as his lordship was implying.

'She had fair hair under all that powder we all insisted on dousing ourselves with in those days, but apart from that she was the image of you when she was young.'

'I'm not a beauty,' Callie disclaimed as she looked for the likeness he claimed to see in that magnificent portrait. She saw something of herself in the lady's large dark eyes and heart-shaped face and for a moment wondered if he could be right, but surely not; she had gone unnoticed for years at Cataret House so she must be a nonentity, mustn't she?

'Such a marked contrast between blond hair and dark eyes and brows must have made her very striking when it wasn't powdered,' she said, and her hand went up to touch her own irrepressibly curly dark hair and how she wished she took after her ancestress in that aspect, as well.

'It was, but she considered her hair insipid and would have envied those raven-dark Laughraine curls of yours, m'dear. Only goes to show we're human and never quite satisfied with what we have, I suppose.'

'True, my father had them then?'

'Come to the picture gallery and find out. It's about time you were introduced to your family and we must see about getting your portrait painted soon, as well. Not sure there's an artist about who can come close to Gainsborough's ability at capturing a likeness nowadays, but we can but try and if we can persuade Gideon to stand still long enough he ought to be added to the line, as well.'

'What do you think a fine artist would make of me

in my schoolmistress's morning gown?' she said with a rueful look at the plain cambric Biddy had ironed so carefully she must have been up with the lark.

'That the jewel outshines the setting, I imagine. You are a lovely girl under all that tightly wound hair and you can't see me get up, you know? It's time you forgot your aunt's notions of proper dress and learnt what suits you. A lady of Raigne needs to be sure of her own style and not follow the herd and I suspect your aunt has spent the last decade telling you that you are plain and nothing out of the common way when the exact opposite is true.'

'Is that what you do, make your own style?'

'Always,' he said proudly.

'I suspect you and the late Lord Farenze of being a fine pair of arrogant and devious bucks in your hey-day, Grandfather,' she observed coolly.

'I can't tell you how it gladdens my heart to hear you say so, Granddaughter,' he told her, and stood up to escort her to the gallery and all the ancestors who would have disapproved of her so deeply if they were still alive.

By the afternoon Callie felt restless and Gideon still hadn't come home. After a brief lunch she went upstairs to discuss her woeful wardrobe with Biddy and the housekeeper. The ever efficient Mrs Craddock produced an array of fine materials and fashion plates by some sleight of hand and Callie's head was soon buzzing with the endless quantities of gowns and accessories she seemed to require. Apparently two muslin gowns and a calico print for summer plus three wool day dresses for winter wouldn't even clothe a governess properly. So a single plain silk evening gown for summer and a velvet one to keep the cold out at Cataret House were laughable even to Biddy, who was learning to be a superior lady's maid at an alarming rate. Lady Laughraine must have enough clothes to turn out several young women in style and it almost made Callie long for the days when she could put on her chosen plain gown for the day and forget it until she took it off at night.

Her grandfather's words about making her own style echoed in her head as she flicked through images of gowns that looked wonderful on the tall and slender creatures depicted, but might not on a shorter and more curvaceous woman who wanted to live a real life. In the end they chose a dozen of the simplest styles and flimsy fabrics in slightly richer colours than the current mode to be going on with. The local dressmaker could make them up and they would do Callie very well, until she had chance to visit a fashionable London modiste and endure her shortcomings being picked over by a professional. For now it was all parcelled up with instructions on which style went with which bolt of fabric and every measurement the seamstress could possibly need taken so she could begin her work. Callie sighed with relief and rang for tea then insisted her maid share it with her.

'Ah, that was proper lovely, but whatever would Cook say if she could see me sitting about with my lady in the middle of the day?'

'Being a fair, as well as patient, woman I'm sure she would be pleased you have a job that doesn't mean scrubbing and stoking a fire and doing whatever hard work needs doing on such a hot day.'

'Do you think she'll find another job, though, Miss Sommers? She was as good to me as Kitty or Mrs Grisham ever let her be.'

'I suspect Sir Gideon paid everyone's wages until quarter-day and I promised Cook and Jane and Seth a good reference, so I'm sure they will find something to suit them.'

'That Sir Gideon of yours is a good man, though, ain't he?' the girl said with a sharp look.

'Yes, he is,' Callie agreed meekly.

'Can't imagine why you ever let him go then, miss.'

'Neither can I, not that it's any of your business,' Callie told her in an attempt to remind both of them she was my lady now.

'Of course not, I beg pardon, ma'am. Are you wanting to rest now, miss, I mean, my lady?' Biddy asked brightly, as if she rather liked the idea herself.

'No, I want to explore the gardens before a storm comes along and batters the flowers to the ground. Lord Laughraine thinks the weather will break today, for all the sun seems bright as ever at the moment.'

'It's terrible hot out, though, miss. You'll melt in the open on a day like today.'

'Not I, but I don't intend going far and will stroll about like a lady of leisure under a parasol. Once you have my best silk properly shaken out and almost smart enough for dinner tonight you can do as you please until the dressing bell rings.'

'I should come, too,' the little maid said doubtfully. Being outside on a day hot enough to fry an egg on the more exposed stone pathways clearly wasn't her idea of enjoyment.

'Nonsense, I won't come to any harm in his lordship's gardens and I don't intend to leave the grounds,' Callie said, and left the room before Biddy's conscience could nag her into coming as well when neither of them wanted her to.

Chapter Fourteen

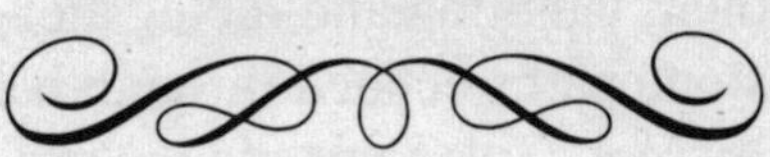

It was hotter than ever out of doors and Callie supposed it would be sensible to find somewhere shaded and sit still and hope for a cooling breeze, but she was far too restless to do that. Raigne felt too grand for Miss Sommers of nowhere in particular at the moment, despite Mrs Craddock's efforts to bring her into fashion. Biddy had done something to the plain muslin that Callie had unwarily changed into after their exertions with the tape measures, as well, and she doubted the girl would do that without the housekeeper's say so. The gown was cut lower and a layer or so of stern petticoats had mysteriously been lost in the wash. Since it was cooler without the lawn undershirt made high to the neck and even a fine shift seemed more than enough today, maybe she should get used to being more fashionable.

She put aside worrying about taking on Lady Laughraine's outer trappings without sharing her husband's bed and let herself marvel at the beauty of nature, subtly controlled by man. Weeks of relentless July heat meant most of the roses had all but done with flowering, but vast old lavender bushes still hummed with sleepy-sounding bees. Daisies and lilies, hyssop and Sweet William bloomed among the shaped yew and tidy box hedges and knots of the older parts of this great whole and suddenly she passionately wanted her children to grow up here.

Her eyes went dreamy and her steps slowed as the sounds of them laughing and racing along these old brick-and-stone paths echoed through her as if they were already real. Gideon would make a wonderful father; all the more so for the barren years of loneliness she had inflicted on them after they lost Grace. He would contain his wild offspring when they were at the edges of what was acceptable, but he would also give them all the love he was denied as a boy. She must make sure she found time to watch them rough and tumble and argue and laugh, then she could thank God that she tumbled headlong in love with such a wonderful man when she was far too young to tell a hero from a fool. Calliope Sommers was so much luckier than her mother and had found a good man to love when she was still in the schoolroom.

That was something else the gossips would whisper over their teacups. They'd say young Calliope Sommers saw what a promising youth Gideon Laughraine was and grabbed him before he was old enough to know better. Some would tut and frown and secretly resent her for catching a man who would do their own girls very nicely, thank you. They were sure to pick apart their long estrangement and find it too delicious to keep to themselves and she sighed at the thought of the stories that would race round the Mayfair drawing rooms at her expense. It didn't matter next to the hope she and Gideon might be happy at last and she hardly let herself believe that could happen, but it seemed as if it just might, as long as they were very careful with each other this time and she didn't believe any more lies.

'I was beginning to think I'd never catch you alone,' a voice she never wanted to hear again said coldly. Callie realised she had wandered down a path that looked over the park and lingered a little too long staring sightlessly at the view beyond the gardens.

'You have been watching then?' she asked as her mother's stepdaughter eyed her as if she were an unsatisfactory cabbage being offered for sale by an impudent market trader. 'What on earth for? We have nothing to say to one another and you have no business here, Miss Willoughby,' she said distantly, shocked to see the woman she would have done a good deal to avoid if only she knew she was coming.

'I am Lady Flette now,' the wretched female corrected her with a snap, as if the whole world ought to know Miss Willoughby had netted herself a title.

'Then I hope you are passing through King's Raigne on a long journey to the distant home of your noble husband, because you are not welcome here.'

'That's why I had to wait until I could see you alone. I knew you would refuse to see me and everyone knows we are related in some way and it will cause a scandal if I am not received here. Sir Roger and I live a few miles east of here and as his family can trace their line back to a Conquest knight, we will not be going anywhere and we have a right to be known as your neighbours at the very least.'

'So you have been spying on me in order to inform me of these facts you seem so sure of?'

'Not spying, just waiting for the chance to make you see reason.'

'I hope you had a very uncomfortable time of it, then.' All the same Callie was shocked to see how thin and careworn the woman was when even she had to admit she had been a rare beauty in her youth. Perhaps her real character was beginning to show through the mask of angelic innocence she once wore so perfectly. 'You boasted how you would spend all your time in London or Brighton once you were wed and never set foot in the country but to stay with princes or dukes, and now you are happy to impose yourself on me when I sincerely wish you had gone to one of those fashionable places and stopped there.'

'Sir Roger prefers a country life,' the confounded woman said as if that explained everything, and perhaps it did if Cecily Willoughby had truly met her match.

'And you oblige him? You *must* be a changed creature.'

'I have no idea what you mean.'

'Then your memory is at fault? You seem very young to suffer such an affliction.'

Lady Flette stopped looking down her nose at Callie's simple muslin gown and old-fashioned parasol and simply looked sour for a moment. 'Sir Roger has told me I must make peace with my stepmother's cousin, whatever quarrels we had as girls. Since you were brought up by a vicar you must be ready to turn the other cheek.'

'No, and isn't the local gossip efficient for you to

even know I am here so soon after my arrival? I dare say you know my husband is Lord Laughraine's acknowledged heir and I will be lady of Raigne one day, as well. I can't imagine any other reason for you to come here and pretend either of us has the least wish to know the other.'

'Your aunt kindly sent me a message to tell me you and your husband would be arriving any day and had been accepted as the proper heirs to Raigne Place for some odd reason known only to Lord Laughraine. My husband was most grateful for the warning, for he likes to be on good terms with his neighbours and Raigne is the most important estate in this part of the world, after all, so who can blame him?'

Was there no end to Aunt Seraphina's malice and clever little twists of the knife even now Callie had thought her out of her and Gideon's lives for good? As well to know the woman would always do what she could to make the lives of those she ought to love most as miserable as possible, she supposed, and resolved not to let that happen again. She had no idea what had occurred to make Aunt Seraphina and Lady Flette believe they had a right to push anyone who got close enough about on a board like so many chess pieces. It seemed to her there were some sorts of human mind it was better not to understand and deplored Gideon's experience of even more malicious and ill-intentioned souls than Aunt Seraphina and this self-serving creature on the darker side of the criminal underworld.

'What a pacific gentleman your Sir Roger must be,' she said so blandly it must be obvious even to the self-absorbed Lady Flette that she thought exactly the opposite and still didn't intend to make the woman's life easier for her.

Callie thought she saw her foe shiver in the sticky heat and concluded Sir Roger Flette was indeed the very opposite of a peaceful husband and possibly even a cruel one. She might feel enough sympathy for any other woman who went in fear of her husband to pretend an amity that didn't exist to make her life easier, but she wasn't saintly enough to pity this one. 'If I was weak enough to welcome you to our new home, do you think my husband would tolerate your presence under any roof he lives under after what you did?'

Lady Flette looked a little conscious and refused to meet Callie's eyes. 'That was years ago,' she said weakly.

'If a century had passed I still wouldn't forgive you for sneaking into my husband's bed as soon as my back was turned.'

'Oh, don't be ridiculous, even a prude like you ought to have got over a girlish practical joke like that one by now.'

Callie stood speechless for a long moment and half wondered if she had fainted again and this was really a bad dream. 'A girlish joke you were lucky didn't get out and ruin your chances of any sort of marriage, let alone one that made you a lady in name, if not fact,' she finally found the words to snap. 'I know there's no point appealing to your better nature, since you don't have one, but how would you like it to be widely known what you did to get me out of Willoughby Manor that day? Is your husband aware you lay in another man's bed before you got to his, madam? No? Then perhaps it's time he found out. Or maybe you would prefer to simply leave Raigne and never bother either of us again?'

'He won't believe your spiteful tale bearing because he's in a very good position to know it's not true,' Lady Flette said scornfully. 'Have you never let that poor wretch you eloped with off that fine drama your aunt and I set up so I could be rid of you? What a poor henpecked specimen of manhood he must be by now if he's had to live with you throwing that piece of playacting at him all these years.'

'It was a lie?' Callie asked hollowly.

'Of course it was. I knew there was something off about that tale of a poor little cousin bereaved of her guardian and child all in one week. My stepmother would never have taken a step out of her way for a worthy distant relative and when your aunt told me who you really were, I had to get you out of the house before someone put two and two together and made a scandal. If it got out that my father had wed a whore back then I'd have lost any chance of a good marriage, so you obviously had to go, and your aunt wanted to set up a school, but all she ever wanted was to get away from her father's stuffy lessons that you soaked up as if your life depended on it. If she could get you away from your disreputable husband, she would have the perfect teacher to help run her school, and it seemed to me that was about your true level in life, so we agreed to help each other. In the end Mrs Bartle came up with a plan to make you think your husband was my lover without much risk my father or his wife would find out. They would have refused to frank me for a London Season if they knew, but I certainly wasn't fool enough to give my maidenhood to that handsome brute you married. I needed it to hook a wealthy husband and he didn't want it even if I hadn't.'

'How cunning of you,' Callie managed to say as if it was an unimportant tale from long ago.

'Yes, your aunt and I got on well, although a country school and you to run it for her seemed to be the beginning and end of her ambition. I suppose a quiet lie endures longest. She must have found some other fool to teach her brats and run her house since you're here with your husband and Sir Roger says you must have lived together incognito all these years.'

'You may tell your husband I am unsure if I wish to recognise a remote connection. I will consult my husband and perhaps your father and stepmother about the matter.'

'That's not what Sir Roger wants.'

'How sad,' Callie said distantly, her gaze chilly as a distant rumble of thunder growled in the heavy air and a line of dark cloud blurred the parched horizon.

'I rode over. I shall be soaked through if I get caught in a storm.'

'Oh, dear, you had better hurry home then, hadn't you? You will beat the storm if you are lucky.'

Lady Flette looked as if she would like to demand the use of a carriage to go home in style, but Callie's bland challenge made her hasten off without a goodbye on either side. At last the impractical sky blue of her ladyship's summer riding habit was beyond her view and Callie pitied the poor animal she would whip into a gallop to get home in time to avoid a soaking. She almost shouted after her that she could take a carriage, after all, but managed to bite her tongue. Give that one an inch and she would never be out from under their feet, however unwelcome she knew herself to be.

'What the devil was Cecily Willoughby doing here?' Gideon demanded the moment Callie stepped in through the long windows to my lord's library, feeling pleased she had managed to find her way round one part of the huge old house and its vast gardens.

'You saw her?' she asked numbly. She should tell him straight away that she knew he hadn't been unfaithful to her, but the words just wouldn't come off her tongue.

'No, I just got in and Craddock told me she had been asking for you, but where have you been since she left, Callie? I was about to turn everyone outside to search the house and grounds in case she hurt you.'

'Oh, no, she's far too much of a coward to risk a fight, and I have the upper hand this time, or should I say the greater expectations? Her husband sounds as if he is obsessed by rank and wealth,' Callie said as steadily as she could, then went to examine her reflection in the watery Venetian glass mirror that told flattering little lies she needed right now.

Considering the upheaval her world had just gone through, she thought she looked remarkably calm and collected, so appearances really were deceptive then. The low rumble of thunder in the distance gave way to a mighty crash right over Raigne. From Gideon's tight expression it didn't bring a release of tension with it. Unable to face telling him what she knew right now, Callie clenched her shaking hands and tried not to flinch as the boom of that first peal of thunder rolled into a constant clash. Lightning ripped the sky so close it seemed all around them rather than a streak across the heavy clouds. She shivered convulsively and Gideon cursed softly and rang the bell, but she couldn't tell him it wasn't the coming storm that made her shudder, but the thought of all she had done to both of them by believing yet another lie. She had been wrong about the words not coming out, there just weren't any words in her head right now that felt good enough to work with.

'A shawl for my wife, if you please, Craddock, and would you like tea, Callie?'

'Yes, perhaps it would help,' she replied absently, feeling as if her composure was about to shatter like glass.

'The cure for all ills?' he said with a shadow of his old smile.

'You really are a good man, aren't you?' she said more or less at random, although it was true, of course.

'What has she said to you?' he asked apprehensively, as if he thought his world might be about to tumble round his ears all over again.

How could she have done this to him? And why couldn't she just come out and admit what a credulous fool she was? A hard knot of misery seemed to have taken up residence in her belly and she doubted any tea could get past it, but he looked so anxious about her now that she hated herself and if feeding her tea made him feel better, she would do her best to down it and pretend it was what she needed. 'Far too good for me, I think,' she added as if he hadn't asked that question about Lady Flette and she really must pull herself together.

'What nonsense is this, Callie?' he asked impatiently. 'Have I gone from devil to angel in the space of a day now? I must tell you that I'm not very fond of either role.'

'I never really thought you a devil,' she told the clammy air by one of his finely moulded ears and this wasn't the time to remember exploring it in slavishly intimate detail when she hadn't yet discovered the meaning of reserved where he was concerned.

'That's not how I remember things,' he argued, the dark times after she lost their child bleak in his gaze.

All those days of her weeping and simply wanting to be left alone sat in the heavy air between them. Then his eyes warmed with curiosity as the hot flash of colour she could feel burning across her cheekbones as they talked of serious, important things refused to chill with the subject. Could he tell that three parts of her thoughts were on how it once felt to love him with everything she was right now? 'I wasn't rational,' she offered with a shrug to admit it wasn't much of an excuse for turning away love.

'And I should have been more patient, more understanding of what you were going through. You were in such terrible pain that I didn't know how to make the world right for you, Callie. The harder I tried, the worse you seemed to feel.'

'And I hurt you deeply, didn't I? I'm so sorry, Gideon, words aren't good enough to say all they should at times, are they? All I can manage is that I just couldn't seem to let you in because my grief was too big to share. I did say I wasn't rational, didn't I?'

'Of course you weren't. Why should you be at such a time?'

'Aunt Seraphina pointed out she had lost her father and her husband within a month and *she* wasn't crying and moping and damning the devil.'

'To do that she would have to possess a heart and I thought she was out of our lives at last. Did Lady Flette's arrival on the scene bring that business at Willoughby Manor back to you again? Is that why you're looking at me as if I have grown two heads? I knew I shouldn't have abandoned you again today, but even I didn't expect your aunt to send her witch's apprentice to stir up trouble between us in her stead.'

'She didn't and I'm not made of glass. You didn't abandon me last time. I told you to go. If you turn all this around so everything becomes your fault, we will never be able to work our way past what I did to you all those years ago, Gideon.'

'Very well, how much of the blame would you *like* me to shoulder?' he asked with a teasing challenge that woke something euphoric and youthful in her she didn't think would ever live again before he came back into her life. 'This much?' he asked; arms wide open as if he'd encompass half the world if he could. 'This?' he added; a tiny pinch of space between his first finger and thumb. 'None at all?' was the next question as he put his hands behind his back and pretended to be far too angelic to know how to sin, let alone actually do it.

'Idiot,' she said, and laughed out loud when he managed to look injured and handsome and nigh irresistible all at the same time.

'Give me a clue then, Wife,' he protested, but there was hope in his eyes and a smile on his lips as he did so and if only they could get past this there was a chance for them, wasn't there?

'Oh, Gideon, I was wrong,' she told him at last in a rush.

'In what way?' he asked warily and she had done that to him, made her impulsive, passionate and hopeful young love wary of every word that left her lips.

'Every single one I can think of right now. Cecily admitted to me today that she lied that morning and my aunt put her up to it.'

'I know,' he answered steadily, and of course he had worked out their complicity a lot sooner than she had. He wasn't a gullible fool, always half ready to believe nothing as wonderful as true love could happen for her. 'It doesn't come as a surprise to me, love.'

'How can you call me so when I was such an idiot? How can you calmly stand there and watch me as if nothing has changed between us?'

'Because it hasn't, has it? I always knew I wouldn't lay a single finger on that little termagant in lust if we were the last two people left on earth, so it's not news to me that I never did.'

She made herself meet his gaze and wondered numbly why he wasn't walking away in disgust. 'I should have trusted you.'

'Why? I was a hot-tempered boy who thought himself hard done by. Why would you take my word on my love and loyalty to you over your aunt's? Oh, don't look at me like that, woman, I haven't grown wings or become a saint. I raged at you every time a letter pleading for mercy fell on deaf ears. I hated you when I lay on the rack for the pain and emptiness of wanting only you night after night and month after month and not being able to have you in my bed. All that stopped me finding you and telling you how aggrieved I was, and how wrong and mistrustful you were, was the thought of you so emptied out and broken as you were after we lost our child. You were too young for me to need you as much as I did, Callie, too close to being a child to carry one yourself.'

'And you were so old and mature yourself at eighteen years old, were you? Oh, Gideon, perhaps you are the bigger idiot out of the two of us, after all,' she told him as she saw all that frustration and agony in his gaze and too much hurt for a man of eight and twenty to carry as if it was his lot in life. 'Instead of expecting you to be strong and certain for me I should have been less unsure of myself. I was taken in by my mother's family and loved and looked after as if I was the most precious being on earth by my grandfather. Given what I've learnt about my aunt lately, perhaps he had reason to be wary of loving her wholeheartedly as I know he wanted to, but I was cared for and encouraged even as you were neglected and blamed for the fact your parents had to wed in the first place.'

'I wasn't some innocent victim, though, was I? I grew up wild and angry and bitter and even when I fell in love with you and you loved me back I refused to see how lucky I was. Instead, I railed at the faults in my destiny and hated my supposed grandfather for making me learn the law instead of sending me to Oxford. Raging at you when I found out who you are put all those doubts about my love for you in your head, Callie. How could I blame you for believing in the woman who helped bring you up when I treated you like a traitor who had been foisted on me by your grandfathers?'

'Is that why you never took a mistress, although you must have been almost as desperate for her companionship as the physical release of taking a lover? You stayed faithful to me because you felt *guilty*?'

Callie felt revolted by the idea he kept his marriage vows because he felt uneasy after accusing her of using his passion for her to scurry him into marriage and solve the puzzle of the Laughraine succession. The thought of him in another woman's arms, let alone her bed, made her feel sick and furious and wildly jealous all that the same time, but guilt? Even for the sake of loving him at a polite distance she couldn't stay here and be his penance.

'No, damn it. I love you.'

'You can't,' she whispered, all those years of longing and hopeless regrets like a weight in her chest she had to squeeze the words past. 'I sent you away. I believed a woman who obviously hates me even when you vowed on everything you held sacred that you were innocent. I can't believe you don't hate me, let alone love me.'

'Can't or won't?'

'No, I want to, heaven knows I want to, Gideon,' she managed to say huskily. 'I just don't see how you can love a woman who put you through hell and then ordered you to leave. In your shoes I would have drunk and caroused my way round London and made certain it got into the scandal sheets so you must see it and know it was all your fault. I deserved to live like a nun for being such a fool, but you didn't need to be a monk to prove it.'

'I did, because none of the women I could have were you. I deserved it because I was furious and hurt when I found out you were the true heir to Raigne and I took the sins of our parents out on you, instead of raging at those who made that mess in the first place.'

'I'm sure you had enough to go round them, as well,' she couldn't stop herself saying with a wry sort of tenderness as she pictured the angry young man she married and wondered how he was so different now. 'Where did all that pent-up anger go?'

'For a month or so I drank myself into a stupor every night and raged at you like a fool with every other sentence, then Poulson, my mentor and now senior partner, and Lord Laughraine hauled me out of my lodgings, put my head under the nearest pump and told me to prove myself a better man than anyone thought me instead of confirming their worst suspicions. It took a great many false starts and a lot of patience on their part, but in the end I learned to pour my anger into what I saw as a fight for justice. A lawyer doesn't need to look far to find one and it took me to some surprising places. There was never a more driven seeker after truth and what I wanted to call justice as I was during the first few years of my legal career.'

'You speak as if you are halfway to your dotage now,' she said with another half-smile for this new sort of intensity in him. It made perfect sense. His exploits as a seeker after truth chimed with the restless Gideon of their youth with so much misdirected energy she was surprised none of them realised how much he needed a worthwhile occupation. Her driven young lover was alive under Mr Peters's cool self-control and her heart raced with joy and something a lot more personal at the thought of all that fire and urgency lying under the disguise of cool reason he now showed the world.

'Of late I sometimes feel as if I am,' he said with one of those self-deprecating shrugs that made her long to explore the new breadth of his shoulders and the tight muscles lower down she was no longer surprised a lawyer managed to maintain. 'But if we stay here that part of my life is over. I couldn't live in danger with a wife waiting at home for me. It wouldn't be fair to you.'

Chapter Fifteen

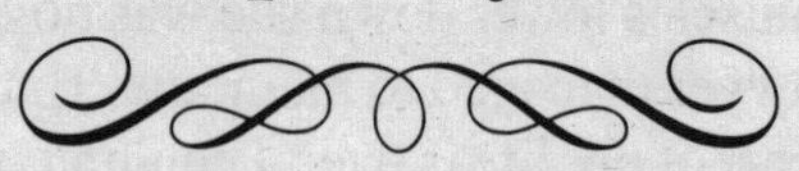

There was the reproach she almost needed to hear at last. He had a wife who refused to be one during all the years he was risking his body and that tender conscience of his for others. Still he took the risks he must have taken, because she wouldn't listen when he swore he was innocent. What else could he do but help the innocent in his own way; being so had not got him an iota of justice from her, had it?

'And if we don't?' she asked, because she couldn't help herself and maybe she hadn't changed as much as she hoped either. How awful if they were locked into the insecurities of their birth for the rest of their lives.

'Then we must learn to live together somewhere else, because I can't endure being wed and not wed to you any longer.'

'What about love?'

'What about it? I've just nailed my colours to the mast, but if you can't love me back I'll take a marriage of amorous friends if that's all you can offer. I'm not proud any more, Callie, but I am your husband and willing to take unfair advantage of the fact church and state bind a man and wife together unto death.'

'I...' Callie tailed off before she could send up her own colours when her grandfather opened the door and blinked.

'Ah, there you are, m'boy. We've been worrying ourselves to flinders about you all day,' Lord Laughraine exclaimed as he came into the room on another peal of thunder, then stood looking at them as if he felt the charge of emotions in the air instead of the vitality of the storm outside. 'Oh, suppose you're having lovers' quarrel and I've interrupted? Leave you to it, then, and see you at dinner,' he said and almost closed the door before he turned back. 'I gave you that suite so you could have some privacy whenever you need it, you know. You could make use of it and let Honey and Bramble hide under my desk in peace. They're gun-shy, but I can't bring myself to think any the less of them when I'm not a great one for slaying innocent creatures, and they feel safe under there in a thunderstorm.'

'Of course they do,' Callie said, and laughed, despite the poor timing of master and dogs, as two spaniels shot out from behind their beloved master to take refuge under the wide and rather ponderous oak table he used to spread his papers. 'Perhaps we could find a guard dog to protect your guard dogs, Grandfather?'

'Perhaps we should, but right now Gideon is frowning at me like a gargoyle and you were enjoying a stimulating discussion, weren't you? Lady Laughraine and I often used to fight like cat and dog in the run up to a storm, seem to recall making up afterwards was a lot more stimulating, though.'

'I could easily love you, my lord,' she said gently, practically feeling Gideon's driven impatience at her shoulder as he glowered at both of them and the dogs for socialising when he was teetering along the edges of reason.

'Good, good, probably don't deserve it, but always wanted to love you, my dear. Sommers didn't think it advisable for the world to know who you were while you were growing up, though—gossip and all that.'

Callie stood on tiptoe and kissed his cheek. 'Thank you for letting him do that then and allowing me to grow up in peace, but right now I really have to go upstairs and quarrel with Gideon, so you will excuse us, won't you, my lord?'

'Aye, minx, take your time,' he said with a gesture of dismissal and went to his desk with the rest of his assorted pack of hounds at his heels and pretended he was deaf to hers and Gideon's hasty farewells.

'Just as well he came in when he did, I suppose,' Gideon said gloomily as he finally followed her into their vast sitting room and she made sure Biddy wasn't waiting in her bedchamber or dressing room to frustrate them again.

'Yes, we could hardly make love in my lord's library now, could we?'

'Don't, Callie,' he rasped in a voice that sounded scraped raw with emotions he'd held in too long. 'Don't offer water to a dying man and not expect to be pounced on as if you're my last hope on earth.'

'I want to try again, Gideon,' she whispered, and looked into his eyes although it cost such an effort. She winced when she saw the guard that he kept on his thoughts was still there like a barrier against the world that he couldn't bring himself to drop. 'I want it so badly it hurts.'

'Oh, Callie, you have to be sure before you say such things to me. I can't draw back and play the white knight if you change your mind. It's been too long since I had a wife. I'm too dangerous to play games with right now.'

'Do you think I haven't longed and ached and hurt for you, too?' she asked in a whisper that felt more like a long gasp of need more than words. 'I've burned. I've needed. I've yearned for you, Gideon, night after night and week after week every year since we parted. It was only ever you for me, will only ever be you. I'm blind to all the rest of mankind because of you.'

'You sent me away, Callie, you couldn't endure to so much as look at me,' he said with a visible shudder.

'I know. I'm so sorry. I hurt so much I wanted you to hurt, too, and that was cruel and little. When I sent you away I thought all the guilt and fury and hurt of losing Grace would go with you, you see? But it didn't go anywhere and it was easier to think that was your fault as well than to see what a silly, jealous little fool I'd been.'

'I should never have gone,' he said bleakly, and for some reason that made her angry.

'Why not? I told you to, so why would you stay when I couldn't do anything but hurt you over and over again?'

'So that's why you turned your back on me?' he asked as if the words tasted bitter. 'To *protect* me? What sort of marriage did we have if you thought you must guard me from your deepest feelings as if I might break?'

'Don't go,' she gasped from the heart. He seemed about to turn away, go downstairs and order a horse to ride back to London despite the still-grumbling storm and the relentless lash of what sounded like all the rain they hadn't had in weeks.

'I have to. You'd best stand aside, Calliope, because I'm not safe right now.'

'No, I won't let you leave and not come back for years. We have to talk about it all. I didn't stump about half alive for the last nine years to carry on doing it a different way when you recalled you had a wife and came home.'

'I knew I had a wife every second of those nine years, Calliope. If you have any sense at all you'll step aside and recall how long it is since I enjoyed the fact of you in my bed. I'm not going to run back to London like a whipped boy, but you really don't want me to stay in this room right now, I assure you.'

'Of course I do,' she argued furiously, confronting him with her hands on her waist and arms akimbo like an angry fishwife. 'I'm a woman. Apparently you can manage without one, but I can't wait another day for a man. I want you. See?' she said with a fierce gesture at the way her nipples had pebbled against the muslin of her much-altered gown.

'Do you think I'm blind or daft, woman? Of course I see.'

'Then why do you only look, Husband?' she snapped as if it was a commonplace thing to have him watch her with such sizzling heat in his eyes they looked like melted metal instead of cool grey with those intriguing blazes of green shot through them. No, they looked like Gideon's, full of lambent promise and heavy-lidded with sensual need. He was here and her heart was racing and her body tight and loose with need all at the same time. How desperately she'd missed him and he was only *looking* at her? 'Never mind what I said,' she added. 'I don't care if we fly blind into passion, after all, Husband, just stop looking and start seducing me, for goodness' sake.'

'We're more like to hit a wall at breakneck speed than fly anywhere,' he protested unsteadily, but his gaze was fierce and his mouth set like an invitation to pure sin as he focused everything in him on her and fire trailed over her body with every hungry place his gaze lingered. Each look set another spark to the blaze flaring between them and they hadn't even touched yet.

'I only want to hit it with you, Gideon,' she said with the fierce heat in her core frank in her gaze and all she'd missed so desperately about him coalescing into pure longing at the heart of her.

One more fractured sigh and she was done with the gap he'd insisted on keeping between them. So close she felt the fine shake of his leanly muscled body before they brushed one on the other and all of a sudden they were melded skin on skin, as if any other sort of existence was impossible and each saw the world through the other.

'Kiss me, I'm not made of glass,' she managed to gasp as the stretch of his body under hers overheated the need inside her to melted honey.

'I can feel that for myself,' he rasped, and she felt

his breath on her cheek and wriggled shamelessly to inch higher and offer up her mouth.

Here was her Gideon, her love, home again with her. She shook like an aspen as his mouth took hers. At first a little clumsy and unpractised, then urgent as they learned all that was heart-achingly familiar and all that was new about each other. Impatient, she opened her lips to lure him in, gasped as pure need, total demand thrust and teased her when his probing tongue delved inside and imitated the beat of life itself, reminding her where they were going. He gasped in much-needed air to trail kisses frantically along her jaw and linger on the line where it met her slender neck before racing his mouth to her ear to learn it again. She was so shaken by the memory and newness in his touch as he found the places he knew would drive her wild, yet seemed to linger in wonder over all that was the same as well as the new maturity of her womanly curves. Was it possible to reach a wild climax simply from the feel of her lover's urgent, sensuous touch on something as every day as her earlobe? She keened a protest, because if she was to fly she badly wanted to do it with him.

His breath was unsteady against her skin and he seemed to fight the same urge to an unconnected climax as she forced herself away from a second ago. His hands were urgent and a little clumsy on her laces and she smiled her approval, although she sensed his gaze had gone as unseeing as her own at this driving urge to mate until they were both utterly undone.

'Never mind them,' she urged, directing his hands instead to the front of the fragile stuff and sighing with delight when the material ripped from stem to stern. She had no real interest where it ended up. This was their now and their next.

Now his hands were busy snapping the ribbon of her shift and who would have thought a woman's corsets could disappear so fast she had no idea how he did it? A brief moment of doubt that he wasn't more practised at this than either of them remembered and she called on her faith in him and ordered it not to fail them this time. Busy about his coat and waist-coat as he had been about her gown, she supposed eagerness and extreme need were all it took. There, it was off in one powerful shrug and they could deal with his neckcloth and fine linen later. She felt his hands, unexpectedly calloused from hard work and long hours in the saddle, revelled in the contrast between the firm touch on the soft skin of her breast as he cupped it, then he dipped his dark head to explore more intently with his mouth and she gasped her delight.

Now she was so glad to be more luxuriant there than she was at seventeen. Her breasts shamelessly revelled in his would-be reverent touch and raised and rounded even more under his fascinated gaze. There, oh, there, he settled his hot mouth on her pleading nipple again and ran his tongue about the tight core, then suckled, and she heard herself moan with the pleasure and need. She was so hot and wet she writhed against his mouth and he made an inarticulate sound of approval and racked up the hot rhyme of his mouth on her to an even more driven and deeper need. She clasped his dear dark head to her and groaned out her pleasure and her driving, galloping need for his hardness inside the hot wet core of her and driving them both insane with completion.

'Oh, love, I need more of you. I'm so ready I'll melt if you don't get on and give it to me,' she whispered into the dark curls under her shaking hand as she rediscovered them and raked her fingers through memories of her wild-haired young love and felt a fleeting sense of smugness that this was another part of him that was only for her nowadays.

'You don't know how ready I am,' he gasped on half a sob and half a laugh.

'Oh, I think I do,' she argued as she wriggled wantonly against the iron-hard fact of his need and gave him a wicked, self-satisfied smile as it leapt even more eagerly under her invitation to set it to work as hard and fast as they could be together again in the most intimate way possible.

'Witch,' he whispered as he managed to steady himself enough to explore her welcome and found it every bit as eager as his need to be inside her for the first time in so long the thought of it made her sob with wistfulness and self-pity. 'Nearly there, my Calliope,' he murmured as if he understood why she felt a moment of acute sadness, even as the joy of being one with him was so close it set her heart racing ever faster and her breath fighting for space in her lungs.

'I missed you so badly, lover,' she confided against his bent down head as he took all the time and restraint he'd found from somewhere to ease her into a position so she could take his rampant need of her little by little, instead of in the frantic rush she could sense he was fighting with every gallant nerve and sinew in his body.

'You're in my head and my heart, always, love,' he told her as he was there at last, first a little intimidating and even harder and bigger than she remembered. She refused to doubt he'd slide home and let them dance to the old familiar beat of this truest and deepest of intimacies.

'Trust us, Callie,' he urged as she gasped in a breath against the undefended state the ultimate act of love gifted to lovers.

'I do,' she told him and met his eyes to let him see it was true as she relaxed and took him in inch by precious inch.

'Ah, love,' he gasped as if he meant it.

She let a pinch of sadness in at the gap of time since they had loved, then let it go to live now. A very fine now it was as he stilled as best he could to take account of it being so long since they had loved. She felt the effort it cost him to hold back in the newly sleek power of his buttocks tense under her touch and the shake in his breath and his touch. Exploring his narrow waist and satin-smooth skin over taut bands of hard muscles, she moved her hands up his back under that confounded shirt they hadn't managed to rid themselves of yet and leaned in to tweak a hard male nipple through the finely woven fabric.

It worked and she felt wickedly triumphant as something broke inside him and he seized her narrow waist to tug her closer to the edge of her perch and thrust so far into her he was fully seated and she could glory in every rampant inch of him, then he stood with her at his level on some convenient surface she had no time to think about now as he withdrew nearly all the way before another deep thrust drove her to hook her legs about his narrow waist and try to urge him to go faster and deeper, before she'd fully taken in the fact they were really lovers once more. Now she was shaking and on the edge of begging when he did it again. She broke into those high, hard spasms of absolute pleasure she remembered and beyond to somewhere new they'd never gone before, even at the height of their youthful glorying in each other's bodies. At the very moment she began to writhe and moan under his bucking body she felt him fly with her as if he couldn't control the desperation in him any longer.

It was glorious and huge, limitless and yet it contained only them; it was their world and their reality. They gasped and bucked together and touched each other tenderly, as if the heat and fire and wonder in their skin and sinews and racing hearts and minds must be shared through every sense they had. Huge spasms of ecstasy raged through her and she lost herself in him. Amidst the heat and hammer and glory was absolute satisfaction and a heady sort of peace. Such exquisite pleasure—she was shocked somehow to find it waiting for them after so many years of drought. Yet also such novelty it was as if they'd never got so far nor been so close until this moment.

Callie still felt delicious little quivers of pleasure echo through her body into his as they calmed and revelled in the warmth and bliss of being together like this again. Once upon a time this had been their time to outbid each other with words and promises. They would laughingly compete to come up with the most outrageously overblown endearments for each other, the richest and most inventive of poetry to murmur in praise of one lover for the other. Now they were silent and waiting, a little bit wary again as all the years apart slotted back into their minds and they discovered how to be a little shy of each other in the most unlikely of circumstances.

'You haven't spent much time in your office reading dusty tomes these last few years, have you?' she half asked, half observed as she let her hands show how much she liked the feel of all that intriguingly arranged muscle and bone under his bronzed and now-cooling skin. The race of his frantically pumping heartbeat was slowing and his breathing almost normal as she ran her hand over his clinging lawn shirt and let out a wifely tick of disgust. 'And you still haven't taken this confounded shirt off,' she admonished him with a shake of her head she hoped he realised was nowhere near the scold she pretended.

'My wife is too hungry for my body to give me time for niceties,' he drawled as if very happy to report that state of affairs.

'Your wife feels it's high time she had a chance to examine that body you are so vain about in detail,' she managed to say solemnly as she tugged and prodded at his prone form until he gave in and heaved himself up from the sprawl he'd slumped into when he carried them into her grand bedchamber and rolled them on to the bed so she rested over his torso and they could lie and wonder at each other all over again.

'Whilst your husband could gaze and gaze at his naked wife for hours on end, if only she would let him,' he retorted huskily and, even as he unravelled the chaos they'd made of his cravat between them, then heaved his shirt over his head to throw into some unloved corner of the room, he was doing exactly that.

'As it's high summer and no hardship to lie about naked with you, I might do that,' she said with a complacent smile for the sheer joy of being on this great bed with him and hours of looking and feeling and touching to gloat over and store up against the day.

'Perhaps not,' he said hoarsely and she laughed as the effects of simply watching her stretch sensuously against the linen sheets left his sex far more rigid than either of them had thought possible only seconds ago.

'We *are* married, after all,' she told him daringly, finding out that all those years of lonely self-denial left a woman a lot more frank and open about her physical needs than even his besotted and passionate seventeen-year-old wife had been.

'We are, but what has that to say about you lying there flaunting yourself like a houri?' he teased as he propped himself up on one elbow to do as she'd invited him to and watch every curve and pulse in her revel in being his lover again after so many years of being so buttoned up and lonely she often wrote into the night just to block out the lack of him in her narrow bed and the terrible gap in her heart.

'That I was so lonely it was hard to tell where I hurt most, Gideon. I missed you—missed this—but having you here, with me, ah, I missed that most of all. I sometimes thought it might be better if I was dead rather than half alive without you.'

'Don't, Callie, I can't endure it,' he said harshly and turned his head away as if to hide from her and how could he do that when they had just made such wonderful love every inch of her sang with satisfaction and joy?

Chapter Sixteen

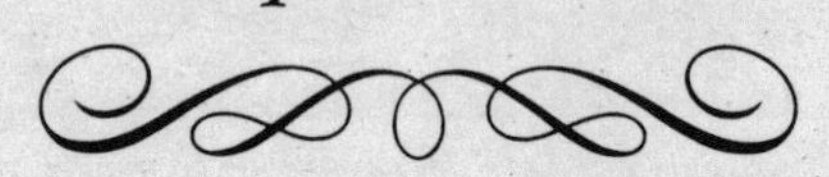

'I'm sorry, that was a silly thing to say,' she argued against herself and tried to soothe his shivering body even as he did his best to hide his tormented expression and seemed ashamed she might see into his heart this time.

'You don't understand,' he grated as if half the demons in hell were sitting on his shoulders and might drive him mad. 'You don't know,' he added under his breath.

'Stop it,' she ordered as she knelt up to pull him back into the soft cocoon of the great bed to simply lie here together as rain beat on the parched ground outside and the rest of the world seemed a long way off. 'Tell me, Gideon, whatever it is that puts shadows in your eyes and tortures you. I have to know about it this time. We can't have those dark little patches of mystery waiting to come between us if we're going to do better at marriage from now on. Don't you see we can't risk hiding our thoughts and fears from each other again?'

Shaken and suddenly terribly anxious about the

suppressed emotions raging under his front of calm self-control, she shook his shoulders and glared at him as a real threat to their marriage seemed alive and terrifying. 'Listen to me, you foolish man,' she snapped as she physically made him look her in the eyes and see how deeply he'd worried her.

'If I tell you, you won't want me near you,' he said, agony in his complicated gaze as he made himself meet hers as if it cost him half a lifetime to do so.

'You did what we did just now with another woman, didn't you?' she accused him bleakly, a stab of that agony sharp in her heart before fury could lash out at him and make him hurt even half as much as she did.

'No!' he gasped, then stared back at her so solemnly she believed him. An almost smile lifted his mouth as he added a caveat, 'Not since I was sixteen anyway and even then it was nothing like we ever had.'

'One day I will have all the details out of you, before I make sure she is living in another country and you solemnly promise me you'll never want her again,' she threatened direly, but still there was that terrible sadness and a refusal to let her all the way into his head in his gaze. She recognised the bleakness in his eyes from the time after they lost their daughter and realised she'd been too wrapped up in her own terrible grief and despair to see it as the strangeness it was, even for the loving father he would have been to their little girl, if he had been granted the chance.

'As if I could want anyone but you,' he said, almost as if he was saying goodbye to a lovely fantasy of them being back together and willing to admit they still loved each other.

'Tell me, Gideon,' she demanded softly, matching him eye to eye, refusing to be fobbed off with a marriage where neither asked the deepest questions in their hearts.

'You will only hate me again.'

'I never hated you. Even under all that darkness and despair I only ever loved you,' she confessed huskily and bravely kept her eyes steady and did her best to show him all she felt for him, then and now, at last. 'If we'd been older, we would have known all we needed was a little time for our world to right itself. Our lives would have been lived well together despite our grief, if my wretched aunt hadn't interfered and I wasn't stupid enough not to see her for what she is. I was such a fool.'

'Not that, my love, never that,' he protested, and paused as if he needed all his courage for the last and biggest secret in his stock of them. 'I was the fool, I simply couldn't stay and keep facing you when I knew you were right and I am a monster,' he confessed on a deep breath, as if owning up to a capital crime.

'I wouldn't blame you for not wanting to be with a woman so mad with grief I didn't even want to live with myself, but I was the one who told you to go, Gideon, not the other way about.'

'I couldn't face you then and I'm not even sure I'm worthy of a second chance at marrying you now,' he admitted painfully.

'Stop it,' she protested as forcefully as she could when she was on her knees facing him in the same naked state as he was. A shiver of awareness and longing for his touch ran through her and there was no disguising she wanted him, whatever he had to say. 'Don't you dare put me on a pedestal Gideon Laughraine. I'm not a goddess to be worshiped or a serene saint to be revered and never touched, lover. I'm a woman and a very fallible one at that.'

'You're certainly not a shy little siren any more, are you, love?' he asked so tenderly it had to be love warming his grey-green eyes.

'No, now get on with it,' she demanded.

'Very well, but you might want to be further away when I tell you.' She shook her head impatiently and refused to let him off a single inch of intimacy. 'When they said Grace was dead I was so relieved I thought I might faint,' he confessed in such a raw voice she hardly recognised it as his. 'When everything went so quiet in that infernal room nobody would let me into while you gave birth to our child and I wasn't allowed anywhere near, I could tell something had gone terribly wrong and I thought you were dead, Callie.'

He raised his eyes and faced her steady and composed and utterly serious, as if awaiting a verdict of death from a hanging judge. 'I wanted to rage and weep and argue with the angels over our perfect little girl and how her life hadn't even begun before it ended, but all the while I was blind with relief and ecstatic that you were still alive. They even said it was an easy enough birth for a first-time mother and I was happy you hadn't suffered as much as I know a very young mother like you can in childbirth. All the time you were so quiet and sad and not my Callie at all, I knew that I'd thanked God on my knees that night because you were still alive. It was a terrible price to pay for you, but I paid it willingly, Callie.'

'Oh, Gideon,' she said with a hard sob as she looked back at that passionate and suffering young man and felt only compassion for his conflicted soul. 'Oh, my love,' she managed as she put her open hands against his hard cheekbones and made him meet her eyes even though they were spilling over with tears. 'What a mull we made of it all between us, didn't we?' she whispered as she explored his dear features with trembling fingertips, as if she had to learn the map of her lover by heart all over again.

'I can't deny that,' he murmured and yet he looked like a man on the rack with suppressed agony, as if he still expected her to turn away and admit she couldn't live with him, after all.

'If you were the one in danger and I had to choose, I would have thought the same and felt as you did, Gideon. It makes no sense at all to me now, but back then it was the very fact I couldn't endure the thought of life without you that made me turn away. It certainly wasn't because I loved you too little, but it felt so deep and dangerous I thought it easier to lose you in the now than spend my life dreading every minute we were apart. You have no idea how bitterly I hated every passably pretty female you set eyes on, or dreaded any of the seductive gestures or looks I knew would come your way as you grew into yourself and made a place in the world apart from me. I was a coward, Gideon. It was better to lose the one person who meant the world to me, rather than risk living like that for the rest of my days and driving you away with too much love for a young man to live with.'

'Love,' he said softly as if it was all he could summon on to his tongue right now. 'Ah, love,' he added shakily and put his hands out blindly to echo her need to feel beloved skin under a butterfly touch.

'Yes,' she agreed on a whisper nobody a breath of listening further away could have heard. 'Yes, Gideon, I do,' she told him bravely, throwing all her defences away and admitting it with all that was once between them and this new love she'd discovered, as well.

'Marry me?' he asked with a parody of James Winterley's one crooked eyebrow that made her want to laugh at just the wrong moment.

'We spent weeks on end dashing about the countryside at great expense so we could wed without let or stay all those years ago, why would we do it again?'

'First, I want to say all the marriage service to you in public,' he counted off on his index finger. 'And I love you so much it hurts.' He spared his touch from her long enough to list on his second finger. 'The world needs to know that us being man and wife is all that matters in the fine tangle our parents and grandparents made of things.' He ended on his ring finger and even the thought of placing a heavy gold band there made her smile like a moon-mad idiot. 'And did I remember to say I love you?'

'I believe you might have done, but it won't hurt if you repeat it at regular intervals for the rest of our lives. So, yes, I will. We'll be written off as a pair of lunatics, but it's a well-known fact they need humouring, isn't it?'

'Indeed it is,' he said with a smile that felt warm and open as the first day they met as almost adults and he dazzled her with it and put himself in her heart for all time as the only lover she would ever contemplate having. 'Are you sure?' he asked, letting her see all the vulnerability and self-doubts he must have struggled with as a boy and young man.

'Do I look as if I have any doubts? Of course I'm sure, Gideon, and we will do better at being man and wife this time, I promise you,' she said solemnly. She had proved life without him was possible, she supposed, but it felt as if she had been wandering for nine years in a barren wilderness now she looked back. 'I learnt a lot while we were apart and I do have a new love in my life, as well,' she told him with a sweet, blank smile and a provocative look.

'He will have to accept banishment to a faraway shore or accept his days are numbered, then, won't he? Please don't run away with the idea I could ever share you, Callie, it would be a very bad mistake.'

She eyed the rock-steady facade he seemed able to throw up between himself and even her when he wanted to hide the passion and fury under the skin of a man of law and took the warning in it with a well-hidden shudder. No, she could never risk being on the wrong side of that wall ever again and shook her head at the very idea and her own stupidity in risking it in the first place.

'It's not a man, it's only my novels that you need worry about taking up my time,' she confessed. 'They made the loneliness of living without you almost endurable and I don't want to give them up even now I have you back in my life, Gideon.'

'Then I shall have to regard them as mixed blessings, since you might have taken the obvious remedy for that solitude and found me out if you hadn't been otherwise occupied.'

'Maybe, but we had a lot of growing up to do. Could you have taken me back without hating me for making you go, love? In your shoes I'm not so certain I could.'

'My life was bare and barren and dry those first few years, Callie,' he said a little too seriously and she wanted to turn away from the bleakness on his dear face and be ashamed of herself for putting him through purgatory on the contrivance of a pair of liars without a conscience between them. 'Don't hide your face from me, my love. I've got years' worth of gazing at you to gloat over now I've finally got you in my bed again,' he argued as he cupped her chin with a gentle hand and made her look at him again.

'I'm so sorry,' she said seriously, no thought of joking them back into laughter and heat and passion in her head this time as she let the bare facts of their split lives into the open. 'I can't even think of the lonely and rootless young man I made of you without wanting to go back and rage at the idiot I was for doing that to us.'

'It wasn't so bad, my darling,' he soothed as his touch went absently sensual again and his fingers began to explore her soft skin and finely boned cheeks.

Heat and longing shot through her body like the occasional darts of summer lightning still left over from the storm outside as steady rain beat against the windows and she felt safe and loved and warm in her lover's arms.

'I found ways of using the law to chase justice and

one night I helped save three lives all at the same time and thought myself the devil of a fellow for a while,' he joked and seemed to realise what he'd been about while his mind told him it was busy remembering. His gaze went silver and hot again and she wanted to simply enjoy all they could have in this glorious old bed once more, but that story sounded too intriguing to quite let go.

'Who were they?' she asked rather breathily as his exploring fingertip trailed slowly down her jaw to explore the smooth skin of her neck and rest at the pulse at the base of it and linger like a kiss.

'Hmm?' he asked as his hot glance followed his touch to gloat over that racing little giveaway, even if her skin wasn't glowing with desire and her body very obviously aroused. 'Oh, them, that's Rich Seaborne's tale. You'll have to wrench it from him some time if your writer's curiosity won't rest now I've woken it up again.'

'Heavens,' she murmured with as much of that quality as she could spare. 'I wouldn't dare,' she whispered with a preoccupied gasp as he stopped looking and set his wicked tongue to that hasty pulse of hers and added fuel to the fire.

'Good,' he managed with far more of a grasp on words than she wanted him to have right now. 'He was the devil of a fellow once upon a time, I wouldn't want you paying too close attention to a rogue like that, even if he is about as tamed and captivated as an ex-rake can be nowadays.'

'Is he now? Somehow I find it difficult to care about your friend and the state of his marriage right now, so be quiet and use your tongue for seducing your wife instead of worrying about someone else's, Gideon Laughraine,' she ordered breathily and, of course, he did exactly as his exacting wife ordered him to, for once.

Chapter Seventeen

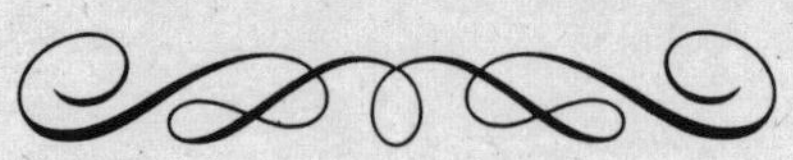

'Over that mysterious illness that afflicted you and your wife last night now, are you?' James Winterley greeted Gideon at breakfast the next morning and he felt himself blush like a schoolgirl.

Of course, everyone knew they weren't ill but intimate last night when they stayed closeted in their grand suite of rooms and had their meals sent up to sit in the grand sitting room between her room and his until they weren't so busy. Why he should feel like a secret lover uncovered before he was ready for it when he and Callie had been wed for a decade was beyond him, but under Winterley's cynical gaze he felt like a boy caught stealing sugar plums.

'No,' he responded shortly and helped himself to his breakfast more or less at random. He would never be over that particular ailment and the very thought of waking up next to his wife again at long last made his hand shake and his eyes lose their sharp focus under Winterley's amused gaze. 'You're not my keeper,' he informed him gruffly.

'Thank heavens. I'd have had my hair turned white by some of your exploits these last few years if I was.'

'Tell me,' Callie's voice cut through the much-fresher morning air and how had she managed to creep up on them like that when Gideon thought his every sense was attuned to her nearness?

'Don't,' he argued before he could think sanely about the effect that would have on her curiosity.

'I'm not fool enough to get caught in a lively debate between husband and wife,' Winterley said before Callie could demand more details and Gideon could think of a way of stopping her finding them out.

'Then you'd best hurry up and eat your breakfast and go away,' she said with an unfriendly look, 'because I'm determined to find out what he's been up to somehow or another.'

'If I go away, all you two will find is your way back upstairs and I have business to discuss with this hangdog husband of yours, Lady Laughraine.'

Callie looked as if she was about to ring a fine peal over the man, then met his challenging glance and laughed instead. 'You really are very like your great-aunt, Mr Winterley,' she said and nodded militantly at him when he shook his head and looked slightly revolted at the comparison. 'Yes,' she argued, 'she had the exact same way of looking at me as if she knew all my secrets and couldn't imagine why I was trying to outfox her.'

'I recognise the description, but not the likeness,' he said with almost offended dignity.

'Ah, well, we shall see what we see,' she said in her best schoolmistress manner and Gideon fervently wished he could distract her from Winterley, breakfast and his own dark secrets for a return to the pleasures of being man and wife for the first time in almost an hour.

'What business?' he asked before his mind could completely haze over with the delights of being Callie's husband again.

'I can't think how any of us were ever fooled by that dry-as-dust manner of yours, Laughraine,' James Winterley said on the brink of a boyish grin before he recalled he was a cynical gentleman of fashion in the nick of time. 'I might be in need of a good lawyer soon, although it might be as well if you recovered your wits first.'

'Why so? Do you have a guilty conscience? I won't touch a paternity suit if you've been fishing in the wrong pond.'

'Come now, Laughraine, I might be a dog with a bad name, but I ain't a fool,' he said with an apologetic glance at Callie, who waved her hand and went on with her breakfast as if she hadn't eaten for days, quite untroubled by Winterley's potential sins. 'And I have never yet laid my grubby hands on an innocent, Lady Laughraine,' the man went on as if he actually cared for Callie's good opinion and Gideon wasn't quite sure how he felt about that idea.

'If you don't want a lawyer to defend you against the wrath of a furious parent and his misused daughter, what the devil *do* you want one for?' he barked.

'I'm thinking of buying a house. No, revise that, Master Lawyer, I'm thinking of buying an apology for a house. More of a few standing walls and half a roof than a house.'

'It sounds like the last place a peacock like you should take up residence.'

'It is, but it has some of the best farmland I ever saw going to rack and ruin round it and a fine set of gallops to train racehorses on. The stables aren't as shabby as the house either, so I suppose I'll have to live in them with my groom and the horses for a while, if I'm fool enough to purchase the place.'

'With winter on its way, it is to be hoped you get even the stables neat and watertight before the worst of the weather sets in so we'd best hurry the business along if you're serious. Are you going to tell me where this ruin is, or am I supposed to guess?'

'It's Brackley House—your uncle called it the old Saltash place.'

'No one has lived there for years and it's at the back of beyond. What can a man like you want with it?'

'Peace,' James said with a closed-in expression Gideon recognised. 'I'm weary of James Winterley and his quest to prove he's worse than his despairing family suspect. I want a place where I can be myself, Laughraine, or as close as I can get when I'm not quite sure who I am. Horses don't care about a man's reputation or the state of his conscience. All that matters to them is he treats them well, feeds them and races the fidgets out of them when they're full of oats and have the devil in them.'

'It all sounds so simple put like that, but I doubt any man's life can be that quiet, even in the middle of nowhere,' Callie put in her fourpenny-worth before helping herself to coffee and giving Gideon a look that said she hadn't forgotten he owed her a long explanation of his own sins and evasions.

'Maybe not,' Winterley replied with a nod that

held surprising respect for her and her opinions and Gideon had to leash his inner beast all over again. 'But that's why I liked the place and will buy it if I can. Your grandfather is a cunning old gentleman, my lady, and I can't help wondering why he pushed me to look at a place that suits my liking for solitude so perfectly and will keep me out of mischief for years. Could he have a scheme up his sleeve to turn us three into bosom bows, do you think?'

'I don't know, could he?' she asked steadily.

'Since I doubt either of you give your friendship because a man likes your company better than your absence, how would I know?' James said with that to-hell-with-you-both look that was beginning to show Gideon here was a man nigh as well defended and poker-backed as he had been himself until recently.

'Perhaps if you're going to be a neighbour, we'd best try to be friends. I certainly wouldn't want you as my enemy, Winterley,' he admitted.

'And I wouldn't want to refuse you if you're going to go on glaring at me like an angry bear, but I promise not to presume on you as a friend or a relative. I do have a certain reputation to preserve as an idle gentleman of fashion, you know?'

'You'll have to get over it if you plan to become a gentleman farmer instead then, won't you, Mr Winterley?' Callie said impatiently and Gideon felt that demand to know what he'd been up to all these years coming dangerously close again.

'Clearly,' James Winterley said with a pained glance at his exquisitely cut summer coat and immaculate linen. 'Unlike your friend Mantaigne I do not enjoy getting dirty. I dare say you two spent most of your time at his noble ruin shovelling out stables and planting potatoes this spring.'

'Something like that,' Gideon admitted with a reminiscent smile as he struggled with the notion this finicky Corinthian felt left out of the adventures he and his half-brother and then Virginia's godson had been wrapped up in during their set time of reluctant self-discovery.

'My great-aunt had a way of making fools out of us all,' Winterley said with an almost affectionate smile. 'I suppose it came from being the most renowned beauty of her age, since she must have learnt the way of winding men round her little finger young and not quite given it up even when she met my great-uncle.'

'She was an astonishing female, wasn't she?' Gideon agreed with an apologetic glance at Callie, who couldn't have known her well and probably had a couple of very forthright exchanges with the lady. 'She made sure I was part of her life, despite having the most potent reason not to want a constant reminder of who I really am around the place.'

'Maybe, although I suspect that's why she wanted to know you in the first place. Virginia adored my great-uncle and any trace of him in you would be a comfort rather than a reminder he'd had a brief affair before they met. He never even looked at another woman once he found her, for all they both had reputations that make me look angelic before they met.'

'I've seen those pictures of her at Farenze Lodge and could have been halfway in love with her myself if I'd met her in her prime. The artist who painted them clearly was.'

'Aye, I often wondered why Virgil permitted him

to paint so many, but I expect he pitied the poor fool, she barely knew there was another man in the world when he was by.'

'How I wish I'd known him better. I envy you that much of your gilded youth,' Gideon said with genuine regret. 'My father hated his real father and kept me away from him, although he hardly acknowledged I existed most of the time.'

'Lucky you,' James replied moodily, and Gideon saw Callie cast him a long assessing look and nearly groaned out loud.

If Winterley thought Lady Virginia was the only female he knew who was capable of interfering in his life for his own good he was about to discover his error. Gideon resolved to keep his wife firmly occupied whilst the man worked out his own destiny and let the marvel of that sink in as Winterley agreed to go back and take a quiet look at the wreck he wanted to buy before he committed himself to the place and Gideon began the dance of pretending his client didn't really want the place at all to get it for him at the best price.

Once the man Gideon was almost inclined to look on as a friend as well as a secret relative had gone about his business Callie gave him a wary look. 'We have to look in those boxes now, Gideon,' she said as if expecting him to recoil in shocked revulsion at the very idea.

'I wrote to you and your aunt made sure you didn't get my letters—what is to be gained from reading my boy's outpourings now, love?' he asked because he felt half embarrassed to think what he might have said in his hurt and desperation when she never once replied to his pleas for any sort of reconciliation.

'And I wrote all my fury and grief and loneliness to you and she did the same to my letters as she did to yours, but I didn't mean that, although sooner or later I think we owe it to who we were then to read them. We have to look to find out what Mrs Bartle did to my parents and tell Mama and my grandfather what they need to know.'

'Isn't it her secret rather than ours, though, Callie love?'

'If he was as callous as she thought, no, I think she would rather not be reminded of their disastrous *affaire*. If that woman played the same trick on her sister as she did on us then it will be her choice what to do about it, but Grandfather needs to know either way. I can only imagine how awful it must be to think your son a villain and pray we never need do so.'

'Imagine it, Callie, a boy of our own,' he said on a long stuttering sigh, then wondered if she could endure to put another in the place of their lost girl. 'Will you hate me if we have another girl, or indeed any child at all in the place of the one we lost?' he asked, suddenly afraid she might not think the idea of either boy or girl in any number she cared to give him waking up Raigne with their chatter and mischief half as wondrous as he did.

'They would never take her place, but I can't imagine anything finer than as many children as we can contrive running about this place and making it into a home instead of a fine museum.'

'Care to start now?' he asked with a tomcat smile

to divert her from the idea of those boxes again as best he could.

'No, we have far too much to do to indulge in bed sports right now and you know it, Husband,' she said severely.

'Aye, I suppose we'd best plan our wedding before we worry about christening a baby of either sex,' he said as provocatively as he could manage and they just managed to give the maids enough time to make up their grand bed before they dived back into it and made that remarriage of theirs all the more urgent.

'Ah, here come the blushing bride and groom-to-be for the second time. So glad you could join us for your prenuptial celebrations,' James Winterley said with a mocking glance at Callie and Gideon that said he knew exactly why they were late.

'My lady insisted on being here for some odd reason,' Gideon replied with a grin that admitted he would be very happy to skip the lavish dinner Lord Laughraine had arranged for the night before his granddaughter and almost nephew married for the second time in favour of a simpler and more intimate one in their grand suite upstairs.

'I did,' Callie said lightly, but with a challenge in her glance at James Winterley that forbade him to make mischief to entertain himself tonight. 'Now I've got into the way of hobnobbing with aristocrats, I was hardly likely to pass up such an opportunity to spend an evening with so many of them, now was I?'

'I don't think pretending to be humble will get you anywhere with Gideon's family now, do you?' the rogue answered with a warning for her not to let herself be intimidated by the great and the good in his own gaze that she found rather endearing. How he'd hate anyone to think he was anything of the kind and she wondered why he was so determined to be the black sheep of the family.

'Apparently not,' she said with a glance around the lovely old room ablaze with the soft light of candles and alive with laughter and eager conversations.

Gideon was soon hauled away from her side by the current Lord Farenze's daughter and his wife's niece and Callie wondered what mischief those two enterprising young ladies had in mind for her after they acted as bridesmaids tomorrow. No doubt they would behave impeccably during the service, but she suspected they'd see it as their duty to plan a few surprises for the newly re-wed couple as they began a belated honeymoon.

'At least the Winterley clan and Gideon's friends have woken Raigne up from what my grandfather calls its long slumber,' she said with an assessing glance at the abundance of life and colour they gave this stately old parlour.

The ancient plasterwork and intricately carved wood had been cleaned and polished until it couldn't look any more mellow and magnificent. Her grandfather was enjoying playing host to his guests so much it made Callie realise how lonely he'd been here all the time she was lonely twenty miles away. This wasn't a night for self-recrimination and regrets over choices she had not made and roads she was too stubborn to take, though, so she turned back to the most enigmatic member of his clan.

'You belong to a fine family, Mr Winterley.'

His smile went grim and the spark of laughter seemed to flatten to self-mockery again. Callie knew she had been thoughtless to remind him he was among those closest to him by blood and still felt he must stand apart.

'I am fully aware what an honour it is they still own up to me,' he said shortly.

'I imagine they have very little choice as the resemblance between you and your brother is striking. The Winterley stamp is so distinctive I doubt any of you could escape being known as one if you tried.'

Callie's eyes were back on her husband now, since he bore that stamp as strongly as either of his distant cousins and was unmistakably a Winterley tonight. She forced herself to take her gaze off his dark head and broad shoulders for a second or two and noticed James was too busy watching his brother's daughter by his first marriage to notice Callie was obsessed with the man she was going to marry again in the morning. There was a fine tension about James Winterley tonight she suspected he would rather she didn't know about. She sensed the whisper of even deeper secrets than she'd thought under his mysteries with a superstitious shiver.

'About this quest you were all set by Lady Virginia. It isn't over, is it?' she asked, and at least that made him take his brooding gaze off his niece and watch her warily. 'I managed to work it out, you know. Your elder brother went first, then Lord Mantaigne and now Gideon has met his demons head on,' she persisted with a wry smile at the thought of herself as chief of those. She knew whatever was secret between Lady Farenze and her lawyers yesterday was in this man's possession now. 'So you're next.' She made it an observation rather than a question. He would deny anyone the chance to manipulate his life if he could, even the great-aunt he loved.

'Must I? I doubt it,' he said sombrely as he stood on the sidelines of all the animated family discussions and pretended he wanted no part of it.

'Never mind the love and marriage the tasks outlined in her ladyship's will brought to your half-brother, her ladyship's godson and now Gideon. You can stand aloof from the rest of the world if you choose with my blessing, but I know you're her fourth knight. Don't shake your head and try to look as if you care for nobody and never have. You loved your great-aunt, Mr Winterley. I have learnt how easy it is to fool yourself you can live without love and hope. I really cannot recommend it as a strategy for not being hurt by trying and failing at love, or any other powerful emotions you're struggling with. No, don't argue—I have nine wasted years of mine and Gideon's lives to cite for what happens when you cut yourself off from all the matters to avoid being hurt again. It wasn't happiness I gained by being such a coward—it was numb endurance. So let's be honest with each other this once. You loved Lady Virginia very much, didn't you?' He didn't nod or speak, but it seemed very significant to Callie that he couldn't deny it, either. 'I know you will do whatever she asked you to. You're a man with too many emotions bottled up in his stubborn head instead of too few, Mr James Winterley.'

'How well you do claim to know me, Lady Laughraine, and I wonder what your husband would say about that?'

'He would say he trusts me, although he's never too sure about your motives,' Callie said with such certainty it made her laugh when he tried to look faintly revolted.

'The moment I heard Peters was Virginia's mystery card I thought here was a man far too buttoned up and rational to tumble headfirst into love and marriage like my brother and his unreliable best friend. As it turns out he's the worst of all. He couldn't fall in love this summer because he'd done it ten years ago, when he should have been minding his books and learning to be a much stuffier lawyer and you're not a lot better, my lady. Apparently it's up to me to prove Virginia can't drive four men determined up the aisle in a twelvemonth.'

'At the beginning of that year I wonder if any one of you thought she would succeed with even one,' Callie reminded him cunningly, then chuckled at his revolted expression. 'If she does manage to work her magic on you, I can see you'll be the most reluctant hero who ever stepped, Mr Winterley,' she teased him because really, somebody ought to. His family treated him with a sort of wary caution that threatened to make her heart bleed for him and for some odd reason of his own he seemed to have let her and Gideon a lot further under his guard than was usual for a cautious rogue like him.

'I'm nobody's hero,' was all he said and she knew he was doing his best to put his aloof persona back together again to face whatever ordeal Lady Virginia had left him.

'Lady Virginia was a fine judge of character.'

'You didn't do as she wanted and take my cousin

back when she came here and begged you to give him a second chance, though, did you?'

'How did you know about that?' she asked, and realised how clever this rogue was when he raised that one eyebrow and let her know he had been guessing. 'Very clever, Mr Winterley.'

'I am, Lady Laughraine. I've refused to dance to anyone's tune but my own since I was old enough to have a choice and I'm reluctant to do as I'm bid even by Virginia.'

'What a precocious and mule-like little boy you must have been. No wonder Lady Virginia doted on you,' she counter-attacked.

'She wasn't the type of female to dote on any of us,' he said as if he was horrified by the notion and looked restlessly about the room for a reason to leave her to play hostess instead of examining him for emotions he didn't want to know about.

'All of us who consider you an intrinsic part of the family are grateful to her for *not* letting you know you had a special place in her heart. You would have grown up unbearable.'

'For a person who only met my great-aunt once, you claim to know a lot about her.'

'I do, don't I?' Callie said with a smile a little to the one side of her handsome adversary. 'Feminine intuition,' she argued blandly.

'Gideon,' he argued suspiciously. 'Or did one of them tell you they only agreed to do as Virginia bid them because the prospect of succeeding in their quests meant I would inherit a fortune so they could finally be rid of me?'

'One of them?' she echoed mockingly. 'You mean one of your band of brothers?'

'I only have one half-brother and he wishes I'd never been born.'

'Somehow I doubt it, but whatever the facts of your relationships, you four are like as peas in a pod—never mind if you're related or not,' Callie said as she turned to face her own returning hero with all the joy and love she felt in him blatantly on display. 'Come now, Mr Winterley, you're an adventurer, aren't you? When did you ever turn down a challenge, particularly one that will be to your advantage if you get it right?' she chided him absently as Gideon took her hand and everyone else in the room went a little less vivid for her, including James Winterley.

Chapter Eighteen

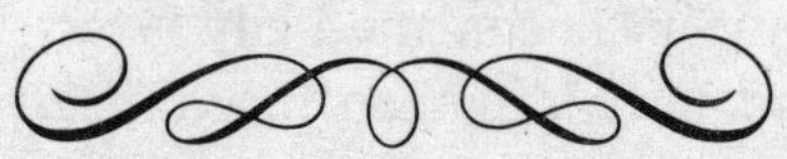

'You look far too serious,' Gideon teased as he smiled down at her as if he couldn't be solemn about anything tonight, because at last she was his openly declared true love again and he was hers.

'This is a very sober occasion I will have you know. I'm going to marry Lady Virginia's latest hero in the morning.'

'I know, and what a woman she was, wasn't she?' he said with sincere love and admiration in his grey-green eyes. 'I was the cuckoo in her nest and she still managed to love me. Heaven knows what she has in store for you, Winterley. You always were her favourite.'

'Ah, so you have been talking to your wife about me, have you? How flattering to think I feature so highly in your private conversations when you can't seem to string together two rational words between you when I come across you nowadays.'

'Actually you are never foremost in our minds when we're alone together. Sorry to disappoint you, Winterley, but you're some way down our list of favourite topics.'

'How else could Callie have got hold of that ridiculous idea, as well, then?'

'I expect that's because it's true, she is a woman of great perception and sound common sense.'

'Rubbish, you're both as deluded as each other, but so long as you're unhinged together I don't suppose it will bother the rest of the world. I wish you very happy, Sir Gideon and Lady Peters-Winterley-Laughraine, but kindly confine yourselves to your own business in future and stay out of mine,' he said, and spun on the low heel of his elegant evening shoes and walked away.

'I *think* he means well, Callie,' Gideon confided with a shake of his dark head for the conundrum who was his cousin and, yes, his friend.

'So do I. Perhaps Lady Virginia was right about him, after all.'

'How do you know she had a special place for James in her heart, love?' he asked idly as he did his best not to look too hard at her and make them both want each other unbearably again before dinner was announced and their absence from their own celebrations became stark and rude.

'Because she left him until last, of course. She started with Lord Farenze as possibly the least stubborn of the stubborn Winterleys and she worked her way down the list until she came to the hardest nut of all. Did she tell you all his fate depended on you?'

'You really must be a witch to know about that bit of her will. I don't talk in my sleep, do I?'

'Not about James Winterley, I'm very pleased to say,' she teased him with a demure look that threatened him with all sorts of stories about what he really did say in his sleep.

'I should never have wed a lady novelist,' he replied and, oh, but she loved this man so much it almost hurt.

'Now I think you should, only think how much it will liven up our dull lives as lord and lady of the manor one day,' she said with all sorts of likely scenarios hinted at in that almost promise of her wildest imaginings adding even more spice to their marriage. 'No, Gideon, we can't. Grandfather would never forgive us if we're not here to be suitably lionised tonight.'

'Do you think any of them would be shocked?' he asked with a wide gesture at the assembled company of Winterleys, Banburghs and Seabornes, most of them intent on their respective spouses and almost as distracted by them in their evening finery as she was by Gideon in his. 'I don't think any of us will be sitting up late tonight, do you?'

'I very much doubt it, but you were right, Gideon—'

'Of course,' he interrupted her in his best parody of a solemn lawyer.

'I was about to say you were right about your friends and all these secret relatives of yours. I do like them, even more so because they seem deeply in love with their spouses. Even Lady Freya Seaborne seems more interested in the person under the fine clothes than which bed they were born in and I hear her brother is very high in the instep.'

'She is a dear girl and not at all haughty since she managed to tame Richard Seaborne, and she has exquisite taste in gowns,' he said with a hot gaze over the one Lady Freya's favourite modiste had so expertly made up in a glowing shade of rose pink to make the most of Callie's creamy skin, almost-tamed dark hair and velvet-brown eyes. The clever cut and draping managed to accentuate her narrow waist and feminine curves despite the fashion and clearly met with his approval. 'You look very fine indeed, love,' he added, but his heated gaze centred on the famous diamond-and-pearl pendant the Laughraine heir always gave his bride on the eve of their wedding and the blaze in his green-and-grey eyes informed her he would very much like to see her wearing nothing else.

'Stop it, Gideon, I won't be able to stand much longer if you don't behave yourself.'

'I have behaved myself for years, Callie, and look where it got me,' he said with all those years bleak in his gaze for a moment and tears swam in her eyes at the thought of the ordeal she had put them through.

'It got us to here and now,' she offered a little hesitantly, as if not quite sure even this was enough to make up for nine years of tortured self-denial..

'Which makes it was worth every agonising moment,' he said more lightly.

'True, but I think I could be with child again, Gideon,' she blurted out the news she had been trying to make herself share with him for days now and not found a moment when they weren't so busy loving she forgot everything but him. Or, if she was being completely honest with herself, a moment when she felt she wouldn't stutter into haunted memories of last time as soon as she opened her mouth.

'I know,' he said so softly she read it on his lips

as much as heard it and of course he did, how could he not?

'You didn't say anything,' she mouthed back at him, the very intimacy of their urgent loving, the re-learning of each other's bodies and minds they had done these last weeks and months piling up to remind her she was a fool. 'Of course you would know. We're not a pair of unworldly children now.'

'I felt it,' he said and his clear gaze was serious again now and she knew he didn't only mean the slight sensitivity in her breasts, or even the fact she occasionally had to wait until he was up and about the business of the Raigne estates before she dared get out of bed and cast up her accounts in a chamber pot.

'Do you mind? I suppose we should have been more careful.'

'I couldn't be, Callie,' he admitted hoarsely, as if it was a fault in him that he wanted her so urgently it was as if they had all those years' worth of loving to squeeze into the rest of their lives as soon as possible. 'I only have to look at you and I want you. No, that's not quite right. I want to make love with you until the rest of the world fades away wherever we both happen to be. I don't even need to look. The truth is that I forgot to take care of you once again, my love, and I'm so sorry.'

'I'm not,' she said, a little bit offended that he didn't think she was capable of telling him to at least try and make sure he didn't get her pregnant if she didn't want to be. 'I want this child, Gideon.'

'So do I, but I want you even more,' he admitted and that painful conversation they had the first night they made love again came back to her and made it impossible for her to keep her hands off her handsome husband any longer.

She reached up to cup a hand to his strong jaw. 'I don't care what anyone else says, this time I want you to be with me when my time comes, Gideon. Why should they keep you out when we each had to go through all that agony last time without each other?'

'I'm not sure whoever decrees a man cannot see his much-loved wife give birth to their child will agree to that, love.'

'Then we'll do it without them. I can't think of anyone I would rather have with me than you. It's our family, I think we both ought to have a say in how it happens.'

'If you don't mind me keeping every doctor and midwife I can lay hands on nearby to soothe my nerves then, yes, my lady, I agree.'

'Well, good, what point is there being destined to be one of the lords of creation if you can't make up your own rules sometimes?'

'None at all, my Calliope,' he said,and reluctantly brought his hand up to remove hers from a wicked exploration of his strongly sculpted jaw in public. 'And don't forget you're named for a goddess, will you?' he asked as he kissed her hand palm upwards to punish her for winding them into a fever of need when there was no time or place to do a thing about it.

'Even better then, maybe I shall decree another faint. Then you would have to carry me upstairs and stay with me to make sure I was all right, wouldn't you, Gideon, my darling?'

'I don't think that would be the reason I left your grandfather to host a wedding-eve celebration without a bride or a groom, do you? Now behave yourself, lover. You may be willing to do that to him, but I don't think I can bring myself to rob him of his triumph a second time.'

'Neither do I, but it's not his triumph—it's ours,' she said seriously as the lingering thought he might feel he'd been trapped into marriage with her in the first place haunted her for a dark moment.

'I know. I would like to claim it was love at first sight, but you did give me a bloody nose and call me a worm when you were six and I was seven, so we'll have to settle for me learning to love you at the grand old age of seventeen when you were more ladylike and almost as irresistible as you are now.'

'I'm quite content to settle for that, in fact…'

'Mr and Mrs Willoughby and Mr Thomas Willoughby, my lord,' Craddock intoned solemnly from the doorway. Callie had noticed him enter out of the corner of her eye and had absently decided dinner must be ready and maybe they could get it eaten and over with as soon as possible, then find an excuse to retire early and celebrate another new start to their marriage and this longed-for new baby all at the same time.

'My mother?' she gasped now and turned to stare at the three travellers blinking in the light of so many candles, then swung round to eye her husband with suspicion. 'If you knew about this and didn't tell me, I shall indeed banish you from my grand bed tonight, Gideon Laughraine,' she informed him haughtily.

'Just as well I had no more idea your grandfather invited them than you then, isn't it?' he said, enough challenge in his eyes for her to know that distrust hurt him.

'I'm sorry, would you like me to faint now, after all, to make up for my mistake, then?'

'No, love, behave yourself and come and greet your mother like a proper baronet's lady,' he said with a boyish grin as he took her hand and tucked it into the crook of his elbow.

'I'm not going to meekly do as I'm bid without question ever again, Gideon,' she whispered as the guests parted to let them through. 'Look where that got us,' she added even as she braced herself to meet her mother's blue eyes and see no feeling in them for her eldest daughter at all.

'Nine years of peace and quiet?'

'No, an eternity of longing and frustration. Now be quiet and behave yourself, Husband.'

'Nag.'

'Buffoon.'

'Ah, there you are, my dears,' Lord Laughraine greeted them. 'Here is...'

'Your mother,' Mrs Willoughby said defiantly, looking straight at Callie and refusing to let her gaze drop away or skim off to take an interest in a more important being as it always had before.

'Mama?' Callie asked, the form of it not feeling quite right on her lips when she had never felt she had a mother before and wasn't quite sure about it now.

'My dear,' her mother said and, heavens above; were those really tears in her eyes? Could she possibly mean it, was she dear to the woman who birthed her, after all? Given twenty-seven years of making it clear she had one daughter more than she was prepared to admit to, was this really the right time to declare herself mother of the bride?

'I'm not sure about this, Mrs Willoughby,' her husband said with a shake of his grey head and a furtive look at the august company his stepdaughter was keeping.

'Seraphina cannot touch me now the truth is in the open at last, Giles. I refuse to kowtow to her demands I stay out of my own daughter's life for one more day,' his wife overruled him with a firmness Callie would have thought her incapable of if she hadn't heard it with her own ears. 'We have discussed this over and over and I won't be kept away from Calliope's wedding a second time.'

The tall young man with his father's mid-brown hair and aquiline nose stepped out of the shadows and bowed to Callie with a rather endearing grin and a twinkle in the bright blue eyes he'd clearly inherited from their mother.

'You must be my big sister, Lady Laughraine, if you choose to acknowledge me?' he greeted her as if he was quite happy to meet her and tactful enough to divert attention from his parents as they stood stiffly waiting for the sky to fall on their heads.

'I always wanted a little brother,' she replied, finding it unexpectedly easy to return his smile and invitation to find this situation funny, at least the bits that weren't a little unreal and full of pitfalls. That one time she and Gideon were invited to Willoughby Manor he was away at school and Mr Willoughby scurried his youngest daughters out of the back door to stay with their paternal grandmother practically the instant she came in through the front one. It said a lot about her mother's determination and this handsome boy's good nature that he was here tonight doing his best to pretend he was proud of her. 'If only I'd known you when you weren't a foot taller than I am, I might have been able to exploit the advantage of being the eldest a lot more thoroughly than I can now.'

'I, on the other hand, am deeply relieved to have been spared yet another sister determined to plague the life out of me in my nursery days.'

'I should have been a braver man and taken you into my home along with your mama all those years ago,' Mr Willoughby interrupted gruffly and Callie was still not convinced he meant it. 'Would have made me uncomfortable and scandalised the neighbours, but my wife never quite forgave herself for leaving you behind at King's Raigne Vicarage when we wed. I ought to have told that confounded sister of hers to do her worst and tell the world what she chose to twenty-five years ago.' He ended with as big an olive branch as he could offer her when he would clearly have preferred to let sleeping dogs lie even now.

'I was quite happy with Grandfather Sommers,' she told her mother. Somehow she knew Mr Willoughby would never have taken her fully into his family and raised her as his own, even if Callie had gone with her mother to Willoughby Manor all those years ago. 'And if I had lived with you all those years I might never have met Gideon,' she managed to lie almost convincingly, because she knew perfectly well her grandfathers would have made sure she did, wherever she happened to be living at the time. How could she have encountered the brooding young Adonis he was at eighteen without falling headlong into love with him on the spot? Impossible, she decided as she glanced at him and found him even more handsome and dashing now than she had then, if that was possible.

'Made for each other,' her grandfather put in indulgently. 'I admit I sent copies of Will's letters to Mrs Willoughby along with her own, my dear, when I begged her to allow the truth to come out at last and the Laughraine succession to rest on you two once and for all. I told her about your second wedding to this rogue and sent an invitation for her and her family to attend it, but it is her choice to do so as mother of the bride. I think you a brave woman to agree to do so, ma'am, and a forgiving one to come back here when it must hold some very difficult memories for you.'

'Thank you, my lord,' Mrs Willoughby said with a composure in her voice Callie had never heard before. 'My sister is a cold and bitter woman, but I suppose she was never lucky enough to have children and a good husband to teach her the value of compassion. I wish she had never interfered between me and your son for my daughter's sake, but I don't think we would have rejoiced in the sort of marriage Calliope has or the one Mr Willoughby and I have made somehow between us over the years.'

Her mother was still a beautiful woman and something told Callie when she wed her Mr Willoughby he was more in love with her than she was with him. Mrs Willoughby had achieved something her sister never would and learnt love as she went. If she had not made much effort to find room in her life for the bastard child of the man she had loved with all the intensity of a besotted girl while she was doing so, was it Callie's place to judge her when she had Grandfather Sommers to love and protect her? Mr Willoughby would never have found it in his heart to do any of that for the child of a man he had to be jealous of.

'Luckily for you, Grandfather Laughraine, I agree with you,' Callie told him with what he called her *I'll deal with you later* look.

'And so do I,' Gideon said as he stepped forward and Callie had to hide a chuckle behind a polite little cough as her mother reverted to type and cast her son-in-law a coy smile and almost preened like a turtle dove. 'Thank you for coming, Mrs Willoughby, you are very welcome and I cannot think of any guest I would rather welcome to our wedding than my wife's mother and her family. I'm sure my uncle has ordered bedchambers aired and made ready against your arrival, since he didn't see fit to inform the rest of us that you were coming.'

'Of course I have, my boy, d'you think my wits are out for an airing just because you're getting married to this girl of mine again? I quite understand if you're too fatigued to stay and eat with us tonight, my dear lady, but if you could see your way to sit down to dinner with us I'll have it put back half an hour in order for you to refresh yourselves. We're only sitting down to a little family affair tonight, Willoughby. No need to stand on ceremony,' the Lord of Raigne said with a dismissive gesture at the glittering company of fifty or so of his and his heir's closest friends and some of the most influential people in the land.

'I'd be glad to, my lord,' the squire said, looking a

little dazed by the sort of the people his host considered family and friends familiar enough to be casual about. 'What say you, my dear?'

'In all our dirt? That's clearly impossible and you must tell Gresley I need her immediately, Tom, before they let her go upstairs and tell the footmen I shall need the largest of our trunks immediately. Oh, and my jewellery box, of course.'

Mrs Willoughby turned to leave the room as if in charge of her own household, then recalled exactly where she was and blushed slightly and recalled her manners, as well.

'If you will excuse us for a few minutes, of course, Lord Laughraine?' she asked with the languishing air of an established beauty Callie doubted she would ever lose now.

After a solemn assurance her host quite understood the necessity to change for dinner after their journey, Mrs Willoughby swept out of the room in a fine bustle at the thought of getting changed and ready to dine in such an impossibly short period of time.

'That's families for you. Are you sure you want to own up to more of that vexed commodity than you thought you were entitled to, Lady Laughraine?' James Winterley asked satirically from behind them again and Callie thought that for a man who claimed to be so indifferent to his own family he was always close by when he thought one of them might be in need of a barbed comments and his reluctant support.

'Do you know, I think I could get to like it,' she said with an impish smile and walked shamelessly into her husband's arms. Gideon opened them to receive her, as if he refused to ever pretend not to adore her again, whatever unladylike stunts she embarked on. 'Can I faint now, Husband?' she asked wickedly, and he laughed out loud.

'Perhaps later, my love,' he said, and kissed her full on the lips in front of all his family and friends.

* * * * *

REDEMPTION OF THE RAKE

To the Monday Volunteers at Croome.

Thanks for being exceptional and making me laugh when I didn't want to.

Chapter One

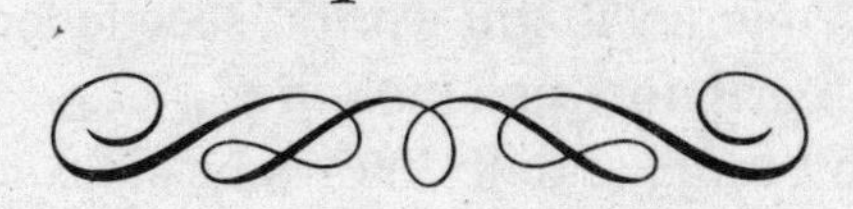

'Mr Winterley is *very* handsome, isn't he?' Mary Carlinge said with a wistful sigh.

'If you ask me, he'd be more at home in London and the *haut ton* must be flocking back there for the Little Season by now,' Rowena replied warily.

'Don't try and change the subject, Rowena Westhope. You're four and twenty and in full possession of your senses, so how can you *not* be intrigued by a young, rich and well-looking gentleman like that one? I don't know how Callie Laughraine managed to drag to him to church again this morning, but I'm grateful to her even if you're not.'

Rowena eyed the tall, dark and, yes, very handsome gentleman and felt a shiver of something she didn't want to think about run down her spine. 'He'll certainly need to be rich, as he's bought the old Saltash place and it's almost a ruin. I suppose he *is* good looking, but he's far too vain and haughty for me to admire him because he was born that way.'

'Either you're a saint and belong in a nunnery, or you're a liar, my friend,' Mary murmured as Mr Winterley glanced in their direction, then let his gaze flit past as if they weren't worthy of it.

'And you're a wife and mother, Mary Carlinge, and should know better.'

'I may have wed Carlinge when I was hardly out of the schoolroom,' Mary said blithely, sparing her husband of six years a fond but dismissive glance, 'but your Mr Winterley is still worth a second look, then a third and fourth for good measure.'

'He isn't mine and he knows he's attractive and well-bred and a fine prize on the marriage mart a little too well for my taste,' Rowena replied as coolly as she could when the wretched man's unusual green eyes flicked back to eye her speculatively.

She had thought herself all but invisible in the shadow of an ancient yew tree, until Mary tracked her down and insisted on asking impossible questions. Now *he* was watching them as if Rowena might put a toad down his back if he didn't keep an eye on her. A decade and a half ago she certainly would have, but it was unthinkable for a sober widow to do anything of the kind.

'Now I like a man who knows his own worth. I'd wager my best bonnet that one is a fine and considerate lover as well,' Mary insisted on telling her, although Rowena didn't want to know her friend's innermost secrets. 'When I finally manage to give Carlinge another son I do hope I'm still young and attractive enough to find out for myself, as long as some discerning female hasn't snapped him up in the meantime.'

'Oh, Mary, no; that's an awful thing to say. We were only confessing our sins before God a matter of minutes ago. You can't possibly mean it.'

'Shush,' Mary Carlinge replied and took a look round to make sure nobody was close enough to hear the vicar's eldest daughter being shocked by things she really shouldn't admit out loud. 'It's as well you lurk in dark corners nowadays and do your best not to be taken notice of. Is that a habit you learnt at your mama-in-law's knee, by the way? If so, it's a good thing she's taken it into her head to go and live with her sister and abandon you to your fate, because you would have stayed with her otherwise and become a boring little widow who breeds small dogs and keeps weavers of iron grey worsted in luxuries.'

'This particular shade is called dove grey, I will have you know, and it was kind of Mama Westhope to take me in when I came back from Portugal with little more than the clothes I stood up in. I stayed longer than either of us intended because she was so prostrate with grief I couldn't bring myself to leave, but it was only until we felt more able to cope with Nate's death,' Rowena defended herself and her late husband's mother, but she had a feeling Mary was right this time all the same.

'Kind my foot, she made use of you, Row.' Her old friend put aside her sophisticated woman-of-the-world manner for a moment to lecture. 'You were little more than her unpaid skivvy and I doubt she's let a single day of the last two years go by without reproaching you for being alive when her darling is dead. No, you have been cried at and belittled for quite long enough, my friend. It's high time you learnt to live again and there's the very man you should begin doing it with,' she concluded with a triumphant wave of the hand to where Mr Winterley was standing with a less-distinguished gentleman doing his best not to know he was all but forgotten at his fellow guest's side.

'Who is the gentleman in the brown coat, Mary? You've become such a fount of information since you persuaded Mr Carlinge to live in his great-uncle's house instead of selling it when he inherited and staying in Bristol.'

'It's healthier for the children, but are you calling me a gossip?' Mary asked sharply. She seemed to consider the idea for a moment, then shrugged and grinned impishly, as if the truth of that silent accusation was undeniable, and Rowena remembered why she loved her old friend, despite her forthright tongue and interfering ways. 'You're quite right, of course. What else is there to do in the country but take an interest in your neighbours and watch grass grow? The man in that rather dull coat is the Honourable Mr Bowood and his father must be Lord Grisbeigh, who is the sort of mysterious grandee the government pretend not to have. He would have to admit to working if they did and we all know gentlemen don't do that.'

Since Mr Carlinge was an attorney and Mary sounded a little bitter about the social distinctions that fed into, Rowena turned the subject to Mary's little son and baby daughter and tried to listen to their doting mother's description of their latest sayings and doings with all her attention and wipe Mr Winterley from her thoughts. For all her talk of taking lovers and the dullness of her life, she was almost certain Mary loved her workaday Mr Carlinge and their lively children far too much to take a risk with fashionably bored Mr Winterley. Or at least Rowena hoped so for her friend's sake, not because the man was tall and broad shouldered and rather fascinating and stirred something in her she'd rather leave unstirred.

'So this is where you're hiding today, is it, Rowena Finch?' the clear tones of her other friend from the old days interrupted Mary's tale of teething and breeching and now she had two pairs of acute female eyes on her instead of one. Rowena shifted under Calliope, Lady Laughraine's dark gaze and flushed ridiculously as Callie's words drew the attention of the very man she'd been trying to avoid.

He looked like a Byzantine prince dressed as a gentleman of fashion and plonked down in an English village to overawe the locals, she decided fancifully. There was a sense of power and fine self-control about him that almost offended her somehow. It was hard to say truthfully how she felt about the interloper, even if a nice little competence and a more useful life than the one she had now depended on it, but no matter, she was done with handsome gentlemen and he would never seriously look her way even if she wasn't. She was a dull and impoverished widow of the very middling sort and he was the brother of a viscount who looked about as tricky and handsome as the devil and that was that.

'I'm not Rowena Finch any longer, as you know perfectly well, Lady Laughraine,' she pointed out with a stern look for the woman she'd known ever since she could remember.

Callie was the last Vicar of Raigne's granddaughter and had come to live with him as a tiny baby. When the Finch family arrived at Great Raigne, so Papa could be installed there as the Reverend Sommers's curate, Rowena was a toddler and her brother Joshua a babe in arms. Callie was an elder sister she never had to long for, because she had one already, rather than a friend.

'I do, although marriage doesn't seem to have done you much good,' Callie said in a voice low enough only to be heard by the three of them.

Mary nodded militantly. 'Callie's right, you should listen to her,' she said and finally took notice of her husband's repeated signals that their carriage was waiting and it was high time they went home. 'I only hope you can make her see sense and come out of her shell, my lady. Rowena won't listen to me and you always were better at getting her to see reason than I am. Only because you're the eldest, you understand? Not because you're Lady Laughraine and all set to be a power in the land as soon as you're not quite so busy being Gideon's wife we hardly ever see you now you're finally home.'

'Very well and I will try to be less busy and make time for my friends. Now go away and let me have my turn at bullying Row for her own good, Mary; your poor, put-upon husband will teach you a lesson and go without you one day if you're not careful.'

'I'll go, then, since everyone is so keen to be rid of me. That doesn't mean I'm going to give up on you and a certain gentleman, Rowena Westhope, so don't imagine I'll let you do so either.'

'It's as well she's gone while we still have a little patience and affection left for her,' Callie observed with a roll of her eyes after the friend they both loved and despaired of in equal measure. 'Mary says outrageous things to disguise the fact she's very content as a country wife and mother. It really is most unfashionable of her, apparently.'

'A lapse you will shortly be sharing,' Rowena said

with a rather anxious look at her friend's pale face and still perfectly flat stomach. The early months of Callie's pregnancy were taking a heavy toll on her energy and spirits, and she couldn't help worrying about her, as well as hoping and praying this babe would be born safe and well and Callie and Gideon could get on with being the doting parents they were always meant to be.

'Don't try and change the subject, Row,' Callie argued as if she was tired of the concerned looks and veiled anxiety of her husband and close friends, and fully intended to worry about someone else today. 'You've been home for nearly a month now and I've barely set eyes on you, let alone persuaded you to join me at Raigne for a comfortable coze. Every time we invite you there's some reason you can't possibly come and Mary says you avoid any dinner invitations or, heaven forbid, party invitations other neighbours send, as well. This simply won't do, my dear.'

'Why not? I'm a widow; why can't I live quietly?'

'Because you're four and twenty, and not four and seventy, and you seem sad and a little bit defeated. Living with your mother-in-law has clearly done you no good at all. That woman was an invalid and watering pot before her son died in battle, so I hate to think what she's like now. The very idea of you shaping to her ways as long as you have fills me with horror. Such a life does nobody any good, Rowena; take it from one who knows.'

The note of regret for all the years Callie wasted listening to her selfish and downright fraudulent aunt instead of her then-estranged husband was too sharp in her friend's voice to be brushed aside as one more attempt to 'bring Rowena out of herself'.

'Gideon always loved you though, Callie. It shone out of you both from the moment you were grown up enough to know what love and passion are.'

'We might have known what they were, but we weren't old enough to understand how to live with them. You're not going to divert me with my own past mistakes today though, because we're talking about you and not me. It's high time you made some sort of future for yourself that doesn't involve writing letters for a bitter and twisted woman, and running errands she's too idle to do herself. And don't tell me you'll be perfectly content teaching other people's children as a governess either, because I know you won't be.'

'Why not, you did just that for nine years and don't seem much the worse for it.'

'Don't I?' Callie said looking as if every day she had spent away from her husband still cut at her now they were blissfully reunited and already expecting another child. 'I don't want you to turn aside from life for such a ridiculous span of time as I did, Rowena. I can't tell you how much it pains me to think my dearest almost-sister has settled for an existence instead of a life because of one youthful mistake.'

About to defend her own impulsive marriage against that accusation, Rowena met her old friend's challenging gaze and let out her breath in a long sigh instead. 'Maybe I'm not as brave as you, Callie,' she said and that felt a bit too true.

'You could hardly be less so.'

'Yes, I could. You were so brave when you lost Grace, then quarrelled so bitterly with Gideon you decided you didn't want to live with him any more. It almost hurt to look at you at the time and he was nearly as good at concealing his feelings as you were. I wish now I hadn't given you that promise not to tell anyone where you were or what you were doing as long as we could go on exchanging letters after you left Raigne. If I was a better liar I might have let it slip to Mama and she would have got the truth in the open long ago. Nine years was far too long for you to be so alone and shamefully deceived by your aunt, Callie.'

'Yet you want the same sort of life I endured for yourself? No, Rowena, you can't let yourself off trying to do better because your dashing lieutenant made you unhappy, and I can't stand by and watch.'

Again Rowena drew breath to lie that she and Nate were blissfully content from first to last, but the act failed under Callie's steady gaze. 'Yes, I can,' she said instead and defied her friend to argue black was white. 'For me love was vastly overrated and I shall not marry again. Apart from that, I agree, it's high time I stopped feeling guilty because Nate is dead and I'm alive and got on with living the best life I can. I intend to advertise for a position as a governess or teacher and look forward to using the fine education Papa and your grandfather gave me at last.'

'At least that fantasy is the ideal opening to play my trump card. Gideon and I have been trying to make you an offer of employment ever since you came home so tired and out of spirits with your life as unpaid companion. Will you work for me instead, Row? Please? I need you and I doubt your fictitious young ladies with rich and doting parents even want a sound education. Very few of mine did. It's true the odd one or two who did made my years away from Gideon bearable, but you don't have to endure the frustration of trying to teach young ladies to be learned and wise when society wants them naïve and empty-headed.'

'You certainly don't need a governess yet, even if this babe turns out to be a girl. I doubt you need a companion either, not now you have Gideon to occupy every spare moment,' Rowena told her friend.

Being offered a sinecure because she and Callie once ran wild about the countryside together felt as wrong as Mr Winterley clearly thought their earnest discussion, if the frown of concern on his face was anything to go by. There was a hint of steel in his not-quite-indifferent green eyes that said he cared about his hostess's welfare, endanger it at your peril. She forced a pang of something uncomfortably like jealousy to the back of her mind and told herself the man ought to care about Callie and Gideon by now, since he'd been at Raigne an unconscionably long time for a house guest and clearly owed something for the privilege.

'I don't have nearly enough spare moments for Gideon to occupy, and I so want to be with him whenever I can. We wasted so many years apart every second seems precious now and I can't find enough of them for us at the moment, or for this little one when it's safely born, God willing.'

'What would you want me to do for you, Callie? Mama Westhope tells me I'm a hopeless housewife, so I'd be very little use to you as one of those.'

'Mrs Craddock would be highly insulted if I even suggested Raigne needed more housekeeping than she and her deputy already provide. No, what I need is a scribe and a clerk I trust and you're perfect for both roles. You always did have a far neater hand than me and by clerk I suppose I mean a secretary. I know most of them are men, but just imagine what Gideon would say if I asked to share his.'

'I wouldn't sully my thoughts, let alone my ears, with your husband's feelings about you being in such close contact with another member of his species on a day-to-day basis. But are you sure you need a female to deal with your correspondence and help with some of your duties? I shall hate it if my return home without much more than a penny to bless myself with put the idea of finding me pretend employment at Raigne into your head,' Rowena made herself say. In truth the very idea of working with her dearest friend and living at Raigne was almost a dream come true. Almost, she reminded herself, as she tried not to meet the eyes of the man who could turn it into a nightmare.

'Yes, I'm sure. I seem so taken up with this little devil the need for help has become a lot more urgent,' her friend confessed with a protective hand on her still-flat belly that gave away volumes about her changed priorities.

'Will you give me a few days to discuss the idea with Mama and Papa and Joanna? If I can persuade my darling sister to take her head out of the clouds long enough to think of aught but her beloved Mr Greenwood, of course.'

'What a fine clergyman's wife Joanna will be and she was always better behaved than either of us. I do hope Hester never falls in love with a serious man though, she'd drive him to drink,' Callie observed with an indulgent glance at ten-year-old Hester Finch rolling over and over in the mown grass in the churchyard and doing her best to shove as much of it as possible down the necks of her mixed assortment of playmates.

'She still has time to grow up and be a lady, more unlikely things have happened. We weren't a lot better at the same age and look at you now,' Rowena said. 'Hes is in severe need of a lecture on the subject of not picking on much smaller opponents right now, though,' she said and went off to supervise her little brothers and sisters after a despairing look from her mother and a promise to consider Callie and Gideon's offer properly.

'Imagine it was made by someone you don't know half as well, then tell me truthfully you don't want the post, Rowena,' her friend called after her.

Rowena turned back to nod agreement, then shrugged ruefully as the squeals of her little sister's victims became too overexcited for comfort. She needed to restore order before there were tears as well as giggles of high delight to disturb the serious-looking conversation her parents were having with Sir Gideon and Lord Laughraine.

Chapter Two

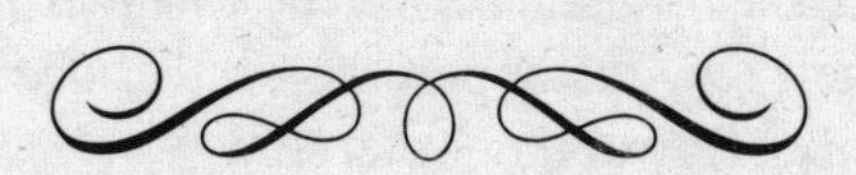

'Reverend Finch and his lady have a fine brood of children. I wonder how they fit them all in to even the most generous parsonage. At least the lovely Miss Joanna will be off their hands soon, since her banns were read today. Which only leaves them with Mrs Westhope to get wed again before the next young lady is of marriageable age, don't you think?' Henry Bowood said so casually James knew he was being twitted on his reluctant fascination with the even lovelier widow.

The man saw too much, always had. James resolved to be more wary and stop watching the widow Westhope from now on. 'Aye, they appear to have had a long and fruitful marriage,' he agreed easily, as if it was of no matter and neither was the retiring beauty who hid in churchyards and sometimes looked as if she knew too much about life outside this lovely rural sanctuary for comfort.

He knew that feeling too well and the Vicar of Raigne's eldest daughter intrigued him. Not that she'd done a thing to catch or hold his interest in the entire month she'd been back in the Raigne villages, he forced himself to acknowledge. He reluctantly turned his attention from the cavorting children and surprisingly indulgent referee to his fellow guest.

'Jealous?' he asked cynically, raising one eyebrow to add emphasis to the question and hoping the spymaster's son would be diverted.

'If I ever felt the want of a family, conveying two of your mixed bag of brats across the Channel and taking them to their new foster parents would have cured me very rapidly,' Bowood countered wryly.

Aye, James decided, it was high time he forgot golden-haired enchantresses with cobalt-blue eyes and all the possibilities they would never explore together and concentrated on the true facts of his life. 'I can't thank you enough for doing that for me, Harry. I could have endangered them now Fouché knows I'm not a simple merchant. You're the only other man skilled and wily enough to get them into cleaner hands than mine and safe at last.'

'You still don't trust me with the location of Hebe's brat, though. The other two you picked out of the gutters once their parents met their end could do with being part of a family,' Bowood said stiffly.

'Better you don't know, considering the lengths the head of Bonaparte's police will go to in order to break the spy ring he's been gleefully taking apart since he got parts of it out of Hebe La Courte before her jailers went too far and killed her. If he has Hebe's child, every single one of us will be at his mercy and he knows it.'

'Not all of us are as soft-hearted as you, James,' Bowood said.

This was no time to feel as if a cold hand had been

laid on the back of his neck, James told himself, even as he wondered how ruthless Harry Bowood would be if need arose. The happy shouts of children and the joyous song of a robin in a nearby tree faded away and he frowned at the terrible memory of his last botched mission to Paris. Even now he didn't know why he had had such a strong feeling he must go there and find out for himself what was wrong. The awful sight of his one-time lover's twisted and mangled body, cast into the darkest alley at the dark heart of the old city when her interrogators went too far extracting her secrets, made him shudder in the mellow sunlight of an English Sunday. Lucky Hebe's child was not yet three years old and would probably forget her lovely, reckless mother in time.

'That's not softness, but guilt,' he confessed bleakly.

'You take responsibility for the orphans of your smoky trade and call it guilt?' Bowood said rather less cautiously than usual. James's turn to eye him sceptically and hope it would remind him to be quieter.

'Why not? The good reverend would say I deserve to feel it after all I have done and not done in the cause of who knows what these last few years.'

'Society is so wrong about you, James Winterley. You have the heart and soul of a monk, not an idle man of fashion.'

'Do I now?' James said, brooding over how a monk would feel about such locked-down mysteries as Mr Finch's eldest daughter. Even less easy with the temptation to knock off her awful bonnet and run his hands through that heavy mass of gold hair until it curled down her back and softened her wary face than this particular idle man of fashion was, he suspected.

'James, the horses have been standing too long,' his brother called impatiently from the lychgate and James shrugged off all thoughts of shocking the Vicar of Raigne's daughter to her buttoned-up core.

'I *could* walk, if I really had to, Big Brother,' he drawled as annoyingly as he could manage, because it hurt to feel the estrangement between them strong as ever on such a fine and family-intimate day.

'No doubt you can, but the question is what you'd do if you ever got those spotless Hessians of yours mired with a speck of dust or, heaven forbid, a scratch?'

'Oh, give them to my valet, of course. I couldn't possibly wear them again after that,' James replied with a weary sigh, as if the depleted contents of his wardrobe troubled him far more than his brother's low opinion.

'Idle fop,' Lord Farenze said impatiently and, since that was exactly the reaction he'd been looking for, why did it hurt?

'James is teasing you, Luke,' Lady Chloe Winterley, Viscountess Farenze, told her husband of six months gently.

James wasn't sure if he loved or deplored her keen wits and kindness most right now. With Bowood always on the alert at his side, he wasn't sure he wanted his estrangement from his brother taken out and inspected. It was what got him into this murky business in the first place, after all, and Bowood was one of the few who knew the truth about that dark time in the Winterley brothers' lives. How could he not when James had fled to his school friend's home and spilt his terrible new secrets into Harry's ears that awful summer when he was seventeen and Luke was married to a vixen? Thank heaven his brother had found such happiness in his second marriage, even if it took him ten years too long to admit he couldn't live without her any longer. The damage Pamela did to the Winterley brothers made James shiver, as if the doxy's ghost was sitting nearby glorying over the rift she drove between them as gleefully as she did the day she made it.

'High time I let Finch and his lady gather up their brood in peace,' Lord Laughraine intervened, ever the bluff host. James marvelled once more that he'd found this haven in the storm his life had become this summer, and his lordship and his heir actually seemed to mean it when they pressed him to stay on now summer was over and Sir Gideon Laughraine was a very happily married man once more.

Riding back to Raigne in Gideon's shiny new carriage through lanes already showing hints of autumn in the rich red of hawthorn berries and glossy blackberries basking in the October sun, James acknowledged Bowood's arrival had taken some of the shine off the quiet country life he'd embraced this summer by buying a tumbledown old wreck of a house up in the Raigne Hills and the neglected estate that went with it. Brackley Manor, made of the local honey-grey stone and so ancient nobody had much idea when it was built, called to something in him. He didn't want to call his instinctive attachment to a house the romantic whim Harry dismissed it as when he found out why James had lingered in this peaceful corner of England for so long. Yet Harry was probably right. The neglect of half a century made him long to see it come alive again under his care and it felt right to build something instead of plotting to destroy it, to restore instead of ruin a home, even if he wasn't worthy of a happy retirement on his acres with a plump and contented little wife and a brood of children to make the old house a real home again.

Harry was part of another world, one where James no longer had a place. He was an unmasked spy; the most useless commodity a government could rid itself of as rapidly as possible. It was good of Harry to acknowledge him as a personal friend after that, he decided, and wondered why he didn't feel the same impulsive warmth and gratitude towards his old friend and the man's clever, devious parent as he had as a hurt and confused seventeen-year-old.

Back then Luke's words echoed so savagely in his mind anyone who extended so much as a finger of friendship towards him after learning of them could have won his affection and loyalty. Now he wasn't quite so sure the offer of an exciting new life and a secret beyond most youthful idiot's dreams was as wonderful as he'd thought at the time. A summer in France, observing the daily horrors and euphoria of a revolution in full swing and reporting back to Lord Grisbeigh, sent him up to Oxford with a feeling of knowing so much he shouldn't that Luke's revolted avoidance of his younger brother hadn't hurt as much as it should. Over the next three years he'd spent each long vacation in different parts of Europe and told himself it didn't matter that Darkmere Castle in all its stern and breathtaking glory was lost to him along with Luke's affection. The summers in Italy and Austria and even one memorable adventure in Russia set him up nicely for his future career of deception and disillusionment, but what if he hadn't run to Harry that day? What if he'd had the courage to stay at home and chip away at the wrong he'd done Luke and, in his hurt pride, the lesser wrong Luke did him by banishing him from his home?

All of it was useless speculation now, but he still felt less trusting and grateful towards his old friend than he probably ought to. Another area of darkness in his cynical mind he didn't want to explore, so did that make him a coward? Time couldn't rub out his last terrible argument with his brother, but it did make his betrayal seem worse. *Did you bed my wife?* That harsh-voiced and unanswerable question was as clear as if Luke had asked it seconds ago even after seventeen years. It shook James to realise half his lifetime had gone by since that day. All he had to offer in reply was a dumb silence that stretched into a coward's admission and Luke turned away from him as if the sight of his half-brother made him ill. *I have no brother, then*, he said and it was as true today as it was then, despite Luke's new wife's efforts to bridge the gulf between the half-brothers that her predecessor made.

'Devil take it, Chloe, why can't I stay?' Luke asked his wife a few days later once she'd tracked James to his host's library where he had permission to spread out the architect's ideas for restoring Brackley to its former glory and adding a few fanciful touches of his own James wasn't sure he approved of.

'Because it's my duty to see each of Virginia's legatees alone before he embarks on his task for the season. I'd like to have seen your face if I let your brother sit in when I gave you yours, Luke Winterley.'

'You weren't my wife then.'

'No, and I never would have agreed to marry you if I thought you didn't trust me.'

'It's not you I don't trust, it's him,' Luke said sulkily and James had to bite back a smile at the sight of his elder brother's thunderous frown even though he hadn't felt much like smiling after seeing the weighty letter in Chloe's slim hand.

'Stay if you must, Luke,' he invited with a shrug it took a bit too much effort to make careless and indifferent. 'It can't come as a surprise to any of us what Lady Chloe has to say to me. I am the only person left on the list Virginia laid down in her will of us fools required to dance to her tune a season at a time. At least there won't be any need to endure another wedding for my sake, after such a surfeit of them so far this year.'

'Why not?' Lady Chloe said so innocently he eyed her sharply and turned his attention to Luke for reassurance he didn't expect the impossible, as well.

'Because I haven't the least desire to be wed and can you imagine me embracing fatherhood as you three did in your own unlikely way?' he asked him directly.

'Hmm, at the beginning of this year I would have said nothing was less likely, since then I've learnt even the impossible can happen if you want it badly enough,' Luke said with a hot glance at his wife that made James feel he ought to blush, if only he still knew how.

'At least you can end it on a certainty, then—I shall not marry. Not even Virginia could bring about that wonder and whatever she wants me to do will not result in marriage. As I have settled in a part of the country where you can see as little of me as you choose, Brother, we can continue as we are and I'm delighted to leave you two to carry on the Winterley line.'

It was a challenge too far, James realised as Chloe blushed rosily and Luke looked like a thundercloud, then stamped out of the room after curtly requesting his wife to get her business with his confounded brother over as swiftly as possible, then instruct her maid to pack for their departure on the morrow, now her last task for Virginia was done.

'Why do you always have to stir his temper like that, James?' Chloe asked with a sad shake of the head that killed the glib reply on his tongue stone dead.

'It's easier than trying to drag up feelings as dead as a doornail between us, Chloe. Don't start a campaign to restore brotherly love between us, for that's a marvel even Virginia couldn't achieve.'

'I don't think any sort of love dies as easily as you think, but Luke is too good at hiding his feelings and you're not a lot better.'

'Maybe not, but some things are best hidden, or ignored until they go away.'

'We shall see,' Chloe told him with a very direct stare to challenge his refusal to take her hope fraternal love might yet blossom between him and her husband seriously. 'Lady Virginia worked three unexpected wonders this year, perhaps there's one to come,' she said, extending her hand so he had to take the letter he'd been avoiding like a coward, or let it drop to the floor.

'And perhaps not,' he replied and accepted it. 'Don't expect too much,' he warned.

'Your great-aunt Virginia taught me too well for me not to, James,' she replied softly, then left him to read his last letter from a woman he had loved as much as he had it in him to love anyone.

Feeling closed in now, James rolled up the architect's plans and shut his notebook. He was too distracted to risk riding his favourite stallion into the hills in search of the peace and quiet he craved, so he strode out of the house by the long windows of Lord Laughraine's library and into the gardens and the wide parkland beyond. Confound it, now his hand was trembling as he checked Virginia's letter was safely in his pocket. He stood still to let nature cure his uneven breathing with clear autumn air. There; he was almost himself again.

The sounds of busy nature preparing for winter only seemed to emphasise the fact he shouldn't have come to Raigne, nor found a place in his heart for this rolling and generous countryside and his poor old wreck in the hills. No point bewailing what was done and out here nobody could see him grieve for a woman who simply loved him nearly nine months after her death. He sensed Virginia was weary with the world even before that last brief illness took her from it, but losing her put cracks in the shell he'd grown round his heart half a lifetime ago and they seemed to have been widening ever since.

A whole season had gone by since he came here, sickened by Hebe's death and looking for who knew what? Now he'd fallen for poor tumbledown old Brackley and become fond of Virginia's latest victim, as well. He could imagine her impatient frown at that description. Lady Farenze's Rogues didn't work—Luke, Tom and Gideon were good men. Three good men and a rogue didn't exactly trip off the tongue. Now, where was he? Ah, yes, that last season: summer. When Frederick Peters, lawyer, turned back into

Sir Gideon Laughraine, heir to a peerage and a magnificent old house and estates. Except Gideon was really Virgil Winterley's grandson and, come to think of it, James had loved Great-Uncle Virgil as well, so that was two more on the list he couldn't help loving if he tried. Gideon's lovely, resolute wife Calliope put another crack in the walls James had built against the world at seventeen and it felt dangerous to care about anyone, but there seemed little point going on pretending he didn't for much longer.

He should leave Raigne before any one of these people who got under his skin while he wasn't paying attention got hurt like poor Hebe. As soon as he'd read Virginia's letter he'd go. He was a landowner in his own right now, even if his house and estate weren't much to boast about right now. On the unkempt Brackley Estate, James Winterley, rake, adventurer and care-for-nobody would be safe from his family and they would be safe from him. Striding freely now, he reached the arboretum Raigne was famous for among plant collectors in the know. It didn't matter if their leaves were native wonders or more at home in China or the Americas, the tired and dusty dark green of late summer was shading into the glorious last gasp of gold and amber and fire of autumn that James secretly loved. He planned a modest version of this splendour at Brackley, then decided a well-stocked orchard would be better.

With a sigh he sat on a neat bench for those who had time to rest after the gentle climb. He couldn't take out Virginia's final letter and face her loss all over again yet, so he gave himself five minutes to enjoy the view like a tourist. The lingering warmth and richness of an

English autumn must have soaked into his thoughts, because he felt much calmer when the screech of a jay reminded him life went on. Out here it hardly mattered if he was coolly arrogant Mr Winterley or a raving lunatic. Mother Nature only required him to be still and not bother her.

Chapter Three

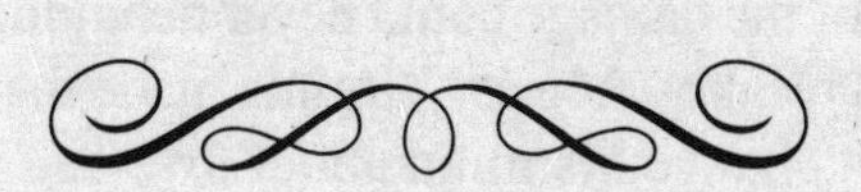

At last James took Virginia's letter from his pocket and examined the outside as if it could take him back to the moment she had finished, folded it precisely and directed it in her familiar, flowing hand. He imagined her getting to the end of her self-imposed task of writing four letters to her 'boys' and leaving them to be read after her death—one given out for every season of the year after she died. Missing her never seemed to fade, however many months he had to get used to it.

Luke had been ordered to do what he'd always wanted and discover all Chloe's secrets, then Virginia's godson, Tom Banburgh, Marquis of Mantaigne, had to face his childhood demons next, before Gideon took on a summer of abiding love and startling revelations. Now it was his turn. It would be a workaday ending to a year of changed lives. The others were lured into doing what Virginia wanted by the promise of James being independent of his half-brother and wasn't that the biggest irony of all? He smiled wryly at the thought of Virginia baiting her hook with a lie. She knew he could buy a house and estate like the tumbledown one he'd acquired without feeling a dent in his ill-gotten gains.

He wondered why she had done it and why he'd failed to mention his fortune. Even a brother who wasn't supposed to care a snap of his fingers for anyone could see Luke had lived half a life since he wedded his first wife Pamela. The woman was ten years dead, but some of the damage could never be undone, James concluded bleakly. At least Virginia made the stubborn great idiot change his mind about love and marriage and his great-aunt's mysterious housekeeper. Now Tom Banburgh and Gideon Laughraine were happy as well and Luke's new wife had given him his letter with a look that said she knew he wanted to sob like a child at the sight of it. Heaven forbid Virginia expected some impossible love match from him because he'd hate her to be disappointed. Not that she was here to *be* anything. He tested the weight of several pages of closely written hot-pressed paper and still hesitated to break the familiar seal of two Vs interlocked that always made him smile at their effrontery.

For goodness' sake, boy, why don't you get on and open the dratted thing?

The voice popped into his head as if Virginia was pacing about this manmade glade waiting to have her say and as impatient with shilly-shallying as ever. James looked round as furtively as he'd done as a boy when his great-aunt caught him in mischief and she felt so acutely present he only just stopped himself peering round this glade to see where she was hiding herself.

Don't be ridiculous, it didn't take supernatural powers to read the mind of a grubby schoolboy then and you're not so different now.

So much for the calming effects of nature and a serene autumn day; fighting a superstitious shiver, James fixed his gaze on the only part of her that could be real today and lifted the seal with a neat penknife she would have confiscated on sight in the old days. Anything was preferable to the madness of conjuring up the beloved, infuriating, marvel of a woman he missed so badly nine months on from her death.

Darling James
Now don't sit there thinking, Who? Me? I love you and always have done. From the very first moment I laid eyes on you as a squalling brat I knew you were special when you decided to trump your mother's cast-iron certainty you would follow her family and came out a Winterley instead. Now I love you for your own sake and you have to accept that, James. You are a good, loving and, yes, a lovable man, and it's about time you realised it.

So why did I do all this? You know as well as I do there's no need to provide you with the fortune you will receive the day Gideon carries out his task to dear Chloe's satisfaction. I hope she and Luke are happy together by now and Gideon attained his heart's desire, by the way? I set the other boys quests they were eager to carry out, deep down, except perhaps for my beloved Tom. I had to push him to going back to the place he least wants to go to for his own sake.

You know almost as well as he does how it feels to be damaged and manipulated by those who are supposed to care for you the most and yet do not. I trust you to watch out for Tom and see he is not going wilder than ever since I made him return to Dayspring Castle and face his demons.

James looked up from his letter with a broad grin at the idea of Tom doing anything wild without his rather fierce new love at his side. The new Marchioness of Mantaigne was sure to outrage the *ton* as carelessly as her husband, but she would love him until their dying day. James felt the lightness of knowing all three were deeply and abidingly happy with their chosen brides and realised Virginia was right, he had worried about them—at least the ones he knew about. Gideon was a new comrade-in-arms and for some reason his wife, Callie, felt almost like a sister. Who would have thought he'd feel fraternal towards such a spectacular beauty as Lady Laughraine, bastard daughter of Lord Laughraine's son and true heiress of Raigne?

That odd idea brought him neatly back to people who didn't know themselves. Callie still thought of herself as a superannuated schoolmarm, even now she was reconciled with her doting husband. He frowned at the idea he'd settled near his newest siblings of the heart to protect them from wolves who saw Callie's vulnerability and tried to exploit it. No, he had fallen for broken-down and neglected Brackley Manor House at first sight and that was quite foolish enough to be going on with. Almost feeling the impatience of Virginia's letter in his hand, he went on reading as if she was here to nag him into it.

As for Gideon, I think you would like him and his wife if you would let yourself.

James laughed and shook his head, she would have

enjoyed the joke that he was perilously close to being both friend and kin to the pair of them after years of walking alone. Nobody could accuse Virginia of lacking humour at his expense.

I know you have the makings of a fine man in you, James, and I trust you to be the strength at the heart of the Winterley family in the years to come. You have a power for good in you that you refuse to trust. I want you to know yourself better than you do today, lest you become a lonely and frustrated man and the true glories of this life pass you by. The pity of it is your mother poured all her frustrated ambition into you as a boy and you were still too fine a human being to let her turn you into a fool and envy your brother his future title and possessions. I only wish she and your father were blessed with more children to dilute her folly.

Still, at least you and Luke managed to love each other as boys. When Luke married Pamela because of some maggot your father got in his head about getting the boy wed and begetting heirs since he knew he was dying himself, she was determined to destroy that love, because she knew he didn't love her. She was incapable of feeling true love for another human being, although she craved it as a miser does gold. I know she did something terrible to you both, but I dare not probe the sore places she left you both. I love the two of you too much in life to risk it, so in death I can say your quest will take longest, which is why I left you until last.

You have to learn to love and trust a lover, my dearest. Be she mistress, wife, or friend, I want you to open your heart to love as you never have since the little witch Luke married cast some wicked spell over you both and froze you in your tracks at seventeen. That's so heartbreakingly young to cut yourself off from the most dangerous and breathtakingly wonderful of human emotions, my love. I was blissfully happy with the love of my life and couldn't wish I'd never met him, even when he died, and grief and fury seemed likely to send me mad for a while. Love is something to celebrate and treasure, never a burden to be avoided at all costs as you appear to think.

So, even if it takes you until your deathbed, darling James, your quest is to learn to love with all the strength and humour and power in that great heart of yours. Don't shake your head; I know you do your best to keep it secret from the rest of the world, but you are a special person and I value you as such. Luke always wanted to love his brother and I felt so sorry for you both when it became clear the main purpose of your mother's life was to prevent him doing so. What you choose to do about your frosty relations with your half-brother is up to you. If you think it right to hold aloof from your family, I ache for you all, but know you have good reason.

James looked up from his letter to stare unseeingly into the soft autumn afternoon. Oh, yes, he had very good reason to stay away from those he loved. It ached in his heart as if a tight band had been strapped round his chest at seventeen and would never be loosed this side of the grave. He shook his head and found himself a coward for refusing to explore it. Revisit that pain and anger and sense of worthlessness, when all that could be done was move on as best he could? No; this time Virginia was wrong. Hadn't he said he'd be her only failure?

'Three out of four is a fine record, darling,' he murmured as he stared unseeingly at the soft, serene blue of the October sky.

And a full house trumps it every time, came the reply so certainly he looked for Virginia's shade again, then called himself a fool for expecting it to show up for him. There was a little more in her missive from some time last year, when she had put her affairs in order while she had the strength and certainty to do so. How he admired and loved the one woman he could safely adore until his dying day. Come to think of it; if she was ordering him to give his heart, wasn't she already too late?

Cheating, my boy, the gruff almost-sound of her voice reproached him and what he wouldn't give to actually see and speak to her one last time? *That's a different sort of love. Virgil and I simply tried to give you and your brother and Tom a firm foundation of love to build your lives on. Love between a man and a woman, full and true and without boundaries, is very different to the deep affection of true family. That love is an undeserved gift that can light up a whole lifetime with the joy and surprise of it, for however long or short a time you are together. I want you to love like that, James, I need you to love truly if I am ever to have peace and join my far-more-saintly Virgil in heaven one day.*

'Now that's blackmail,' James muttered with a frown at the circling buzzard that had taken off from the perch where it had been dreaming in the sun at the top of the tallest oak in Lord Laughraine's beloved woods. 'I've made love to some of the loveliest women in this land and quite a few further afield and not fallen in love with a single one of them. If I couldn't love any of them, I'm beyond heavenly intervention.'

No, just looking in the wrong place, the not-quite sound of Virginia's distinctive voice in his head insisted stubbornly.

James felt that restriction where his heart ought to be again and did his best to ignore it. Did she expect him to find a saint? The very idea made him snort with derision. Even the slightest hint of the saintly martyr in a woman would make him play the devil more than ever. No, he didn't have it in him to give himself wholeheartedly to any deep human emotion, let alone loving a woman who'd preach at him and pry into his sooty soul. Shaking his head at the very idea, he forced himself to read the final farewell of the most matchless woman he'd ever met.

Whatever you do, live well and never close your heart to loving those around you if you can't let go of your pride or your tender conscience long enough to truly love a partner for life. I was lucky to adore your great-uncle from the moment I met him and perhaps that's not a miracle given to many of us sinners. You must believe that if I could have had a son I wanted him to be just like you, James. Know that now and please shrug off the self-loathing you struggle with for some reason you never would confide in me.

I find it hardest of all to stop writing to you, but now my pen is in need of mending and I am weary of this wide and wonderful earth of ours at last. Don't grieve for me any more, love. I'm more than ready for a new adventure the other side of this little earthly life, if God will allow a sinner like me into heaven where I know Virgil already abides.

Farewell, my love; be happy and true to yourself. I pray one day you will be truly loved by the right woman, despite your conviction you do not deserve her,
Virginia

James blinked several times and watched the buzzard lazily circle its way up to the heavens on a warm thermal of autumn air and call for its mate to join it. Soon two birds were mewing in that circle, gliding and calling in the still air as if all that mattered was the miracle of flight and one another. For wild creatures with only their next meal and the urges of nature to answer perhaps it was. For James Winterley there was good earth under his feet and a mass of mixed emotions in his heart. He must go back to Raigne soon and show his sister-in-law and his hostess he wasn't bowed down with the task Virginia had laid on his shoulders. Truth was he didn't know how he felt about it. How could an unlovable man end up like the other three? Impossible, so he shook his head and decided he'd been right all along, he was destined to be Virginia's only failure.

Perhaps he should give back the small fortune Gideon had passed to him as Virginia's lawyer? James had plans for it, so, no, he'd accept the sacrifices Virginia's nearest and dearest had made to get him off their hands. It would be an insult even he couldn't steel himself to make if he was to throw the money back in their faces and tell them he didn't want it.

'Are you a hermit, mister?'

James jumped and looked for the source of that voice, so attuned to ghostly intervention he wondered for a moment if it came from a cherub instead of a child. He looked harder and spotted a grubby urchin peering down at him from halfway up a vast and curiously branched tree.

'No, are you a leech?' he asked as casually as he could and watched the girl squirm a little higher. Was there some way to get close and catch her when she fell without alarming her into falling in the first place?

'Of course not, do I look like such a nasty, slimy bloodsucking thing?'

'Only by hanging on to an unwilling host and defying the laws of gravity.'

'You're a very odd gentleman. I watched you for ages until I got bored and decided to see if I could get to the top of this tree instead.'

'So that's my fault, is it? I suppose you will tell your unfortunate parents so if you survive the experience?'

'No,' the pragmatic cherub said after a pause to think about it. 'They will know it's a lie,' she finally admitted as she carefully worked her way up a little further and James's heart thumped with fear as he let himself see how far from the ground she truly was.

'How perceptive,' he managed calmly as he strolled over so casually he hoped she had no idea he had his doubts about her survival if she took a wrong step.

'Yes, it's a trial,' she admitted with a sigh that would normally have made him laugh out loud, but he was holding his breath too carefully to do any such thing as a branch writhed and threatened to snap when she tried it too hard.

'I can see how it must be,' he somehow managed to say calmly. 'Sometimes knowing what you know and keeping quiet about it has to be enough, don't you think?'

'What?' the adventurer asked rather breathlessly, as if not quite willing to admit her lucky escape had scared her so much she hadn't been listening.

'You know you can climb that tree, so perhaps that's enough.' He did his best to reason with her as if every inch of him wasn't intent on persuading her to come down before she fell and he must try to catch her.

'There's no point me knowing I could do it if nobody else does.'

'Yes, there is. You have the satisfaction of achievement and I'll know.'

'No, you won't. I'm only halfway up.'

'Which is about ten times as far as anyone else I ever came across can get. Being further up than anyone else can be has to be enough at times, don't you think? I believe that's the sign of a truly great person—knowing when it's time to stop and be content.'

His latest critic seemed to think about that for endless moments before she took another step either way and he felt slightly better when the whippy branches above her head stopped swaying from the intrusion of a small human into its stately crown.

'Do you really think it's a big achievement to get this far?'

'Of course it is; Joan of Arc couldn't have done better.'

'She got herself burnt,' the urchin said doubtfully.

'There is that, of course. Well, then, whatever great woman you think the most highly of couldn't have done, as well. No woman of my acquaintance could touch you.'

'What, not even one?' she asked as if she didn't think much of his taste in friends.

'One might have done, but she died nearly a year ago now and I suppose by then even she was getting a little old for climbing trees. She would have been up there with you like a shot otherwise,' he assured her.

'And you think she would have thought this is far enough?'

'I'm certain of it, she was the most lionhearted woman I ever came across and even she would say it's enough to prove your courage and daring to yourself at times. Now I do wish you'd come down, because I'm getting a stiff neck and I'm devilish sharp set.'

'Why don't you just go, then?' the girl said rather sulkily.

James wondered if he'd blundered and might have to risk both their lives by climbing up after her. If the girl insisted on going too high for him to be able to break her fall, even if he could judge the right place to try, he might have no choice. A lot of those branches simply wouldn't take his weight, though, so he wondered if he could shout loudly enough to attract the woodsmen and hope they were lean and limber enough to do what he couldn't.

'There's roast lamb and apple pie for dinner,' he said as if that was all he could think about right now. He hoped the mention of food would remind her she hadn't eaten for at least an hour and eating might trump adventures even for intrepid young scamps like this one.

'I wish I was going to your house for dinner.'

'I suppose if we'd been properly introduced I might get you invited another night. I've heard rumours about plum cake being available for hungry young visitors at any time of day, but I don't suppose you like it.'

'Why not?'

'Only boys like plum cake, don't they?'

'No, I'm as good as any boy and twice as hungry.'

'So girls don't prefer syllabub and sponge cake after all, then?'

'I don't.'

James was delighted to see the girl look for a way down almost without noticing she was doing it. She might make it back down to earth without killing herself on the way now, but he tried not to let his relief show lest she went further up the tree, because she couldn't let him see she was almost as scared as he was she might fall right now.

'What don't you like? So I can tell Cook when you come to dinner,' he went on as if he hadn't noticed she was thinking better of her plan to reach the top of the slender tree.

'Cucumbers and rice pudding.'

'Oh, dear me no, I can't think of a worse combination.'

'Not both at the same time, idiot,' she said scathingly and felt less confidently for footholds on the way down and his heart seemed about to take up residence in his mouth as he watched her fumble, then find one.

'How, then?' he made himself ask as if he hadn't a serious thought in his head while she hesitated between the next unsteady foothold and an even less likely alternative. Luckily the first held long enough to let her find a better and he sucked in a hasty breath and tried to look calm and only mildly interested when she found the nerve to look down again.

'Rice pudding is worse, it looks like frogspawn and tastes like it by the time it gets to the nursery all cold and shuddery,' she told him rather shakily.

'I know exactly what you mean, but it goes down much better with big spoons of jam. I would never have got through school without wasting away if my brother hadn't insisted I have jam with my pudding or succumb to a mysterious ailment unique to our family.'

'I wish one of my brothers would think up stories to get us out of having to eat cold rice pudding on its own,' she said wistfully and moved a few feet closer to the ground.

James estimated she was still about thirty feet above his head and worryingly unsafe when the girl's elder sister appeared at the edge of the clearing, looking visibly shaken and pale as milk. She seemed about to distract the girl with a terrified exclamation and part of him whispered it would be good if she turned out to be a widgeon and released him from the spell he'd been in danger of tumbling into since the first day he laid eyes on her.

This wasn't about him, though, so he shook his head

and glared at her to keep quiet. He'd done his best not to know the Finch family better after spotting this disaster of a female hovering on the edges of it after church a few weeks ago. And who would have thought he'd let himself be cajoled and persuaded inside one of those for the good of his sooty soul quite so often?

'I don't think my brother would save me from rice pudding at every meal now we're grown up if that makes you feel better,' he shouted cheerfully enough.

He held his breath as the next branch the child tried gave an ominous crack. Again she skipped hastily on to the next and both watchers let out a quiet sigh of relief. The girl in the tree had frightened herself with her own daring and he had to keep her calm enough to take the next step to safety and the next, until she was low enough to catch if she fell.

'Why not?' she quavered bravely and how could he not put all he was into saving a girl who seemed as reckless and brave as Virginia must have been as a child?

Despite her mass of golden hair and bluest of blue eyes, she reminded him of Hebe's little daughter Amélie. The defiant determination not to cry and admit how frightened she was put him in mind of the poor little mite he'd smuggled out of Paris at the behest of Hebe's mother. The Terror had taken her husband and sons, now treachery had robbed her of her daughter, but she was still brave enough to part with her grandchild. Now it was up to him to see that the child had a better life than her mother and the responsibility felt terrifying at times.

'We argued,' he admitted, although it wasn't exactly true. The problem was he and Luke hadn't even had the heart to argue, they just let each other go and that was that.

'Me and Jack argue all the time,' the girl said matter-of-factly.

'Is he your only sibling?' he said with a warning glance at the one he wanted to know about least right now.

'What's a sibling?'

'A brother or sister.'

'Oh, no, but Nan's only a baby and can hardly walk yet. I'm next, then there's Jack, he's two years older. Sophie is fifteen; Josh is at Oxford. Joanna is quite old and she's getting married in November. Rowena has been grown up for years and years; she lived with her mama-in-law for ages but she's home now. I hope she stays with us. She's *really* old, but much more fun than Sophie. It's nice to have one big sister who doesn't scold all the time.'

James couldn't spare a glance at Mr Finch's eldest daughter to see how she'd reacted to that quaint summary. 'Your parents must be busy with such a large and enterprising family,' he managed coolly.

'Oh, Papa and Mama are always busy. What with Papa's pupils and all those services, Mama says it's a wonder we ever see him.'

'You must be Reverend Finch's daughter, then?'

'Why do people always say that as if it's a surprise?' the girl grumbled.

'I really can't imagine,' he said wryly.

His breathing went shallow as the child stretched a grubby bare foot to find her next precarious hold. At a crash of unwary movement behind him he turned his head to bark a furious command at Mrs Westhope and saw a gangling stripling stumble into the clearing. Shock at the sight of his sister perched halfway up the wretched tree was written all over the boy's ashen face. James drew breath to shout out an order to be silent just too late.

'Good Lord, this time she'll kill herself, Rowena,' the boy shouted furiously.

The girl in the tree started, snatched at a much-too-slender branch to steady herself and screamed when it snapped off. This time there wasn't another close enough to grab and save herself. She did her best to stumble on to another slender branch and shuffle her way back to the relative safety of the trunk. James's heart seemed to jump into his mouth as he tried to calculate where best to stand to break the child's fall, at the same time as briefly snatching off a prayer she wouldn't need him to in the first place, since it was so hit and miss. The force of even her slender little body made the fine branches whip away or break as she grabbed at them. He winced for the scratches and bruises they would cause even as he reminded himself far worse would happen if he didn't get in the way and stop her fall.

'Stay back, you'll do no good,' he ordered the boy who looked about to dash forward and get in the way.

James had to forget him and hope his elder sister would stop the boy. She must have dragged her brother away, because James could pick the best spot to try and catch the child. He braced himself against the impact of the solid little body now hurtling towards him in a flash of flailing arms and grubby petticoats. A pity she couldn't grow wings like the buzzards he'd been watching earlier, he found time to reflect as stalled time passed sluggishly. He did his best to second-guess gravity and snatch the girl from the shadowy arms of death by adjusting his stance as she fell. An image of this intrepid child lying lifeless and broken if he failed flashed in front of his eyes to truly horrify him, even as he stepped back to compensate for a little flail she managed, as if trying to slow her flight on the way down. He couldn't quite think her a hell-born brat as every sense he had was intent on saving her from as much harm as he could.

Time flooded back in a rush. The girl's speed crashed into him with all her slender weight behind it. He frantically closed his arms and caught her close. In the flail of limbs and hammer of his own heartbeat he knew he was between her and the dry, hard-packed earth. For a long moment it seemed they would escape winded and a bit bruised. Then he felt his foot slide on the smooth bark of an outstretched tree root, as if the wretched thing was reaching out to claim them even now he had the girl safe. Unable to flail about and get his balance because of the child in his arms, he had no hold on solid ground. He twisted and turned as best he could to save the girl injury and fell heavily to earth with a bone-jarring thud and actually heard his own head slam against the next tree root with a vicious crack. Almost at the same time a harder, sharper slap of sound rang through the wood like a death knell as James fought hard to hold on to his senses.

Chapter Four

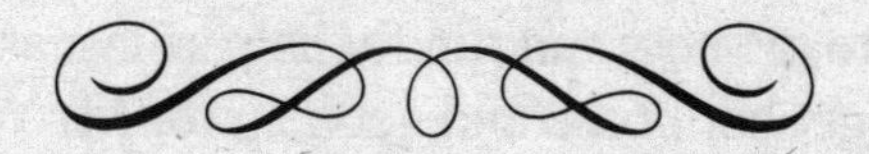

'Oh, Lord, Hes, what have you done?' Jack Finch yelled.

Rowena let go and they dashed to the dark-haired stranger who still held Hes, despite a blow to his head that still seemed to echo round the clearing. Perhaps he'd been mortally wounded by the shot that followed his fall so closely it might almost have been one sound.

'Be quiet, Jacob Finch,' she ordered, knowing shock and his full name would silence him while she took her little sister from Mr Winterley's arms and willed air into her lungs. 'You can let her go now,' she told the all-but-unconscious man. Her little sister was whooping for air with dry little groans that terrified Rowena that she'd never restart her much-tried lungs without wiser help than she had right now. 'Let her go!' she demanded this time.

He did one of those terrifying saws for air that echoed Hester's and she wrested her suddenly frighteningly small sister out of his grasp. She spared a preoccupied moment to be relieved his much-more-powerful lungs were forcing air into his labouring chest now they were free of the slender weight.

'Come on, Hes, breathe,' she shouted desperately.

'How could you, Hes?' Jack shouted, terror making him sound so furious he could hardly get the words out. 'How *could* you?' he repeated on a sob.

'Hush, Jack,' Rowena managed to say as calmly as she could when her own nerves were stretched almost to breaking. 'Sounding as if you'd like to strangle her won't help her recover. She's alive and breathing, so leave her to me now and run for help as fast as you can. We must get her home and get help for Mr Winterley. We owe him our sister's life,' she reminded him when Jack shot Mr Winterley an impatient look, as if he was the last thing on his mind.

'I startled her and made her fall in the first place, didn't I?' he said, an agony of self-reproach in his eyes.

'And did you make her go up the tree she's been expressly forbidden to climb time and time again? You know you didn't, so just run to Raigne as fast as you can now, love, and we'll worry about who did what later. Tell the grooms to bring a hurdle or the best sprung cart they can find, but go now, love, and hurry. They need a doctor and Raigne is closest.'

'I suppose someone has to fetch him, even if Mama and Papa are home and I don't suppose they will be.'

'No, go to Raigne and tell Sir Gideon what happened. He'll know exactly what to do and which order to do it in.'

'Don't alarm Lady Laughraine, boy,' the stranger managed in a broken whisper.

'Do as he says,' Rowena ordered brusquely. 'Now go.'

With one last look round as if he'd like to go and stay at the same time, Jack went as fast as his legs would carry him and Rowena managed a sigh of relief. A fleeting idea that the powerful male at her feet cared too much about Callie's serenity flitted though her head, but she banished it to a dark corner and concentrated on facts. If that really had been a gunshot so close she had felt the echo in her own ribcage, two semi-conscious adventurers and an over-bold poacher were enough for one woman to worry about right now.

Hester's stalwart little lungs were gasping in air as eagerly as if it was going out of fashion now and colour was coming back into her pallid cheeks. Rowena went on rubbing her narrow ribcage as she leant Hester forward to help as best she could. She stared down at the stranger, feeling helpless in the face of his deeper hurts. Now Jack was gone and with the worst of her fears for Hester calming, she had time to feel the horror of what might have happened, if not for this supposedly idle gentleman. Had he sustained some terrible injury as he strove to save Hes, or maybe he'd been shot although he twisted to save her sister from a terrible fall at what seemed like exactly the right moment at the time?

Considering the loud crack his head made when it hit the tree root, how could he not be badly hurt, Rowena? If he'd taken a bullet as well there would be blood, though, wouldn't there? She examined every inch of him visible; his closely fitting coat of dark-blue superfine was only marred by grass seeds and the odd leaf that dared cling to it. His dark hair fell in rougher versions of the neatly arranged waves she'd seen gleam like polished ebony as the late summer sun shone through the plain side windows in church only last Sunday. There was no sticky trail of blood matting it to dullness when even this far into the woods light came in leaf-shaded speckles.

She made herself glance lower and concluded such pristine breeches would give away a wound all too easily and as for his highly polished boots, what was he doing wearing such expensive articles of fashion in Lord Laughraine's woodland? No, he seemed unmarred by bullets and she knew too much about such wounds to be mistaken. He wasn't flinching away from the ground pressing against one or moaning in agony. She doubted he'd do that if he was badly injured, though, for the sake of the child sitting so close she would feel as well as hear them. Some instinct she didn't want to listen to said he'd put Hes's welfare before his own. Under all the Mayfair gloss and aloofness this was truly a man. Trying to pretend otherwise every Sunday since she had come back to King's Raigne and found Mr Winterley a welcome guest at the great house had been a waste of effort.

Never mind that; he must be horribly uncomfortable on that unyielding root. She dare not move him for fear of causing more harm. One of the better military surgeons once told her that well-meaning efforts to help an injured man often did as much damage as the wounds inflicted by the enemy. She wanted to remove her light shawl and cushion his poor head, but would that do more harm than good?

Since he didn't appear to have been shot she could discount that as a reason for his continuing unawareness. Perhaps she had misheard in all the shock and confusion of Hes's wild tumble anyway and there never was a second sharp crack ringing through the now-silent wood. He did take the full force of a surprisingly substantial little body hurtling towards him after all. She suspected Hes could have broken one or two of his ribs when she slammed into him almost as hard as a bullet might. The thought of a gun being fired in anger took her back to the terrifying noise of the battlefield and the long, terrible tension every wife endured when waiting to find out if she was a widow. She shuddered at the tragic end to that waiting for her and all the other wives and lovers facing the full stop put on a man's life by war, then drew in a deep breath to banish old terrors from her mind and concentrate on new ones instead.

'Will she do?' the man made the huge effort to ask in a rasping whisper.

Even the breathy rumble of it told Rowena there was more to his hurts than simply being winded by her little sister's plunge into his arms. She shifted the small body in her arms to peer at Hester's face and saw a trail of tears on her grubby little face that almost made her break down herself. She couldn't put her sister aside to check on the gentleman who had rescued her. While she was grateful to him, this was Hes, her sister, and she came first, even when she was sitting between two injured souls and none of it was his fault. She wiped away her sister's tears with her fingers and kissed her grubby cheek.

'I don't think much harm befell her ladyship here, as long as she does as she's told for a day or two and doesn't climb this particular tree ever again. I think all will be well with her, don't you?' she said softly and Hester managed a wobbly smile.

'I won't,' she managed to gasp between breaths. Her little sister was a daredevil scrap of mischief far too headstrong for her own good, but Rowena loved her so much it physically hurt right now.

'Pleased to hear it,' he said, went even paler, then finally lost consciousness.

'Is he dead, Row?' Hester managed to wail in an almost-normal voice.

'No, love, but remember he's been hit on the head and probably hasn't managed to get enough air into his lungs quite yet.'

'He looks dead.' The little voice sank to a fearful whisper.

'No, I'm sure he will be perfectly fine in a day or two and Jack is sure to be at Raigne soon. You know he can run like the wind when he chooses. So help will be on its way before long and Dr Harbury will probably insist he stays in bed for a while. Mama and the doctor are sure to insist you stay in yours until we're sure no harm was done and you deserve it, so don't look at me like that,' Rowena added as her little sister shuddered and seemed unable to bounce back to her normal state of barely suppressed mischief.

'You know how much I hate being shut inside on a lovely day.'

'Let's hope for rain, then,' Rowena murmured hardheartedly, with an apologetic look at the serene blue sky and a shiver. Somehow she dreaded the coming winter and all the long and lonely dark nights it would bring with it even more than usual.

'I hate that even worse.'

'I know, all mud and stickiness and damp stockings.'

'Ugh, don't,' Hester said with another shiver and clung to Rowena in a way that made her more anxious about her little sister and at the same time guiltily annoyed at Mr Winterley for worrying them with his long and somehow painful silence.

If not for him, she could carry her little sister home and put her to bed, then send for the doctor herself. If they didn't have to wait for someone from Raigne to take responsibility for Mr Winterley, they could be halfway back to King's Raigne Vicarage now. Rowena would love to hand over the care of their most-adventurous child to her mother and father and take time to be shocked and shaken herself. She shouldn't dream of being so selfish, she decided, with an apologetic look at the unconscious man. If not for him, Hes would be dead or so near to it they must pray for a miracle to save her from a fall from such a height. Now he was suffering for his heroism while Rowena wished him at Jericho.

She was a bad and ungrateful woman and ought to do penance. Luckily Papa wasn't a fire-and-brimstone vicar who thundered hellfire and damnation at his parishioners from the pulpit and expected constant repentance from his family. Flinching away from the poor man because he lay almost as still and pale as her husband after the terrible battle at Vimeiro that day was cowardly and wrong, though. He was deathly pale under the unfashionable tan that gave him away as a contradiction. Even she knew pinks of the *ton* prided themselves on having a pallor that set them apart from those who toiled for a living, or country squires who rode their acres so they could afford a spring Season in town to marry off their daughters.

The bronzed smoothness of this man's skin was tight over high cheekbones and she suspected he was forcing stillness on himself now. Perhaps he was suppressing his injuries so as not to shock her little sister with his moans of torment? She refused to think about the chance that really had been a gunshot aimed with deadly accuracy. After all, she had to sit here with her shocked little sister and a semi-conscious and injured man until help came. The idea hostile eyes could be looking for a chance to try again felt intolerable right now, so she wasn't going to admit it was possible on a sunny autumn day in safe little England.

Mr Winterley must have a very low opinion of her after today. She had stood paralysed with fear while he acted to save the life of a child he must only have had a vague idea existed until today. Rowena shivered at the thought of his contempt for such a useless female and fought not to pass on her disturbed feelings to Hes. Struggling with her horror at being so close to a wounded man after scouring the battlefield for her husband's mangled body that awful day two years ago, she gently laid the hand she could spare from hugging Hester on the man's forehead, as if touching him might tell him she was sorry. His skin felt warmly familiar under her hesitant fingers. Seeing his faint hint of a frown smooth out, she made a gentle exploration of his temples and further back and was relieved to see no blood issued from his finely made ears. Not sure how she knew that was a good sign, she sighed and wished she knew more about how a vigorous male should react to the world around him.

Even with that last awful image of him in her head, Nate was little more than a boy in her memory rather than a mature warrior like this one. Why had her imagination painted him as a battle-hardened knight and not an idle gentleman of fashion? Somehow this vital man had lessened her husband in her memory and she'd meant to find out about his hurts, not compare him to a corpse on a godforsaken battlefield a thousand miles away.

Rowena caught in her breath and reminded herself she must be cool and logical, despite her fear that a mortal wound might lurk under this man's crisply curling black hair. His fine and fashionable haircut wouldn't guard his head from attack. She recalled the noise as he hit this confounded tree root with horror; it sounded like the crack of doom when he hit the earth with Hes locked in his arms. What a shame he wasn't wearing the fine beaver hat she could see on the bench where Lord Laughraine usually sat after walking up to his favourite viewing point. It might have shielded his head from the worst Hes and the tree could do. She gently winnowed her fingers though the midnight unfamiliarity of his thick dark hair and felt a slight tightening of his skin. He was awake and suffering as she suspected, so she padded her fingers a little further away so as not to hurt him, then snatched them away altogether. Surely it was wrong to feel so in tune with a stranger that you knew where he hurt even when he was pretending to be unconscious? He frowned almost imperceptibly and she automatically smoothed it away and saw a faint smile relax his stern mouth.

She had touched a perhaps mortally injured man and found him warm and human under the bravado and show of a Bond Street beau. Far from being cold and glaring in death, or alive and somehow desperate to feed off her vitality, he was himself. She stopped again and he shocked her a little by raising the hand nearest to her reaching one and meeting hers as if he knew exactly where she was by instinct and didn't need to open his eyes. He wanted her touch, it was as plain as if he'd sat up and told her so. And she wanted to touch him back; that was equally plain, since her hand closed gently on his as if it belonged there without any permission from the rest of her. Perish the thought—she reminded herself how firmly she had resolved never to marry again after she found Nate dead that day—but she couldn't bring herself to slide her hand out of his and break the contact even so.

Tempting to tell herself the warmth spreading through her was caused by the simple human contact of another hand on hers—tempting, but not very honest. A tingle of something more exciting and less understandable ran under it, a feeling of heat and homecoming. She felt shocked to realise this was the first physical contact she'd had with Mr Winterley, a man who stayed with lords and ladies as casually as she might with her sister and Mr Greenwood once they were wed and ready to receive visitors. Even as she did her best to remind herself of the gulf between them, the feel of his hand against hers without pressure bridged it. So she sat and let warmth flow from her hand to his and back again, rather bemused by the intimacy and telling herself her lungs had an excuse to be breathless after such a shock.

Birds were still singing in the distance and Hes was squirming to be let out of the fierce hug Rowena still held her in with her other arm and that made her recall where they were and what had happened. She couldn't simply let her little sister go or leave this man's side to watch over her as the wary widow in her wanted to. It would be so wrong to desert a warrior in disguise while he was brought low like this. Although she hated the way his gentle grasp on her hand tugged her back into a world of feeling she thought she'd put behind her with Nate's death, none of it was his fault. Well, part of it was, but she doubted he'd reached across the gap between them for the comfort of her touch and done it on purpose.

'Be still, little love, you'll hurt yourself and Mr Winterley if you flail about so. You're not going adventuring again until Dr Harbury says you're over your latest attempt to kill yourself,' she murmured softly and Hester stilled.

'I never meant to hurt him, Row,' she whispered, on the edge of an overwrought storm of tears as the seriousness of what had almost happened finally sank in.

'Oh, my love, I know that and so will he when he's awake,' Rowena said, using her sister's distress as an excuse to slip her hand out of Mr Winterley's light grip and stroke the wild white-blonde curls off her little sister's face. She met her little sister's teary gaze and did her best to reassure her there was no need for hysterics. 'You are a dear, you do know that, don't you?' she assured her sister with a fond smile as blue eyes so like her own gazed back at her sorrowfully.

'I don't think many people would agree with you right now, Row.'

'This gentleman obviously liked you enough to save your life,' she said lightly.

'That was nice of him, wasn't it?'

Rowena saw Mr Winterley's surprisingly expressive lips twitch as if he was amused by Hes's artless comment. Even in such pain as he must be in to lie here as if he'd truly been felled by that blow, he still managed to find her sister endearing.

'Yes, love, very nice,' she confirmed.

She let her gaze flick over his compelling face and person once again, lingering on his perfectly barbered dark head and beautiful coat. Such fine tailoring should be forbidden gentlemen with so many natural advantages, she decided severely. Ruffled and slightly battered by his adventures, he didn't look like a heartless dandy any more and that seemed a little unfair for some reason she couldn't quite fathom.

'There's someone coming,' Hester whispered.

'Thank heaven for them, then, love.' Rowena breathed, a little of the tension easing from shoulders she hadn't realised she was holding so stiffly until now. He wasn't going to die in her care; this man wasn't going to let life slip out of him between one breath and the next as Nate had moments after she found him on that bloody and blasted battlefield, as if she wasn't worth struggling to live for.

'I will,' her sister promised so solemnly Rowena believed her.

'We'll do it together,' she murmured and the man let his mouth relax for a moment, as if he was about to speak, then thought better of it.

'Why are they coming creeping through the bushes like that, Rowena? Jack must have told them where we are and what the matter is and that they should hurry.'

Rowena glanced at the watch Nate's mama had given her for a wedding present, as if she knew they must count the hours. Now she realised how little time had passed, her heart jigged like a frightened horse in panic. It was too soon even for Jack to have run all the way to Raigne, found someone capable of organising a rescue, then got here before Hes's lungs had quite settled into their usual unhurried ease.

'Maybe one of your friends escaped from their books and won't show their face for fear of being sent home,' she said as cheerfully as she could.

Memory of that sharp echo ringing out as this man hit the ground with Hes in his arms sniped at her and a superstitious shiver slid down her back. The thicket of evergreens a past Lord Laughraine had planted to preserve game looked ideal cover for a hunter of men now. Even the air in the mellow autumn woodland seemed to have gone wary; birds stopped singing as if they were listening and there was the angry flick of a squirrel's russet tail halfway up the tree that had caused all this trouble in the first place. Nothing stirred but the branch echoing the squirrel's flight, yet it felt as if half the world was listening for what came next.

'I'm frightened, Row,' Hester whispered, as if she felt like a pheasant in the sights of an expensive shotgun, as well.

'This gentleman isn't in a fit state to hurt you even if he wanted to. We have proof the boot is on the other foot and he must wish you well, since he's saved you a hard tumble and more broken bones than I can bring myself to think of right now,' Rowena joked as best she could.

With another glance at the unfriendly evergreens she counted how many seconds it might take her to snatch her little sister up and run for safety. No, she couldn't leave this man staked out here like a sacrifice, even if it wasn't a little bit too far to take the risk. Mr Winterley had saved Hester's life, even if he had brought an enemy into this wood with him. Nobody had tried to shoot her or Hes or Jack in all the time they'd lived here, so the danger was his. What a poor return it would be for saving Hes if they left some villain to murder and rob him as brutally as she'd seen the dead and wounded on the battlefield stripped and plundered that awful day, irrespective of which side they fought for. Even if she was that ungrateful, this odd feeling of connection to the man would keep her here. So should she let Hes go and tell her to run home as fast as her shaky legs could carry her? No, she might be caught and used against them and, knowing Hes, she'd refuse to go.

Her little sister had heard the furtive movement as if a marksman was finding a snug spot for an ambush, as well. Rowena shuddered at the idea of Mr Winterley coldly murdered, yet he was Lord Farenze's brother and wouldn't that bring every single instrument of the law down on his killer? It seemed too big a risk for a sane man to take, but a leaf stirred where no wind could reach it and she sensed a predator waiting for a clear shot at his quarry even so. The safety of two other beings felt heavy on her shoulders. Mr Winterley's face was still blank and serene as if he lay unconscious, but the flex of his hand nearest to her, shielded from view by her skirts, told her he was aware as any man could be after that savage blow to the head.

'Can you see that patch of dried-up moss and oak leaves yonder, Hes?'

'There's nothing wrong with my eyes,' Hester said impatiently.

'Then go and gather the driest and softest bits and bring them here so we can make a cushion with my shawl for the poor man's head to rest on,' Rowena said and hoped the silent listener had no idea she was thought to be a sensible woman the rest of the time.

'Didn't you say he should be kept…?' Hester's still slightly shaky voice tailed off at the sight of Rowena's fierce glare. She hoped the fact she was being moved out of the line of fire wouldn't dawn on her reckless sister. 'Oh, very well, it really is taking for ever for Jack to get back with Sir Gideon or his lordship and that tree root must be very hard,' clever little Hes said with her bottom lip stuck out, as if she felt sulky and furious and a bit bored.

Rowena tried to make it seem natural to shift round a prone man, then hover slightly hysterically. She took her time forming her least favourite shawl into a square and wondered aloud if it would ever be the same again if the man bled all over it.

'Not even the most careful laundering will get the stain out of wool and it's not as if I have dozens of them to be ruined,' she twittered fussily.

'Here, this ought to make him comfortable as the Sleeping Beauty,' Hester said as she trudged back with an armful of leaves and moss and some bleached and dry grass harvested from the edge of the clearing.

Rowena bundled the driest of her sister's offerings into her shawl, then wrapped it into a makeshift pillow. Keeping between her sister and harm, she thrust the neatly wrapped bundle at Hes, then knelt at Mr Winterley's other side to frustrate his attacker.

'The instant I lift his head you must put my shawl between his poor head and that nasty tree root,' she ordered as if she and Hes were nearly as dimwitted as one another.

'Yes, of course, sister dear. How you do fuss,' Hes said with such a huge sigh of long-suffering patience Rowena frowned at her for overacting. Nothing stirred behind her, though, so maybe it was working.

'Right pocket,' Mr Winterley murmured when Rowena bent even closer. She felt almost as fluffy and distracted as she was pretending to be as she fought off the feeling of being too close to a sleek and magnificent predator. 'Get your sister out of here,' he added so softly she bent over him like a ministering angel to hear him and her hair tumbled out of the last of its pins and hid even more of him from prying eyes.

Close to he was lean and vital and ridiculously tempting as she breathed a little too heavily in his ear and heard him grunt with pain when she lifted his mistreated head. Hes pushed the improvised cushion under him and Rowena watched as fascinated by him as the silly debutante she was doing her best to ape. He smelt of clean woods and a faint, cool undercurrent of spice and lemon water and man. The scent pleased her somehow as Nate's linen rarely had, even when she laboured hard to keep it clean herself when they were on the march and he said the laundresses were too rough with his precious shirts. How unfair of her to contrast a man intent on fighting his country's mortal enemies with this idle fop. Cross with herself, she flinched away, then saw him frown as if in pain and called herself every sort of a fool under her breath.

Chapter Five

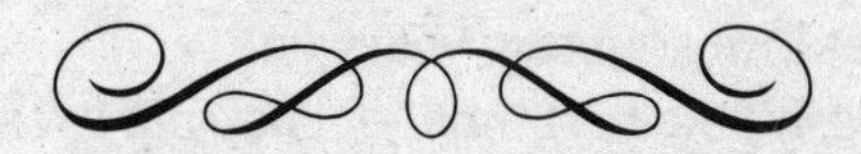

James willed the ringing in his head to subside and pushed the darkness away. He distracted himself from feeling awful by wondering where a vicar's daughter had learnt so many unladylike curses. He hoped the imp on his other side was too busy wondering if he was dead again to hear and resolved to have words with the woman when they were free of an audience. He knew from the warning tingle at the back of his neck the man who had shot at him was out there. The worm was probably puzzling about what to do next, but James couldn't dismiss him as that shot was so true that, if not for this iron-hard tree root and the impulsive girl who felled him, he'd be dead. He'd be dead meat if he was standing where he was when the shooter aimed and no doubt the man had a second weapon and nerve enough to try again.

How the devil had his enemies tracked him down? He'd thought it safe to be James Winterley when he had to come home with his tail between his legs. Nobody took a useless society fribble seriously and it was a relief to saunter through life as if he hadn't a care in the world. If he was being honest, and it might be as well if he was considering how close to God he might be, he took perverse pleasure in living down to James Winterley's raffish reputation. He'd been very young when he gained it; a confused and angry boy at odds with himself and the world. Fifteen years on from his riotous start to adult life as the Winterley boy, the spare half-brother, he could almost pity his younger self. Or he could if he wasn't saddled with the low standards the boy set him so many years on.

This wasn't the best time for chewing over past mistakes, but even that cover had failed him if the skill of the stalker so close he could almost taste him was anything to go by. He lay still as a corpse behind the coward's shield of Rowena Finch's glorious hair and delightful body and did his best to plan a speedy exit from this open space without either Finch girl getting hurt. It was more of an effort to keep his face blank when he felt a slender hand insinuate itself into his coat pocket and heard the rustle of hot-pressed paper under the fair Rowena's searching hand. *Not that*, he wanted to shout at her. *Don't touch Virginia's letter.*

He managed to crack open his eyelids by the smallest distance and saw her wrinkle her nose in distaste at having to search a gentleman's pockets. The sight somehow calmed the worst of his fears and that was a beginner's mistake. Between one breath and the next a woman as full of life and promise as this could be dead as mutton. Why had he thought that one certainty of a spy's life less true here? Raigne had cast a spell over him, but he should never have stayed so long. But how could he have thought it would be easy to give up his unseemly profession and live near here in peaceful obscurity either?

'Got it,' Mrs Westhope murmured as she bent close to cover the movement of her lips with a front of fussing over his injuries as she slipped the lethal little pistol out of his pocket with the finesse of the finest pickpocket in the land.

'Take your sister and run, then,' he muttered as urgently as he dared.

'No,' she whispered emphatically.

'This isn't some rustic coney-catcher ready to shoot me for my boots.'

'Who is he, then?' she asked as if she had a right to know.

'None of your business,' he grumbled so faintly she pressed closer, as if shielding him with her body was all the answer she need make to that grumpy denial.

Somehow he must fight the blankness that blow on the head threatened every time he tried to move. She was risking so much and all he really wanted was to reach up and cup her chin, see a flush of consciousness across her fine-boned cheeks and a softening spark of desire in those extraordinary cornflower-blue eyes of hers. He wanted her to bend an iota of space closer still and kiss him as if she meant it. Had that blow on the head truly driven all the sense out of it? Until now he hadn't thought he had enough masculine idiocy left in his pounding head to lust after this luscious mixture of a woman, but now it was sending messages to the rest of him he didn't want to hear. He must make her go, before she got killed, or noticed the state his body would be in if she didn't move further away.

'Get her out of here,' he risked demanding loudly as he dared.

'And risk whoever is out there attacking us?

Don't be more of an idiot than that blow on the head made you.'

'Is he coming awake at last, Row?'

Hearing the panic under that question, James hesitated and Rowena seemed caught between admitting it and laying them open to his enemy, or denying it and making her little sister more disturbed by the whole business.

'Wha…?' he moaned artistically and made the decision for her.

'Do be still and stay quiet, sir,' the fair Rowena ordered so sternly he suspected she would prefer to slap him.

'Who…?' He gasped, as if fighting unconsciousness, and now at least he could snatch a glance round the wide clearing and take in the slender options available.

'You saved my little sister's life,' Rowena proclaimed dramatically. He frowned under cover of her tumbling hair as she bent over him again to act out her fantasy heroine.

'Da…?' he managed. Maybe the watcher would believe him addled by the blow any listener must have heard, since it sounded like the crack of doom inside his head.

'I think our patient is asking if you are truly unscathed by your latest misadventure, Hes. Show yourself to the gentleman, dear, and prove you're truly in one piece, although you don't deserve to be after what you did.'

For a moment James dreaded the fearless girl being cowed by her lucky escape. Even if it might stop her being so reckless next time she wanted to defy gravity, he didn't want that. Then he caught the little devil peering at him over her grubby handkerchief with enough mischief in her eyes to supply the proverbial cartload of monkeys and had the deuce of a time not grinning back.

'Good...' he managed as if that was a small part of his worries taken care of.

'Perhaps his mind was affected by that blow,' the woman said hopefully. James thought that was taking drama too far, but it wasn't her mind so she probably didn't care.

'I'll never forgive myself,' Hester wailed, then buried her head in her handkerchief to muffle the noisiest pretend sobs James had heard in a mercifully long time.

At least she was suffering for her art, he concluded, with a fierce frown at the elder sister to make his impatience clear. He spared a moment to wonder why Rowena's tumbled mass of fair locks felt like a soft golden lure against his cheeks, then told himself not to be such a fool. It was hair, admittedly of the silken and shining kind, and as thick and soft as a lover's wildest fantasy, but still a workaday feature most women of her age enjoyed in one form or another. Reminding himself that blow on the head hadn't addled his wits entirely, he cleared his senses of Rowena Westhope and tried to use them on his enemy. Something told him the man was furious and impatient, and James couldn't spring up and dash for cover without warning his co-stars, so he made as if to sit up to divert them from amateur theatricals.

'No, sir, you must remain still until help comes. I couldn't live with myself if you did some terrible harm to your poor head because I lack the wit to keep you lying quiet,' the lovely Rowena said earnestly, fixing a steely gaze on him and daring him to argue.

'Grab her and run when I say so, then,' he demanded as softly as he could. Something in her wide blue gaze made him think it was highly unlikely the minx ever did as she was bid without an argument. Seeing a similar talent in the blue eyes her little sister fixed on him reproachfully, James shifted to test his reflexes. No better than satisfactory, he concluded, but they would have to do. 'Now,' he urged and wondered if he was about to faint and make this too easy for the shooter as he lurched to his feet.

He wasn't giving in yet; not after all the years of warding off blows and knife blades in dark alleys where the likes of him lurked. He imposed his steely will on his wavering legs and managed to keep pace with Rowena and her wriggling captive. At least this way a shot would hit him first. They were too close for even the best marksman to be certain of shooting him and not one of Finch's beloved daughters, and James sent a desperate plea to heaven to guard that good man's offspring from a death James probably deserved and they didn't. The hasty movement jarred his bruised and protesting head and spine, and he winced and waited for a kill shot to smash into him. Breath sawed in his labouring lungs as if he'd run a mile instead of a few yards. He thought for a moment he'd been shot and his body was keeping going in the long moment when terror blocked agony for mortally wounded men. He'd seen it, inflicted it even, yet he'd never felt it and by some miracle he still hadn't.

There were no more hurts to his person than Hester Finch had inflicted by accident when they reached the opposite side of the clearing. They sank into the sheltering hollow of a mighty oak tree's roots. It took the lack of any blood coursing out of any of them to convince him his foe hadn't risked picking him off, then getting away before anyone could give chase. This was no time to sink into the leaf-cushioned sanctuary and give in to the headache pounding at his temples, though. No rest for the wicked, he reminded himself ruefully, and managed to cling to his right senses by a hair's breadth.

'You're safe?' he gasped as if he'd run a mile instead of less than fifty yards.

'Aye, but how much do your enemies hate you?' Rowena asked impatiently, as if all her talent for pretence had been used up.

'Enough,' he admitted. Hester patted his shoulder solemnly, as if to console him.

He couldn't help the surprised guff of laughter it shocked out of him. She smiled wisely at him as if she understood his confused thoughts, which was more than her sister did from the impatient frown knitting her surprisingly dark brows.

'Some of them dislike me almost as much as my friends,' he joked. The girl's silent sympathy took him closer to tears than a grown man wanted to be, especially with a deadly enemy nearby.

'You can watch that way while I cover our backs,' Hester's unimpressed sister ordered him, expertly cocking his deadly little pistol, then turning away to ignore them both.

'She would learn how to shoot before she went to Portugal with Nate,' Hester explained with a shrug, as if that covered her sister's ability to defend them to the death.

'Nate?' he managed lamely.

'Her husband, he was a soldier,' the child said matter-of-factly.

James supposed that was what a generation or two of war did—made death part of day-to-day life and cut off a young woman's hopes and dreams in a moment. He risked a sidelong glance at the young widow and saw her intent glare into the middle distance, as if she'd cut herself off from them and her past. Somehow that moved him far more than the most delicate of flinches or a bravely blinked-away tear. The girl with the bluest of blue eyes he'd ever encountered had lost so much yet she had fire and courage enough to tie her knots and carry on. Wasn't it about time he did the same?

'I'm sorry for your loss,' he muttered.

'So am I,' was all she had to say to a stranger.

There was nothing else *to* say, so they sat still and tense for what seemed an age. Conscious he was being watched like a mother hen by the girl he'd set out to save only minutes ago, James tried to stay alert, or at least awake. Hester and her sister had saved his life as surely as he had saved Hester smashed bones and a broken head. If not for the outrageous deeds of Miss Hester Finch, James Winterley would be dead. As a corpse he'd be beyond hearing the robin shouting an urgent song from the nearest hazel thicket. In his half-dazed state, he knew he was lucky to be glaring into thin air to catch a hint of movement. He sat with the thought of all he might not be right now haunting him and was thankful he had senses left to gauge the world with. An assassin this good would never miss the mark he had made alone on that bench and as unguarded as he'd been since he was seventeen. Lucky for him the watcher turned up late and he imagined the man waiting for the perfect mark while he was trying to talk Hester out of her tree and constantly shifting for the best place to catch her if she fell.

It would have been an almost perfect crime; in their panic over their sister, Rowena and Jack wouldn't chase the killer of a stranger and by the time anyone else turned up the attacker would be long gone. James was glad he didn't sit in the man's shoes as he shifted uncomfortably in his own and went through a list of his enemies in his head. Did it all begin the day Pamela had taught him the real meaning of shame? Or when Luke had asked the question he'd been dreading and James couldn't meet his eyes and lie? That blow must have been worse than he thought because he regretted his past although it was too late to change any of it now.

'I believe help really is on its way this time,' Rowena announced in almost a normal voice. 'I can actually feel hoof beats coming through the ground after so many weeks without rain,' she added as if putting it that way was nothing out of the ordinary.

'Just as well you can, then; my foot's gone to sleep,' James muttered gruffly.

'If only that was all we had to worry about. Who is he?' she whispered sharply as soon as Hester was too busy craning her neck to see who was coming to listen to her.

'I don't know,' he admitted, trying not to shake his head and addle what brains he had left.

'You have so many enemies you don't know which one hates you most?'

'Yes,' he admitted baldly. If she knew how dangerous he was, she'd avoid him in future, if there was any future for him in the Raigne villages.

'Then I pity you,' she said in a low voice that sounded cold and final.

'Right now I feel quite sorry for myself,' he said wryly and shocked a rather delicious chuckle out of her.

'Who are you really?' she asked as if unable to control her curiosity any longer.

'Death,' he returned solemnly, the pain thundering at his temples making it sound like a perfectly sensible idea to him.

'James! What the devil have you been up to?' Luke's voice bellowed as he rode towards them as fast as he dared go on the hard-packed earth.

'Luke,' he said wisely, as if Rowena ought to know him. 'My brother; he'll see you both safe,' he confided and let the thunder engulf his senses again with a huge sigh of relief.

Chapter Six

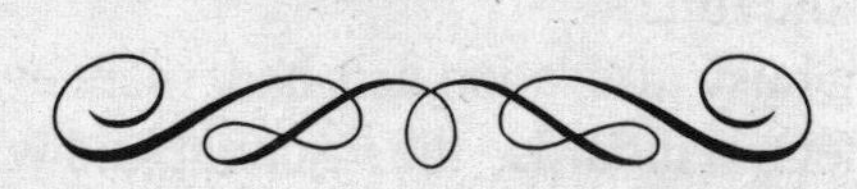

At least now Rowena knew Mr Winterley's first name, thanks to the lordly gentleman looking down his aristocratic nose at all three of them. He jumped off his horse and strode towards them, frowning as if this had to be somebody's fault and his brother was the most likely culprit.

'What's he done this time?' Lord Farenze asked roughly and made Rowena's hackles rise.

She'd quite thought she despised James Winterley for being handsome, rich, aristocratic and fashionable, before he fell at her feet and became a simpler nuisance. Now that she heard someone else unfairly criticising him she felt protective and angry on his behalf and realised it would be too easy to take more interest in Mr Winterley than was healthy.

'Your brother just saved my little sister's life and dodged an assassin's bullet before hitting his head so hard I wonder he still recalls his own name,' she snapped.

This time Mr Winterley came back to a sort of semi-consciousness more quickly. She saw him tense, then relax at the sound of his brother's voice raised in anger. He was hunched into the hollow like a hedgehog curled up in winter now and something about the defensive curl of his powerful body tugged at her heart. It didn't seem right he should fall into such a pose as if by second nature. Whatever this stiff-necked lord thought of his brother, even Mr Winterley had the right not to be wrong all the time.

'What a busy afternoon he's had, then, even by my little brother's standards,' the viscount said with a half-smile that betrayed affection for the man at his feet, even if he didn't want either of them to know about it for some odd masculine reason.

'Never mind that, he needs a doctor,' she informed him sharply.

'You can safely leave that to me, Miss…' He let his voice tail off as he waited for her to shuffle her name into the mix so he could dismiss her.

No, that was her own prickly uncertainty talking. He was waiting with grave courtesy for her reply and she wanted to shout that introductions were of no matter when a man was suffering, if not in grave danger. Then his lordship's gaze fixed on his brother even as he spared a small part of his mind to interrogate her and she could pity the chilly distance between them, as love was clearly buried under it somewhere.

'Mrs Westhope,' she told him as Hes wriggled against the fierce hug she was holding her with, as if to reassure herself the Finch children would never be estranged like these two haughty aristocrats. 'And this is my sister, Miss Hester Finch.'

'Mrs Westhope; Miss Hester,' the man acknowledged them, seeming so reassured by the even breathing of his own sibling he could spare Hes a smile and Rowena liked him a little better for it.

'Sir?' Hester said with a wobbly curtsy and quaint dignity Rowena wondered at.

How did the harum-scarum scamp go from wild savage to composed young lady between one minute and the next? Rowena wondered all over again at the changes a girl went through when she was no longer a little girl nor yet quite a woman. Hes was on the edge of all that promise and confusion, so perhaps it wasn't surprising she clung to childhood even as it slipped into something more complicated.

'I beg your pardon, ma'am,' the gentleman said with just enough of a bow not to hurt Hes's tender feelings, so perhaps he was human after all. 'Luke Winterley, Viscount Farenze, at your service,' he introduced himself.

'I know—is he your brother?' Hes asked, pointing at the man on the ground.

'My half-brother.'

'Is he the Honourable Mr Winterley, then?'

'No, my father didn't live long enough to inherit the title. My brother is a mere mister and regularly tells me he's proud of it. One day I might even believe him.'

'Papa says none of us can help the bed we're born in,' Hes replied sagely.

'True, but it's high time we got my brother to the nearest one, then waited for the doctor to tell us if his wits are addled by what *your* brother says was a blow fit to fell an ox.'

'How will he know?' Rowena shocked herself by asking.

'Good question.'

Now came the sound of anxious voices and the ring of iron-shod hooves on the dry pathway and the rescue party came into view. Jack jumped from the foremost cart before it halted, so he could see if Hes was unscathed by her latest adventure and, since she was dancing with impatience at Lord Farenze's side, be reassured she was lively as ever.

'Oh, hurry up, do,' Hes urged on the men following her brother. 'And make sure you don't hurt him.'

'I don't know why you're giving the orders; no thanks to you he isn't dead,' Jack objected.

Rowena knew he was so shocked he'd lost control of his temper and his tongue from sheer anxiety, but poor little Hester didn't.

'I didn't mean to; I never meant to hurt anyone,' she protested and seemed to realise how close she'd been to death today and what she owed the stranger who had stepped between her and the ground this afternoon.

'Don't say another word,' Rowena told her half-angry, half-ashamed brother as she hugged her sobbing sister close. If the truth were known, she felt a little overcome by the fear and drama of the last few minutes herself and, now they were all safe, had time to feel her own head aching as if in sympathy with stubborn Mr Winterley's greater hurt.

'But...' Jack stuttered out with a helpless look at Lord Farenze.

'I said, not another word, Jack Finch, and I meant it,' Rowena said sternly.

'Best do as you're bid, lad,' his new friend urged. Lord Farenze spared poor Jack a rueful shrug before rapping out orders.

Rowena secretly want to sob with relief with her

little sister. It felt so good to hear someone else take charge, she was in danger of being swept up by the force of Lord Farenze's personality, until he ordered her and Hes and Jack on to one of the carts from the Home Farm.

'No, we must go home. Our parents will worry themselves into an early grave once rumours we were involved in an accident start spreading.'

'No, can't go alone,' the supposedly unconscious James Winterley mumbled as if being brought back from somewhere much nicer by a persistent and annoying fly. 'Not safe.'

'Go back to sleep,' his brother barked impatiently. James Winterley smiled faintly, then seemed to do as he was told for once. 'Now, where were we, Mrs Westhope?' his lordship said with such ironic authority Rowena only just managed not to put her tongue out.

'Oh, very well,' she conceded, not because she thought they were in danger. After all, what had any of the Finch family done to provoke an assassin into lurking in bushes waiting to kill them? She told herself she'd relented because the idea of them going home without half a regiment to protect them seemed to agitate the stubborn idiot who had saved Hes. He really ought to let his brother take charge and give in to his raging headache. 'But we must send a note to say we're safe as soon as we get to Raigne.'

'Very well, now can we hurry?' the viscount asked wearily.

Lifting Hester into the cart, giving Jack a hand, then jumping up after him, Rowena braced herself for a rough journey. There were no springs to shield them from any dips in the woodland ride and she told herself to be glad this was Lord Laughraine's well-maintained parkland and not a rutted farm track.

'Pass the little maid up to us, Miss Row,' the stable boy urged and she saw how he and the slightly older driver padded the seat between them with their coats and was touched, so how could she refuse to let her little sister go?

'There now, Miss Hes, whatever 'ave you bin up to this time?' the boy asked with an urchin grin of complicity that restored Hes's spirits far better than sympathy.

Rowena exchanged a rueful, resigned gaze with Jack and wedged herself into a corner of the cart where she could use the sides to compensate for a rough passage. It reminded her of days on the march with Sir Arthur Wellesley's Peninsular Army. Her horse went lame for several days and she had eventually had to walk at the tail of the army with the rest of the wives, baggage and camp followers, instead of riding with the column. To a recently naïve girl from a country vicarage that journey was an education. One of the more raucous women offered a ride in the cart she used to carry anything she could buy or sell to the soldiers.

'What about the children?' Rowena protested weakly at the time, feet aching and blistered as never before.

'Too good for my cart, are you, my lady?' the woman mocked.

'No, it's not that,' she protested fervently, just in case it was.

'Then get in and don't argue, those mites can outrun you barefoot any day of the week, let alone this one,' the woman said with an almost-fond glance at the assorted tribe of urchins who'd attached themselves to the army along the way.

Rowena hoped they managed to survive the terrible retreat from Corunna as this cart rocked over a winter rut in the ride and she swayed with it as she'd learnt to on that rough and seemingly endless journey. Being shocked and frightened by what happened today in quiet England seemed almost an insult to the women still out in Spain and Portugal, clinging to the hard life they endured on the march to live with their men. Did many of them regret the dance or the chance encounter with a soldier that had led them to the life they had now? Shivering again, she struggled to think how she might feel right now if Nate had survived the Battle of Vimeiro. Their marriage hadn't exactly been the soaring romance she expected, had it?

By the end Nate would cuff her if his shirt was clean but not ironed, until she learned to dodge his fists. He blamed her for the lack of a fire or anything to cook on it, the state of the weather or even the proximity of the enemy. When her monthly courses came, she must sleep on the floor as she was unclean, although after a while lack of good food and the stress of being on the march and living with a bad-tempered husband dealt with that and they stopped. Nate took first choice of any food going because he was a man and needed it more. In fairness, she supposed he was partly right; they shared hardship on the road, but he had duties to carry out and enemies to fight, as well.

She knew Nate had felt grown up and glorious at Shorncliffe training camp when they were first married, but in the field he soon lost any illusion about the glories of war. Even she had thought it an adventure to set off for the Peninsula with her dashing young husband after two years of living a rather aimless life of tedium and scratch parties in Kent, then Ireland. She couldn't blame Nate for being unprepared for the hard truths of war when she was horrified by them, too. She mourned Nate as a heartbreakingly young man who met a hard end, but had never been able to admit to her parents she was guiltily relieved when her marriage was over. Did that make her a coward, she wondered, as the procession of carts slowly emerged from the woods and into the mellow autumn sunshine?

'I can see Dr Harbury's gig in the stable yard,' sharp-eyed Hester shouted over the rattle of iron-shod hooves and wheels on the smooth hoggin roadway.

'That's good news, Miss Hes,' her friend the stable boy said with a grin and a nod at the forward cart that contained Mr Winterley and his intimidating brother. 'We don't want Mr Winterley's brains addled when he's a pleasant-spoken gentleman and says he'll take my little brother on as stable boy soon as he's stocked his yard proper like. I hope he still remembers he offered our little 'un a place before he fell out of that tree.'

'*He* didn't fall out of it, I did,' Hester insisted rather proudly.

Rowena sighed and shook her head, wondering why her little sister thought she'd done anything to be proud of today.

'Did you now, miss? And you wi' no more'n a rip in your pinafore to show for it as well, but I suppose the angels bore you up like Moses, did they?' the older groom asked, as if he might believe it of any other child but this one.

'No,' Hester said, as if considering her own story

and deciding it was best edited a little after all. 'He caught me,' she admitted, with a wave at the cart now turning into the stable yard with a real live lord in it straining every muscle to save his brother from the worst of the inevitable jolts in their path.

'You've even better reasons than the rest of us to hope his brains ain't bin addled by you falling atop of him, then, ain't you, Miss Hes?' the elder groom observed sagely.

'Yes,' Hester admitted quietly.

'Indeed she has,' Rowena agreed as their cart wound into the yard last. She jumped out to lift her little sister down with a severe look she hoped would back up the groom's robust opinion of Miss Hester Finch's adventure *du jour.*

At the head of the procession Mr Winterley was being very carefully lifted out of his cart by his brother and two burly coachmen, and on to a hurdle someone had strewn with an exotic mix of silk-and-velvet cushions.

'Do you want to do yourself permanent harm, you idiot? No? Then keep still, for heaven's sake,' his exasperated brother barked when Mr Winterley did his best to see what was happening behind him.

'Look after them for me, Luke,' the man was begging softly when Rowena led her brother and sister forward in case he was straining to see them.

Whatever she thought of the gulf that lay between the vicar's brats and a rich and important lord's brother, she wanted the man to be well and arrogant again, not brought low by saving the little scamp now clinging to her hand like a limpet, as if the full magnitude of his possible injuries had finally hit home.

'Why?' Lord Farenze asked coolly.

Rowena shot him a glare for what he seemed to think about her and a man she hadn't been properly introduced to. As if she'd indulge in clandestine meetings with rakes, she decided disgustedly. She might as well have been a nun for the last two years and had wished she actually was one for an unhealthy chunk of her married life.

'Fouché,' Mr Winterley mumbled furtively in reply to that impudent query, just as if Bonaparte's infamous head of police might be hiding behind the mounting block, listening.

'What's that viper got to do with anything?' his brother asked and even Rowena wondered if the man was out of his wits from that crashing blow after all.

'Not you, me,' Mr Winterley muttered restlessly, as if he wished he could jump up and march away and take that danger away with him.

Not all the wishing in the world could overcome the concussion he was struggling with much longer, Rowena reflected, marvelling at the strength of will under that idle man-of-fashion disguise. Watching his drawn face, she could believe he really thought they were in danger from his clenched jaw and the faint frown knitting his dark brows. So what could an English gentleman have done to earn the enmity of that much-feared French official? And what did that make of his front as a dandified idler with nothing to worry about but the cut of his coat and the fall of his neckcloth? If that was a lie, he must be a very different man under all that show and perfection.

'Where the devil is the doctor? Tell him to hurry, as my brother is clearly out of his wits,' Lord Farenze barked at anyone close enough to hear that damning name.

No, he isn't, Rowena wanted to argue, but saw a warning in his lordship's steely grey-green eyes even as the words trembled on her lips.

'Harbury, thank heaven,' Lord Farenze added with such a fine pantomime of the terrified brother even Rowena believed him for a moment.

'My lord, Lady Farenze has a chamber prepared for Mr Winterley in the Old Lord's Rooms and I've been making sure Lady Laughraine lies down as I insist she must in her condition after such a shock.'

'Good man,' his lordship said with the masculine unease at matters feminine that seemed to dog even the most sophisticated and definite of men as far as Rowena could see.

'And you two can wait in the kitchens,' she announced to her own brother and sister in quite the grand manner, because then they might not find a reason to argue until they were in there and unable to resist the treats soft-hearted Cook would think they needed after such an adventure.

Luckily Jack and Hester simply did as they were bid with a sigh of relief. For some reason Rowena didn't want to be excluded from Mr Winterley's sick bed and learn his fate second-hand. Lord Farenze looked as if he might order her away as well, then shrugged and loped after the procession that was getting ahead of them so fast she had to trot to keep up.

'Lay him on the sheets, we've stripped off everything that could get in your way,' ordered composed and capable Lady Farenze.

Rowena had seen her at the heart of an eager circle

after church and thought her almost as beautiful as Callie. Unwilling to add herself to the awed hangers-on, she had stayed with the children while her father and mother did their duty, or marched her smaller brother and sister home when they got bored with pretending to be angelic.

'Callie claims you are a capable young woman, Mrs Westhope, so I hope you'll stay and help, since my husband looks nearly as likely to faint as his brother is right now,' Lady Farenze informed her as if there was nothing untoward about two ladies taking over a gentleman's sick bed. 'Luke, you'd best wait with Lord Laughraine in the library. Cribbage has sent for Sir Gideon, but he set out to visit Raigne Hill and Holton Badger this morning, wherever they might be, and I'm told he'll be some time.'

'If he's got all the way there, it'll take at least two hours for someone to find him and bring him back.' Rowena spoke up as she knew the area and they didn't.

'So we're left to cope with Lord Laughraine, who isn't as young as he likes to think he is, and you, Luke Winterley. You're clearly anxious as a mother hen and we'll do better without you, love,' Lady Farenze informed her stern and powerful husband. He gave her a rather helpless shrug that spoke of genuine fear for his not-so-little brother. 'Go and make sure his lordship isn't getting in a similar state about his favourite guest and stop anyone bothering Callie until she's feeling better,' his wife urged with an understanding of her husband's finer feelings. Rowena couldn't help but envy her as a wife, considering she never knew what Nate was thinking or, come to think of it, even wanted to know after the first few months of marriage.

This man shrugged once again and did as he was bid; Lord Farenze seemed to trust his wife's judgement and that was something to put aside and think about later, she decided, and let her gaze flick back to the cause of this upheaval. Now *he* would never trust anyone as his brother did his wife. The thought that was at least one thing she and James Winterley had in common was nothing to be proud of either.

'It's safe to open your eyes, James,' the lady told her patient and shot him a stern look when he recovered his fainting senses remarkably quickly.

'He always was as stubborn as a brick,' Mr Winterley informed her with a wry grin.

'He loves you,' she said with a very straight look.

'God knows why, damned if I do,' he muttered, then seemed to recall they weren't alone and closed his eyes again, as if to shut Rowena out.

She told herself she had no right to feel insulted as the doctor bustled into the vast suite of rooms an elderly Lord Laughraine had built when he could no longer go upstairs.

'I must now put you through a very thorough examination, Mr Winterley,' he warned his patient. 'I dare say Lady Farenze and Mrs Westhope will be more comfortable in the next room whilst I do so,' he added with the authority of his profession.

'You will call us if my brother-in-law tries to escape, won't you, Doctor?' the lady asked with a backward look at that gentleman to say she knew he would if he could.

'Cribbage and I can manage one fainting gentlemen between us, my lady,' the doctor assured them. Lady Farenze looked dubious, but led the way into the grand sitting room and shut the door behind them even so.

'I suspect James will want to curse freely, but you can tell me what the exasperating man has been up to this time while we're waiting,' the lady said as she turned her full attention on Rowena.

'My little sister is adventurous,' Rowena said carefully.

'You and your family have my sincere sympathy,' Lady Farenze said with a shudder. 'My niece is much the same age, so I'm qualified to ask exactly how "adventurous" your own firebrand has been today?'

'She has long been forbidden to climb certain trees in Lord Laughraine's plantation,' Rowena said carefully.

'Ah, that sounds like an irresistible challenge to me.'

'Exactly, but if we let her do whatever she pleased, she'd probably kill herself inside a week. At her age, something expressly forbidden seems nigh irresistible, however.'

They exchanged a resigned look at the contrariness of their own particular hostages to fortune. 'So there was a certain tree?' Lady Farenze prompted.

'One of the tallest in the wood and that makes it more of a challenge. I don't know if you have been right to the far western corner of that particular plantation and seen it, your ladyship, but it has slender, upright branches and a straight trunk so there is little anyone could do to recover a hold if they let one slip.'

'I begin to see how your little sister and James met. He pretends to be so careless and aloof, but I know perfectly well he'd never walk away from a child in trouble as your sister must have been as soon as she got very far up that tree.'

'She lost us far too easily and it took me a while to realise where she must be heading, so I have to be glad he was there for her when I was not, for her sake,' Rowena admitted even as she glanced at the closed door and wondered if Mr Winterley would recover as rapidly as her new friend believed, if her calm manner was anything to go by. 'A fall from such a height could easily have killed her,' she admitted with a shudder.

'If he's not careful the world will find out what a soft heart James Winterley keeps hidden under those fine waistcoats and that touch-me-not air.'

'He isn't quite what he seems, is he?' Rowena blurted out carelessly, regretting it when Lady Farenze's shrewd dark eyes sharpened and she raised an eyebrow in a sardonic trick she might have caught from her husband's brother.

'I suspect James has secrets even Luke hasn't dreamt of, but what made you see through his useless man-of-fashion act?'

'Something he said,' Rowena admitted uncomfortably.

She didn't want to lie to this wise and surprisingly friendly woman, but would if she had to. It was as well nobody but Rowena, Lord Farenze and the man himself knew Bonaparte's feared intelligencer might want James Winterley dead for some obscure reason.

'He must be further out of his wits than I thought if he's been dropping clues to his real self so carelessly.'

'I doubt he'll be that far out of them this side of the grave,' Rowena said impulsively, then regretted it as her ladyship looked even more intrigued. 'You must know him better than I do, of course,' she added hastily. 'I dare say I imagined too much from a few words murmured when Mr Winterley wasn't in his right senses.'

'And I suspect you're a very acute observer, Mrs Westhope. I shall be wary of saying or doing anything out of the way in your presence.'

'Oh, no, please don't be. Mr Winterley and I were in a situation that heightened our perceptions and that's all we'll ever have in common.'

'I seem to have made you feel uncomfortable on top of an afternoon I wouldn't wish on my worst enemy. I'm so sorry and promise to be no more wary in your company than with any other lady I would like to make a friend of. Lady Laughraine thinks a great deal of you, so it will be a shame if we cannot like each other because of a few clumsy words on my part.'

'You're very kind,' Rowena said uncertainly.

Lady Farenze looked incredulous, then laughed. 'No, I'm not. I'm ham-fisted and Luke would roll his eyes at the ceiling and try to cover up for me if he wasn't so busy pacing the carpet in Lord Laughraine's library. I'm very new at this viscountess business and I doubt I'll ever get into the right way of it.'

'You took charge of the situation when we got here and none of us was quite sure what to do first.'

'Oh, that was easy. I was housekeeper to the last Lady Farenze for a decade while I was busy raising my daughter as best I could. No, I must remember to call her my niece now, mustn't I? At any rate, Verity gave me plenty of practice at dealing with the consequences of mischief to her and anyone caught up in it.'

Rowena stood open-mouthed for a moment before

she snapped it shut. 'I thought you were a lady in your own right?' she said at last.

'I am, for what it's worth. When my twin sister died giving birth to Verity, my noble family and I parted company, since they wanted to put the poor little mite out in the snow and I wouldn't let them. I warned Luke I'd never be a credit to society, but he insisted on marrying me anyway.'

'As he's a noble and sensible gentleman, why would he not?' Rowena said and chuckled when her ladyship looked unconvinced. 'I'm so glad Callie has you as a friend. She is very sceptical about being "my lady" and has found it hard to get used to, as well. She loves Gideon so deeply it was heartbreaking to see them apart all that time as well and having you and your husband and brother-in-law here diverted her from fretting about Gideon's rank and having to be chatelaine of all this one day,' she added with a gesture at the treasures all around them.

'And there's the baby to cope with as well,' her new friend said frankly.

Thank goodness she wasn't mealy-mouthed about such a natural thing as Callie being with child so soon after being reunited with her husband. The lady had only been wed six months herself, if Rowena was remembering the tale Mrs Finch had passed on of how Callie's distinguished visitors fitted into her new life aright. She hadn't taken much interest at the time, doubting she would ever meet the fine lord and lady her mother referred to in person. Distinctions of rank and wealth didn't seem to mean much after her brief time in Portugal and she tried to avoid social gatherings where the sum of a person's ambition was to get a nod or even a faint word of acknowledgement from the great or the good.

'What with fretting if this one will be born well and healthy, and so many changes, I suppose it's no wonder Callie feels overwhelmed by all the changes in her life,' she agreed.

'Yes, it's better when a person has time to grow accustomed to one huge change before the next one comes along. I find it difficult at times to be my lady again rather than Mrs Err…and of no importance whatsoever. You have a talent for putting such things in perspective, Mrs Westhope.'

'My husband used to say I lacked imagination, then add there's no point being practical when the world is falling apart round you.'

'He didn't deserve you, then, did he?'

'Perhaps not,' Rowena replied, thinking of all the months of silent reproach Nate's mother piled on her for defects Nate must have complained of in his letters home. It really was high time she found her own place in the world and put all that behind her. 'We didn't suit very well.'

'You must have been very young when you wed.'

'I was eighteen and Nate was twenty.'

'Neither of you long out of the schoolroom, then.'

'Callie and Gideon were even younger when they wed, but they were truly in love.'

'And it's easy to be confused by a man and his feelings and desires when you have little experience of adult life yourself, is it not?'

'Some men are confusing whenever you meet them,' Rowena admitted unwarily.

'Which reminds me—one of the most baffling ones

I ever met is lying on the other side of this door. Shall we risk outraging his masculine sensibilities and see what the good doctor thinks? I don't know what they imagine we'll be shocked by, even if it's taken them all this time to get him undressed.'

'It's more their sensibilities than ours they fuss over, don't you think?'

'Aye, at heart men are far more pernickety about such things than women.'

'True,' Rowena agreed, rather relieved to find that a lady of such rank thought so, too. 'I suppose it's because women have to cope with as many, if not more, bitter truths than their husbands do.'

'And I suspect you've been closer to the edge of what it's possible to endure than most of us, but I won't press you for details. We'll talk about them another day, when you're not wrung out by events, and anxious about your sister and her rescuer.'

'Thank you,' Rowena said faintly.

'Being a housekeeper for so long has made me a very managing sort of female,' Lady Chloe Winterley admitted.

'Not at all,' Rowena said politely, thinking sometimes it felt quite pleasant to be gently managed for your own good.

'What a kind liar you are. Callie was quite right, I do like you. She said I would if I could get you to stop remembering your so-called place in life and be yourself.'

'I like you, too, but I doubt Callie told you I'm pliable and meek by nature, since she knows I'm nothing of the sort.'

'I'm making allowances for the shock your sister

and James gave you this afternoon. Am I right in thinking you were every bit as headstrong as your endearing little imp of a sister in your day? I was reputed to be much the same, but that's not how I recall it at all.'

'How very odd other people's memories are at times.'

'Infuriating, isn't it?' Lady Farenze replied with an urchin grin and led the way back into the state bedchamber.

'My lady, I must protest! Mr Winterley could have been stark naked for all you ladies knew of our progress.'

'Nonsense, Dr Harbury, and I'm a married woman even if you did happen to be such a slowcoach. I'm married to Mr Winterley's brother, what's more, and I doubt he has anything Luke doesn't, even when he's not respectably covered. So stop fussing and tell me what damage my brother-in-law has done to himself this time. My poor husband will need your services if you don't let me tell him the worst soon.'

'Mr Winterley has taken a severe blow to a vulnerable part of the head. He should remain perfectly still for the rest of the day and tomorrow, and not make any sudden movements for the rest of the week. Moving too sharply or being startled at such a delicate stage in his recovery could set off a series of events I don't like to contemplate.'

'Harbury thinks I'll end up a mooncalf if I'm not careful, Chloe,' Mr Winterley informed his sister-in-law with a tired sort of irony that wrung Rowena's heart.

His eyes were shut again and there was a set look to his mouth that said his head was hurting nigh unbearably. She had no idea why she was here all of a sudden. Some instinct had whispered his well-being was crucial to her, but that was ridiculous, wasn't it?

'How would we tell the difference?' Lady Farenze teased the patient lightly.

'Good point,' Mr Winterley said with a rueful smile.

Rowena wondered if he secretly worshipped his beautiful sister-in-law from afar. Unlikely, she decided, past a wistful feeling she wasn't going to think about. He didn't seem the sort of man to yearn after the unattainable, and Lord and Lady Farenze were deep in love and shared a strong bond even a stranger could respect and envy. The beauty and promise of such a true and mutual love tore at her heart for a moment. All nonsense; some people were unable to make such a strong connection with another being and she was one of them.

James Winterley was even more self-sufficient than she was and she sneaked a sidelong glance at him. It wasn't his manly beauty that made her shiver with something a little too intriguing for comfort. Nate had been a fine-looking man and Rowena was flattered by his attentions, but that was a place she must not revisit. There was something so vital and acute in the man's green-grey eyes when he opened them to lock on her as if he'd felt her attention, that the thought jarred through her she could have been deeply intrigued by him if things were different. So what did he see; a plain female of four and twenty with her hair down her back and her eyes haunted by this afternoon's events? Whatever he saw, he frowned as if he could read her mind and didn't want her gratitude.

She glared back militantly, for what else did he expect? He met her stare with an urgency she didn't understand and she shook her head, trying to make him realise she wouldn't talk about those terrifying moments in the wood when he was the target of hidden but relentless malice. Although she supposed she ought to tell his brother, if that would keep the stubborn great idiot safe until he was himself again, she decided with a frown. From the flare of fury in his gaze Mr Winterley had read her thoughts and wasn't that a disaster in the making? She held his gaze, because she'd promised herself she would never be cowed by another man once the sting of Nate's death faded. If she wanted to tell Lord Farenze his brother was lying when he shrugged off that one whispered word, she would. While Mr Invincible Winterley was laid up with a hurt he'd got saving her sister, she had a right to make sure he didn't get killed by his enemies thanks to Hester's adventure.

'Life is different for all of us now, James,' Lady Farenze warned him, as if she'd seen and understood too much of their silent exchange. 'You can't pretend to be as detached as one of the ancient gods of the mountains any longer.'

'Why not?' he asked with a frown that looked desperate and grumpy, instead of a formidable weapon when he was his usual haughty self.

'You're part of a family now, whether you like it or not.'

'I don't,' he grated out between tight lips.

'That's too bad, James, because we're not going away.'

'Don't be so sure. You need to talk to your husband if you think he's ever likely to admit me to it in anything more than form.'

'You are an idiot, James Winterley,' Lady Farenze told him brusquely.

He had tried imposing his will on his sister-in-law instead of Rowena this time. He must be having a deeply frustrating afternoon, she decided, as her new friend met his furious glare with a kindly smile, as if he was excused bad manners as he had the headache.

'My patient might turn into one of those in truth if we don't leave him in peace now, Lady Farenze,' the doctor cautioned fussily.

'If we do, he'll be out of bed and off before we're hardly out of the door. Someone he can't order out of the way like a bad-tempered general must stay with him until he's either asleep or ready to admit he's in no fit state to go anywhere today.'

'That will be me, then,' Lord Farenze observed from the doorway and frowned even more formidably than his brother when his wife looked sceptical about the idea.

'James is supposed to be kept quiet and calm for the next couple of days, not wound like an overstressed spring, Luke Winterley.'

'I'm not often accused of being a rattle-pate,' her husband argued and Rowena wondered if she was about to be caught up in a family argument, before both the lord and his lady decided this situation was irresistibly amusing at the same time and laughed instead.

'Ignore them,' Mr Winterley advised as he opened his eyes to gaze at his brother and sister-in-law with baffled affection, 'they can't help it.'

'No, I really don't believe they can,' she agreed softly.

It was hard *not* to envy the love that bound this pair

so closely together that it made her wonder how it felt to be so deeply in thrall to another human being. She was surprised to see a similar puzzlement in Mr Winterley's eyes and let herself see a deeper man than she wanted to know about behind his air of sophisticated aloofness.

'Did you see anything?' he asked so softly she was sure nobody else heard. Luckily the lovers were occupied with each other and the doctor was busy tutting disapprovingly at such odd behaviour in a sickroom.

'No, if not for that shot I wouldn't be sure I didn't imagine him,' she whispered.

It was true; there was only a hint of stealthy movement behind those thick branches, yet she knew someone was in that stand of evergreens eager to harm him as surely as if he'd marched into it without any effort at concealment. She hadn't imagined that shot as he fell to the ground with Hes clutched to his chest either. Remembering that terrible moment with a shudder now, she knew falling over that root had saved his life, so perhaps Hes was the heroine of this tale after all. The man was in acute danger from at least one enemy and if he wouldn't take it seriously, she'd make sure his brother did.

'Promise you'll be wary from now on?'

'I'm not the one someone is shooting at,' she replied impatiently and their quiet exchange must have reminded the lovers this wasn't a farce laid on to amuse them as they turned suspicious eyes on both of them this time.

'Promise?' James Winterley urged her as Lord and Lady Farenze looked as if they thought they'd missed something vitally important.

'Yes, and I'll keep a watch on Jack and Hes, as well.'

He sighed and closed his eyes, frowning against the fierce headache he must be suffering from. Silly to wish she could stay and soothe his tension away as she had in the woods. She had to get Hes and Jack home and admit what nearly happened to her parents, before the family heard the tale second-hand and much embroidered by the gossips.

'If you're sure Mr Winterley hasn't come to any great harm, I should like to get my brother and sister home if Dr Harbury will allow it?'

'Bed's probably the best cure for the shock they both had today. Tell the little rascal this gentleman will do, as long as he refrains from sudden movements and does as he'd told. I'm sure you don't wish to be unable to walk or talk properly for the rest of your life for the sake of taking a few days of idleness to prevent it, Mr Winterley.'

His patient waved a resigned hand and went back to his headache, but Rowena knew he'd have his brother to contend with if he tried to get up too soon now.

'If you will make sure Miss Hester Finch is quite recovered before she goes home, Doctor, you can save yourself the trouble of another call,' Lady Farenze added.

Rowena knew her new friend was making sure his bill landed on her husband's desk rather than Reverend Finch's. The lady clearly knew how it felt to stretch a budget so finely an unexpected bill from the doctor could land you in debt.

Chapter Seven

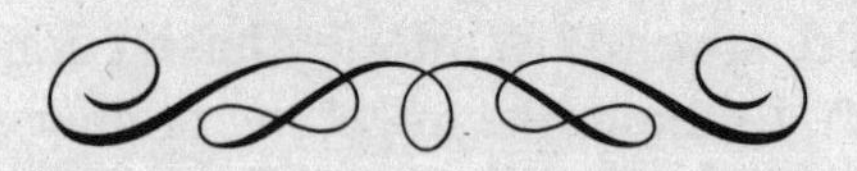

'So what's he really like under all that gloss and style, Row?' Joanna Finch asked her elder sister once everyone else was in bed late that night.

They were sharing a room as they had most of their lives until Rowena married, and it felt familiar and strange to exchange the little details of daily life before they slept once more. At twenty Joanna was angelically fair, slender as a wand and incurably interested in her fellow beings. Her shining happiness at the prospect of marrying her curate in a matter of weeks made Rowena feel middle-aged and jaded rather than barely four years older than her next sister in line.

'I have no idea who you mean,' she lied and avoided Joanna's interested gaze.

'Why, your Mr Winterley, of course, and are you ever going to tell me what really happened in the woods this afternoon?'

'He's not my Mr Winterley.'

'Don't be difficult, Rowena,' Joanna said in her best imitation of their mother in a rare stern mood.

'I doubt he's anyone's Mr Winterley but his own.'

'Ah, so that's why you're so prickly about him; he's a kindred spirit.'

'I really have no idea what you mean,' Rowena informed her sister gruffly and hid behind her hair.

Of course she needed to tease out the tangles it had got itself into during a long and difficult day, so it might as well make itself useful and hide her from Joanna's gaze. Maybe she *did* feel oddly connected to the man, but that meant it was even more sensible to avoid him until the feeling went away.

'The gentleman sounds hard to know and over-fond of his own company, so a perfect match for you.'

'Nonsense. You always accuse me of being aloof whenever you can't get what you want to know out of me fairly.'

'I can't imagine what you mean, sister dear. I do know Nathaniel Westhope wasn't the man we hoped and you can't go on letting him spoil your life from beyond the grave. Please don't poker up and defend him as if everything was perfect between you, because being dead doesn't make him a saint. Papa can say what he likes about not judging our fellow beings lest we be judged in return, but I can't help it. He hurt you.'

'I'm sorry he's dead; I have to be when he was so young, Joanna. We tried to live with each other for four years, but we were an ill-matched pair,' Rowena admitted stiffly. There seemed little point pretending her marriage was happy when Joanna and her parents knew she was lying. 'I haven't been a good sister to you since I came home either, have I?'

'Oh, nonsense, you couldn't be a better one if you tried from now until doomsday, but you hide so much of yourself from the world it feels strange to have you back and feel you're close and far away at the same time.'

'I suppose it must be, but the years we spent apart changed us both. You're a beautiful woman now and Mr Greenwood's betrothed; I'm past my first bloom and Nate's widow, and some things between a husband a wife must stay unsaid, even to a beloved sister,' Rowena said, all the things she couldn't tell an eager bride-to-be about her own marriage uneasy on her mind.

'Doesn't not saying them make them more important?' Joanna challenged. 'You should tell someone and, if you're too wary or protective of me or Mama, why don't you confide in Callie? She's kind and compassionate and life was hard for her until recently. You can't protect her from the big, bad world when she already knows far too much about it.'

'She's *enceinte*,' Rowena said and wondered if she would confide in her friend even if she wasn't.

'And must be added to your list of people to keep at arm's length for their own good, I suppose? I doubt she'll take to being on it any better than I do, by the way, unless she's changed out of all recognition and I see no sign of it so far.'

Rowena thought her friend *had* changed. There was a reserve about her the Callie Sommers of ten years ago would have scoffed at. Rowena felt more akin to her than ever and they had managed to exchange letters over the years when time, overseas postings and Callie's wicked aunt permitted—which probably meant the old cat lifted the seal with a hot knife and read them before deciding whether to pass them on or not. If anyone knew how it felt to be set apart from the rest of your kind by bitter experience, it was Callie. Even so, with a child already on the way, how could she add her trivial ills to the worry Callie and Gideon must struggle with until this baby was safely born?

'She can't be that offended, or she wouldn't have asked me to work for her,' she said to divert her sister from her favourite occupation—ruthlessly improving the happiness of those she loved.

'I doubt she needs a nanny, since neither of them will let the baby out of their sight.'

'I expect you're right, but this is nothing to do with the baby, or only indirectly.'

'Then for goodness' sake tell me, Row, and stop being so mysterious.'

'You do know I'm hoping you'll be so fascinated by your Mr Greenwood's secrets you'll forget everyone else's from now on, don't you?'

'Sorry, but I shall never be that distracted, even by Antony. You have to tell me about Callie and Gideon's offer now you've trailed it so cunningly, even if you only did it in the hope I shall forget to fish for those precious secrets of yours.'

'You're as persistent as a gadfly, Joanna Finch,' Rowena said with a half-serious frown.

'Tell me what they've offered you, then,' Joanna said with a long-suffering sigh.

'They want me to act as Callie's secretary. She has so many new duties to perform and wants to spend more time with Gideon and her grandfather. Do you promise to keep it a secret if I tell you what else I would be doing?'

'Yes, so long as Antony doesn't need to know.'

Rowena considered her sister's priorities. The Reverend Greenwood was a good and compassionate man, so if he ever did need to know it could only be for a good reason. 'Callie has written a novel. It will be published next year and she hopes her true identity will not get out, so hence the need for secrecy.'

'How clever of her; what if it leaks out anyway, though? We both know lady novelists are frowned at by the high sticklers and mocked by the critics.'

'Gideon is so proud of her I doubt if he'd mind who knew or what they thought about it. Anyway, the printer is eager for her next book and I can help with that. Callie has most of the manuscript roughly written, but Gideon says she needs help with making a fair copy and I am to be her scribe for any further books as well as helping with her duties as her grandfather's hostess and future mistress of Raigne.'

'Excellent. I don't think the life of a lady's companion or a governess would have suited you at all, so at least you will have to let go of that silly idea of advertising for a position. I know you've acted as Mrs Westhope's unpaid companion these last two years and we both do our best to keep our little brothers and sisters out of mischief, but I want you to be happy, Rowena. With Callie and Gideon you will be valued and treated as part of the family and at least now we won't have to worry about you being all alone and far away from everyone who loves you.'

'You do know I'm the eldest and quite capable of worrying about my own future, don't you? I believe your Mr Greenwood is destined to be a bishop before he's forty with you behind him pushing and prodding, Joanna Finch,' Rowena said, not sure when her sister had got to be so observant and a little scared of what she might see next, if she let her.

'Antony has a fine mind and a great heart. If the world needs him to shine in such a role, then he has the humility and gentleness to weather it better than a good many men of the cloth,' Joanna said as if life was that simple and maybe it was, for a couple of fine people who simply loved each other beyond question.

Rowena hid a smile behind her now-shining blonde curls before she parted them carefully and began to weave them into night-time plaits. 'And the perfect wife to help him do so?' she teased.

'Well, of course, that goes without saying.'

'What do you imagine I'm going to do with this?' James barked at the footman who entered the grand bedchamber of the Old Lord's Rooms with his breakfast the next morning.

'Eat it, sir?' the man said with an admirably straight face.

James almost laughed, until his stomach rumbled insistently and made it clear a bowl of thin gruel and a cup of weak tea wouldn't suffice. He sighed, shook his head and eyed the so-called meal with the contempt it deserved.

'I'll fetch Lord Farenze,' the footman said with the air of a man with a broader pair of shoulders to drop his burdens on in his sights, then left the room before James could argue.

'George says you won't eat your nice gruel,' Luke said as he strode into the room a few minutes later.

'And you know what you can do with it, don't you?' he responded grumpily.

'Feed it to the pigs? I met Callie's maid coming downstairs with a tray like yours and every bit as untouched, poor girl.'

'Poor indeed if she's faced with that for breakfast until she's safely brought to bed.'

'I'm sure Gideon will prevent her and his child wasting away long before then, but I'm still not going into battle with Mrs Cribbage for you.'

'I might as well get up and do it myself, then.'

'Since you're going anyway? Think again, little brother. Chloe got George to remove all your clothes from the room you were occupying, then gave orders you're not to have them back until she says so.'

'Do you enjoy living under the cat's paw? Damned if I do.'

'Of course I do and don't imagine you'll persuade me to oppose the best way to stop you galloping off on the first horse you can heave a leg across without falling off the other side by questioning my wife's wisdom.'

'Even if I was poleaxed by that tap on the head I'd stay on better than that, but why are you suddenly so keen on my company you can't let me go?'

'Maybe you're the grit in my oyster,' his brother answered with a wry smile.

'More like the caterpillar on your cabbage.'

'Cabbage, what on earth is that?'

'You can't fool me; I was brought up at Darkmere, as well. It was boiled cabbage to go with our boiled fish every Friday or go without. I hope you still recall the taste and order something less awful for your own brats.'

'Eve never suffered it, so I doubt we'll start now,'

Luke said with such a contented grin James had his suspicions confirmed.

'When's it due?'

'We think April, but Chloe wanted it kept quiet until Callie feels better. She's probably realised she'll get gruel and weak tea for breakfast if we don't.'

'Rubbish, you'd starve yourself rather than let your wife go hungry.'

'I would, but Chloe got over the worst of her sickness before she insisted we came to Raigne, so I won't have to. I'd fight sterner foes than Mrs Cribbage for her, but that's what love does to a man; you should try it some time.'

'You can't wish me on some poor female who's done nothing to deserve it.'

'Rubbish, the right wife could be the making of you.'

'I'm not sure I want to be remade and I'm better off alone.'

'Thinking that way made me lose years of happiness with Chloe,' Luke said flatly. 'I'm not sure I can ever quite forgive myself for them.'

James felt guilty about the gulf between Luke meeting Chloe and realising he'd never be happy without her. James didn't come between them, but he didn't have to, did he? His youthful sins did it for him. His brother had taken a decade to learn to trust another woman after Pamela turned him into a bitter recluse and he'd certainly played his part in that.

'And I refuse to take a wife simply because you three renegades have done so.'

'Yet you could be happy with the right one, James. There's a deal of good in you, if only you'd admit it.'

Virginia's mistaken opinion echoed in James's head and made him wonder how two people he loved could be so mistaken in him. 'No, I'm a lost cause. Remember what damage I can do without even trying very hard and leave me be, Luke. Make sure they send in a decent breakfast before you do, though; I need better than this if I'm to go the devil in any style at all.'

'You're not going anywhere.'

'I must; I'm dangerous,' James said with bitter desperation.

'Ah, so we're back to Fouché again, are we?'

'Who?'

'You know exactly who. What have you really been up to all these years, James?'

'I would have thought that was obvious,' James drawled uneasily.

'I should have paid more attention instead of taking the gossip and scandal at face value, but I'm looking now. Are you finally going to tell me what's been going on while I was busy raising Eve, feeling sorry for myself and missing Chloe? Or do I have to lock myself in here with you and badger you until you do?'

'Just this and that—mostly that,' James managed wearily.

'It's not as if Virginia didn't try to warn me,' Luke admitted with a dogged patience that made James even more uneasy, 'but I refused to take her seriously. More fool me.'

'Does it matter? We've been going our own way for a decade and a half and I see no reason to change.'

'First Chloe and Eve made me think hard about who I am and then I got round to you, little brother. That's when I realised your life doesn't add up. After that I wondered if your enemies could possibly be even slower on the uptake than I am, what do you think?'

'No, and that's why you have to let me leave. That blow on the head must have knocked some sense in because I know now that it's high time I left Raigne and went back to town where I'll do less harm.'

'Why? Where could you be safer than in the midst of Lord Laughraine's household with most of your family around you?'

'Gideon's lady is carrying the child they waited nine years to risk making and now you tell me Chloe has my next niece or nephew growing in her belly and you want me to put them all in peril for the sake of my own worthless hide? Not while I've breath in my body to draw the jackals away. Help me go, Luke, I can't have them on my conscience, as well.'

'You care too much and not too little, don't you?'

'Nonsense, you know very well I tread a bit too lightly through life.'

'So you've been tugging on Fouché's smoky tail for fun, have you?'

'Oh, no, that was for revenge,' James admitted unwarily.

Bonaparte led his people with an iron hand in a velvet glove, but Fouché was his bared left fist; his enforcer. Hebe's death had made James lash out at the man who caused it, even if he didn't actually wield the knife.

'Reckless of you,' his brother observed quietly.

'Yes, I was a fool.'

'Now I've thought you many things in my life, James, but never a fool.'

'Think again,' James replied wearily.

'I asked the wrong questions that day, didn't I?' Luke shocked him by asking out of the blue. The one he did ask all those years ago echoed in James's head even now. *Did you bed my wife?* 'I don't care if Eve is yours or mine, James. I love her and never mind which of us planted her in Pamela's belly. If the trull was only put on this earth to give birth to Eve I thank her for it and for abandoning Eve as a baby so she's untainted by whatever made Pamela as she was.'

'You're better than I am, then. I curse her name every time I recall she existed,' James admitted unwarily.

'Ah, so my Chloe's right, then; Pamela did something truly wicked to the boy you were back then.'

'Man enough for her purposes,' James muttered uneasily. He'd spent half his life trying not to talk about it. Now Luke was forcing him to recall things he wanted to forget.

'Tell me, then it will be over and done with at long last.'

'I'm a human butterfly, Luke; when did one of those ever stop to consider the damage it did as a caterpillar?'

'However hard you pretend to be a flibbertygibbet with no feelings or conscience, I know you're the opposite at heart and I'm not going anywhere until I have the truth.'

'You have a wife and daughter and another life on the way to protect and cherish. Let me go my own way again and concentrate on keeping them safe.'

'Stop being so melodramatic, little brother. You always did take yourself too seriously.'

'What I'm tangled up in *is* serious.'

'Then the sooner you tell me, the sooner we can make it less so.'

'You think it's that easy?' James was so shocked he almost laughed.

'We're brothers—hurt one Winterley and you hurt them all, but we can consult Gideon later. For now tell me what really happened to you with that she-devil I wed when I was wet behind the ears. At the time I swallowed Pamela's version and I suppose that proves how young and stupid I was myself. Tell me the truth now, little brother, so we can move past it and get on with our lives.'

'I was a stupid boy, Luke. You know what callow youths are like at that age,' James said in a cowardly attempt to hint at the tale, then leave it at that.

'I do, but you were never all that foolish, even at an age when a boy struggles to live in a man's body.'

'I must have been, mustn't I?' James said bleakly.

'I was the fool. I refused to see how wicked Pamela was until she decided being my lady one day wasn't enough for her any more and shattered my illusions.'

'She was your wife.'

'And I was a young idiot. Eve made me grow up, but you had to do it alone.'

'I hope you don't pity me?' James asked incredulously.

'You wouldn't let me if I wanted to. So are you going to tell me what you really got up to with my first wife behind my back?'

'I don't remember,' James almost shouted because it shamed him to admit it. 'I simply woke up one morning with her…' He paused, unable to go on because, whatever else she was, Pamela had been Luke's wife at the time. 'The night before I drank so much I collapsed into bed and slept like a fool. I don't even remember staggering upstairs and getting undressed. Whatever I drank and however I slept, I still woke up in the usual state an untried boy of seventeen wakes up in and well, I'm sure you can fill in the details for yourself,' he finished saying weakly, feeling the hot flush of shame he'd lived with ever since burning across his cheeks in a cool, darkened room seventeen years on.

'You're telling me she took advantage of a devilish need most lads of seventeen have to struggle with every day of their life?'

'Yes, damn it. Even when I woke to find her doing so, I couldn't stop myself enjoying it. Until that moment I would have given my eye teeth to wake up thus with any other woman but her and my cock wasn't listening when I screamed at it to stop. She laughed at me and carried on and I wasn't man enough to stop her, Luke. There, now you know the worst and that we can never be friends again, so there's no need to tell me so.'

'When did it happen?'

'A week or so before she left you and went to live with her sister until Eve was born. I bolted for my mother's house as soon as I'd got my clothes halfway on my back that morning and felt steady enough on my feet to run down to the stables, throw my saddle on a horse and ride to Kent as fast as the poor beast could carry me.'

'Eve is not yours, then.'

James hated himself for putting his brother through

sixteen years of doubt because he had lacked the grit to tell his whole tale instead of whatever travesty Pamela twisted it into.

'I know it in my head,' he admitted as the idea of Eve as his flitted guiltily through his head as it had done now and again for the last sixteen years and wanted to settle down, despite the impossibility of her birth at full term seven months after that rough awakening to life as a man instead of the boy he suddenly knew he'd been until that moment. 'No thanks to me your daughter is truly yours, so can I have my clothes now?'

'No, I'm not letting you stick your head in an enemy's noose because Pamela avenged herself on me in the most cunning fashion she could think of over a decade and a half ago. We have to trap the man on your tail, then get on with our lives and after that you can rebuild that ruin you're inexplicably fond of and breed horses or whatever you intend to do.'

'*We* don't need to do anything.'

'Do you think nobody else has the wits to ward off a dangerous enemy, then, little brother?'

'And how can you call me that now you know what I did?'

'I expect Pamela made sure you were so drunk you hardly knew your own name the night before she carried out her scheme to divide us for good. Maybe she helped your youthful desires along with some devilish concoction as well; she did it to me once after I'd told her I didn't want her or her sick fantasies any more. She loved having power over men and used to shock, tease and seduce me until I hardly knew black from white. You did what any boy would when she had him under her power in so many ways that morning. A great many would not have torn themselves away so quickly either. Most boys would go back for more and no doubt she expected you to do the same. She told me you were her long-time lover and only stopped visiting her bed when she was so fat and ugly with the brat the Winterleys got on her between them you couldn't endure to mount her any longer. That's why I reacted as I did when I challenged you and you simply admitted you'd slept with her.'

'I was simple indeed, wasn't I?'

'You were seventeen, James. I was cynical enough by then to know there was nothing Pamela wouldn't do to convince herself she was irresistible to our sex. I said I asked you the wrong question, but now I blame myself for asking it at all. I did things with her it sickens me to think about. You being taken advantage of one morning when you were half-drunk and probably drugged is less than nothing next to them.'

'That's it, then? I'm to consider myself absolved?'

'Maybe you'll feel better if I say you've already suffered for what you could have done very little to stop at the time.'

'I could have invented my own personal Arctic to spoil her morning ride.'

'Be a seventeen-year-old lad again and tell me that. No, you have to forgive yourself and let this idea of yourself as a shamed outcast go. I know it will cost a huge effort because you were born stubborn and melodramatic. I blame your mother.'

James roared with laughter at that favourite phrase of his own mother when Luke did something she didn't like as a boy, which was most of the time. He felt a great burden fall from his shoulders and his brother's remark seemed exquisitely funny. It was so good to laugh with him for the first time in so long it almost hurt.

Chapter Eight

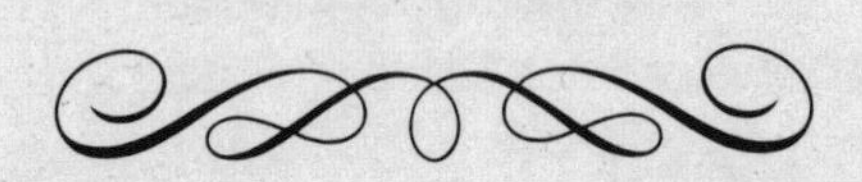

Outside the fine range of windows she hadn't even taken in as belonging to the Old Lord's Chambers when she came out here to think in peace, Rowena let out a long sigh as quietly as she could and wished there was a way to stop her ears burning. Or to not be here and not overhear what she'd just overheard. It had looked exactly the spot she needed when she slipped through the half-open oak door and into the mellow old knot garden in search of peace and quiet. Deserted and calm and slanted with October sunlight and shadows, she thought it the ideal place to sit and consider Callie and Gideon's urgently restated opinion she was the right person to help them through a very different life to any they were used to and could she start tomorrow?

She wrung her hands like a tragedienne as that problem faded into obscurity and she tried to think of a way out of here without letting them know she'd heard them. The silence inside argued the brothers were either thinking of what they'd told each other, or his lordship had gone away so she only had James Winterley's wolf-like senses to cope with now. If she so much as shifted on her stony bench he might hear her and she didn't dare put a foot to the ground. So she sat and agonised about what to do next. Should she admit she was here and apologise for knowing what that wicked woman had done to a mere boy?

Never, her inner coward protested and the rest of her agreed so fervently she nodded, then furtively looked about her, as if even that unwary movement might give her away. How could she face sophisticated, mocking Mr Winterley's gaze with the knowledge of all he'd suffered at seventeen and not blush like a peony? If anyone else knew, some crass idiot would turn his tale into a vulgar romp and make out he was a lucky devil to wake up being pleasured like that. She thought of her brothers and shuddered at the very idea some ruthless harpy might do the same to them without their consent or much cooperation one day. She couldn't be an elder sister or a soldier's widow without knowing young men had lust-bedevilled urges they either battled with or succumbed to. Even so, to take what wasn't willingly given like that seemed every bit as wrong in a woman as it was in a man.

She shuddered and did her best not to recall how that felt. Nate had at least been familiar to her and her husband. Still, memory of the first time he ignored her *No* made her shake so hard right now she nearly forgot where she was and moaned out loud. How helpless and violated she'd felt when her husband took her anyway and seemed to enjoy the marital act far more when she didn't even pretend to want it. Forcing himself on her might prove he was a potent and powerful man who only wanted women, so he did it and proved himself a liar. Looking back, she could pity as well as despise him, but if Pamela Winterley was in front of her right now there wouldn't even be an iota of mercy for the drab in her heart as she accused her of…of what exactly?

Destroying a young man's hopes and dreams for the sake of revenge? But revenge for what? Surely all Lord Farenze did was be her husband? As heir to Viscount Farenze after his ailing father, no doubt he was a very desirable *parti* when they married and even if he hadn't loved her, he would never have abused her. He was too much like his younger brother to dream of it—where had that certainty come from? She reminded herself it didn't matter what the Winterley brothers were really like; she wasn't in the market for another husband and certainly not the only one available now his brother had remarried.

Anyway it was clear to her this Pamela had had no excuse for acting as she had. Part of her was deeply shocked the woman abandoned her baby daughter without so much as a backward look, as well. Whatever her twisted reasons for leaving her husband and family, the harpy left a seventeen-year-old boy ashamed and isolated and adrift in the world. Her heart went out to him so hungrily she wanted to go back and hug that boy and reassure him it wasn't his fault; and he would always be a better man than he thought he was.

Oh, but that was nonsense as well, wasn't it? He was who he'd made himself and wouldn't thank her for her pity, heaven forbid, so somehow she had to get out of here before he found out she knew. It was so quiet, could he be asleep? Dr Harbury would certainly hope so. She tried not to think about the leap of fear her silly heart had taken when a whisper that the good doctor predicted dire consequences if his patient didn't take the week of rest reached her. No doubt the man had a head like rock and would walk away looking debonair as soon as some kindly soul handed him his dandified clothes.

'Here's your breakfast,' Lord Farenze's voice announced on the other side of those heavy brocade curtains and dashed her hopes of a timely getaway.

'Ah, that's better. Put it here, Huddle, then make yourself scarce. Unless you're going to defy my lordly brother and bring me my breeches?'

'Er…'

'I thought not; now get out before I waste this tea by throwing it at you.'

'Yes, sir,' Huddle said with a grin even Rowena could hear in his voice.

'You're only a paper tiger, aren't you, little brother?' Lord Farenze's gruffer voice observed from a little too close for comfort and she sat here, silently dreading he'd push a curtain aside to stare out whilst his sibling ate.

'Don't tell anyone, will you?' James Winterley replied through whatever his lordship had managed to cozen out of Cook. 'And stop stealing my toast,' he demanded.

Rowena let out a silent sigh of relief when she heard his lordship step further away and argue amicably with his brother over what sounded like an enormous breakfast, or whatever it could be called at this hour of the day.

'That's much better,' James said when he could eat no more and Luke had demolished what was left.

'What's to be done about your other little problem?' Luke asked as if that was all they ever need say about Pamela and maybe he was right.

'I'd hardly call it little.'

'No, but we agreed about your tendency to high drama just now, didn't we?'

'This isn't something to solve with a lordly declaration and an impatient sigh,' James said, sobering as he recalled the mess he'd be dragging his family into if he didn't leave now.

'What is it, then? You owe Gideon an explanation, since anything that troubles one of us affects us all and it's high time you realised it.'

James wondered if he could plead a headache or deny anything of the sort, but Luke was right, he couldn't do this alone now. He'd tried so hard to make sure his family was untouched by his other life; put walls round his true identity whenever he went to the Continent and took complex routes in and out of his other identities. Only three people knew him in both guises—four, now he must include Luke; the other two were patriots, but most people could be bought for the right price. He must have looked pained at the very idea Bowood and his father would give him away if the inducement was high enough, because Luke now looked ready to believe in that headache after all. Tempting to let that be his excuse for waving it all away and trying to sleep his day away, since Chloe and the doctor deemed he must and he might as well restore himself to the best condition he could before he tracked down his latest enemy.

'Promise only to tell Gideon and try to swear him

to secrecy?' he managed past that temptation and the secretive habits of half a lifetime.

'True marriage goes far deeper than you know, James. I can't promise Chloe or Callie won't know something is afoot simply because we do.'

'I don't want any of you involved.'

'Too late. I'm your brother; Gideon and Tom are kin of the heart thanks to Virginia's interference and you can't keep us at arm's length any longer.'

'Oh, very well, but don't forget you insisted on knowing, I doubt there's any need to remind you I kicked up so many larks at Oxford I had to be bailed out by you, is there?' He began his tale at the beginning.

'I said I'd paid your debts for the last time and you told me you'd beg in the streets for your bread rather than ask for another penny.'

'Knowing we'd fallen out, a man I knew at Oxford took me home that summer and although I didn't know it at the time, his father is the kingpin in one of the unseen wheels the government likes to deny it has.'

'And he recruited you at not quite eighteen years old? I wish I'd known so I could put a stop to such dangerous nonsense.'

'No, as the second son what else could I have done? I'd have made a terrible priest and would have been court-martialled for insubordination if I had gone into the army or navy. Being a spy and adventurer suited me and I was good at it, before I lost my temper this spring. I certainly don't need the fortune you three worked so hard for under the terms of Virginia's will.'

'Then why the deuce didn't you tell us? We had to dance to Virginia's tune all year to secure it for you.'

'You were all having so much fun I didn't like to spoil it.'

'Why didn't you give *me* a hint you'd become so warm in the pocket.'

'Would you have believed me?'

'Before I had to come to terms with loving Chloe, probably not; I was too much of a cynic to see beyond my own troubles and thought supporting you explained why my stepmother outruns the constable long before every quarter-day.'

'As if I would take her pin money, not that I could rely on it as she gambles it away nearly as soon as she gets it. Did you never wonder why Father kept her at Darkmere and refused to let her visit London or Bath, despite all her pleading and fits of temper? He even persuaded Virgil she should only be given use of the Dower House in Kent on condition she didn't leave it for more than a sennight at a stretch. She wagered every penny she could get hold of by fair means and foul all their married life and I've been buying up her debts since he died. How she manages to run them up in Haslet Hall Dower House is a constant source of wonder to me, but she does it despite the precautions he and I put in place to stop her.'

'I suppose it was her debts I paid when you were at Oxford?' Luke asked, then seemed to be going through this new information in his head since he shook it as if it hurt. 'And that's why you really took to such a dark trade? You needed the money to pay off her debts.'

It was almost a relief for James to interrupt Luke's self-flagellation to tell him the life he had led as a pretend horse trader was so long ago it seemed that boy was someone else. 'At least it began as pretence before

I got too good at it. I moved on to trading goods when I realised the poor beasts ended up dead on a battlefield or discarded once they were broken down by forced marches. Even I couldn't feel guilty about sacks of corn or coffee and flagons of wine and olive oil, so I flourished like the proverbial green bay tree. Easy to acquire information along the way when you're bargaining for a cargo or bidding for a contract.'

'As long as nobody knows you're an Englishman.'

'The trick is to become whoever you're pretending to be at the time—so that talent for drama you accused me of has come in useful.'

'You always had a gift for languages and how I used to envy you as I struggled through the classics. Someone must know who you are if they really were after you in the woods the other day, though, so could a disguise be less sure than you think?'

'Perhaps one of my aliases came up when they beat it out of a friend and Fouché reached his own conclusions,' James said with a heavy sigh.

'And you took your revenge for whatever they did before he betrayed you?'

'She,' James corrected dourly, 'and, yes, I broke into the man's home and stole a letter that will make Bonaparte incandescent with fury if he ever sees it.'

'Of all the reckless things you've done that has to be the most headlong; didn't you think before you stole it?'

'You didn't see what they did to Hebe la Courte,' James said grimly, the image of his one-time lover and friend as vivid as the moment he first saw her broken body in the gutter.

'One of your lovers?'

'Yes, although it's many years since we did our best to be in love with each other. Once we gave that up we were good friends and loyal allies. When Fouché's men had finished with her, not even her own mother knew her at first when I carried her body home for burial. That poor woman is in hiding in her own country now and her last hope depends on me.'

James's saw his brother's eyes sharp on him and wondered if he'd given away too much, but this was Luke and possibly the only man he could ever confide it all in.

'I put Hebe's child in danger when I lost my temper. I wanted to avenge her mother's death and all I managed to do was endanger the poor mite further.'

'Did you leave her with her grandmother?'

'I tried to persuade the lady to leave, but she says she's too old to settle in a barbarous country and learn gibberish. She let me bring her daughter's child here, though, although it nigh broke her heart to part with her.'

'You must have loved the woman to lose that temper of yours so spectacularly.'

'We clung to each other at a time when both our worlds were rocked to their foundations. I loved her, but not as you love Chloe. Enough to wish they'd tortured me instead and you know what a selfish fribble I am at heart.'

'Don't, James; that act is over between us and please don't try and convince me you don't care because you care too much, don't you?'

'Do I? By taking a petty vengeance for Hebe's death I put too many innocent lives at risk. The poor mites have already suffered enough in this stupid war and I should have put their safety first. That one act of stupidity erases everything I've tried to do.'

'Not you; you'll find a way of keeping this Hebe's daughter and any other orphans you have secreted about the country safe. It's what you do, isn't it? Protect those who can't protect themselves. Carry on doing it until we've found out who did their best to kill you the other day and you can all start a new life at Brackley. I couldn't understand why you wanted a tumbledown old place miles from civilisation, but it will make a perfect home for a former spy and whatever mixed bag of orphans you managed to pick up along the way, won't it?'

'How did you know about them?'

'Come now, James, we grew up together. Now we've seen past Pamela's wicked schemes to keep us estranged I know perfectly well you couldn't walk away from an innocent victim of the murky game you've been engaged in all these years.'

'Aye, well, never mind me. It's a good house for all the neglect and far enough away from neighbours for them to be headlong and carefree for a while, or I thought so until someone followed me and tried to end my unlikely idyll before it could begin.'

'Could that be the very reason they did so?' Luke suggested and confirmed a suspicion James had been toying with, that this had more to do with his collection of waifs than his murky past.

'I've lain here racking my brains for hours on end, but I can't see how or why anyone would care where they are or what I intend to do about them. What threat do a handful of children nobody wanted to think about once their parents were dead offer anyone?'

'Maybe your enemy is closer to home?'

'Bowood and his father are the only ones who know who I am and they promised me when this began it would stay that way. My information gives them an edge, but they would hardly admit it came from me. Can you imagine the derision if Beau Winterley was revealed as their source? They'd be laughed out of every club in St James's.'

'Someone still seems to know.'

'True, and what does he want with me?'

'I don't know, but he's not getting it. Are you sure your waifs are safe?'

'Aye, trust me for that,' James said grimly. 'Those who have them are tried and trusted and have no idea who I really am.'

'However many children have you made yourself responsible for, then?'

'My profession makes widows and orphans. Sometimes a remaining parent is strong enough to make a life in a safer land. Some of the children went to wider family and others are so happy with foster parents they will stay until they're grown. Hebe's little girl and two others are too small to need aught but a good nurse and a safe home for now.'

'Until Brackley and Papa Winterley are ready for them?' Luke teased.

'Or they are ready for me,' James argued quietly. There was a fear in his heart he'd fail when it mattered more than ever before to track down his enemy and make the future safe for the three children the war had left him.

Chapter Nine

Horrified yet fascinated by what she'd overheard this time, Rowena wished she could think of some magical way not to be here and at the same time marvelled at what she knew about the real James Winterley. She'd taken a surface gloss as the sum total of a man and how could she be so lazy? A crack was running through her view of herself and perhaps Mary and Callie were right and she was less than the eager, adventurous girl who had fallen in love with a scarlet coat. Her husband had been nothing like she thought, but was that any excuse to measure the world by his standards?

If he did but know it, James Winterley had shaken the safe little box she had built round herself long before Nate's death. It was a small space for a grown woman, but breaking out of it felt so risky she wanted to curl up somewhere and reassemble her barriers. Coward, she accused herself. Humiliation and disappointment had made her a smaller person and James Winterley a greater one. That dreadful woman changed his young life for her own vicious reasons, but he had still embraced the adventures that led to and lived the best life he could.

She felt as little and useless as she had that day a so-called camp follower offered a place in her cart, because she was sorry for the soft-footed wife of an officer wilting like a hothouse lily in the midday sun. That woman had more real love and pity in her heart than the officer's lady; James Winterley did whatever he could for victims of his shocking profession and what did the vicar's daughter do? Run away, Rowena thought with terrible weariness. Before she took a long, hard look at Mrs Rowena Westhope she needed to get away from Raigne, though. There was too much risk she'd stumble on James Winterley escaping his brother and he'd know she'd overheard—unlike him, she had no talent for acting.

As the only other person fully aware of what was going on yesterday, wouldn't it be safer to stay away from her family, though? The very idea of them tangled up in nation spying on nation seemed ludicrous, or it had before James Winterley arrived. Part of her wished they had never met Mr Winterley in Lord Laughraine's woods. Except Hester would be dead or terribly wounded and poor Jack convinced he'd caused a tragedy he could never quite forgive himself for if they hadn't.

She caught herself about to shake her head at the very idea and give herself away if either Winterley saw a shadow move in a supposedly deserted courtyard. Given the thickness of those rich brocade curtains and lining, was it possible to sneak away so softly neither would notice? Now they were less intent on prising secrets out of each other it seemed unlikely and she should have gone when they were busy, except she had this terrible curiosity to hear everything she could about Mr Winterley's real life. She felt guilty for being here, but perhaps better she heard them than someone less likely to keep his secrets.

Could they hear her listening? Foolish to think so, but the robin calling his territory from a nearby holly tree halted his song and the silence seemed too alert. She held her breath, as if that could help. The numbness of knowing something she shouldn't was fading and terror threatened to take its place. Maybe she could persuade her family to take a late holiday by the sea until Mr Winterley left? Great-Aunt Deborah lived in Ramsgate and sea air was said to be good for over-stretched nerves, and hers felt so close to breaking point right now it wouldn't even be a lie.

The impossibility of persuading her family to leave King's Raigne vicarage when Joanna was about to marry her Mr Greenwood and there was so much to do at Glebe Farm made her want to groan. She must get out of here without alerting the brothers, then she could pretend she didn't know James Winterley was more than the proud dandy she had thought him on Sunday. She *was* wearing soft-soled shoes and had got to this bench without alerting two acute males in the first place. Now even her shabby old gown might betray her presence by rustling too loudly if she dared tiptoe away. She waited for a chance to leave when they were talking of more important problems than Rowena Westhope and her galloping heartbeat and wildly jangling nerves.

* * *

'Promise you'll not leave this house, James?' Luke demanded. 'At least until the doctor's been and we can consult Gideon. Best if we send for Tom as well, since we'll need every advantage we can get to frustrate this shadowy enemy if he's going to hide in bushes and take shots at you when we least expect it.'

'Leave Tom out of this. With him at Dayspring Castle there's one less to worry about.'

'He won't be any more flattered than I am to be thought such a babe in arms.'

'Never mind his pride; I'm happy he's not here, even if you're not.'

'I suppose we can leave him to his own devices for now.'

'Good, convince Gideon I can look after myself, then, and make my life endurable.'

'Consider it unendurable, neither of us will let you slide out of our lives again.'

'Taking my name in vain, are you? I heard my name as I came in, so might I suggest you talk with the doors and windows shut from now on?' Sir Gideon Laughraine's pleasant tenor voice interrupted their brotherly argument and made Rowena's heart thunder so loudly she was amazed they couldn't hear it.

She measured the distance between her bench and the door on the other side of the courtyard. It seemed too far to risk with three pairs of acute masculine ears on the alert for outsiders, but after Gideon's comments, how could she not? Sighing at the feel of constricting skirts as she wrapped them even closer round her legs, she wondered if anyone would miss her if she stayed here until darkness fell. The call of nature would betray her even if one of the gentlemen didn't look out and catch her sitting here like a statue. There was nothing for it; she had to leave as quietly as she could right now. So she slipped silently on to her knees and began her escape.

'Gideon's quite right,' James admitted. 'All these years of guarding my thoughts so carefully I hardly even knew I was having them, then I forget I wanted the windows open. I must have thought it would keep my wits sharp and you two at bay. I might as well have let my man stifle me by keeping them firmly shut for all the good it did me.'

'It's easy to relax here and forget a long and bitter war is still being fought on the Continent,' Gideon said. 'And you've been fighting it alone long enough.'

It was more a statement than a question and James wondered how much of his true self he'd given away to his acute not-quite cousin. Wherever had the close-mouthed operative he'd prided himself on being once upon a time got off to? He was so ham-fisted he doubted he'd hear a mouse in the room; except he could hear something like one outside right now and a very furtive, overgrown one it was, as well. Luke picked up his shift of attention and raised his eyebrows.

James shot Luke a look to say, *Keep talking and don't let Gideon stop me*, got out of bed, paused to get his land legs when his head swam, then called on the skills he once prided himself on to tread so softly his mouse wouldn't know he was on its tail. The heavy curtains seemed too secure a barrier for a moment, but there was a sliver of light where the curtain was pulled too far over. He set a wary eye to the gap and did his best not to gasp as his iris adjusted to the sunlit courtyard beyond. For a moment he despaired of seeing more than box-edged knot gardens—he wondered why they were called knots when they were plainly gnarled old box balls run together—with pots of late-blooming flowers and a venerable lemon tree in a wheeled tub. He wondered about throwing wide the curtains and confronting their listener for a moment. Patience went a long way in a career like his, though, and he listened to his brother and Gideon act as if he was still in bed, and arguing he should stop there, and waited.

He was rewarded by the sight of a very feminine *derrière* wiggling into his narrow view at much the same level as those ancient knots. His mind couldn't quite take in the fact Mrs Rowena Westhope was doing her best to pretend she wasn't out there and never had been. He refused to look deeper into his certainty it was her as she shuffled so carefully along on all fours she was almost as quiet as that mouse. He frowned at the thought a narrow gown of dull grey-blue stuff really wasn't suitable raiment for a lady rejoicing in such superb assets as the lovely Mrs Westhope had in her armoury. Never mind her clothes, or that deep cornflower-blue gaze of hers now; what the devil was the confounded woman doing escaping Lord Laughraine's best inner courtyard with all his deepest secrets buzzing about in her busy head?

Maybe he should hop out of the open window and challenge her in his nightshirt. She deserved no consideration about the spectacle that would make, he decided, with an odd twist of amusement to the hard line his lips had set in before he imagined that scene in his head. He doubted she'd succumb to ladylike hysterics, but it would be intriguing to watch her struggle to produce any sort of polite response to such a thoroughly impolite situation. This was no time to be amused by the sight of her shuffling so determinedly in the direction of the side door either. That dull and never-touched-by-fashion gown of hers would probably be ruined by its latest expedition, as well. Good—it belonged in someone's ragbag and a sensible female would have consigned it to one long ago. So what *was* he going to do about the owner of all the shabby lack of splendour creeping past his vantage point at the pace of an ailing snail? Try as he might he couldn't see her as a traitor ready to sell her country to Bonaparte for enough golden guineas. Was that a dangerous blind spot, or an instinctive knowledge of the woman that ought to worry him on a different plane altogether?

Now only her feet were left for him to watch and he still didn't know what to do about her. How was it possible to feel moved by the sight of those much-mended indoor shoes of hers leaving the courtyard in such an unusual manner? She must have donned them to visit Callie, her long-time friend and ally, instead of the sensible walking boots he vaguely recalled yesterday from his first real encounter with the most adventurous members of the Finch family. She caught her gown on some obstacle out of sight and her feet paused. He could imagine her tense and frown while she shuffled about as best she could until she freed it silently and was ready to creep on again.

Since even all that shabby woollen stuff hadn't managed to hide the shape of her superb legs, he found it unforgivable of his own masculine urges to notice how fine and seductive her ankles looked as they finally wriggled out of sight. Best if he stayed here for a moment, he decided ruefully. Even the confounded nightshirt Huddle insisted on for an invalid wouldn't cover the effect seeing Mrs Rowena Westhope's feminine curves so unexpectedly displayed had wrought on his manhood. Of course, if he'd managed to get himself to bed in his usual state of nature he wouldn't even have this much fine linen to cover his blushes. And why couldn't he take this incursion into his deepest and darkest secrets seriously enough to feel violated and infuriated by the dratted woman?

Because you want her too much to care, he chided himself and wondered if that blow on the head had done more damage than he thought. *From the first second you set eyes on her with that hideous you-can't-see-me bonnet on her head to fend off wolves like you, you wanted her speechless with wanting under you. Even beset as you were yesterday by flying children, gauche youths and hidden assassins you still wanted her*, his inner critic insisted like a stern confessor. That didn't alter the fact Mrs Westhope now knew too much about him and his secret life. She held his life in the palm of her hand and somehow he must stop her sharing it.

He caught the softest of snicks as she somehow managed to open the door on the other side of the old courtyard wide enough to get through it from her peculiar position, then a faint shuffle of soft shoes and much-washed petticoats as she stole through it. She shut it so softly he might not have heard if he was sleeping instead of pouring his heart out to his brother. Of course, then there would be no need for her to creep away, or for him to wonder what the devil he was going to do about her. Such a dire problem sobered him and at least now he could turn and meet the question in two pairs of remarkably similar grey-green eyes without looking for a piece of furniture to hide behind, so there was a bright side to every cloud, wasn't there?

'Perhaps you would shut the window for me now, Laughraine? You might do it more quietly,' he managed to say almost casually.

'Aye,' Gideon said and did it with a cautious silence that made James wonder how unsafe the missions he once undertook for his noble clients were.

'Are you going to tell us who it was?' Luke asked after Gideon checked the outer doors of this vast suite were shut tight.

'We might as well wait until Gideon's finished,' James advised and clambered back into bed.

Somehow he had to ward off the memory of Rowena Westhope's improbably blue eyes and the way that gown was designed not to show anything about her to advantage. *You didn't manage to disguise her feminine charms from a rake, though, did you?* Perhaps the large bruise on the back of his head he was trying to ignore was worse than he thought, he mused, as he was arguing with an inanimate piece of cloth.

'That blow on the head must be worse than we thought,' Gideon said as if he could read James's innermost thoughts and what a disaster that would be. Mrs Westhope was one of Sir Gideon and Lady Laughraine's oldest friends, a vicar's daughter and a widowed lady of unimpeachable reputation all rolled into one inconvenient package. 'I doubt you've been that careless since you were in your nursery.'

'My fault,' Luke said with a heavy sigh. 'I should

have left James to walk his own path, even if it does lead straight to the devil.'

'Haven't you heard that the devil looks after his own, then?' James rallied enough to say cheerfully, even as the idea of that unimpeachable widow of his knowing his deepest secrets gnawed at that conviction.

Chapter Ten

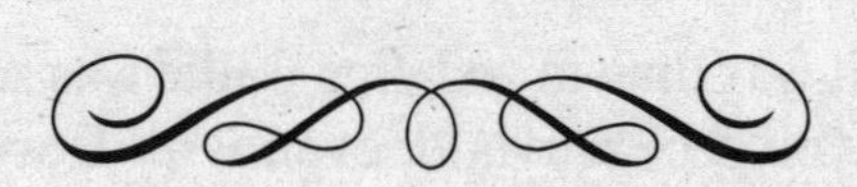

Two days later Rowena was still struggling with her new knowledge of James Winterley and feelings she didn't want to understand. She had taken up her new post, but she'd be a fool not to, wouldn't she? And Callie needed her. How could she say no when Gideon had begged her to come as soon as possible? Except today Mr Winterley had been declared his usual annoying self and freed from a captivity that must be nigh unendurable. It was so tempting to argue her work could easily be done at the vicarage and run away until he'd gone, but she refused to play the coward again. She didn't want to face him, but he intrigued her and that conclusion left her more uncomfortable about him than ever.

So she sat in front of Callie's notes for her next book and fretted over meeting him face to face. Best to pretend nothing had occurred and, apart from her appalling lapse of manners and common sense, it hadn't, had it? She was jolted out of her endless arguments with herself about what was right and wrong only when the light began to fade and it was too late to escape an invitation to dine. What a relief Mr Winterley elected to dine in his room one last time, almost as if he'd grown fond of it, or was avoiding her as gladly as she was him, but that was impossible—he didn't know she was party to his most intimate secrets, so why would he avoid such an insignificant female as Mrs Rowena Westhope?

When it was time to go home Callie was so anxious Rowena would be waylaid, even with Horsefield to drive the gig and Lord Laughraine's offer of a groom as outrider, that meeting Mr Winterley at the breakfast table instead was an uncomfortable possibility.

'I don't care if you've walked to the village alone every other night of your life, Rowena, I don't want you to do it tonight,' Callie insisted, almost hysterical with worry. 'Or any other night until that prowler is caught and locked up for good. Ann Goode was accosted on her way home two nights ago by some man trying to do heaven alone knows what and I won't risk him doing it to you.'

'If it means so much to sleep in your own bed, I could escort you as well, I suppose,' Gideon offered with so little expression Rowena knew he thought her foolish to insist on going home when she could stay here and make his wife feel better.

'I doubt the man will linger in the area after Ann screamed so loudly he was chased off by the blacksmith and half the men in the village joined in.'

'It's what he said to her,' Callie admitted with a visible shudder. 'That he knows who she is and where her family live. No wonder the poor girl went to stay with her married sister in Bristol until she's sure he's gone.'

'Some simple madman, I dare say, my love. The constables are alert and will move him on or take him up. There's no need to fret,' Gideon argued half-heartedly.

'I'll be safe as the crown jewels with so many escorts, Callie,' Rowena said in a last attempt to get home.

'You can call it a silly fancy on my part, but I feel as if there's someone wicked out there tonight watching us,' her friend said with a superstitious shudder.

'You have too much imagination, love,' Gideon said with a would-be wry smile. 'I hope you'll humour my wife and stay to make her feel better, despite the small army you can call on if you really must go, Rowena?' he added with a pleading look.

'I must send a note to Papa and Mama, or they might think I've been kidnapped,' she joked weakly.

'Heaven forbid.'

Gideon could hide his feelings a lot better than he had as a boy, but the signs were there if you knew him well. He was uneasy about something more than his wife and baby. If they were alone she would challenge him, but Lord Laughraine and Lord and Lady Farenze were here, so she agreed to accept a nightdress from Lady Farenze, since Callie's would be far too short, and hoped Mama would send a change of clothes come morning. Still, at least James Winterley wasn't in the room to silently mock her frustration.

Rowena followed Lord Laughraine's housekeeper through a maze of corridors and obscure staircases it would take Ariadne's ball of string to rediscover in the morning. Why on earth wasn't she being lodged in a more straightforward corner of this rambling mansion? Still, at least she'd have peace and quiet at the end, simply because nobody would be able to find her in order to disturb her up here. She had a vision of herself wandering the less well-known corners of the Raigne like a lost spectre from a three-decker novel, before common sense informed her Mrs Craddock and Gideon knew where she was. The housekeeper would send someone to wake her and guide her to safety in the morning, or maybe Gideon had a map drawn out for bewildered guests to receive with their morning chocolate.

They reached their destination at last and Rowena fought a distinct feeling of anticlimax as she did her best to look grateful for a room furnished with leftovers for the night. Maybe this was where they lodged visiting governesses? There was a shelf full of ancient tomes and a spartan washstand that didn't have a single idea above its station.

'It has a lovely view of the Park,' Mrs Craddock told her uncomfortably, as if she had no idea why Lady Laughraine's friend and Reverend Finch's eldest daughter had been allotted such an obscure corner of this huge house either.

'I shall be very comfortable here,' Rowena assured her with perfect truth. She was used to sharing a bedchamber with Joanna or squeezing into the narrow cot in a room barely large enough to hold it that her mother-in-law considered good enough for a daughter-in-law who had failed to provide her with a single grandchild. 'Thank you for making it so pleasant and a fire is a welcome luxury now the nights are growing cold again.'

'Aye, it will soon be Christmas,' the housekeeper said with a frown. 'I must remind Cook to buy more fruit for the puddings in the morning.'

'I shall be snug as a dormouse up here tonight, so

please don't worry about me,' Rowena said and Mrs Craddock left her in this oddly secluded eyrie with a last doubtful look.

'Dormouse indeed,' she thought she heard the housekeeper mumble as she went. 'I'll not have any mouse in this house while there's a cat left in the country worth its keep. Cook needs to candy oranges, as well.'

Rowena smiled at her preoccupation, but a household this grand must think well ahead and this Christmas would be the most joyful for many a year. The years of unhappiness Gideon and Callie had endured, and Lord Laughraine's lonely life until they came back had been far too long and weary. Her troubles seemed small next to their grief and loneliness, so she sat staring into the fire and tried to put them in perspective.

If she undressed and tried to sleep, she would lie sleepless for hours now Joanna wasn't here to be anxious about her tossing and turning when she was unable to get Mr Winterley's intriguing life story out of her head. A few minutes sitting here mulling over the day and she caught herself nodding. The second time she must have missed that stage out and woke with a start when a distinctly masculine arm reached past her to make up the fading fire. With a squeak of shocked surprise she blinked owlishly up at the man who'd haunted her dreams ever since she came home and tried to gather her senses.

'Ah, Mrs Westhope; I'm so glad you're awake. Now we can talk properly at last, but it was such a novelty to look at you without being glared at in return I didn't like to wake you. When you began to shiver in your sleep it was clearly my duty to warm the place up,' James Winterley's dark velvet voice drawled as he stepped out of the shadows to stir up the glowing ashes with the poker. He must have seen her eye that sturdy length of good iron longingly and shook his head reproachfully, then grinned. 'Now that's downright unfriendly, Rowena—unladylike, as well.'

She was so shocked he felt free to use her given name that she sat dumbfounded for a long moment and stared back as if he was an apparition. 'What the *devil* are you doing here?' she gasped when she could get the words past her thundering heartbeat and a sleepy sense this scandalous intimacy felt right.

'Perhaps I'm finding out if that sooty gentleman truly looks after his own,' the wretch suggested, as if he'd strolled into a *ton* party and was thinking of settling in for a few hands of cards and a pleasant supper.

'Well, he doesn't. Now go away, before I ring the bell and have you put out by force.'

'Not quite as easy to do as you think, perhaps, but you won't even try.'

She itched to smack the insufferable smile off his face as he came even closer. The candle she had left burning on the mantelpiece picked up the intriguing masculine planes of his face, yet didn't manage to reveal his thoughts and that was unfair as she couldn't quite throw off sleep and a sinful dream she didn't want to think about.

'I never could resist a dare; ask the maid who comes to find out why I'm ringing a peal at this hour of the night if you don't believe me,' she said as she rose to her feet at last and backed away from his overwhelming physical presence.

She was getting closer to the bell pull, of course,

not retreating from a masculine threat she couldn't dismiss as predatory although she wanted to. Much too conscious of the sensual tension in her own body in this ridiculously intimate space, she glared at him and reached for the bell nobody was likely to hear if she rang it.

'I wonder which of our reputations will suffer most, Mrs Westhope,' he mused as if he was discussing two strangers shut in the intimate darkness of an obscure guest room.

'You don't have one to lose,' she accused rashly.

'Then I'll be no worse off if we proceed as the scandalmongers expect. I'll probably be thrown off Laughraine lands, and my brother and Sir Gideon will help if we're caught, but that should suit me very well, don't you think?'

'I can't see how it could,' she said uneasily, because if she hadn't overheard him and his brother talking the other morning she could have no idea how much he wanted to be gone.

'You listen at windows when you should be at home minding other people's business, though, don't you?' he asked silkily.

'That's a monstrous suggestion.'

'Of course it is, so shall we get down to seducing each another, since you claim there's nothing else to discuss?'

'No,' she said, feeling she was living in some sort of dream. Not that any time or place could be right for her and a shameless rake. 'That's an outrageous idea.'

He looked unimpressed, so she glared at him. She wondered if it was best to admit her sins and hope he'd leave, though. As if he had the slightest intention of trying to have his wicked way with her anyway, her inner critic argued scornfully. A hot thump of excitement deep within her still startled her into shooting him a panicked glare.

'And I refuse to become any man's mistress,' she blurted out as if he'd demanded she become his right now. Deeply buried feminine instincts she preferred to think she didn't have were whispering he'd make loving wondrous, but that was silly.

'If seduction is off the menu we can get our unfinished business done all the sooner, I suppose,' he said, as if it was normal to invade a lady's bedchamber and demand a meeting in the middle of the night.

'We have nothing to discuss,' she said and shook her head.

'Interesting,' he said huskily, bending closer and seeming larger and even more vital. 'A widow who thinks seduction overrated, yet you won't talk about something that might make me go away. What a delightful conundrum and I've the whole night to solve it.'

'You can't stay—indeed, you must go this instant.'

'I don't have anywhere else to be,' he argued languidly, as if this sort of assignation was nothing out of the ordinary for him. 'I'm still abed, you see?' he went on remorselessly. 'Lady Laughraine and my sister-in-law ordered me there on pain of not being allowed my clothes back until tomorrow so many hours ago I almost gave up counting. So I can't be here, can I? And nobody would look for me before morning even if I was and this is the last place they would look even then. So you see, we have the night ahead of us and nothing to do but explore each other, since you don't want to talk of eavesdroppers and what they hear when they're pretending not to.'

'Stop it,' she demanded, trying to persuade her inner demons they weren't horribly tempted to agree. 'We only truly met three days ago. We're strangers, despite this shocking intrusion.'

'Yet you know more about me than any other being on earth but Luke.' All the lies stacked up on her tongue fell away as he bent closer to look down at her as if he could read her soul and it was more sooty and complicated than her status as widowed daughter of a country clergyman argued it should be. 'As close kin, my brother has some right to know my secrets. You do not.'

'I have no idea what you mean,' she replied feebly.

'Liar,' he said so softly she looked up and saw the shine of his intense gaze even by the light of a single candle.

It was like confronting a dark force of nature. She had to grasp her hands together to stop them reaching for him and something she didn't understand wanting. He was such a very physical presence, a man so beautifully proportioned his air of restrained fitness called to a dark part of her she didn't know she still had. Despite his accusation she knew too much about him, she doubted anyone would ever do that. Part of her wanted to explore every inch of his body and the intriguing, complicated mind that made him such a dangerous man to be alone with at such a bewitching hour of the night. The other part wanted to run away.

'Even if I had the slightest idea what you're talking about, Mr Winterley, and I don't, I know how to keep secrets.'

'There are men with ways of prising them from a

woman you don't want to know about. Think yourself fortunate I'm not one of them.'

'Are you trying to frighten me?' she whispered and could have kicked herself when a visible shudder racked her to her toes.

'Is it working?' he murmured.

'Yes,' she admitted and moved closer to the fire and further from him.

'Good, because you need to be frightened, Rowena. You entangled yourself in my life to satisfy your curiosity and your life may depend on you keeping a still tongue in your head.'

'Oh, don't be so melodramatic. Your brother was quite right about you,' she snapped.

She saw his half-smile of satisfaction and realised what she'd admitted. No use pretending she hadn't been outside his room listening now. She gave a rueful shrug to say it didn't matter; she'd never repeat it, but he didn't know her well enough to believe it.

'You acknowledge you were there, then?' he asked warily.

'How can I do otherwise after saying that, but how did you know?'

'I witnessed your retreat; a very novel and intriguing one it was, too.'

She flushed at the idea he'd seen her creep away on hands and knees. 'Why didn't you challenge me then instead of invading my room in the middle of the night?'

'Perhaps I was enjoying the view too much to get the words out,' he drawled mockingly, but there was that hot gleam in his shadowed gaze again and it wasn't right to feel warm and a little bit hungry at the sight of it.

'I really can't imagine why,' she said, then blushed when he looked at her as if she was some unknown species. She realised he meant he'd enjoyed the spectacle of her wriggling her way across the moss and stones. 'Oh, you mean...?' She gasped and stopped as the thought of him watching her retreating *derrière* and finding the sight arousing made her feel hot and ashamed and needy all at the same time.

'I mean...you have a very fine figure, Mrs Westhope. Oh, yes,' he said with outright desire in his intent look this time. 'How many years did you say you were married?' he asked after a pause she was almost tempted to fill with a nervous titter.

'I didn't, but it was four. My husband was killed at Vimeiro.'

'And didn't he make it clear you have a fine collection of feminine assets?'

'Not that I recall.'

'You would if he had.'

'Yes...no...oh, I don't know—and it's none of your business. I promise never to repeat a word of what was said in that room the other day. Now leave me be,' she said with a sigh that admitted he probably wouldn't.

'You'll know that's impossible if you use the brains Gideon swears you possess, despite all evidence to the contrary.'

'That's very rude, but I suppose it was rude of me to listen to a private conversation and you're paying me back with my own coin. My word is my bond, just as a gentleman's should be.'

'I wouldn't take the word of one in these circumstances. Thanks to your snooping, you hold my darkest and most dangerous secrets. There are those who would cheerfully kill for half what you know.'

'But we're strangers, why would they suspect I know more about you than anyone else? As a mere acquaintance, your enemies will hardly worry themselves about tracking down a plain country widow and bullying your secrets out of me.'

'And you actually believe that's all you are?'

She nodded, because it seemed so obvious more words were unnecessary, not because something hot and baffled and new in his gaze silenced her.

'To put it plainly, since you seem so deluded about the realities; you are completely mistaken about yourself, Rowena. In fact, you're so wrong I can only wonder at your husband's idiocy. You are a rare beauty, my dear Mrs Westhope. I'm sorry to have to tell you this as it clearly comes as a shock, but any sentient male will notice you, even in your armour-coloured gowns and trying-to-be-invisible bonnet.'

'That's very rude of you, too,' she was surprised into protesting.

'No it isn't, it's the truth. Deep down you must know it, since you take so much trouble to disguise your looks and figure from masculine predators like me.'

She gasped at his skewed version of her and tried to read enough of his thoughts to see if he was most angry with her for being, allegedly, beautiful, or himself for finding it a snare. Surely he couldn't be right, though, could he? She was well enough, if a little faded by the side of her sister Joanna, but she'd never have been one of the toasts of St James's even in her prime. Her doubts must have been showing since he seemed so irritated by them.

'Didn't they have any chain mail available the day you bought this instead?' he demanded, fingering the worn stuff and it felt as if he'd touched her instead for some fanciful reason. 'You hide in plain sight, don't you? First there was the brown-grey you wore to church the first week you returned to King's Raigne. I hope you ruined the slate-grey you wore to creep about outside my window, although I suppose you'll replace it with another in your favourite non-colour if you did.'

'If I can afford it, I will.'

'Don't bother; they don't work. The contrast between gown and wearer accentuates the deeply desirable woman under all that armour.'

'You're exaggerating.'

'No, I'm considered a connoisseur of feminine beauty and you could snatch Paris's apple from Venus any day.'

'Women are not *objets d'art* to be curated as if men own us, whatever the law says about us being mere chattels of our husbands.'

'Such passion,' he said with a sharp intelligence in his glance she wished was focused on anything but her right now. 'Did your husband try to own you, Rowena?'

'Mind your own business and don't call me Rowena, James Winterley.'

'How did you learn my first name, Rowena dear? Not from hiding behind the nearest evergreen or sibling at church every Sunday since you came home.'

'I overheard it,' she confessed defiantly.

'My point exactly—what gives you the right to know so much about me when we hardly know each other?' he asked harshly and Rowena couldn't meet his steely green gaze however hard she tried.

'It's not a matter of rights and, believe me, if there was a way not to know what I heard you say that day, I'd happily take it, Mr Winterley.'

'James,' he corrected.

'I can't call you that,' she protested a little too loudly.

'Shh, Rowena, you just did and remember, the most unlikely people creep round this house listening to private conversations.'

'Oh, will you never forget that? No, of course you won't, but please believe I'm sorry I overheard what I did and will never say a word to anyone else.'

'Being sorry won't change what you know,' he said bitterly. 'I wouldn't have you know of my youthful shame for all my ill-gotten gains either, but it's done now and nothing will take that away.'

'It was never your role to *be* ashamed, James,' she told him gently, letting those wayward hands of hers reach for him after all.

It didn't matter; he didn't see. He'd already turned his back and marched into the shadows of this odd room, up here where nobody came by accident. Gideon had conspired with him to leave her cornered and alone up here. James Winterley had his betrayals to brood over and now she had one of her own. Lesser in every way, she acknowledged as tears stood in her eyes because one of her oldest friends had left her to this man's mercy. Perhaps Gideon was right; listening to a gentleman confess his secrets to his brother was unforgivable and put her beyond the pale. Never mind being there by accident and already hearing too much; as soon as she realised what she was overhearing she should have made a fuss about getting up and going, instead of staying until she'd heard everything she could, then creeping away like a thief. So why didn't she? Because once she'd started listening she wanted to know all she could about him. That idea jarred against the pact she had made with herself when Nate died never to feel more for a man than mild liking ever again.

'Why not?' he asked at last, his voice sounding rasped by the secrets he'd kept for so long. 'She was my brother's wife. How can I *not* be ashamed until my dying day?'

'Because that would deny your brother the right of forgiveness and I hope you're not that selfish or arrogant.'

'I am, apparently. Luke wants to let me off my sins, but I can't forgive myself.'

'And that gives your first sister-in-law a twisted power over you both from beyond the grave. She sounds the sort of person who would gloat and treasure the pain she caused you both as a miser does gold.'

'She would at that,' he admitted with a shrug that told her he was clinging to his self-inflicted need to do penance, despite anything his brother could say to let him off it.

'Yet you still hand her such a prize?'

'I did what I did,' he said bleakly.

'No, she did what she did, for whatever evil reason, and it sounds as if even she would have been hard pressed to say what her motives were, but she chose her victim well, didn't she? She must have known how it would hurt you and your brother to be estranged.'

'We're only half-brothers, Mrs Westhope,' he said stiffly.

'You think that makes a difference? If so, that blow

on the head must have been worse than we thought and you should clearly be in bed,' she told him to change the subject.

'Yours or mine?' he invited outrageously, but his heart wasn't in it.

'I shall remember how much I owe you and ignore that distasteful remark,' she said stiffly. She stood her ground so he had to halt his restless pacing and he stared down at her as if still trying to decide what to make of her.

'You owe me an apology,' he said at last.

'I meant I'm indebted to you for Hester's life.'

'Oh, that,' he said with a dismissive wave. 'I would have done the same for any child. I might even have considered it for you.'

'I would certainly have killed you if I fell on you from such a height. Luckily my tree-climbing days are well and truly over.'

'But not your listening-at-windows ones,' he replied drily.

'I've never done it before,' she admitted. 'And can safely promise I never will again.'

'Never make promises, Rowena, you don't know when you'll have to break them,' he warned her as if he spoke from bitter experience.

'Idiot,' she said as if she had known him half her life, so why did it feel as if she had?

'Because I hate to break my promises?'

'No, for not letting yourself give them in the first place.'

'I'll admit it's hard to in my line of work,' he said ruefully.

'Yet you're not in it any longer, are you? You've been

discovered and couldn't go back to it if you wanted to. I don't think you do, though, do you? Something tells me you're weary of lying and pretending, Beau Winterley.'

'A man about town spends his whole life lying and pretending. I might as well do it for an end as perform it free for my acquaintance.'

'Either way sounds like a bleak existence to me.'

'Isn't that brutally forthright, even for you?'

'Say truthful rather, it's a waste of your intelligence and talent.'

'If I do anything useful it will tumble around me the moment my past is revealed. Spying is a dirty game and I'll be despised for sullying my noble name as soon as those who secretly work for our enemies let it leak out I'm not quite the vain idler society thinks me.'

'Then don't be Beau Winterley any more. Be yourself.'

'How?' he asked and spread his arms as if to display the trappings and instincts of a gentleman of fashion and make her realise he was what he was and could be nothing more.

'By forgetting the quarrel your late sister-in-law forced on you and your brother, and becoming the man you would have been if not for her.'

'You don't know me, madam,' he reminded her stiffly. She flinched and wished she was half as well armoured as he thought.

Yet didn't the strength of his protective cover prove how vulnerable the man under it was? Would it be dangerous to know the real man under that careless-dandy front of his? Yes, dangerous for her. He was right. She didn't know him, not by the measure of everyday detail that was true intimacy, and he was the last person she should be close to.

'I know myself and I promise never to reveal a word of your secrets to another human being and now can we go back to being strangers? We must meet as such every day you remain at Raigne and I truly mean you no harm,' she said, coming up behind him as he stared out into the night, so absorbed in the darkness it seemed safe to reach out and touch his shoulder and show him he wasn't as deeply alone as he suddenly looked.

She saw his face in the dark mirror of the glass reflecting candle and firelight back at them. He looked austere and brooding as he tested her words for possibilities. For a tense moment she wondered if he was going to shrug her off. Then he raised his hand to cover hers and there was the warmth of him, above and below it. She let out a stuttering sigh to go with the secret one that shot to the deepest, most secret heart of Rowena Westhope and echoed back longing for a very different assignation from this one.

'Good intentions don't get a man in my shoes far,' he told her gruffly, but he left his hand over hers and warmth and a great deal more seemed to flow between them for a long moment.

She was watching him so closely it was only seconds after he saw something below when she looked past him to share the shock of knowing they'd been seen, like this, like lovers. Slowly, almost as if he didn't want to break the bond of man to woman any more than she did for a mad moment, he lifted his hand and she snatched hers away. They would have been outlined against even the soft light of a single candle and the fire's glow so clearly she had no doubt they looked intimate and furtive, if a little careless for lovers.

'Who was it?' she whispered as if they might be able to hear as well as see them, four floors below and through a closed window.

'How should I know? The most unlikely people linger in that confounded courtyard at all hours of the day and night hunting my secrets,' he said brusquely and swept the curtains together as if that might rub out the watcher, instead of making them more certain they had seen something furtive and wrong.

'It's the middle of the night,' she said, still shocked that someone—staff, or family—saw them highlighted up here like a pair of stage lovers.

'Exactly,' he said with a hard look to say that made it even worse. 'So you'll have to marry me,' he said as if it made perfect sense.

'I'll have to do what?' she asked past the buzzing in her ears that made her wonder if she was about to faint for the first time in her life.

'Marry me, it's simple enough.'

'No, it definitely isn't,' she told him crossly, regaining her composure as the absurdity of her ever being his Mrs Winterley sank in.

'Well, someone just saw us together in the middle of the night and I doubt they will keep it to themselves. You're the vicar's eldest daughter and I'm such a devil of a fellow I'm surprised he hasn't locked you all up.'

'Don't joke, it's not funny.'

'I know,' he said grimly, as if she was the one who had been taking this too lightly and not him.

'Papa and Mama can weather the storm.'

'What about your next sister and her worthy young curate? Will they withstand it when it comes to settling in his first parish with a scandal haunting them? Mud sticks, Rowena. It will stick to your other sisters as well, especially when they make their debut.'

'Nonsense,' she argued uneasily, 'Sophie is fifteen and Hester has years before she'll even go near a ballroom, thank heavens. By then any whispers about me will be forgotten.'

'Don't be naïve. Still, at least I'll be able to protect you properly when we're under the same roof,' he said as if it was a sane and sensible idea and why hadn't he thought of it before he had to?

'That's even more ridiculous,' she argued, feeling as if she was wandering in one of those nightmares where no rules applied. 'You can't marry me simply because we once shared a moment of danger or a scandal.'

'Whoever was down there just now saw me with you in the middle of the night,' he said, counting off reasons why she should marry him on his fingers and making that nightmare even darker and more twisted somehow. 'You were in the woods with me the other day and the idiot who shot at me must think you saw more than you did, as he's been accosting fair-haired women in the twilight.'

'I couldn't tell him from Adam if he stood in front of me.'

'You might if he'd found you last night instead.'

'It would be reckless to expose himself to recognition like that, you're imagining it.'

'And did I imagine that gunshot?'

She shuddered at the memory of it so close she could almost taste it. Her breath caught at the idea he might be dead right now if not for Hester. 'No, but it's you he means to harm, not me. How could assaulting me at twilight help with that?'

'I doubt he intended you to survive,' James said dourly.

'Even if he meant to murder me he wouldn't get far in a place where everyone knows everyone else.'

'He's an opportunist rather than a strategist, but there are ways of killing silently I hope he doesn't know and you won't find out.'

'No, I know too many already,' she said, all the different sorts of death she'd seen on campaign haunting her as the numbness began to wear off and she finally took in the fact Beau Winterley was asking her to marry him, no, not asking—demanding she did so whether she wanted to or not. 'And that's not a good enough reason to marry me either.'

'I can think of a better,' he said with the wolfish smile that had made her distrust him on sight. 'Which leads on to reason three. I am a noted admirer of beautiful women and we've been thrown together on a daily basis. It will be assumed I'm trying to win you to my bed, virtuous widow or no,' he added rather wearily. 'As soon as those rumours about us being pillow mates start to do the rounds, my enemy will assume whatever I know you do, too. You will have to marry me so I can protect you from him.'

'No. I shall *never* marry again. Even if I had the slightest intention of doing so, I wouldn't wed a man who imagines there's an assassin lurking round every corner and does his best to seduce every attractive woman he meets.'

'Not if I was married to you I wouldn't,' he muttered crossly. 'I'd be too busy fighting off the wolves eager to snatch away the woman who captured my fickle heart.'

'I'm not a chicken to be fought over by a pack of idle predators.'

'Try telling them that.'

'I won't need to, since I won't be marrying you and I'm quite happy to miss the rest of the dandy set, by the way. If you're anything to go by, their charm is wildly exaggerated.'

'I must need more practice, then,' he murmured and how had he got so ridiculously close without all her warning instincts screaming an emphatic *No*?

'Not with me you don't,' she snapped, but her legs refused to obey when she ordered them across the room.

'With you before all others. Marriage is a leap I never thought I'd make either, so let's find out how it will be if we work at it.'

'We can't,' she told him and gazed into his fascinating green eyes like a mesmerised rabbit staring at the fox about to gobble it up.

'I think you'll find we can,' he whispered with a warm invitation to find this furtive midnight tryst fun in his gaze, before he came even closer and her eyes went out of focus as he lowered his head and kissed her, and she let him.

Not just let, but revelled in every second, she decided with the small bite of sanity she had left. For a moment she held her breath as the gentle persuasion of his kiss rocked her to the tips of her toes and they tingled traitorously. Need spread through her like a hot flame and she'd never dreamt she could burn for more and as deep as this. Even when she thought she was in love with Nate, she never felt raw need sweep her under. Memory of what kisses led to sobered her and she would have drawn back. He laid a soothing hand on her back and she heard him catch his breath as her body shaped to his touch without asking. He hummed approvingly against her mouth and what was the point denying them such delicious pleasure? And it *was* only a kiss, wasn't it?

Did I say only? she asked herself after he'd seduced every single sense she had. *It's like no kiss I ever dreamt of.* This was a new world of heat and mouth-watering chances for more and she wanted to explore every last one. *I take it back, it's dangerous as a spark in a powder keg,* her inner woman whispered to the one who didn't do this and didn't enjoy lovemaking. *You're enjoying it now*, the houri argued smugly. Rowena moaned softly as James teased at her lips until she parted them so he could slip his tongue into her mouth and explore even more.

He built it so beautifully, this blaze at the heart of her. Made her feel so cherished and appreciated and feminine her body went pliable and wanted to cling to any part of him it could reach. His hand shook slightly as he cupped her chin to angle their mouths even more intimately, as if however close they got to each other could never be enough. She wriggled in agreement, then went as stiff as a peg doll when his starkly aroused sex met her flat belly through all these layers of fine wool and linen. The invasion and even pain of having Nate like an invader inside her was stark in her memory and she winced back to stare at him as if they'd nearly done something terrible.

For a moment he looked dazed and lost in that sensual world he'd been building for them. James Winterley, Beau Winterley—lover, spy and elegant man of fashion—seemed vulnerable and shocked because an obscure country widow no longer wanted him as brightly and brilliantly as he wanted her. He looked almost as boyish and hurt as he must have that morning his first sister-in-law ripped away his innocence. She raised a hand to soothe the frown and puzzlement away, then hesitated and drew back. Not even for the boy he once was could she invite this complicated man into the bed so close by and endure such wretched intimacy again.

'There may be more for us to work through than I thought,' he acknowledged rather breathlessly at last. Despite the battle it must have cost him to calm his unsatisfied sex he looked almost himself again, except for a thoughtful frown between his dark brows as he gazed at her with a parcel of questions she didn't want to answer in his intent gaze.

'You still want to marry me?' she managed past this feeling her heart was trying to beat its way out of her chest.

'Why wouldn't I?'

'Because I can't... I don't want to...' was all she could manage to explain.

'You're not cold, that's a certainty you needed not waste your breath trying to refute. Man-haters don't kiss one like you just did, Rowena Finch.'

He paused, waiting for her to lie, but what was the point? Instead she tried to hide a shiver as the real coolness of an English autumn night whispered in past the last hot twist of regret deep within that said he was right.

'I never have until you,' she confessed.

'We've made a fine start, then. Whatever Westhope did to you, we'll forget it together,' he told her with such deadly seriousness it felt like a vow. 'There's a lot of territory to cover between a kiss and climbing into bed together. We're going to explore every inch of it until you're ready to trust me and I promise you nothing you did with your husband will ever compare with what we can do together.'

'You still can't marry me,' she argued as she tried to ignore the idea it might be a wonderful journey with him.

'I don't see why not,' he said in his old, arrogant way and that made it easier to tell him he was mistaken and must leave before the night was spent and she hadn't had a wink of sleep.

Chapter Eleven

Even next morning Rowena couldn't get the sound of James Winterley's parting words out of her head as she woke up with *You still have to marry me* echoing in her ears.

'Never again and certainly not to you,' she'd argued.

'Well, that's told me, hasn't it? You have no idea how lovely you are, do you?'

'No, not that it matters,' she ended, with a fearsome frown and a very firm goodnight.

She lay back against the fine linen and lace-covered down pillows and allowed herself a long sigh. James was a strong man with a deep-down integrity and it was unfair to compare him to Nate. She hated the fact Nate was dead, but at least she didn't have to be his wife any more. She'd be fifty times a fool to put herself at the mercy of a man again; a hundred times if that man was James Winterley. She was about to spring out of bed and find the mallet she would need to drive the ridiculous idea out of his thick skull when a maid breezed into the room with a cup of chocolate in one hand and a jug of hot water in the other and informed her breakfast would be served in half an hour.

'I'm Sally, ma'am, and Sir Gideon said I was to help you dress, then guide you to the Yellow Morning Room so you can break your fast. I really don't know why he got us to get this funny old room ready for you in the first place, though. It's half a mile from the rest of the family and I had to stop and remember which turn to take a few times and I live here. If we get lost, we can always go down the garden stairs and out into the Old Lord's Privy Courtyard, then back in, I suppose.'

'That might be best,' Rowena agreed absently as the little maid tutted over the crumpled state of her clothing.

She was put in this obscure guest room so James Winterley had easy access to it and nobody would know if he came and went via the very courtyard she bitterly regretted entering the other day, wasn't she? At any rate Gideon had questions to answer. As for the wretch who had tried to compromise her into marriage last night, he'd best hope one headache had gone before she gave him the next. At least Sally didn't seem shocked or conscious with her, so whoever saw her and James last night had kept their counsel, so far.

'Mr Winterley didn't disturb you this morning?' the maid asked and Rowena was glad she had her back turned. 'Only a message arrived for him at dawn and he's gone away for a few days. He must have left at sunup and his room is on this side of the house, so I thought you might have heard him go.'

'I heard nothing,' Rowena said, wondering why Raigne suddenly seemed empty.

'He's took that big stallion none of the stable lads will go near, so it is to be hoped he's really right as ninepence again like he says. If he falls off that great beast he'll be soft in the head for the rest of his life if he ain't dead as mutton, or so my dad says and he's a village blacksmith and knows a thing or two about horses, and being bashed on the head.'

'I dare say,' Rowena said faintly. The wretch infuriated her like a very handsome wasp when he was here and worried her half to death in his absence. 'The chocolate is delicious, thank you.'

'You're welcome, ma'am. Oh, and that viscountess the missus is such great friends with nowadays said you was to call in her room and choose a day gown to wear until Mr Horsefield shows up from the vicarage with your traps.'

'How very kind of her,' Rowena managed doubtfully.

'So if you slip this old thing on over your underpinnings and puts the shawl over the back we won't need to do up more than a few of them dratted buttons, will we?'

Rowena went behind the plain screen and washed, then did as she was bid. Sally found the way back to more sensible parts of the house and left her to Lady Farenze's maid, who pursed her lips at the extravagant choice of morning gowns being offered to a lady's companion, then nodded approvingly when Rowena chose the plainest. The stern-looking lady's maid made Rowena sit and have her hair brushed and dressed before the gown was thrown over her head.

'Oh, that was lovely, Culdrose,' she said with a grateful smile. 'I can't tell you how long it is since anyone did that for me.'

'You have beautiful hair, Mrs Westhope,' the maid told her and shook her head slightly as if she knew it was a mixed blessing for a respectable widow.

'It can look brassy if I'm not careful, but this style looks so neat and elegant I shall try hard to remember how you did it.'

'I'm here to help if you can't, madam.'

'My, you are honoured,' Lady Chloe said lightly as she peeped into the dressing room and nodded her approval of the simple gown and elegant new hairstyle. 'You look younger and a lot less like a governess. Lady Laughraine will be pleased.'

Rowena was a few years younger than Lady Chloe, but a stranger would probably set them the other way about until now. A picture of James Winterley enchanted by her transformation sent her into an impossible dream for a whole minute. No, the idea was laughable; nearly as funny as her doting on him. She reminded herself Papa or Horsefield would bring her box to the big house this morning and she could wear her own clothes again. That should put a stop to any more foolish ideas a sophisticated gentleman of fashion might fall in love with a countrified quiz, if she tried harder not to be one.

Two days later nobody had mentioned Rowena's dubious night visitor and the strain of waiting for the gossip to bloom was giving her a headache. Well, in fairness it wasn't only the suspense that was doing that. At the end of an afternoon when mist never quite lifted from the lake or let the turning leaves blaze through the dullness from the woods, Rowena was beginning to think she might earn the ridiculous salary Callie was going to pay her after all. Bored and still queasy at midday, Callie had been alternately argumentative and tearful all day. Now she was sitting in the parlour she'd made her own, trying to be brave. It almost broke Rowena's heart to see her friend wrestling with her hopes and fears for this new child of hers and Gideon's.

How would it feel to know another life was growing inside you? The other Mrs Westhope said Rowena must be barren, but the lack of a child had more to do with Nate wanting her so rarely, thank heaven. Yet another reason to refuse James Winterley when he next demanded she marry him, though. Even if Lady Farenze produced boys in strict rotation for the next two decades, no noble succession was ever secure enough. It behoved a man like James Winterley to sire sons and she was a very poor bet on that front.

'Do you think James will be all right, Row?' Callie interrupted her dark reverie on what sort of wife the man really should marry.

'Cats always fall on their feet,' she replied cynically.

'My, you really do dislike him, don't you?'

'Not really, but he should not have risked his health by riding off on that great beast so early and staying away so long. How does he think my little sister or Jack will feel if he's discovered face down in a ditch because he hasn't the sense to do as the doctor ordered and be careful for a few more days?'

'Don't,' Callie said with a shudder.

'I'm talking nonsense, Callie. Sooner or later he'll come back as infuriating as ever and hungry as a hunter. He has a very healthy appetite.'

'Yes, he's a great favourite with Cook, especially

now I am turning up my nose at all sorts of things I usually love and wanting those I can't abide.'

'Mama had the oddest cravings for charcoal when she was carrying Nan. Papa came up with the compromise of burnt toast, but we were all glad when her passion for it wore off.'

'I hope I soon get over wanting salt on my pudding, then, poor Gideon thinks I'm teetering on the edge of lunacy.'

It was said with such a heavy sigh, Rowena wanted to hug her friend and reassure her all Gideon wanted was his adored wife to be happy and she could eat the wainscoting in the Great Hall if she chose to. Treating her as if she was fragile for the next six or seven months wasn't likely to leave her facing the birth with hope and joy in her heart, though.

'Gideon would fetch a tear from the moon if he thought it would make you feel better,' she pointed out, 'but you must stop trying his love, Callie. It's strong and sure as ever and driving him away again won't do you or your babe the slightest good.'

'I can't lose a child and a husband again, Row, I really can't,' her strong-willed friend wailed as if that forlorn outcome was written in stone. It was so tempting to take her in her arms and let her cry, but Rowena managed to resist her woebegone face and teary eyes.

'Stop being a tragedy queen, Calliope. With Gideon at your side you can face anything you have to and why are you so convinced lightning will strike twice? I'm so sorry you lost Grace, even more so that your wicked stepsister and aunt came between you and Gideon when you needed each other so very badly. I can't imagine where my wild, reckless playmate has got off to, though. You're moping about the place like a Gothic heroine, although you have the finest man we know as your husband; your grandfather dotes on you both and now you're going to be blessed with a child. Don't spoil the happiest days of your life by imagining the worst all the time like this, love.'

'You don't understand; you haven't lost a child,' Callie accused tearfully, even as she waved a hand in apology.

'No, but my mother and father did quite soon after we came to Raigne and now they have too many children to cram into the vicarage all at once. Why don't you speak to her, dearest? She is the most practical woman I know, but she feels deeply under the vicar's-wife serenity she's had to assume to cover it up.'

'I will, then, and I'll try to look on the bright side from now on, I really will. I've been horribly selfish, haven't I?'

'No, but you will be if you go on wafting about making us all low spirited for much longer,' Rowena tried to joke when she badly wanted to hug Callie and cry with her.

'Then I won't. Joanna's wedding is only a few weeks away, then there's Christmas to look forward to,' Callie asserted, sitting more upright and trying hard to be cheerful. 'You're quite right, Row; it's time I got on with my life. Grace is with God and none of it was my fault or Gideon's. Tomorrow I shall start writing again, since doing it makes me feel like me, if that makes any sense at all? You may have made a rod for your own back.'

'I do hope so, I could certainly do with something new to read,' Rowena said, as if she didn't have Raigne's vast library at her fingertips, and Callie laughed.

* * *

It was nearly dark when Rowena decided she couldn't pretend to be wandering about the herb garden for no reason much longer. James Winterley could fall off his horse and finish the damage the Finch family started any time he liked. At least then he couldn't order her to marry him and add her to his list of rescued dependants. Quite why she was so intent on saving him from a rifle bullet that day in the woods escaped her right now and she could cheerfully bash the man over the head if he stood in front of her now, if only she could reach, she amended practically. The idiot man could hardly have had a wink of sleep the night he left and who knew what danger that might put him in? She began to wonder if he was ever coming back and why she cared one way or the other.

'And why did you leave in such a hurry?' she mused out loud. 'Was it to get as far away from me as you can in case I change my mind and say yes?'

A small part of her felt desolate as she tried not to fall over a stone urn in the semi-darkness. She flushed at the notion she was waiting for him like a lovestruck girl and stumbled into a box ball instead. She quietly cursed him for being such a distraction she was in danger of doing herself serious damage and marched towards the stable path as it was less cluttered with dimly visible objects and a quicker way back to the house.

'Careful, Rowena,' a husky male voice warned softly and she nearly jumped out of her skin. She was teetering on the edge of a tumble again and he did nothing to stop her pitching on to the gravel in an undignified heap, so she glared at him after she flailed her arms and somehow recovered her balance without his help.

'I'll be careful when you show some vestiges of common sense,' she struggled not to shout back. 'I dare say you've been riding here, there and everywhere for the last three days after such a crack on the head it's a wonder you're not a simpleton. Was it a shooting party you had to get to so urgently; or a tryst with your latest lover; or simply a meeting with your dissolute friends that couldn't wait a moment longer?'

'Since when do you care what I do?' he asked flatly, as if he was her devoted suitor and had a right to feel aggrieved she had rejected his offer.

'Maybe I don't want to feel guilty when you finally kill yourself,' she said shiftily as temper died abruptly and she wondered about that herself. 'The doctor said you must be quiet for at least a week after such a blow to the head and you ignored him.'

'Do you worry about anyone who has a trifling blow on the head or just me?'

'Nobody else acquired their injuries saving my little sister's life,' she muttered and almost turned away before a small movement of the bundle he was carrying stopped her.

'Where are we this time, Uncle Monday?' a child's sleepy voice whispered.

'In a safe place, Sprout, now go back to sleep,' he soothed the small child Rowena could now see snuggled trustingly against his shoulder and why did she look oddly familiar even in this poor light?

'I'm sorry,' she murmured as the child did as he bid with a touching faith in his power to make the world go away Rowena wished she could share.

'Oh, dear, are you really, Mrs Westhope?'

'Yes, and if you're not careful the world will find out you have a heart after all.'

'You won't tell anyone, will you?' he joked and continued towards the grand suite Gideon and his great-uncle had given him for as long as he wanted.

That could be a silent challenge to James Winterley's enemy, she decided; he is our honoured guest, take him on at your peril. Reluctantly impressed, she stepped ahead to open the small door on to the path from the Old Lord's Rooms since his hands were full. Could this be poor murdered Hebe's daughter; the child he thought safer with someone else? Idiot, she chided him silently, the child obviously adored him and could have no better protector if she was a princess instead of a dead spy's love child.

'Thank you,' he said absently as he passed inside, probably expecting her to take herself off meekly until he was ready to bombard her with impossible demands again.

'You're not fobbing me off that easily,' she muttered and heard a surprised chuckle that somehow warmed her and that warmth whispered how much she'd missed him and made her squirm all over again.

'Thank the Lord you're back safe at last, Mr James,' Huddle greeted his master, then shot a startled glance at Rowena, as if trying to place her before he checked over the great idiot standing between them for further damage.

It was the longest sentence she'd heard the taciturn man utter and she wondered how deep in James's confidence the man was. Not all that far, if the startled expression on Huddle's face was anything to go by when he saw the child asleep in his master's arms. He stood back to let him into the suite and something about the dark-haired little waif so confidently nestled into James's shoulder made Rowena hesitate on the edge of propriety.

'Is she your daughter?' she was horrified to hear herself ask.

'Hush,' James cautioned and looked even wearier, if that was possible. 'Only by adoption,' he murmured. 'Now kindly forget you ever laid eyes on her and leave. Huddle, we'll need the contents of my saddlebags to settle the mite for the night,' he added.

The man took another look at the child, then went with a resigned shake of his head. Rowena had thrust herself into James's private business again and fidgeted under his steady gaze. The child shifted in his arms and he soothed her with a tenderness that brought a lump to Rowena's throat.

'Is someone still watching you?' she whispered.

'I evaded him and you can trust Gideon not to let strangers into his uncle's kingdom now he's forewarned. Whoever the rogue is, I had warning he was after the children in time to get them to safety.'

'You're late,' Gideon's voice muttered an abrupt greeting when James shifted his sleepy burden to open the inner door to the vast suite an old lord had made down here.

'Did Bowood get through with the other two?' James responded. Rowena could hear the slur of exhaustion in his voice and why must he carry the world on his shoulders like this?

'Aye, now come in before someone hears or Callie finds out,' Gideon urged and tugged James through the door, looked shocked to see Rowena trot behind him like a devoted collie dog and frowned. 'What the devil are you doing here?' he muttered as he bolted the heavy door behind them and motioned towards the faint glow of light at the other end of the dark panelled corridor.

'Mrs Westhope does seem the handiwork of that dark gentleman rather than the Reverend Finch's least saintly offspring at times, doesn't she?' James Winterley drawled insultingly.

'In fairness there's stiff competition for that title,' her supposed friend replied.

'Thank you for being no help at all,' she snapped at the man she had, mistakenly, regarded as a good friend until he took James's side instead of hers.

'Well, he's right. You should keep out of this dark business.'

'Since you employed me, then persuaded me to live here most of the week, you can hardly blame me for being here instead of at the vicarage. I *am* involved and there's no point ripping up at me when you should be getting the child to bed as she's obviously exhausted.'

'Touchy, isn't she?' James asked Gideon as if she wasn't here.

'Practical,' she argued stalwartly.

'Luckily Callie's one-time nurse is back in the area and looking for employment. She may have more of it than she wanted right now, since she's already got the boy and girl your furtive friend brought in this afternoon. One more sleepy head won't bother her overmuch after the trouble we've had getting those two little demons to sleep, but no wonder Bowood refused a bed for the night and galloped away as fast as his horse could carry him,' Gideon said as he led the way past a vast sitting room and enormous bedchamber.

'Stay here,' James ordered Rowena softly as he followed Gideon into one of the smaller bedchambers built for servants to an irascible old lord of Raigne.

Chapter Twelve

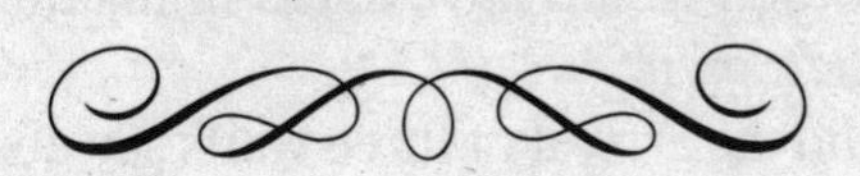

'As if I'm a lapdog,' Rowena muttered darkly and went back to the dimly lit sitting room, surveying the glowing fire and the makings of a hot toddy on the hearth.

Gideon had done his best to make his friend welcome after a long ride. Rowena found herself wishing she could be the one waiting for James Winterley's return; perhaps even leaning into his side as he pulled her close and told her about his adventures and quietly enjoyed the comfort of his own fireside. He could demand she married him until they were old and grey, but he'd never share so much of himself with her.

So that was the impossible dismissed, now what came next? She sank on to the chair nearest the marble hearth. Why did it surprise her that Mr Bowood had taken so much trouble to bring two of James's orphans here? She considered the idea more deeply and realised she saw the man as the very antithesis of James. He was truly heartless and cold, where James only thought he was. She did her best to tell herself the man was James's friend and she didn't really know him, but she knew enough to be suspicious of any supposedly disinterested act or gesture and look at it harder for hidden motives. For some reason the man wanted James to see him as a devoted friend and even clever, witty and supposedly hard-bitten James Winterley had his blind spots. Mr Bowood and his sire were there when James was at his most vulnerable and something told her better men would have acted in his interests instead of their own.

What did the arrival of three waifs say about James Winterley and the game he'd been entangled in since he was too young to know better, then? It said he had a generous heart to go with that restless, reckless spirit of his. That he was a man who saw the bleakness of destroyed lives and did something about it. It said he was too complex to dismiss as she'd been trying to dismiss him ever since she first laid eyes on him.

'You're still here, then?' he asked when he finally came into the room, rubbing a weary hand through midnight-dark hair that already looked as if he'd been dragged through that proverbial hedge backwards.

'As ordered,' she reminded him and got to her feet.

'I never expect you to listen.'

'Sometimes I do.'

'I know,' he teased and why was it a relief to see laughter in those extraordinary steel-shot green eyes? Because if he could laugh, he must be feeling his usual infuriating self and she didn't want him to suffer any damage from rescuing her sister.

'And now I shall go and change for dinner and wish you goodnight.'

'No, you won't.'

'I shall do as I please.'

'I know, but I shall still see you at dinner.'

'You can't, you're exhausted,' she protested.

'The world needs to know I'm ready to join it once more.'

'But you rode heaven alone knows how many miles today and you shouldn't put your health at risk for the sake of the gossips.'

'What are they saying, then?' he asked warily.

'That you are stubborn as a donkey I dare say. Nothing about us,' she admitted with a weary sigh, 'but half the area wants to shake your hand for rescuing Miss Hes from certain death and the other half isn't so sure she didn't deserve to break a limb or two to teach her a lesson. I don't intend to hear any of them.'

'Nor me,' he said with a wry smile and she unwarily smiled back. Was it possible to lose yourself in a man's eyes? She experimented with the idea for a moment longer, then forced herself to look away.

'So there's no need to prove anything to the neighbours or make me refuse you again and your waifs are quite safe for the time being. Why have you gathered them here, though, James? Has your enemy threatened them in some way?'

'A rumour Bowood intercepted and brought to my attention,' he said shortly and Rowena wondered how much he trusted the man who had got him into his dark trade in the first place. As an outsider so much of what his nondescript friend had done seemed off-key and more than a little suspicious, but James was a loyal friend and how could she argue against a man he'd known for so long when she was nearly a stranger?

'You never spoke more truly though, *for the time*

being isn't enough for me or them,' he went on bitterly. 'I meant to make my property safe and find more folk I trust to keep it so before they came, but the bailiff's house at Brackley is sound, if old-fashioned. We'll make it habitable between us.'

'What are you talking about? *We* won't be doing anything together.'

'I'm talking of that marriage we need to make to protect you and the children. You're up to your lovely neck in my sordid life, Rowena, and someone knows, so how can you not marry me? You know what will happen if you wander about the countryside, begging for my enemies to steal you away and extract my secrets from you by guile or force, don't you? I'll have to hand myself over to men who want me.'

'Why should I matter to you more than any other chance-met female?'

'You don't see consequences to your actions; you blunder about in the dark paying no heed to the ruthless men on my tail. You must marry me, Rowena—it's the only way I can make sure you're safe from those jackals for life and silence the gossips.'

'Put like that, how can I resist?'

'I knew you'd see reason.'

'I was being ironic. The last thing I should do is marry you, Mr Winterley.'

'It's probably as well you don't need to work on your technique for refusing the offer of a gentleman's hand and heart, since no more of them will be offering.'

'We are *not* going to be married,' she said slowly and emphatically. 'And that's the most absurd reason for marriage you have come up with yet.'

'Did you love Westhope so much you can't put another man in his place?' he asked as if the idea hurt. That couldn't be, though, could it? He had every eligible female of the *ton* to consider before he got to her and she refused to be second best twice.

'No, by the time he was killed my husband and I were strangers living in the same tent rather than man and wife.'

'He was a fool, then,' he said, as if that was the most significant part of the short history of Nathaniel Westhope and his not-very-beloved wife.

Rowena shrugged. With James's acute gaze on her she was uneasily aware he had a trump card in his hand if he chose to pressure her into saying more. She knew his deepest secrets, so what right did she have to hers? She just hoped he wouldn't play it.

'Was the man blind or simple?' he asked with flattering incredulity.

'Officers lead their men into battle, Mr Winterley, not the other way about,' she managed to say with a social smile and a would-be careless shrug.

'Try telling some of them that,' he said cynically.

'The go-ons wouldn't listen,' she said, recalling the forthright opinion troopers held about such cowardly officers behind their backs.

Nate was never one of that shabby crew, but the terror in his eyes before battle whispered he could be, if he let himself. She admired him for not hanging back, despite his fear, but her knowing he wanted to was another reason to lash out at her. She wished he'd been brave enough to admit the life he'd longed for wasn't for him and sold out. At least he'd be alive, even if there wasn't much left of the happy marriage they set out on. James's gaze was intent on her now;

even weary half to death and troubled by the burdens on his broad shoulders, he was a force to be wary of. She should leave him to his schemes and puzzles and protect herself from another man who couldn't give her the love she once longed for.

'Never mind the past; we can have the future instead,' he said a bit too seriously.

'I won't marry you. Please accept my decision and guard your new family instead.'

'Is that it? You don't want responsibility for the trio of brats who depend on me? After helping with your tribe of younger brothers and sisters for so long, I suppose you're weary of the task?'

'I love every one single of them. They're unruly and take advantage of Mama and Papa being so busy with parish duties to get into mischief, but there are no better people on this earth.'

'And that's exactly what I thought you'd say,' he said smugly.

'Then why ask such an insulting question?' she asked impatiently.

'Because I wanted you to hear yourself deny it, of course.'

'Oh, you...you *wretched* tease. You're a great deal too clever for your own good,' she informed him snippily, but to be reminded how much she would have loved a family of her own at this very moment was a goad too far.

'If that was true, I wouldn't be in this mess,' he argued with a weary shrug.

She felt one strand of her iron determination to resist him snap and wrenched her gaze away, before he could do even more damage. Whatever he'd done during his piratical career, he had rescued the three vulnerable children now asleep in the bedchamber along the hall. Rowena tried to squash the idea the dark-haired mite he'd carried in just now might be his in more ways than one, despite his denial. He had talked of an ex-lover being murdered when she shouldn't have been listening. What if that sleepy child he rode so far to fetch was his? The gnawing ache in her chest at the very thought of him making that waif with a passionate and now-dead royalist Frenchwoman couldn't be jealousy, could it? Jealousy argued she cared far more deeply then she wanted to admit about James Winterley. Uneasy at the notion, she asked the question she'd been longing to since she overheard him admit at least three orphaned waifs now depended on him.

'Why did you do it?' she said, daring him to wilfully misunderstand.

'Because nobody else would,' he said, his eyes steely. 'Spies and informers are expendable. I admit some would sell anything they could lay hands on for a profit. Others are so cunning I counted my teeth after every encounter, but some do it for an ideal, a dream that would fail if they ever achieved it. Never trust a person with a burning cause, Rowena, they rarely do themselves good and harm those they should put first.'

Ah, so they were back to the woman he'd loved, were they? The one he had found dead. Hebe somebody, she recalled, wishing she could remember the rest of it. Even at the time she overheard that story a hot jar of envy towards his ex-lover had shot through her and now she wasted time telling herself not to be ridiculous. Best not to reason her way through this with his acute gaze on her, though; she had an uneasy feeling he'd read her mind.

'And these children are part of that harm?' she asked.

'Their family put a cause before their safety. I can't believe they risked so much for an unattainable goal,' he replied.

'Why not? You did. Or was it about adventure and profit for you?'

'I have no family of my own,' he said as if making excuses. Most men would crow loudly about taking in three orphans. This one thought he hadn't done enough. How could she defend herself against such a puzzling mix of masculine arrogance and idealism?

'Your brother and your niece, as well as Gideon and Callie, would argue that.'

'None of them depend on me.'

'None of mine do on me in the strict sense of the word, but I'd fight Bonaparte in single combat to save them from harm.'

'So would I,' he admitted in a rusty voice and shot her an exasperated glare as if it was her fault he'd had to admit it.

'So you went into that dangerous and shadowy trade to protect your brother and his daughter the only way you could, didn't you?'

'I wanted an adventure as well, green fool that I was.'

'I wish I'd been there. Someone needed to make you see what a gallant, mistaken idiot you were being. You would have done better to stay and make peace with your brother.'

'Maybe, but there are large holes in your argument,

Rowena—not least being I'd hardly have listened to the infant you must have been when I was a rash youth of twenty.

'I was ten years old and you might have had to listen if we knew each other then, because Mama was quite right, I was as fearless and unruly as Hes at the same age.'

'What a confession, but I didn't even listen to my great-aunt and she was the most intrepid female I ever met. But why do you try so hard to be prim and correct now, when it must go against every instinct you possess?' he ended with a frown.

'I grew up,' she admitted bleakly.

'Hmm,' he said as if he wasn't quite sure, but his gaze lingered on her womanly curves, then centred on her lips as if they looked tasteable. 'In certain aspects I can't argue, but in others…?' He let his voice trail off doubtfully.

'We're supposed to be talking about you,' she said haughtily.

'Not at my behest.'

'No, because you like to pretend you don't have a heart, don't you? Let alone a deep love for your family and loyalty to waifs you probably never set eyes on until they were left alone.'

'Your theories wound me, Mrs Westhope,' he drawled in best Beau Winterley style.

'Don't play the society fop with me, James. Not if you want me to take one word of your ridiculous proposal seriously.'

'So you're tempted after all?'

'Not by you,' she told him rudely, 'by those unlucky children.'

'Unlucky because they're orphaned and away from their native land? Or because they're landed with me as sole protector?'

'Both,' she snapped succinctly.

'Ah, that's me put in my place, then,' he said mournfully.

'Hah, that's about as likely as pigs learning to fly.'

'Oh, I don't know. I even feel like a henpecked husband right now and you haven't even said yes yet.'

'Nor will I—not unless I'm convinced those children are in danger if I don't sacrifice us both for their sake.'

'For me it wouldn't be a sacrifice,' he said with that frankly masculine assessment of her outward face and form in his wickedly knowing gaze once more.

'And for me it would be a revolution I didn't ask for and don't want.'

'Revolutions have peculiar outcomes, Mrs Westhope, look across the Channel to our French cousins' example if you doubt me. They start out as one thing and end up somewhere else completely.'

'I would rather not, thank you.'

'Then let's get back to planning our wedding as swiftly as possible.'

'I am not going to marry you,' she said between gritted teeth.

'Then why should I tell you another thing?'

'Because I already know too much and you're too much of a gentleman not to.'

'I doubt if that's it.'

'So do I,' she agreed darkly.

'To prove you wrong, I shall tell you anyway—in the hope the plight of my waifs will soften your hard heart where mine cannot. So you're right; I can't help being a cynic about the way nations turn their backs on the inconvenient leftovers of war and gallop on to the next battle. Still, that's all by the bye now. I took the three children down the hall from their own countries only when it was clear there was no other way to keep them safe. Now I have been sent a message from the most unlikely source to say the sanctuary I found them with good families is not secure. I have a ready-made brood to protect and care for and heaven help us all if you will not. Will you be mother to them and help me give them a future, Rowena? I'm not sure I can do this on my own any more.'

Suddenly he looked very serious indeed, as if her aid was truly vital. It couldn't be, he hardly even knew her, but it didn't feel that way, did it? She shivered with the conviction she had seen deeper into the truth of James Winterley's soul than he'd permitted another living being to look. Which brought her back to the lovely and tempestuous Hebe he shared far more with at a time when he must have been desperate not to be alone.

'So do you want me to be a nursemaid with added benefits or a glorified governess?' she demanded as furiously as she could, to cover another stab of jealousy at the thought of him and the Frenchwoman so passionately absorbed in one another they might have made a love child. 'Your ways of proposing marriage must leave your path strewn with women eager for any alternative.'

'I've never done it before. I was cured of wanting a wife at a very young age.'

'Yes, I suppose you must have been,' she mused.

His gaze shifted from hers and she wondered if he would ever get over the idea she knew more about him than he wanted her to. She had a worrying conviction she needed him to understand he wasn't the only one betrayed by those who should cherish and protect them, so she decided to let him into a part of her own life she didn't want to revisit either.

'I'll trade you a secret for all those I stole from you outside that window, James. I never enjoyed the so-called delights of the marriage bed, not even when Nate was trying to be a considerate husband at the outset, and the rest of our marriage made me vow never to put myself in the power of a man again. The idea of a ready-made family is more of an asset to your cause than a drawback, but not even the plight of those children is a strong enough incentive to make me say yes and risk losing everything I am again.'

'Your husband was a fool,' he condemned with such flattering contempt for Nate's judgement that she must remember not to find it warming and intimate.

'I'm a cold woman,' she assured him as earnestly as she could when the tension between them made a flush of heat burn along her cheeks.

'Are you indeed?' he drawled sceptically.

Rowena began to wonder if she'd offered an unconscious challenge to a red-blooded man like him by not being openly besotted with him. Maybe she should let him kiss her again to show him she was right. If she marched out of the room and left this discussion unresolved he'd never leave her be; if she stood in his arms and found the private wasteland she found whenever Nate made himself take his wife to prove he was a man, he'd soon see how ridiculous it was.

'Yes, and I can't imagine your pride would let you offer me a white marriage. Can we drop the subject now and get on with dressing for dinner?' she asked with one last try at getting him to see sense without making herself freeze in his arms.

'Hungry?' he asked in that big-cat growl of his.

'Ravenous,' she replied, wondering about the coldness she staked so much on as he loomed over her in the semi-dark and a warmth that was nothing to do with the fire spread through her.

'Somehow I find you warm and enticing, despite all your warnings. You seem the very opposite of chilly to me, Rowena Finch,' he whispered as he bowed his head to look deeper into her eyes. 'Can I kiss you again and prove your husband wrong?'

'Oh, very well, but please get on with it. We don't want to draw attention to ourselves by both being late for dinner if you insist on joining us in the dining room tonight,' she agreed as if deeply reluctant.

Diverting him from his fixation on marriage with chilly kisses didn't seem such a good idea now and how unfair of him to call her Rowena Finch. That girl was wild and impulsive and all too eager for life, not a wary widow. Who knew what bringing her into the mix might do to it?

'I've never had such an irresistible plea for seduction levelled at me in my life, but I'll do my poor best,' he said with such laughter and invitation to share it in his fascinating eyes she forgot all her plans to discourage him.

She couldn't look away, not even when he came closer and she told herself she badly wanted to. A flash of fire engulfed her; a tentative meeting of true self to true self she didn't believed was even possible until now. Rowena felt his mouth on hers in one of those gentle kisses he specialised in before he unleashed the fire underneath them. He began with another almost-innocent meeting of mouth and mouth, yet something shot between them that was more than she'd ever felt in her life. Gasping with shock, she parted her lips softly, licked at the taste of him on them and heard him groan softly before he let go of the reins and took her mouth in a long, satisfying kiss that left her breathless and unaware of anything but a blaze of need for this never to end.

She wanted to explore the world through him; needed to stay in this intimate shell of 'us' he'd drawn round them once more. She let out a long moan of denial when he tensed under her exploring hands and seemed about to raise his head and let Mr Winterley and Mrs Westhope back in, when they should just go on being James and Rowena until there was no separation between the two. Dipping one more kiss on her very ready lips, he broke away as if it cost him far too much.

He was still so intimately close she could feel the heat of him, and even the smell of overworked man and horse and too much road wasn't enough to repulse the new Rowena he'd brought to life the other night. She managed to distract herself from the proximity of so much fit muscle and bone and bronzed skin touchably close by wondering how he stayed so fit whilst aping the idle man about town. She still had to catch her breath in an audible sigh at the sheer temptation of him a mere fingertip's distance away. She wanted to breach that gap and shamelessly nuzzle into his powerful body, to be as man-mired as she could be simply by proximity. That need ought to shame her. Yet he looked as shocked and stranded as she felt when he stared down at her with so many James Winterley questions in his eyes.

She supposed she should be grateful he was betraying a whisper of his inner self by breathing as if he'd run a marathon. Hard to tell in the light of the now-flickering candle if that really was hot colour burning on his high masculine cheekbones, but the way he was looking at her, as if he wasn't quite sure what had happened when they touched either, told her it was. She felt him test those moments of elemental need against a map he'd drawn himself as a hurt and guilty boy of seventeen. Would he deny this was anything out of the ordinary if she dared ask? Was it? She felt the gap in her heart, knowing so little about the true art of making love with a man. It was a shift of self-revelation to join the rest of them she'd suffered these last few days. Was that what really happened when two compatible adults stepped over the border of acquaintanceship to become lovers? If so, she and Nate had never been compatible or in love to start with.

'Someone's coming,' he whispered huskily, as if saying it out loud was near impossible.

How much more he knew about amorous encounters than she ever would, she decided numbly. Half the household could have been lined up outside to march past the disgraceful spectacle of James Winterley blasting every notion of how men and women were together into the ether and she wouldn't have known. That gap between them made her feel raw and exposed and far too vulnerable to whatever he might say next.

She shuddered uncontrollably at the thought of I-told-you-so derision in his eyes even as she stood back to wrap her arms about her torso as if to protect herself from a killing blow. The gesture was too revealing; he frowned as if he found the idea she wanted to protect herself from him repulsive.

'I'm not your late husband. You need never fear me, in or out of the bedchamber,' he said stiffly, as if he really believed she thought he'd lash out at her in frustration.

'I know you'd never hurt me,' she said impulsively. 'At least not deliberately,' she qualified and knew she'd put up a barrier between them with her cowardice.

'Ah, but what about by accident?' he asked cynically. 'I do a lot of the damage by meaning well and refusing to leave well alone.'

'You wish you'd left me alone, then?' she asked past a choke of what mustn't be tears.

'No, would that I could sincerely say I do. Better for both of us if I thought we could simply be a rational couple agreeing to jog along together as man and wife, but I can't lie that well. Later we'll talk more, but here comes Gideon and we haven't time,' he said and watched her with wary eyes she only knew were green shot with silver from infatuated memory by this dim light. They were like his brother's and Gideon's in everyday terms, but James Winterley's gaze was sharper and, at least she could admit it in the privacy of her own head, infinitely dearer to her than either gentleman's.

He was building walls round himself in front of her eyes and she wondered if he could pick her gaze out from her sister Joanna's or even Mama, whose unfaded blue gaze showed exactly where her daughters got their deep-blue eyes. Probably not, she decided practically, bracing against the hurt of being one more entranced female to this man.

Chapter Thirteen

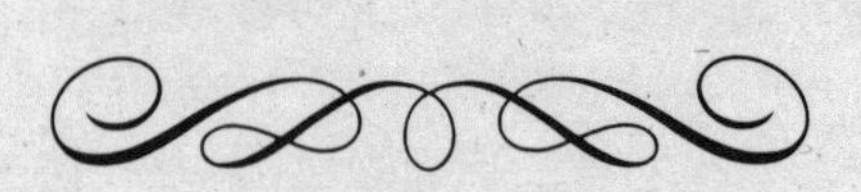

'I couldn't order dinner to be set back, since we put it about you were keeping to this room all day to convalesce for the heady excitement of dinner *en famille* tonight,' Gideon announced with a quick frown at the sight of them at opposite sides of the fireplace as if they wouldn't dream of kissing each other. 'You look downright villainous, James. Even from here you smell of horse and roads so strongly I can't but wonder how you have the gall to stay in the same room as a lady, given the dandyish fellow you pretend to be.'

'My status as a man of fashion is clearly under threat,' James agreed wearily.

The truth was he didn't know who he was any more. If he became Papa Winterley and retired to Brackley Manor to raise other people's children, he wouldn't have time to saunter about the *ton* as if he cared for nobody and he badly wanted to be Rowena's Finch's last husband, as well. The sound of his own voice saying '*my wife* thinks this' and '*my wife* does that' echoed in his thoughts. It sounded so right he wanted to start now and who would have thought it? Not the James

Winterley of even a week ago. Now she had him so damned confused he could hardly remember his own name when he looked deep into her blue, blue eyes and lost his grip on the world. Just as well the candle was flickering as if it was thinking about going out and Gideon was standing there like a deaf dowager then. At least he couldn't stand and stare into her eyes like a mooncalf when he stank like a midden and wasn't quite sure if he was on his head or his heels.

'You'd best put Beau Winterley back together then, hadn't you?' she snapped.

'Indeed,' he said with a clumsy bow. Gideon looked amused by his downfall, but stood implacably inside the door like a strict chaperon.

'Hmmph,' she murmured and how did women put so much meaning into that sound?

She snatched the candle from the mantelpiece and swept out of the room without a backward look. Impossible to stand in front of her and make her listen as instinct urged him to; she'd suffered enough from a stupid male determined to impose his will on her already. The idiot was getting confoundedly in the way and how he wished he could have come across the ardent innocent she must have been at eighteen. *And how likely is that, James?* that inner voice almost like Virginia's scoffed. *At eighteen she must have been breathtaking, so she was never likely to be left on the shelf, now was she?* True enough, he decided and almost nodded, except if he did Gideon would know he had a complete set of bats in his belfry.

'Luckily for both of us there's no time left to ask what you two were up to,' Gideon said with a warning not to hurt Rowena Westhope if he wanted to be welcomed at Raigne ever again behind his cool stare.

'I was begging her to marry me, if you must know,' James admitted in a driven voice and decided it was as well Laughraine couldn't see the flush of heat on his cheeks. She probably hadn't glared at him like an insulted princess because he had stopped kissing her, then numbly warned her Gideon was on his way. No doubt she was thinking up ways to be insulted by those magical, word-stealing kisses right now. Drat the woman, but his life had been turned upside down from the first moment he set eyes on her. And he'd said enough during that shamed confession to Luke to earn every ounce of her regal contempt. The truth was, she had him so confused he felt his world had been turned the other way up and he was trying to work out how to navigate it.

'She said no again, so there's no need to look smug and order the banns read. Wish I'd never set eyes on the confounded woman,' he muttered unwarily.

Gideon surprised him by laughing uproariously, then slapping him on the back. 'You're clearly in love, my friend. Welcome to my world of frustration and mystery. I wouldn't live anywhere else now I've found Callie again, but it'll take a cynic like you a while to settle to the task of loving your chosen lady for life, I suppose.'

'I'm not in love,' James protested. The idea of it made him want to call for Sultan to be saddled again, so he could ride as hard and as fast as he could in the opposite direction, even if both of them were beyond dashing anywhere much after today's exertions. Then there were his three very good reasons to stay and those mysterious threats to them he couldn't quite get to the bottom of.

'It has all been a bit sudden for a noble idiot like you to take in properly, I suppose,' his suddenly jovial host said with a wise nod, as if he was expert in matters of the heart, even though he could hardly claim to be anything of the sort when he'd mislaid his beloved wife for nine years. 'Your man tells me he has a bath waiting for you, my friend. I dare say you'll feel better able to face the world and your future wife when you're clean and shaven and dressed exquisitely once more.'

'She said no and how can I be in love with her, Gideon? I only met her properly a few days ago,' James protested as if he hadn't heard and really, what did appearances matter when your world was upside down anyway?

'Since you have the use of your eyes, although I wonder about the rest of your faculties, you must have noticed our lovely Mrs Westhope the moment you strolled into her father's church in Callie's wake the first Sunday after she came back to King's Raigne. I'm deeply in love with my wife, but Rowena is a diamond of the first water, despite all her efforts not to be. That makes it more like a month and, if you're going to try and fool me you hadn't noticed her from the off, don't fool yourself as well,' Gideon said, sounding like a doctor advising what symptoms a new sufferer of a disease could expect. 'Anyway, it doesn't matter if you've known her a decade or ten minutes. Callie and I grew up loving each other so I suppose you'll argue it's not the same for us, but I still recall the moment I looked at her and thought, *That's it, she's mine and I'm hers*. You could ask your brother how it was with him if you're looking for evidence love takes time, but I think you'll find he struggled against that admission from the first day he set eyes on Lady Farenze. Don't try to prove how stubborn Winterley males are by making yourself unhappy for nigh on ten years when you could be the exact opposite, man. Happiness is within reach; learn by our mistakes and grab it with both hands before it evades you.'

'You two are a lot more worth loving than I am, Laughraine,' James made himself say earnestly to his friend and secret relative. 'You've no idea about some of the things I did and saw after I left Darkmere all those years ago. How can a man like me ever be safe to love a woman like Rowena Westhope? I should never have asked her to marry me. She knows too much about me for her own good and I thought it the best way to protect her, but staying away from me could be the most sensible thing she'll ever do.'

'I doubt Rowena needs shielding from real life for her own good, James, and don't forget I've moved among the dregs of all levels of society during my chequered career. There's not much about the lowest depths human life can sink to that I haven't seen first-hand. And you're wrong to think love is an honour you must deserve; it's a gift. Two of the men I admire most in the world have been given it this year, despite their sins. I hope you're man enough to simply thank God, then seize your own undeserved happiness with both hands and make it a royal flush out of us four for Lady Virginia.'

For a long moment silence stretched between them in the now even-darker room and James struggled to come to terms with that radical idea. Gideon might be right. It was almost too incredible to take in, the notion of all he'd denied himself at seventeen being gifted to him anyway, despite all his efforts to convince himself he didn't want it. He shook himself like a great dog to dispel the hope about to lure him into a danger more acute than any he'd faced before, then wrinkled his nose in disgust as visible clouds of dust and a great deal worse scattered from his travel-worn person even in this muted light.

'How she'd crow if she got us all leg-shackled before her year ends,' he said with a shrug to admit it was possible, now. 'Meanwhile that bath is getting cold and I wonder you let me stay in the same room as Mrs Westhope in this villainous state for so long. What a poor host you are, Laughraine.'

'Now I thought I was being a very good one; letting you greet the woman who's been on pins about you in private. I'd best take my duties as my uncle's deputy more seriously in future and play the chaperon next time you go away without her.'

'Don't you dare,' James said stiffly and marched off towards his much-needed ablutions with Sir Gideon Laughraine's mocking laughter echoing in ears that burned as consciously as a guilty schoolboy's.

Rowena was glad Sally, the usually talkative maid who seemed to have been assigned to her, proved a deft and surprisingly quiet dresser tonight. Whether the mistress of the house had told her to mind her tongue or the girl sensed something new and a little bit dangerous in the air tonight, she had Rowena deftly dressed and downstairs in Lady Laughraine's sitting room so fast that she hardly had time to notice she wasn't wearing one of her own dull and inconspicuous evening gowns until she got there. By then it was too late to find her way back up all those stairs to resume her protective cover.

She glared at the clinging pearly-cream crêpe whispering so luxuriously around her legs and what felt like every inch of the rest of her and shifted the elegantly simple gown so she could hold it away from her body in the hope it might hint less broadly at the shape of the woman underneath it. No doubt she failed as that made her even more self-conscious by lovingly shaping the dress to her back and what she hoped was a neat enough *derrière* after all the walking and running after her brothers and sisters these last few weeks. She frowned as the thought she cared one way or the other what James thought of her rear view, if she let him see it thus outlined, made her feel as if an outrageous stranger was living inside her skin.

'Don't you like it?' Lady Farenze asked anxiously from her seat on a *chaise* next to her politely standing husband when she saw Rowena stare down at her borrowed plumage as if she hated it. 'It's one of my favourite gowns, but I really can't wear it now I've grown so fat and I thought you might like to borrow it tonight,' she added with such overstated pride in her still-tiny baby bump that Rowena had to hide a smile and be gracious about the loan of a favoured gown for such a quaintly deluded reason.

'It's lovely,' she said limply, sitting down with a sigh of relief as the wretched stuff settled round her and couldn't outline her figure so explicitly she wondered Luke Winterley let his wife out in public in the clinging monstrosity.

She was shocked by the conclusion that wolfish gentleman gloried in other men seeing what a prize he'd won in Lady Chloe Farenze and envying him every sleek curve and refined inch of her. His lady had been through so much to reach the blissful state of happiness she obviously enjoyed with her husband now that he was intent on showing the world how deeply he valued her, and what fools others were to turn their backs on such a goddess and leave her to risk everything she was for her newborn niece ten years ago. Chloe looked almost bemused to be feeling such joy, especially now their first child was on the way and openly declared now Callie was feeling better. There was a special glow about her old friend as well tonight and Callie clearly felt she was over the worst of her sickness at last. Rowena silently conceded it must feel wonderful for them all to be so deeply loved and looking forward to being parents to complete their happiness, as well. She did her best not to envy them their open delight in the loves of their lives tonight.

'Ah, Winterley, so you've deigned to join us at last, have you?' Gideon drawled mockingly when James strolled into the room as if he'd had nothing more crucial than the arrangement of his cravat to worry about all day. 'I'm sure Brummell would be proud of you now, so please don't even consider spilling soup on that perfect neckcloth, will you? I'm not prepared to sit like an actor in a frozen tableau while you spend another hour preening in front of the mirror until you're perfect again.'

'You should know as well as I do that Brummell asserts once perfection is achieved, a true man of fashion must act as if he's unaware of it, Laughraine, so I can safely promise not to move a muscle even if I shower myself in the stuff,' he drawled.

Rowena felt her hands tighten into fists at the spectacle of Beau Winterley back to his impeccable, satirical self once more. She fought a deep sense of sadness and straightened her fingers with an effort. The real James was so much more than this elegant clothes horse and he would never truly know it if she wasn't there to tell him so at regular intervals.

'Careful, Little Brother, I might not be the only one tempted to do that for you if you go on pretending to be as careless as a lamb in the springtime much longer,' Luke Winterley warned him with a quick nod towards her and a significant glance at the butler who was patiently waiting to tell Callie dinner was served.

'Come then, my dear,' Lord Laughraine said as if this was a day much like any other. 'Since these four insist on smelling of April and May and it seems a pity to break them up and leave them sighing at each other across the table, we might as well lead the way and let young Winterley bring up the rear, so to speak.'

'Thank you, my lord,' Rowena agreed with a relieved smile and gladly took a seat by his lordship while James seemed happy enough between his sister-in-law and Callie.

He acted as if he hadn't a care in the world for the rest of the meal; managing to look long-suffering and henpecked when Chloe declared it time he retired to splendid isolation before he overreached himself again. Not by a single word or gesture did he give away the fact he was exhausted and deeply anxious about a future even he admitted was uncertain. Somehow Rowena managed to return his polite goodnight with a faint nod and a murmured word that might have wished him peaceful slumber, if he chose to interpret it that way.

She half expected him to appear in her secluded room as soon as Sally talked her into a headache and departed with Chloe's precious gown over her arm. At least it hadn't mattered she was wearing a deceptively simple travesty of a gown this evening. The married couples present only had eyes for each other; Lord Laughraine was too much of a gentleman to ogle a lady and Mr James Winterley wasn't looking. It had been a confusing day and she was glad it was over and delighted he hadn't been anywhere near her since that confounded kiss. It was relief that made her feel so weary; he'd been away so long it was no wonder she felt a sense of anticlimax now he was back and infuriating as ever, despite the danger and anxiety of the last few days.

The man had clearly given up persuading her to marry him. Maybe he wanted his wife to present the same indifferent face to the world as he did and she couldn't be like that, so wasn't it a good thing he'd taken her *no* at face value and given up the whole ludicrous idea? She thought back to who she'd thought she was before she met him and wondered if she'd really grown up much beyond Hester's current level of reckless unawareness. Mama was right after all, she admitted to herself, once upon a time she *was* very like her headlong little sister. Now James Winterley's wretched, wonderful, bewildering kiss had reminded her how it felt to be so rash that living in the moment was more important than any consequences. He'd turned her into a woman she didn't recognise and she burned for him to do it again—with interest and any added benefits he could come up with. So wasn't that even more reckless than Hes's determination to climb the tallest tree in the forest and to blazes with the danger?

Pulling on her old flannel dressing gown, Rowena felt as if even this plain old friend was whispering impossible things about her and James Winterley as it wrapped round her too-sensitive body like a second skin. Her senses were humming with awareness hours after James made it emphatic for both of them she was a healthy young woman with a full complement of needs and desires. As for that abomination of a gown Lady Chloe had made sure she was wearing next time they laid eyes on each other…

Of course she was very glad to be rid of it and back to her everyday self. Nor did she want to think how it felt to sit through dinner and in the drawing room afterwards, conscious it was outlining every inch of her in far too much detail. Once James took himself off to bed, Callie and Lady Chloe yawned and Lord Laughraine claimed he was too old to sit up half the night gossiping and the house settled for the night sooner than Rowena wanted it to. If only she was at home she'd have Joanna to talk to, for a little while longer and, considering her future husband was the breathless joy of her sister's life right now, perhaps it was kinder to be here and leave her sister to dream of her Mr Greenwood until she could actually lie next to him and live it instead.

How would it feel if James Winterley was warm and close and intimately near her right now, then? The shiver that ran through her at the very idea of being this close to the wretch had nothing to do with feeling cold. Tonight she felt as if every inch of her was on pins; she was awake to her body as she hadn't let herself be for so long, simply because James kissed her again and looked at her as if he meant it. Most of her couldn't forget he'd left her wanting more and gone to sleep in his grand bed in the grand room in this grand old house either. Or quite forgive him for it. Had the kiss they shared here been nothing more than a brief meeting of lips to lips to him and far too easily dismissed from his mind as just one more possible lover untaken? Probably, if he could fight the exhaustion that must be like a physical weight on his shoulders long enough to think of her at all.

Doing her best to dismiss James from her mind, she wrapped the warm comfort of her old wrapper closer and stared at the window as if he might be awake after all and see her. No doubt he would raise one of his dark eyebrows in a mocking salute and congratulate himself she was awake because of him. *Enough of that, Rowena, let the wretched man think what he likes.* She wasn't sitting here gazing at that unlit window especially to think about him. So why hadn't she snapped herself out of his arms and slapped the grin off his piratical, stubble-marred and devilishly handsome face earlier and made it clear to him he was no more appealing than the villainous stable tomcat? Sighing at her own idiocy, she told herself to go to bed and face the wall so she could try and forget her window overlooked his latest lair. And it didn't matter if he'd kissed her as if his life depended on it, then ignored her for the rest of the evening. Except she still sat and wondered what he was dreaming of in that profound darkness below, drat the man.

She reminded herself Nate dazzled her when she first laid eyes on him, as well. She had been visiting Worthing with her maternal grandparents. It was such a polite place compared to raffish Brighton that seventeen-year-old Rowena was bored and trying not to be disappointed by her first grown-up trip away from home. The arrival of the invalidish Mrs Westhope's dashing young son felt like the sun coming out on a dull day. Her head was already full of the dash and glamour of Callie and Gideon's passionate romance, although it had come to a sad end by then and, thinking Ensign Westhope must be as intriguing inside as out, she refused to listen when Mama and Papa cautioned against marrying him, then travelling the world at his side.

Maybe it was the memory of Gideon and Callie's elopement that made them give in and consent to the marriage as the lesser of two evils. Rowena stared moodily into the night and pulled the curtains to behind her. She snuggled into the seat cushions so she could watch the much grander Lord's Rooms below without the interference of light from the fire and her candle. However good James was at making her feel a stranger to herself, he was exhausted and as set as ever on guarding himself from the rush and drama of life and idiots like her. She ought to be glad he'd seen sense. Hadn't she spent the last two years promising herself she was done with marriage for ever? So why did trusting another being with so much of herself suddenly seem almost attractive? *Idiot, wasn't that what you thought last time?* wise Rowena argued. *Ah, but this man is different*, her inner fool argued. Not that it mattered how *she* felt about the idea. He had clearly changed his mind and was probably congratulating himself on a lucky escape.

And no wonder he'd gone cool on the idea of marrying her. He knew how fragile her disguise of a sensible widow was. If she'd managed to be chilly and unaffected in his arms tonight, he'd be more inclined to want her. Men loved a challenge, didn't they? Until she melted all over him like ice cream in July she was one of those and now she wasn't. She sighed and glared at those unresponsive windows. Let him find a correct and chilly aristocrat to marry instead, then. They'd soon see how much he enjoyed sharing the small part of himself he'd allow anyone to know about with such a stony-hearted lady.

She shook her head rather sadly at the idea such a passionate man could force himself into the mould of a cynic and think it fitted him perfectly. For a moment she let herself dream how heady life could be if only they loved each other. Released from the shackles he put on his powerful emotions, James would be an eager lover as well as her best and most-treasured friend. So that was the man he could be—a man indeed and a fine father, as well as a lover other women would envy. In her fantasy marriage of true minds he would be hers every bit as surely as she was his and all those other women could have of him was envy because she would be his beloved wife.

'And any moment now you'll be wafted off to fairyland on a million butterfly wings, Rowena Finch,' she told herself sternly and shook her head. 'You're *not* the fine stuff such dreams are made of,' she admitted rather sadly and took herself off to bed, in the hope that particular one wouldn't haunt her with all the untold possibilities dreams must have, but harsh reality lacked.

Chapter Fourteen

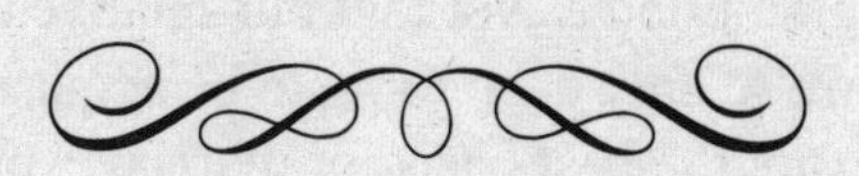

'We need to visit your father,' James informed Rowena as soon as he tracked her down to the library the next morning.

'Why?' she asked, trying to pretend she was too deep in Callie's scribbled notes to listen when really her heart was beating at the double because he was in the same room.

'For the good of my soul?' he drawled and she raised her eyebrows and stared at him sceptically. 'At least it got you to look at me,' he added smugly.

'Why?'

'Your ten-year-old sister might be able to get away with that unimaginative technique for avoiding the subject, you cannot, Mrs Rowena Westhope.'

'Why not?'

'Ah, a note of variation. Because you are a sensible lady of mature years, not a harum-scarum girl.'

'I'm only four and twenty.'

'That ancient? You poor old soul.'

'Go away, I'm busy,' she said with a glare that ought to make him leave, but he settled down on the corner of her work table and if he possessed a quizzing glass he would have eyed her through it to make her feel ruffled and out of sorts, but there was no need when she felt that way already.

'I suppose you think I'm too old for you?' he said at last and was that a note of seriousness behind his annoying Beau Winterley drawl?

'Of course I don't. Not that our relative ages matter when we're only ever going to be acquaintances.'

'Hmm, not the best basis for marriage, but I think from our previous encounters all the evidence says you're wrong.'

'I am not going to marry you, Mr Winterley. How many times do I have to say it before you have the good manners to listen and leave me in peace?'

'It's not a question of manners,' he argued rather stiffly and had she managed to offend him at last?

She had to hope so, because if he didn't go away she might give in and she didn't want to be lonely and needy inside another marriage and then there was that promise she had made herself and she hadn't done that without reason, had she?

'It is from where I am sitting,' she told him with the horror of feeling too much for an indifferent husband this time instead of too little making Mrs Rowena Winterley unthinkable.

'You won't accept the fact you're in danger from my would-be assassin; you don't take the threat of whoever saw us the other night using my presence in your bedchamber in the small hours of the night to blacken your good name and that of your family seriously. What will it take to persuade you to marry me?'

'And what will it take to convince you I shall *never* remarry, least of all to you?' she burst out.

It felt unfair and a bit cruel that she had to sit here and listen to all his reasons why they ought to marry. He would never say he loved or truly needed her. She wouldn't say yes unless he did and even then she would have to think hard about whatever it was she felt for him. That was that, stalemate.

'You not taking fire in my arms; you not feeling your heart race when I'm near as mine does every time we're in the same room. Don't even bother to deny it, I can see the pulse beating at the base of your throat from here, despite your latest suit of armour and that basilisk glare.'

'You are unpredictable,' she managed to say as if that explained her reactions to his closeness and not this choking feeling she might be turning away something wonderful, but she simply had to do it. If she didn't, she might find herself married to another man who didn't really want her once the novelty of the idea wore off.

'I'm a man,' he said flatly, as if that explained everything and maybe it did.

'Exactly. A man I am not going to marry. Nobody has mentioned seeing you in my room that night and if they were going to they would have done it by now. Contrary to your dire predictions no one has shot at me or molested me in any way either. We do not need to marry and I won't marry you, Mr Winterley.'

'You have a very odd way of discouraging suitors, Mrs Westhope,' he said distantly, but it was working this time, wasn't it?

'Because you don't listen.' She stood up at last

to rage at him more or less eye to eye. 'You think because I am a vicar's daughter and a humble lieutenant's widow I'll do as you say if you say it often enough, don't you? The mighty Beau Winterley has the blue blood of generations in his veins, so what he says will be, must therefore be. No, it must not. Not with me and not with my family. I won't be mocked by your aristocratic friends and see them sneered at by the society beauties who warmed your bed before I got anywhere near it. I won't guy myself up in fine clothes to try and do you credit when they all know I am out of my proper place in life and no gowns will ever disguise the fact. I won't be paraded as a curiosity, the upstart who caught Beau Winterley when he wasn't being careful enough to run hard in the opposite direction. If Papa was a country solicitor instead of a cleric you would be looking for a clerk or apprentice surgeon to marry me off to, but now you have the ridiculous idea of marrying me yourself in your head, you are too arrogant to let it go.'

'Finished?' he asked coolly.

'Yes, I rather think I am,' she said and turned away to hide the fact she felt more hot and bothered as he became more aloof and tightly composed.

'For someone who claims to have such contempt for me and my kind, you set great store by the opinions you force on us out of ignorance, do you not?'

She raised a hand to deny it as words seemed to desert her at last. Tears caught in her throat and stopped her speaking, but he wasn't going to let her off that easily anyway.

'I would have thought Mr and Mrs Finch would have more effect on their eldest child, you having spent the longest time on this earth with them, but you missed out on their loving kindness somehow, didn't you, Rowena?

'Yes, and Joanna is about to marry a humble curate so you can't propose to her instead, although she is twice the woman I shall ever be.'

'Please don't suggest I wait for Miss Sophia or, heaven forbid, little Hester, because the very idea of such an April-and-December coupling for either of them makes my stomach turn. I respect your family too much to propose anything of the sort. Would that I could say the same for you, madam.'

This was what she wanted. Exactly what she set out to do when she woke up this morning after dreaming of him and those impossible things all night long. Far better for him in the long run if he believed her at last and went away. A match like them could only endure if they loved so strongly they couldn't bear being apart, and he didn't love her and she really hoped she didn't love him.

'I suppose you will be safe enough here at Raigne, Gideon will see to that and send me word soon enough if whispers start doing the rounds about the Winterley rogue and Mr Finch's lovely daughter. Then you will have to make up your mind to wed me or leave me estranged from myself and the rest of my family, won't you? What a dilemma for such a stern and steely lady.'

'Good day, Mr Winterley,' she said between lips that felt numb and awkward and at least he didn't know how hard she was having to fist her hands behind her back to stop them reaching out and begging him not to go.

'Is it, Mrs Westhope? Is it really?' he asked as if

she might know, then swung on his highly polished heel and left her to her solitude and a grey silence that somehow seemed to go on for ever.

October was over and done with for another year and November had half sped by and it seemed both an age and the blink of an eye since James Winterley left Raigne for his ruin in the hills. In little more than a week now her sister Joanna would marry her Mr Greenwood in King's Raigne Church. A whole month had passed since Hester fell out of that tree and Rowena met James Winterley's steel-shot green eyes full on for the first time; almost a month since the kisses that woke up this wretched siren within her that refused to let her sleep peacefully in her eyrie of a night for aching for him sleeping and waking. The idiot wanted all sort of impossible things from him and he wasn't even here to deny them to her now. Ten miles of good West Country soil lay between them now, oh, and his cool smile and warily aloof manner the day he took her *no* at face value. At times she dearly wished she'd refused Callie and Gideon's offer of an occupation she loved, as ten miles between her and James Winterley wasn't nearly enough to put him out of her head.

Seeing Callie's vivid imagination at work was a delight, of course. Making a fair copy of her friend's scribbled notes or her own, after she had sat and listened to Callie's dictation of her latest book, made her the first reader and that felt a privilege rather than a job. Rowena was enthralled by watching her friend's characters develop as the story went on and Callie melded their adventures into a satisfying tale. It was also intriguing to watch Callie come to terms with her new life as Lord Laughraine's heiress and wife of the official heir to Raigne. So much work and organisation went on behind the scenes to keep this grand old mansion functioning as the heart of a rich and vast estate. As a vicar's daughter Rowena was used to the busyness and daily hard work of both of her parents, but this was on another scale altogether. Coping with what should be done as it always had been, what ought to be brought up to date and all the time running this vast ancient pile efficiently would have been too much to expect of Callie on her own, even if she wasn't carrying a child and perhaps the next heir to Raigne.

'And that's without this need I have to carry on writing. It makes no sense to go on with it now I have Gideon back in my life and Raigne to occupy me even before this little one comes along to terrify us all,' Callie observed one day as she rested a hand on her very slight baby bump and listed all the ways she needed her secretary-cum-friend to be alert and healthy and happy so she could keep on helping her. 'I really don't know how I'd manage without you now, Rowena dearest, but if you don't stop losing weight and looking tired and pale and altogether like something the cat wouldn't even bother to drag in, I might have to.'

'It's November and nearly winter so of course I'm pale; why shouldn't I be at this time of year?' she defended herself. Callie was right, though, it was ridiculous to waft about like a wraith when she had such an interesting life and lived close to her family and friends in the Raigne villages, too. She was treated like a member of the family as well and how many lady secretary-companions could boast that?

'Of course I don't expect you to be brown and weather-beaten at this or any other time of year, Row, but you really are getting too thin and those dark circles under your eyes worry me. You haven't been sleeping well, have you?'

'Sometimes Mama endures several weeks of either waking up in the middle of the night and being quite unable to go back to sleep, or not being able to sleep in the first place until it's almost time to get up again, so maybe I'm following in her footsteps. She says it goes away as suddenly as it appears after a while and she's never quite sure what brings it on in the first place.'

'Worry, perhaps? Or having her deepest-held and dearest convictions about herself undermined so badly she's forced to take them out and re-examine them? It could even be the fault of a certain enigmatic gentleman we could probably both smack round his handsome head for disappearing off to his wreck of a house with those three little mites and their nurse so he can prove how little he needs any of us.'

'No, I don't think Mama worries about him any more than she might over any stranger who chose to live apart from his kind,' Rowena replied as carelessly as she could.

'Ah, but she isn't the one we're really talking about, is she?'

'I am.'

'No, you are trying to and I refuse to co-operate. I'm not prepared to let you act the serene widow woman content with her lot in life any longer, Rowena Finch. We both know it's a lie and I'm done with living one of those, even for the sake of my best friend's so-called peace of mind.'

'I *am* a widow woman.'

'Not a very contented one.'

'That's my business, Callie,' she had to argue, because it felt like a very personal and private sort of business if they had to talk about James Winterley.

'I kept my counsel when James left so hastily. I even managed to keep a still tongue in my head when you became so cheerful about his defection it almost hurt to look at you. Gideon told me not to interfere.'

'Without much success, as far as I can tell,' Rowena muttered darkly.

'Rubbish, I've been as tight-lipped as an oyster for nearly a month.'

'No, you haven't, Callie.'

'True, but I have done my best to bite my tongue every time I noticed you and my almost cousin-in-law are looking about as happy and rested as each other.'

'Does he really look that bad?' Rowena asked before she could guard her tongue and the I-told-you-so expression on Callie's face said she had betrayed herself. 'Mr Winterley has three children to care for and protect now, little wonder if he's not quite his usual self,' she added with a would-be carelessness she knew wasn't going to do her any good.

'You might have seen for yourself how he looked if you hadn't suffered a chill that day he brought them over to meet Chloe and Luke's niece and daughter, and you kept to your bed all day.'

Rowena nearly fell into the trap of admitting she'd been heartsick and not ill and watched him arrive from where she stood a step back from one of the big windows of the informal sitting room above Raigne's grand Tudor porch. From so far away he looked much as he always did. Not as self-possessed with a small child holding on to each hand as if they had no intention of letting go. Even the very little one he brought back that last night at Raigne was wailing in her nurse's arms because she wasn't being carried by the right adult. Best not to admit even to herself that it hurt not to be the female at his side, Rowena decided, even if the poor woman was effortlessly outshone by this wonderful new father the three waifs had no intention of losing sight of. Unfortunately Callie's eyes were too sharp not to see her flinch and she seemed more determined to get Rowena to admit she felt something for the slippery devil, other than deep exasperation, of course.

'I wish you'd stop pretending you don't care, Rowena,' Callie said gently. 'I want you to be happy and neither of you seem to be so without the other to exasperate.'

'But that's ridiculous, Callie. We're not in the least bit like you and Gideon. Mr Winterley is a good-looking, elegant and well-bred gentleman and I dare say a great many females find him irresistible, but I'm not one of them.'

'Liar.'

'I can't be, can I? He has those three waifs to care for and seemed perfectly happy without me.'

'I knew you'd watched him arrive. I should have sent you a message when they were going so you could see him leave as well, if you weren't such a coward you won't admit how much you wanted to see him in the first place.'

'Don't, Callie.' Somehow it hurt far more than it should that James taught her to long for him, then went away, even if she'd told him to go. 'It isn't something I'm proud of.'

'Yet if only I could go back and make myself listen to you nine years ago, I would do it, Rowena. You were so right when you insisted Gideon loved me and I could never be whole and right again unless I let him know I loved him back. However sad and unlike myself I felt when I came to King's Raigne to pack up Grandfather Sommers's things and leave the vicarage empty for your family to move into, you said what you had to as a dear friend to both of us then, young as you were. That was brave of you, so I'm doing the same in the hope you'll listen as I wish I had. Never turn away love, Rowena. Nine years of being lonely and sad and less than Gideon and I could be together taught me what alone truly feels like. It's bitter and life sapping. Don't be a fool for the sake of pride, will you, love? It's not worth the agony.'

'This is a different situation; Mr Winterley and I are not in love,' Rowena argued.

'Only because neither of you would recognise it if you ran straight into it at full tilt. I never met two people so obviously made for each other as you and Mr James I-Don't-Need-Anyone Winterley, Rowena Westhope.'

'Nonsense, I'm nowhere near as cynical as he is.'

'Are you not?'

'No.'

'Then prove it by not hiding like a coward when James turns up this afternoon to consult Gideon and Luke and whoever else they've dragged into this business. Or don't you want to know how the task of tracking down the man stalking him is going?'

'Is someone still doing so?'

'If you don't care, it can't matter one way or the other, can it?'

'Never mind me, what about him?'

'Oh, yes, what about him?' Callie replied with a small untrustworthy smile she probably thought Rowena hadn't seen. 'I believe Sally will have repaired your pearl-grey satin so well by now that nobody will know it was ever ripped in the first place, so you might as well shroud yourself in it and join us all for dinner tonight and find out for yourself.'

'You haven't said if he's safe or not yet,' Rowena said grumpily.

'You're not going to find out unless you ask him yourself, then, are you? I can't see him managing not to know he's being spied on twice, can you? So you might as well join us and see for yourself.'

'Very well, but I can't promise anything more.'

'I shall simply have to trust he's less stubborn than you are, then,' Callie said with a sigh that said it was touch-and-go.

'Mrs Westhope,' James Winterley greeted her impassively as she walked into the drawing room before dinner with as little time to spare as she dared leave. She had stern words with her knees when they wobbled as she risked a very slight curtsy, but hoped she was the only who knew about them.

'Mr Winterley,' she answered with a regal nod.

Oh, heavens, he was a handsome devil, wasn't he? Memory had let her blur the clean lines of that powerfully sleek body a little, taken some of the truth and integrity out of his green-grey eyes and wiped away the frown between his dark brows. Was he looking more honed and somehow darker; a little less immaculately elegant? He could still sit as the model for a secretive brooding hero and set the hearts of half the nation beating faster, so what did little details like that matter to a besotted idiot like her? They still did, though, unfortunately.

'Oh, for goodness' sake, have done with all this unnecessary formality,' Gideon broke in impatiently, 'it's like sharing a room with a pair of bodkins.'

'Good evening, ma'am. How do you go on?' James said with such a carefully polite smile it made her want to run upstairs to the obscure chamber she'd become fond of and hide again.

'Very well, I thank you. And you, sir?'

'I think they give bodkins a bad name, Gideon,' James's brother said and rolled his eyes at the ceiling.

'Hush, all of you,' Callie warned from her seat on the sofa next to her husband. 'Here comes your visitor and what will he think if you three start quarrelling again?' Were they arguing before she came in? Now Rowena wished she'd come down earlier.

'Ah, Bowood,' Gideon said genially as he rose to his feet and stepped forward to meet the new arrival. 'I don't know if you recall Mr Winterley's friend, the Honourable Henry Bowood, from his earlier visits, Mrs Westhope?'

'Mrs Westhope,' the man said with a nicely judged bow and a polite smile.

'Mr Bowood,' she greeted him as gracefully as she could manage with James's gaze so hard on them. She tried hard to work out why his face seemed so familiar. She remembered him being eclipsed by James that morning at church when she was trying so hard to fool Mary Carlinge she was completely unmoved by Beau Winterley and told herself Mr Bowood had an ordinary enough face. No doubt she had seen echoes of it in another nondescript one she couldn't recall right now.

'I first met Harry Bowood when we were disgusting brats at Eton,' James said, more at ease with the outwardly forgettable man with light brown hair and light brown eyes than she'd ever be.

'Speak for yourself, Winterley. I was an endearing brat, you were the disgusting one,' the man teased and Rowena almost wanted to like him.

Mr Bowood would never stand out in a crowd. Which was an excellent skill in an agent, she supposed, and led her to wonder how James survived as one. This Bowood and his father had dragged James into a life that almost destroyed the bits of him that weren't already blasted by his late sister-in-law. Impossible to warm to him and did she only feel like this about him because she had overheard a private conversation? Perhaps; there was a hint of caution in Lord Farenze's manner, as well. She probably only detected it because she felt the same about a man who used friendship instead of cherishing it, but a shiver iced down her spine all the same.

'You're misinformed, old friend,' James said easily.

Evidently he bore the man no grudge for the life he'd lured him into as a boy, so why did Rowena feel there were dark undercurrents to this apparently sociable dinner? Apart from the ones that lay under James's refusal to look at her directly and her unease with him. She sent him away, so she ought to be very happy he'd listened.

* * *

She sat between Callie and Lord Laughraine at the round table the family used for dining informally later and tried to pretend she was content and this was a night much like any other. Except it wasn't. James was here. Even without this feeling Mr Bowood was testing the air for secrets, she'd find it hard to say what she ate. If not for her conversation with Callie earlier, she would excuse herself when it was over.

Luckily Lord Laughraine decided this was a night to plead his age and apologised for keeping country hours not long after the tea tray was banished. She met his still-bright dark eyes with a laugh in her own and he winked to agree he was only tired or infirm when it suited him. Glad she was coming to know this charming but iron-willed nobleman better, she bid him a demure goodnight and accepted the candle Cribbage handed her. She hadn't met James's eyes fully all evening and wasn't sure if that was good or bad. Keeping a close guard on her tongue should have tired her out, but she felt wide awake and restless when she reached her quaint bedchamber.

Chapter Fifteen

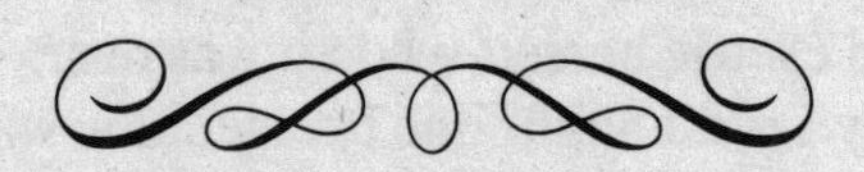

Despite the grey gown everyone seemed to be condemning as ridiculous on a lady of four and twenty, she looked vital and a bit too alive to meekly go to bed, she decided as she stared at herself in the watery old Venetian glass mirror over the mantelpiece. For the first time she took James's aspersion seriously and wondered if he was right about the grey attracting attention rather than diverting it. There was a glow in her eyes, colour in her cheeks and the slightest trace of a smug smile that said *he* was here. Never mind if they were physically apart and she'd said terrible things to make him go away, the fact James was nearby made her feel alive to the end of every last finger and toenail.

She shot the mean sliver of light shining from between the tightly shuttered windows of the Lord's Sitting Room a hard stare. Was James deep in conversation with his fellow spy down there, or closeted with Gideon and Lord Farenze so they could exchange ideas about his enemies? Maybe one of the children who had clung so determinedly to James when he arrived had woken up from a nightmare and, given the childhood they endured before he rescued them, they had every right to them. She couldn't steal down the crooked backstairs. It would be folly to tap on that shuttered window and expect him to welcome her when he opened it.

Resuming the grey-grey sort of day gown he despised, as it would make less noise than the armour-coloured satin, she stole down all the same and hoped Gideon had given Mr Bowood a room on the opposite side of the house. She edged round the deepest shadows of the courtyard and only stubbed her toe once. Glad the lemon tree had been taken in for the winter so it wasn't there for her to fall over she edged towards a risk she'd promised herself so sincerely not to take. He might be horrified to see her, he could even laugh, but she had to find out what he really felt when she turned up uninvited in the Old Lord's private courtyard, outside the same window she had sat by on that fateful golden day when it wasn't anywhere near as cold and eerie as it was now.

Although her slippers were soft and well worn, he must have heard something of her stealthy arrival, or maybe he knew more about idiots creeping about in the dark than most men did. She saw the light waver, then leap when he grabbed a candlestick, and held her breath for it to go out in his haste, but of course it didn't. For anyone else it would, but for James Winterley it stayed alight, the next question being where was it alighting him to? Past the vast sitting room and down the nearest echoing corridor. He must have blown the faithful flame out once he was sure of his way and wouldn't wake the children by falling over some precious antique in the dark. Now he was waiting for her to make her next move and even the house seemed to be listening for the latest human folly to stalk its venerable byways.

If she stayed still and furtive he'd come out to investigate, but if she made a noise someone else might hear her. Still thinking about those choices, she nearly jumped out of her skin when his hand reached for hers out of the blackest of the shadows. It took every ounce of willpower she had not to gasp and jump halfway out of her own skin and give them away to anyone nearby. Then he found her mouth as if he knew where it was as well as his own and used those long fingers of his to gently press her lips together in a silent demand she keep them closed. Before she even knew it had reached out, her hand was locked in his as if it belonged there—each made for the touch of the other. Ridiculous when even in the silence of their furtive journey back the way she came he couldn't quite mask his irritation with her.

Tempted to yank her hand away and creep off alone, she recalled what Callie said about how it felt to be truly on her own and decided to listen. She heard a slight catch in his breath as he checked their progress and used every sense he had to test the night for outsiders. Safe enough, he let her know somehow and now they were off again. She let her own senses get to work; they were back at the ancient oak door now and she reached out to reassure herself she'd shut it behind her and it was still so. Yes, here it was, all fissured and greyed with age, almost as strong and hard as the iron that bound it together. Had the hinges truly been as well-oiled and smooth running as she thought?

Would even a slight groan of metal on stone give them away and undo his caution?

As the door opened as easily as if it let in her lover every night, somehow she knew he'd stayed away for the very reason he asked her to marry him—to protect her. It was what he did; he left his brother and his home and took to his dangerous trade because it was the only way he could find to protect Lord Farenze and his baby daughter. He gathered up orphans and spirited them away from danger because of those protective instincts of his, so why wouldn't he ask a dull little country widow to marry him because he thought he'd endangered her by one-too-many appreciative looks? Or was it because of that day in the wood when she and Hes had frustrated a madman of his quarry and he thought the lunatic might come after her for revenge? Even more humiliating somehow if he chose to marry her for such a chance-met reason. That was why she sent him away as if she didn't care all those weeks ago, wasn't it?

She huffed out a sigh at the very thought of them. The memory of that bullet snickering past his dark head the second after he'd snatched Hes out of the air and fallen towards the earth with her kept her quiet as a mouse. Danger still stalked him. She almost forgave him those ridiculous protective instincts as she let herself know she'd rather take the next bullet than feel it slam into him and ice her world to real greyness for ever.

At last they were outside her bedchamber's ancient door. She felt as if all she couldn't say for the last month would tumble out of her mouth when they could safely speak again and tried to put a guard on her tongue. No, apparently they weren't here for that. James had a far better use for their mouths. Here it was again, a headlong tumble into them. His mouth was ravenous, as if he'd been starving for her all this time. How could she have done this to them? They would have had so many more weeks of life together if she hadn't made him leave without her for his wreck of a house in the hills above Raigne, but he was such a forgiving soul she stroked the side of his face and welcomed him wholeheartedly to try to make it up to both of them for so many days and hours of sadness and folly.

They could have a nice refreshing argument about whether her protective idiocy or his was the stronger later. Now her hand wanted more time to smooth his midnight-dark curls into the back of his neck where he almost let himself be vulnerable. Deep down something protested she was giving too much of herself away, but she ignored it and tugged him closer. She stood on tiptoe to meet his even-closer kiss as his mouth opened on hers and the heat simmering inside her for so long flashed into a blaze at last. Maybe he felt the little flicker of doubt she let herself sigh over as she went under, the check of hurt he might do this, then walk away because she had hurt him. A whisper of memory—how it felt to be married to Nate and dread the next moment he wanted to use her. James raised his head a little and peered down at her in the dimness of the firelight and shook his head as if he hadn't the words left to tell her he was sorry for going away because she told him to, sorry for not coming back sooner and even sorrier Nate hurt her and she hadn't forgotten yet.

'You'd better be,' she murmured as he neatly manoeuvred her towards the bed and she hardly even noticed they were close to being completely undone by each other already. 'Hurry,' she ordered as the rest of their clothes were shrugged off with a haste his valet would never forgive her for if he caught sight of his master's beautifully tailored coat and waistcoat shucked off with all the care of a sack of corn being emptied at the mill. Her grey gown would never be the same again, she decided with a giggle she hadn't known she had in her until now. Lud, but she was tired of grey. She must have muttered that thought aloud because he grinned and raised one wicked eyebrow as he took in the glow and shade firelight cast over her flushed skin and there wasn't a dot of that dull shade in sight.

'I could get to like it,' he argued with a preoccupied fascination with her body that made her feel gloated over as well as alive in every inch of her as she'd never been before. 'We have to try and find a way to hide how you really are from the world if I'm to stay sane for the next fifty years,' he explained huskily.

'Hmm, no need to hide it when you're not here to be mad or sane about me, now is there?' she asked before he followed his gaze with touch, got closer until he sipped at the scent of her at the base of her throat, then nuzzled in hungrily as if he wanted to make a sensory map of Rowenaland, then settle there for life.

'You told me to go and, anyway, I would still know,' he argued as he raised his head to look deep into her eyes and her pulse leapt at all the fiery need she saw in his.

'Then don't leave me again,' she ordered and put

a stop to argument by leaning up to kiss him and silence his *buts* and *maybes* with something far more important.

So they learnt the primer of true intimacy in one greedy gulp and went on to advanced education the moment he stopped torturing her with butterfly touches and hot kisses to places she hadn't known a woman wanted to be kissed until now. How had she ever thought she could live without the regular luxury of having him fully inside her and as close as a man could be to a woman? The idiocy of all the defences she'd tried to put up against him made her despise her old self as a new one was born. The fact was she truly loved this man and whatever she'd felt for Nate was a cheap candle next to the power of the sun. As she loved James beyond reason and limits, she had to love whatever they did together to be close as lovers had to be. It was as simple and as complicated as that, but only for him could she forget what she knew and be a lover and a woman in every sense of the word.

'Rowena?' he gasped as his desperation rose hard and rather awesome against her where she was most on fire. She shifted against the hot wet ache he'd already stoked to a raw blaze with the wickedest kisses and caresses a woman could know and she was on the edge of knowing something extraordinary about them both.

'I missed you so much,' she confessed. 'From the first second you got into the saddle of that wretched great horse of yours and rode away, I felt as if you took the only part of me that mattered with you.'

'Contrary female, you're the one who insisted I went to Brackley and left you behind.'

'You believed me.'

'Almost,' he conceded absent-mindedly. 'Better if I'd seduced you right there and then and got the truth out in the open between us, I suppose, but Gideon or his uncle might have come in at any moment and you deserved to stew for a week or two for driving me away like that, lover.'

'Did I?' she asked as his hands did incredible things to her sensitised skin and senses.

'You did, I didn't,' he told her severely and this wasn't the time to see the sadness as well as the laughter in his unique gaze and admit it all. 'Do you take it back?' he asked as if he could doubt it with her lying here next to him naked as the day she was born and shivering with longing and maybe a little bit cold wherever he wasn't.

'Yes, James, every last word,' she gasped and it was too much to expect him to say he felt more for her than any of this other loves, even as they neared the deepest intimacy a man and woman could offer each other and she'd heard men would lie to please a lover. For a moment that was a snag on her delight, a little bit of herself he couldn't share, then she let even that go and simply dived in to being with him in the closest sense there is. This was a night to be reckless and if she took a step back now she might never forgive herself for not having loved completely even once in her life. Reckless or not, he seemed to revel in giving her pleasure, in teaching her touching and being touched was an art form she hadn't even dreamt of before she met him. His long, sensitive fingers explored parts of Rowena she didn't even know needed exploring until now. She arched against the pleasure of every inch of her warming and rousing for more. Even as memory threatened he caressed her into a little ecstasy that had her senses riding high and screaming for more all at the same time.

There, he was hard and heavy even as she felt even softer and more melted and needy inside. She shifted a little to make it not easier but sooner; to tempt him onwards and to the devil with chivalry and all the gallant James questions she could sense on the back of his tongue even now. She wanted him hard and awesome and high inside her now and he was taking this so slowly, as if they had all the time in the world. She knew from the force building inside her that he was quite wrong and keened her passionate disagreement.

'Hush, it's been a long time for you and I need you to trust me,' he soothed as if he could hold that force at bay for her until he chose to let it rip, but still she writhed and gasped and at last he was there, at the very centre of her and she felt deliciously stretched and completed and somehow even a little bit smug.

'I can take you though, can't I?' she gloated against his sweat-slicked throat this time and felt his pulse thunder and the iron self-control it was taking him to still his sex hard and high inside her and let her ease into loving him as Nate never had. She stopped the contact of her mouth to his hammering pulse and lay back and frowned at the thought of how invaded and somehow belittled she'd felt during this very act with her husband and how cared for and right and glorious it was to feel James at the very centre of her secret core. Somehow she knew there was even more to look forward to than being open and hot and happy about him being right here, inside her where only he belonged.

'Forget him,' he said harshly. 'If he wasn't dead I'd

have to kill him, first for being here before me, then for teaching you to expect too little of your lovers.'

'Only you,' she protested and he kissed her this time and as soon as their lips touched again she forgot Nate and all his gritted teeth and harsh fumbling.

Now he moved and, oh, it was exquisite, almost on the edge of being too much pleasure for a woman to endure without fainting, she decided as he set a rhythm that was old as time and new as this very second. She picked up the beat of it and matched him as they went from trot to gallop and her legs wrapped about his neat buttocks and urged them both on almost by instinct. Together, headlong in a heart-racing, wonderful race to whatever came next. That mystery she'd sensed before beckoned irresistibly as he changed the rhythm of loving her with his body and somehow managed to go harder and even deeper within her as she felt him strain every honed sinew and muscle he had to hold back until she knew where they were going, as well. It felt a little lonely for a moment when he rose, poised and jaw clenched as if almost at the edge of human endeavour, then she let herself know this was James, the man who put her pleasure before his own, so she relaxed and let the glow spread, then flex, then convulse into something beyond her, beyond either of them.

Her mouth went wide and she gave a long gasp of absolute delight, then she opened her eyes to watch his because she didn't want a single bit of her to be alone any more. Even in the semi-darkness she saw the intriguing grey centre of them silver and how could she know the rest was even more vividly green than ever by firelight? In daylight she would see them flare and burn brighter green than ever, but now she gloated over watching him and guessing all that as he shuddered and bucked and gasped for joy even as she did the same. Completion of one by another felt like a perfect gift between them and if they could watch each other slip into this huge, generous ecstasy together, why would they want to miss a moment by shutting their eyes? The sheer, lovely pleasure of it all seemed to last almost for ever, then it was over and she knew it could never last long enough. Those moments of absolute unity she had no idea lovers could give each other until this very moment were so precious she didn't want to let a single second of it go to waste.

Now he seemed to recall he was a gentleman, though, and moved his weight off her, even as she wished him a little less of a one for a moment. She curled into him as he heaved himself to one side and lay still and breathless, as if getting out of bed ever again could be beyond even his whipcord strength. The reality and might of his body under all that fine linen and perfect tailoring was both a novelty and a familiar delight to her. She padded questing fingers over the light dusting of dark hair across his chest and downwards where it arrowed towards his manhood, as if she needed any more encouragement to be fascinated by the source of so much delicious fulfilment for his lover.

'I dare not stay all night,' he warned her in a rusty voice that sounded as if he really didn't want to say the words. 'The children wake sometimes,' he explained with a shrug that shifted her attention from the newly discovered wonders of James Winterley and made her look into his ridiculously handsome face instead.

'You keep forgetting I have five younger brothers

and sisters,' she told him, some of the hurt she felt at being cut out of his and his waifs' lives even by her own contriving openly on display and she was too sated and undefended to care.

'And you forget they could be in jeopardy as well as you, if this mysterious villain I'm trying to unmask ever realises how much you mean to me.'

'How much do I, then?'

'More than you want to, I suspect,' he said stiffly and there it was again, all the hurt and alienation he'd lived with since he was little more than a boy and she'd only added to it by sending him away. She couldn't bring herself to poker up and agree he was simply a passing fancy, a source of feminine curiosity she had satisfied by finding out how a true lover of women took a bedmate.

'Impossible. You don't think I'd break a vow I made never to do that again when Nate died for anyone less important than you, do you?'

'I doubt you ever did that properly when he was alive, so are you going to tell me all about it before we go any further together or not?'

'I suppose you think it might even the score a little between us, sir?' she asked lightly and even as she said it she knew it was the wrong thing to say. 'No, don't turn away from me. I was defending myself by dragging up the memory of what a truly monstrous female did to the boy you once were. I really don't need to keep you at a distance any more after I let you so far into myself, do I?'

'I hope not,' he said very seriously.

It felt like a promise, so she cherished it as one and

leaned up to meet his eyes whilst she told her story, because somehow she knew she had to convince him she wasn't holding part of herself in reserve now and she did so badly want to be as close to him as she could get, for as long as he would let her.

'I think Nate was at war with himself,' she finally admitted with the true seriousness she felt her late husband deserved, one last time. 'Soldiering made everything worse for him somehow. We married when he was not quite of age and I was eighteen and I doubt he knew a great deal more about the big wide world than I did. He probably knew less now I think about it properly. Living in a large country parish means not much of the basic sins and glories of the human kind can be hidden from a tribe of children who escaped their books too often to be kept away from real life.' She paused to think about that notion and shook her head. 'Even so, I had a head full of dreams back then. I watched Callie and Gideon fall in love and expected the same thing at any second while I waited to be grown up enough to wed my hero.'

'Most very young women share that hope,' he said as if that should comfort her and it did, mainly because he hoped it would. A new and much bigger hope was beginning to touch her heart now and she felt her heart race at the vulnerability of feeing real love and longing for it in return, even as she smiled up at him and trailed a wickedly adventurous finger down his jaw.

'If only I'd met you back then instead, everything might have been different,' she said and that splinter of joyous anticipation wouldn't quite go away and let her turn away from his gaze as she went on. 'I didn't, though. Nathaniel seemed the embodiment of those dreams to the silly girl I was, so I decided to marry him, even though he wasn't you and I should have known better.'

'He had no choice in the matter, then?' he objected and wasn't it lovely to have such a stalwart partisan to defend her, even if she didn't deserve him?

'Not much. I realise now I was a hope rather than a dream for him, one he couldn't resist giving himself to become the man he felt he should be.'

'Ah, I'm getting an inkling what you meant when you said he was at war with himself. I take it your husband was not a natural lover of women?'

'No,' she agreed, relieved he understood what she meant and she didn't have to expose poor Nate's tortured battles with himself more openly. 'He married me because he wanted to love me enough to overcome his urges not to, if you see what I mean?' she said as delicately as she could because from here Nate seemed a sad and rather lost boy, not the angry tyrant he'd become when saddled with a wife he never truly wanted.

'I do and, whatever the naysayers think, it's more of a sin he spoiled both your lives by fighting his true inclinations than if he'd accepted them and spared you both misery.'

'So do I now. At the time I wasn't so generous.'

'How did your life with him go, then? Come on, Rowena, you might as well tell me and get it over with. You know my deepest and darkest secrets, it seems only fair you tell yours in return,' he said with a smile that made a joke of that secret knowledge and who would have thought he could ever do that, even with a lover?

Again that stubborn jolt of yearning for more than he could give tugged at her heart. If he could joke about his dearest secrets with her, there was a chance of something more lasting than mere passion and convenience between them, wasn't there? Maybe this was a time not to think about boundaries and *if*s or *maybe*s, perhaps it was time they let what they had grow until they found out what it could be?

'Very well, then, I suppose you're right. The painful truth is I disliked the so-called joys of the marriage bed even more than my husband. Luckily Nate found me less and less desirable as time went on and I can hardly blame him. I did my best to avoid offering him any encouragement and after the first year or so he left me alone, except when he was drunk. Then our situation was my fault and I suppose it didn't matter to him that he hurt me. When he was posted in this country or Ireland we could cover up how hollow our marriage was even from each other with all the little social comings and goings officers and their wives organise to stop themselves thinking how serious army life is under the glitter and polish. Then we went to Portugal to fight a real war, as Nate called it, and the gaiety no longer hid the truth that staying alive day by day is the whole business of being on campaign. By then if there was no fire to cook his dinner on that was my fault, if his washing couldn't be done I hadn't tried hard enough. When I bled every month, at least until our lives got so hard it stopped, he found me disgusting and that was definitely my fault.'

James's fingers flexed into fists for a moment. Then he seemed to force himself to relax as he read the unsaid parts of her story and knew she was too well acquainted with violence already. 'I always said he was a fool, didn't I?' he asked with a caress down the clean lines of her jaw to remind them he wanted her rampantly and abidingly and cared about her feelings and hopes and fears, even if he didn't quite love her.

'So you did, Mr Winterley, so you did,' she whispered and it wasn't the same sort of driven need to find out everything in his arms as it was earlier. Or at least it wasn't at the outset. This time it began gently and reassuringly, but any kiss with this man must go beyond a simple need for comfort, at least as long as they were both breathing and had enough privacy to nurture it.

'I meant to leave you be for the rest of the night,' he whispered after they'd tested the magic once more and found out it was still wondrous. 'Have I made you sore?'

'No, and I'm no virgin for you to be so delicate about making love to me again. You made me feel like one tonight, though, James, and I thank you for that. But does it matter to you that I've already been bedded by another man?'

'Of course not,' he said so abruptly and with such a fearsome frown of disgust at the very idea it might that at least she knew he was telling the truth. 'I wish you never had to endure the loneliness of being initiated into what ought to be lovemaking by a dolt. The idiot had the enchanting girl you must have been at eighteen in his bed and chose to make her feel unwanted and unloved, instead of cherished to the finest extremity and desired endlessly with every chance he had. That only matters to me because I wish I could have fallen on you like a starving man then as well as now, my lovely. I begrudge him the painfully young Rowena Finch he didn't treasure to add to my collection of Rowena moments we're going to create together for the rest of our lives.'

So he intended to marry her again, did he? And was prepared to call her his lovely, but not his beloved? She told the sliver of secret hope still stubbornly alive and eager for more; maybe in time he'd do better and it could live on a little longer.

'Joanna will be married next week,' she heard herself say for no reason at all as far as she could tell.

'Hmm, would they agree to share, do you think? Or shall we ask your papa to make use of the special licence we're going to need if we're to get ourselves up the aisle before Advent on a different day?'

'Don't you want to keep us a secret, then?'

'It may come as something of a shock to you, madam, but there is a fatal flaw in the argument that a man and wife can be secretive about owning up to one another for very long.' He let his hand rest possessively on her naked belly for a long sensual moment and the sharp heat inside her leapt into vivid life at much the same rate as his fascinating green eyes blazed with all sorts of wicked possibilities. 'Never let it be said I corrupted the Vicar of Raigne's eldest daughter for more than a week or two before I got her up the aisle and made her my wife,' he said, as if he was as virtuous and upright as Joanna's Mr Greenwood, who had always known he wanted to be a clergyman one day and only dared hope he'd find a wife like Miss Joanna Finch in his wildest dreams.

'You kept away from me for a month and don't try to tell me it was because I lied about wanting you. You didn't want to risk breaking your splendid isolation, did you, James?' she made herself ask coolly.

'Oh, but I did,' he whispered. 'I've wanted to risk that from the first moment I met your astonishingly blue eyes full on as you condemned me across half a churchyard. Ever since that day your little sister was busy terrifying the life out of us and you stubbornly refused to let my latest enemy shoot me it's been more a certainty than a risk, but I had to convince you it was inevitable we would end up like this somehow,' he assured her with a lazy wave at the naked bits of them even the most enthusiastic lover could expose on a November night when he was far too warm and sated to get out of bed and make up the fire.

'You made a very fine job of hiding it right until that last day, then.'

'Of course I did, woman, that's what I did before I knew you properly. Why would I want my world turned upside down in the first place, let alone admit you could do it between one icy blue gaze and the next? It took weeks of trying to force you out of my life to prove it can't be done. I was trying to stay away from you for your own good, as well. I have a snake on my tail, Mrs Westhope, unless you have forgotten?'

'I thought you must have done, to risk asking me to marry you again.'

'This particular enemy knows too much about me. It feels more of a risk to leave you free to wander the countryside at will with him ready to use any means he can come up with to get me at a disadvantage. I can't stand not knowing if you're safe or not any longer, Rowena, the chance he'll work out how much I want you haunts me night and day. It's a risk, this life I'm hoping you want to live with me and my waifs. I shouldn't even suggest it again if I was truly a gentleman, but somehow I can't help myself.'

'How flattering,' she said, trying not to let herself sigh for the romantic proposal every woman had a right to hope for from her lover, didn't she?

'And, of course, you're far too unforgettable for comfort as well,' he added as if even admitting that much cost him an effort.

'Never was a man more reluctant to take a wife, however many times you've told me I'm going to marry you. I'm not sure I like being grudgingly accepted as part of your new life, Mr Winterley.'

'I'm making a complete mess of this, aren't I?'

'Yes, I've had more romantic offers of marriage.'

'Never a more sincere one,' he argued with what looked to her like a fearsome frown at the idea of Nate outdoing him in any way. 'Will you marry me, Rowena Finch?'

She seriously considered how her life would be without him in it after finding this world of warmth and wanting and mutual need she could have with him. It would be bleak and barren and almost unendurable, she concluded. It was a huge risk to say yes, but how stupid not to take it when she looked at the alternative of living without him.

'Very well, James, I will,' she agreed, without any of the assurances of undying love his brothers-in-arms had made earlier this year to their lucky wives.

Which made her more desperate than Lady Farenze, Lady Mantaigne or Lady Laughraine to marry her hero, she supposed; or more realistic, perhaps? Better to have what you could get than wish for the moon. All the same, she felt a passionate envy of those women for marrying such besotted husbands biting at her heart as she tried to pretend she already had what she wanted.

'I'll do anything I can to make you happy, Rowena,' he promised her so gravely it made tears stand in her eyes.

'I know you will, James,' she replied softly and did her best to meet his eyes with a serene acceptance that promise would go as far as he could let it and no further. 'Simply concentrate on staying alive and that will do me very well,' she told him because it was true.

'I fully intend to, but marrying you means I have to hunt this fox down and make sure he can't threaten you or my family before we finally settle down to raising our children,' he promised and she saw sharp purpose in his expression and shivered briefly for the man about to be outfoxed by a better one. Then she remembered how close the cur had come to killing James that first day in the woods and knew she wouldn't waste a moment's pity on his foe when the man was exposed for the cowardly vermin he was.

'It's as well I already know the best and worst of family life, as you come equipped with a family before we start,' she said with a smile because she was looking forward to knowing his waifs and perhaps being accepted as their mother one day.

'You don't mind them, do you? I can't bring myself to hand them over to the nearest orphan asylum, even though they're driving me halfway to the madhouse with their antics already and even the eldest is only four years old.'

'Of course not; I always wanted a family and if Nate and I worked harder at our marriage I might have to ask you the same question. The truth is I like children, but please don't tell my brothers and sisters. They're hard enough to manage as it is.'

'I suspect they already know,' he said and maybe all this would turn out well for his children and them as well, she decided, rather dazzled by the tenderness in his smile.

Chapter Sixteen

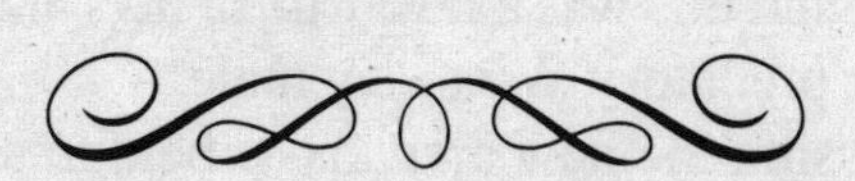

Stretching herself sleepily a few mornings after James became her lover, Rowena woke and stretched deliciously. Her body still felt sensuous and sated hours after he left this secretive little eyrie of theirs just before sunrise. He'd come to her bed every night and stayed as long as he dared, whatever limits he'd put on their time together at the outset. The children's nurse must know her employer spent his nights somewhere else and no doubt had a very shrewd notion whom he spent them with, but she'd said nothing.

Even from her eyrie on the other side of Raigne from the main drive, Rowena heard a minor uproar this morning. With a quick frown to try and silence Sally's endless stream of chatter so she could listen harder for a clue to who it might be, Rowena nodded absently at one of the morning gowns Chloe sent from Darkmere with her husband, claiming they were too tight for her now and it seemed a shame to waste them when they would be out of fashion before she could fit into them again, if she ever managed to do so. Smiling at the idea of slender-as-a-wand Chloe Winterley grown so fat she couldn't make most of her peers green with envy, Rowena took a last look at herself in the ancient silver mirror and decided she looked a bit too pleased by what she saw as the effect such a cunningly cut gown would have on James dawned. She must go to London in the spring and pick gowns of her own to drive him demented with as she thought Chloe was lying and this was a favourite of hers and her own particular predatory Winterley male.

Dismissing the new arrivals as benign since they were making no effort to hide their arrival, she dreamt about the future for a few self-indulgent minutes. No, there were more serious matters to consider than a visit to an exclusive modiste to order the wardrobe of fine gowns James vowed she'd have if he had to pick it out himself, since she was so attached to her chain mail he didn't trust her not to resume it as soon as he took his eyes off her. No doubt he knew a little too much about exclusive London dressmakers, so he most certainly wouldn't be choosing her gowns. Where was the mystery in that?

Anyway, this morning she was clad in a soft rose-pink wool gown and a fine muslin underslip that was exquisitely embroidered and buttoned to the neck. Somehow such an outwardly demure gown managed to invite the right man to find and intimately explore the woman underneath so delicately Rowena wondered if it was altogether wise to venture outside her bedchamber in it.

'I think I'm getting the way of this new style Lady Laughraine says you should wear your hair in at last, aren't I, madam?' Sally asked earnestly.

Rowena eyed the sleepy-eyed, elegant creature in

the dressing mirror and nodded at her as if greeting a stranger. It felt odd to take trouble with her appearance again, to love the feel and slide and texture of fine cloth and even better cutting against her newly sensitive skin. If not for James, she would go back to dressing for purely practical reasons and slide back into her old self like a pair of worn slippers, but he was here. He was always close now, however far away he might actually be, and the woman she was with him outshone any version of herself she ever dreamt of as dowdy Mrs Westhope. Yes, she was glad to be the Rowena in the mirror, the one who looked out on the world with a certain confidence and trust it wouldn't throw bricks at her. Progress, she decided with a wry smile and it turned smug at the thought of what this gown would do to her own personal predator.

'You help me look very fine in my borrowed plumage, thank you, Sally.'

'You always did look fine, even in all those muddy greys you would wear, ma'am. You didn't seem to know it until Mr Winterley offered for you and you said yes, though.'

'Maybe you're right,' Rowena said with a blush when she thought of the time and place of his proposal she really must learn to control in future.

She had said yes to him a little bit too often since to feel quite comfortable when she and James went to see her father yesterday for their premarital talk with their vicar and, if she hadn't loved her husband-to-be before they went, she would have done afterwards. James was so endearingly serious about it all that even Papa congratulated her sincerely for finding the right man to marry this time.

'I shall be keeping a much closer eye on Rowena's husband this time, my boy,' he joked with a thread of seriousness underlying it. 'And you played into my hands in buying a property within such easy reach of the Raigne villages.'

'At the time I purchased it I wasn't aware I'd be marrying your daughter before the year was out, but I'm glad you and Mrs Finch will be nearby, should Rowena need you,' James responded and Rowena shivered. He meant he wanted them close in case the man on his trail succeeded in killing him and she was left alone and so bereft she couldn't even bear to think about it.

'I wonder who has arrived, Sally?' she asked, trying hard not to admit a part of her would be frozen and dead for ever if she lost James now.

If he was going to die at the hands of an assassin you'd think he'd have the consideration to do it before I fell in love with him, wouldn't you? The well-dressed woman in the mirror looked more composed than the real Rowena felt at the very thought of ever having to live without him. *Then you'd best make sure he doesn't do anything of the kind, hadn't you?* the annoyingly serene-looking creature replied in her head and was she now going insane from loving the wretched man when he didn't love her? Sometimes she thought he couldn't make love to her so intensely and tenderly without loving her, but in that case why wouldn't he say so? Since he hadn't, she had to live with the notion he was too honest at heart to pretend an emotion he didn't feel.

Rowena frowned at the woman reflected back at her and made one final check she looked neat as a pin before going downstairs to find out what the noise had been about and show the world she was very happy to be marrying James in little more than a week, even if he wasn't in love with her.

'Thank goodness you're all still here,' possibly the tallest and most vital lady Rowena had ever seen was saying to her host when Rowena reached the foot of Raigne's grandest staircase.

'I might agree if at least half of me wasn't still tucked up in bed and dreaming at this hour of the morning,' Gideon said as he ran a hand through his dark hair and yawned.

'Where's Tom?' James asked with a frown as he joined them in the hall and at least now Rowena had a clue to the lady's identity.

James took Rowena's hand as if he couldn't be in the same space and not make skin-to-skin contact, even if this was all they could have right now, and she didn't care if the lady turned out to be Empress of all the Russias as his warmth scotched some of her doubts about loving him more than he'd ever love her.

'With the second coach,' the Marchioness of Mantaigne replied placidly, her gaze on their locked hands and her smile triumphant. 'I can't wait to tell him his godmother has done it again.'

'Of course she has,' said Gideon as if he'd never doubted it, whatever it might be. 'Second coach; however many of you are there?' he demanded hastily when he noted Rowena's bewildered expression. Why was he trying to divert her from whatever the Marquis of Mantaigne's godparent had done?

'All of us,' the lady said. 'Well, not Partridge and

Prue, and Tom persuaded the boys to leave the dogs behind somehow. The others insist nobody's going to kidnap them and why should they chase about the countryside with a pack of hell-born brats ripe for mischief if they don't have to.'

'Who was kidnapped, then?' James's voice cut through the hubbub. 'My apologies,' he went on more smoothly, 'James Winterley at your service, Lady Mantaigne.'

'I'm still doing my best to forgive Tom for that, but I'm glad to meet Lady Virginia's last boy, Mr Winterley.'

Before James could cut through Rowena's confusion, one of the most handsome men Rowena had ever set eyes on strode into the hall. The look he cast his lady was rueful, tender and bemused all at the same time, as if he'd stumbled on a huge adventure when he met her and was still trying to get used to his good fortune, so of course he was the Marquis of Mantaigne and even Rowena had heard of him.

'Causing havoc as usual, my love?' the former rake about town asked ruefully before he stepped forward to greet Gideon, then James as if they were truly his brothers.

Something about the three of them standing there told Rowena James belonged to a close and powerful family, whatever rubbish he talked about walking alone, then Lord Farenze strolled down the stairs to join them and there were four strong men linked by birth and friendship. All these years of James avoiding those he loved because of the evil creature his brother married the first time around made Rowena want to do a dead woman harm. So she caught James's eye and smiled up at him as trustingly as she knew how instead.

'Rowena, this is my adoptive brother, the Marquis of Mantaigne, and his lovely lady,' he said, 'and I suspect Raigne is about to be invaded by a tribe of less lovely Trethaynes, unless that's the sound of an invading army thundering down the drive. Tom, Lady Mantaigne, this is Mrs Westhope, shortly to be my very own Mrs Winterley.'

'I am very pleased to meet you, Mrs Westhope, but I hope you'll call me Polly,' the lady said with a disarming smile. 'I don't feel like Lady Mantaigne even after six months of—' Polly was interrupted by a troop of boys all talking at once.

'Enough!' Lord Mantaigne's voice rang over the chatter of six boys and another almost-responsible adult. 'Now line up ready to be introduced properly.'

The lads sorted themselves by height and shunted one another up or down the line with not-very-subtle nudges and loudly whispered insults.

'These unappealing brats are Tobias, Henry and Josh, Jago, Joe and Benjamin, and this is our very good friend Lady Wakebourne. My apologies for leaving you until last, ma'am, but we both know these urchins will only stay still for so long.'

Lord Mantaigne managed to look proud of every fidgeting one as Rowena tried to work out if any of them were his.

'The first three rascals are my brothers; Jago, Joe and Benjie plague the life out of Lady Wakebourne on a daily basis and she still hasn't disowned them,' Lady Mantaigne clarified and all six preened as if they'd been pronounced of the blood royal.

* * *

After that the morning passed in something of a blur. Callie was willing, but still a little too fragile to join the mayhem, so Rowena helped Polly and her formidable friend amuse six headlong boys and James's trio of waifs while James and Lord Farenze and Gideon went into an earnest huddle with the Marquis of Mantaigne in Lord Laughraine's study.

'It only needs my brothers and sisters to find out what they're missing and we might as well call in the builders and upholsterers and be done with it,' she told Polly while Lady Wakebourne was busy trying to bring order out of the chaos and Rowena and her new friend could talk as privately as they ever would among such chatter and excitement.

'They need to run off their pent-up energy,' Polly said with a long-suffering sigh. 'Even I had no idea how restless they'd be on a long journey and they're sure to be fidgety and very likely unruly during your wedding, but I couldn't leave them at Dayspring after what happened.'

'There really was a kidnapping, then?' Rowena whispered as the boys whooped with delight as Lord Mantaigne, Gideon and James entered Raigne's famous Long Gallery with James's elder brother. James's three little ones raced after their new friends and Rowena was relieved they'd stopped clinging to him as if he was their only hope in an unsafe world.

'Do you know much about James Winterley's past?' Polly asked cautiously.

'I know he's not who most people think he is and has at least one dangerous enemy.'

'I'm glad he's told you that much about himself,

since even Tom had to prise bits of the tale out of him and surmise the rest and they're close as brothers. I don't want to spend the rest of my life wondering which bits of his life James Winterley has confessed to you so I don't put my foot in my mouth every time I open it.'

'That would make life difficult,' Rowena said, trying not to laugh.

'Well, it would,' her new friend told her with a wry smile. 'I'm doing my best to be polite and restrained and ladylike for Tom's sake, but I don't want to pretend with my friends and I hope you'll be one of those?'

'I'll be delighted if you want me to be.'

'Good, then let's talk about kidnappers while the men take this mob outside to run off some energy and try to pretend nothing's wrong.'

'Will they be safe?'

'Men or children?'

'Both.'

'They'll all survive, I dare say. Would you want to take them on?'

Rowena surveyed a quartet of fully mature aristocrats and shook her head. One by one they were astute and powerful men—together they were formidable.

'Neither would I, but now I can tell you a pair of hired men snatched Benjie and Josh a few days ago. I suppose they thought the littlest were least trouble.'

'How did you get them back?'

'They climbed up the chimney and down the roof, then threw themselves on the mercy of our local smugglers. The boys think it the best adventure they've had in weeks.'

'And what happened to the kidnappers?'

'Tom won't tell me, the protective great idiot.'

'Men,' Rowena said on a sigh.

'I know.'

They were silent for a moment as they watched their particular ones through the windows. They stood watchful and united as the shrieking, giggling crowd of children ran amok and they guarded them with every protective instinct they had plus most of Lord Laughraine's outside staff stationed round the park.

'I can't imagine how I ever lived without him now,' Lady Mantaigne admitted at last. 'I'm almost disgustingly content with my new life and so lucky I can hardly believe it at times, but we're not here to talk about me, are we?'

'I don't see why not.'

'You do know about the last Lady Farenze's will, don't you?' Polly asked obscurely and Rowena struggled with the idea she'd stepped off the edges of the known world when she agreed to marry James and become part of this family.

'No, but what can it have to do with me?'

'Just what I would have said six months ago. Lady Virginia Winterley, the previous Viscountess Farenze, left a task for each of her "boys" to undertake by rote throughout the year after she died. Maybe she wanted to keep them from moping about the place grieving for her, or perhaps she wanted them to unknot their lives and learn to be happy. Tom thinks she left the hardest problem until last...' She paused as if she couldn't think of a way to say this without wading into deep waters.

'James Winterley?' Rowena asked and it wasn't really a question, because of course he was the most complex and tricky of four very complex and tricky gentlemen.

'Exactly,' Polly said with a fond smile at her own particular rogue even though he couldn't see it and grin besottedly back for once.

'James doesn't love me,' Rowena blurted out wistfully.

'How clumsy of him to let you think so.'

'No, truly, he doesn't. I think he's as fond of me as he will ever let himself be of a woman, but he doesn't love me.'

'He knows exactly where you are all the time and I've seen the way he watches you when you're not looking. Tom taught me a lot about true gentlemen and Lady Virginia's four fine specimens in particular. That man loves you, Rowena, whether he's willing to admit it or not.'

'It's as well I agreed to marry him, then, isn't it?'

'It's terrifying when you let yourself see how surely your happiness lies in the hands of another, isn't it? I promise it's a risk well worth taking.'

'*You* were terrified?' Rowena asked sceptically.

'Of course I was. Tom's a marquis and I'm a pauper. He enjoyed his untrammelled bachelor existence with all the verve and dash he's now putting into being my husband and leader of a ready-made family. If I didn't love him so much, I'd never take that leap with Tom Banburgh, of all the men I could have fallen in love with. The wonder is he managed to love me back somehow.'

'I don't see that as much of a wonder,' Rowena said with a wry smile.

'Good, now we'd best see if they're up to their handsome necks in mischief yet and rescue your tots from my brothers before they get involved in one of their foolproof ideas for making trouble.'

Chapter Seventeen

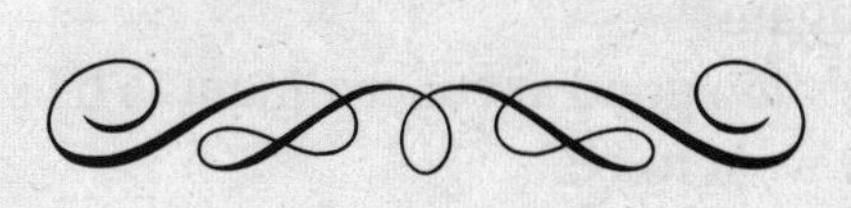

'I'm not sure about this,' James muttered. 'It's too much of a risk letting them run wild in the open.'

'I have men on watch and the neighbourhood is on the alert for strangers,' Gideon argued. 'Stop worrying—we're all in this now and you must trust us.'

'I do,' he said, still uneasy as their assorted orphans ran riot through Raigne's famous King Harry Oaks and he wondered if they'd end the day unscathed by their own efforts, let alone any his enemy had planned.

'Then trust yourself, James,' Gideon added with a straight look to remind him they both knew how to play dangerous games.

'This time it's important,' he admitted.

'Then use us. We have skills that could weigh the odds in your favour so you'd be a fool not to when you need any advantage you can get.'

'I suppose so,' he admitted reluctantly. He'd never worked with people he cared so deeply about before. Not even when he and Hebe made the world go away in each other's arms and look where that got them.

'Let's pool information, then. We can move on to

trust and the importance of it working both ways later,' Tom said lightly, but there was a steady challenge in his blue eyes James found it impossible to shrug off.

'So have you decided who is after you yet, James?' Luke asked coolly.

'No,' he replied with a frown.

'Has anyone caught sight of him prowling about the place again?'

'No, he's too good at concealment to be seen when he doesn't want to be.'

'Luke says you suspected Fouché has a hand in it,' Tom said as if yet to make his mind up if that was far-fetched or not.

James shrugged and cast a moody, longing glance back towards the Long Gallery where Rowena was probably scheming with Tom's wife not to be left out of this deadly business as they spoke. A rosy image of his three waifs grown strong and secure in their care and leading a growing pack of green- and blue-eyed urchins into mischief mustn't distract him right now. He'd learnt the hard way to stay aloof from those he was protecting. After Pamela had made that shattering move against him and Luke he'd been lonely, hurt and longing for home and he knew now that he'd rushed into a mad affair with Hebe to hold all that at bay. She was a year older, but far more experienced and ardent and almost as lonely as he was. They enjoyed each other until he led their enemies to her in his haste to forget in her arms one night.

After a breathless chase over the rooftops of Paris and a tense ride to safety through a nervous countryside to the sea, they both vowed never to bed a fellow agent again. They stayed friends, though, and years later Hebe must have loved the man who fathered her child to keep him such a secret. James's gaze drifted to the dark curls of three-year-old Amélie and he wondered again who fathered her and if there was even the slightest sign of him in his daughter.

'Bonaparte doesn't trust him as far as he could throw him, so why waste time on me?'

'Is a letter all you took that night?' Tom asked cynically.

'You think I tupped his woman? Perish the thought.'

'Somebody else's, then?'

'No, it was a business trip,' James said shortly, 'I was sent to stop the holes in the Paris network and brought Hebe's child home instead.'

'So you didn't pull any other wild stunts?' Gideon asked.

'It was important to get the child away before someone used her in the bloody game we were playing.'

'So you went to look for a spy who spies on his own side?' Tom asked.

'I did, but I was warned my cover was broken before I could find him,' James said grimly.

'Wasn't that convenient for whoever made those holes? Perhaps you know more than you think,' Gideon suggested.

'It's my job to know what I think. If aught happens to me, you three will look after my orphans and the others I tried to help, won't you? Your old senior partner-at-law has a list, Gideon. I had to trust someone and he's the most cunning lawyer I ever met, bar you.'

'Thank you, but, no,' Gideon said calmly. 'If we make such a promise, you might not fight as hard not to be killed by this mystery assassin.'

'He will; he's in love,' Tom argued.

'That explains a lot, I suppose,' Gideon said and Luke just grinned.

'No, it doesn't,' James asserted with exaggerated patience.

'Won't admit it,' Gideon said and made James's fist itch.

'Can't let himself say so,' Tom added as if he wasn't here.

'Too much of an idiot to know what's in his heart,' Luke joined in and James glared at him.

'Never mind me. This is about them,' he said with a wave at their responsibilities.

'Until we know why they're in danger, we can never be sure they're safe,' Tom said soberly.

'So kindly get on and use the brains you appear to have been born with,' Gideon demanded. 'I refuse to spend the next thirty-odd years worrying when your murky past will catch up with us.'

'And you have a life of your own to live now, Little Brother,' Luke reminded him and James's gaze went back to the windows of the Long Gallery and his hope Rowena was still safely in there quizzing her new friend about Virginia and her influence on all their lives.

'I've never used my own name when I was on a mission,' James mused. 'Even Hebe had no idea who I am and I was far closer to her than I should have been. My cover was good enough to fool Bonaparte's spies and you three all these years. Why did it fail when it mattered?'

'Who else knows you're not a bored aristocrat or a casual buyer of this and that?' Gideon asked and made James think about loyalties he hadn't wanted to question.

'Only the man who originally recruited me and his son. Bowood took over his father's work when the man was ill a few years ago. There was a leak then, but Harry caught an informer double dealing and we thought he'd stopped it once and for all.'

'Who holds records of operatives and what information they provide?'

'Nobody else knows; or so they assure me.'

'Then they have phenomenal memories, or are lying.'

'True, perhaps I'm not as clever as I think I am.'

'Or it didn't matter enough to question their records until now.'

'Probably not,' James conceded, distracted by the sight of Polly and Rowena strolling towards them.

'Love,' Tom greeted his wife simply and kissed her while Gideon watched the grove from this vantage point and James tried to avoid Rowena's acute blue gaze.

'Mrs Westhope,' he greeted her warily.

'Mr Winterley,' she challenged back.

'I wish I'd never come here,' he said and felt clumsy as a spotty youth with his first lover. Of course she took that remark personally and glared at him accusingly. 'They would be safe if I'd stayed away, barring my three, I suppose,' he explained.

'Their lives so far haven't been very safe,' she argued. 'But they're loved now and that makes up for a great deal. You spent years protecting your brother and niece in the only way you could and now you have them. It's time you let someone care for you, James.'

'I can look after myself and I've done little to deserve being cared for,' he said wearily.

'I shall put it down to love, whatever clever arguments you marshal. Fool yourself if you want to, but you can't fool them any longer,' she informed him coolly, with a wide gesture at the assembled men and children. 'Or me,' she challenged directly.

'I have to, Rowena,' he informed her in a raw voice, knowing even now some cold-eyed assassin might be sighting his rifle on her. 'I can't afford to love and nor should you.'

'Even a pauper can love and be loved, but not Mr James Winterley? I pity you,' she told him sternly and began to walk away.

'You can't go,' he protested as he grabbed her arm to stop her heading into the parkland. 'Have you any idea what a weapon you'd be in my enemy's hands?'

'And you pretend we're just lovers who like one another a little?'

Anyone waiting for a chance to slip the knife between his ribs could watch them staring at each other as if it was impossible to look away. Breaking the contact with an effort he felt in every inch of his body, he cast a hasty look about him to check woods and hollows for his foes. Half the Imperial Guard might be concealed in there; they would be too far away to hit much, but a spyglass could tell anyone interested that he couldn't take his eyes off his betrothed and how had he let that happen?

'Do you want my soul as well as my attention?' he protested painfully.

'No, that's enough to be going on with. I didn't want to care about you either, you know?'

'Then apparently we're fighting the same battle.'

'Not on equal terms,' she argued. How could he not want the fiendish woman as she stood there defying every notion he had about independence and isolation? 'You came here armed with elegant indifference and an aloofness it would take a cavalry charge to destroy.'

'You're more than a match for any armaments I have.'

'No, I'm not and you hold the love of your own family in reserve,' she said as if they were discussing the weather and he'd underestimated her yet again. She knew they were probably being watched and had staged a dare to his enemies as well as him.

'Maybe I do,' he admitted shakily because Rowena had more courage in her little finger than he had in his whole body.

He waited with every muscle tensed in protest at her risking so much, fearing the bullet that could whine past them or find its mark this time and end his life one way or the other. Shoot her and he might as well be cold in his grave for all the good he'd ever be.

'I know you do, but I refuse to stay on the edges of your life until you recall there's a wife-shaped gap in your life. Live in the now or don't bother to fight that battle, James,' she dared him and he could see the resolution it cost to demand he take them seriously as two people who could love and honour each other for life. 'Don't tell me this is the wrong time. It will always be wrong if that's how you're going to think. I won't stay around waiting for there to be a later for us, when you're not quite so busy.'

'The Laughraines and Winterleys are entwined branches of the same tree now, whether they like it or not, and you're like a sister to Callie and Gideon, so you can hardly avoid me.'

'I can, but they probably wouldn't let me.' She pointed out Gideon and Luke standing next to Polly while Tom was busy catching falling leaves with the children. 'Do you think you're the only one risking everything here?'

'No,' he admitted, looking round his tight circle of friends and knowing what a privilege it was to belong with them. 'Are you telling me you're willing to take that risk? When I'm not worth the effort?'

'Only if you meet me halfway,' she declared, then swung on her heel to march back the way she'd come. Alone, unguarded and vulnerable to the calculating gaze he could almost feel on his back.

Chapter Eighteen

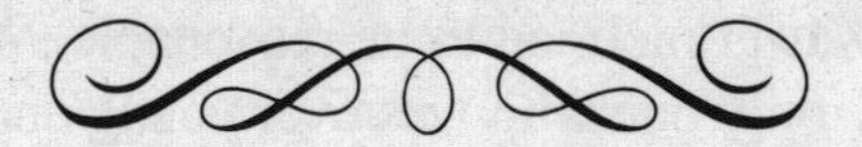

Either James must chase Rowena, or not trust his friends to keep his family safe. The cunning witch was even trickier than Virginia. He hesitated, met Gideon's enigmatic gaze with a nod and hurried in Rowena's wake. He had to lengthen his stride to stand a chance of overtaking her before she ran for home at the vicarage instead of Raigne. She could lose him in the thick woodland between here and King's Raigne village if he let her get away.

'Damned fool woman,' he cursed under his breath, then caught her arm in time to stop her running down the first track through the woods to King's Raigne vicarage. 'Are you trying to kill yourself?' he asked when she swung about and faced him furiously.

'Leave me alone,' she demanded through gritted teeth.

'No, you'll run smack into one of my enemies and defeat me.'

'Then trust me, James; let us be more. We can beat this creeping jackal together.'

He hesitated, every instinct screaming he couldn't

let her take such a risk, but if he didn't, what was left? The thought of his life without her was terrifying, so blank and comfortless that he knew she was right and he was a coward.

'If I love you, it could get you killed, Rowena,' he told her gruffly.

'And it might help me be more alive than I ever dreamed possible,' she said with a look that told him she still wasn't inclined to be reasonable. 'You think you're the only one who was ever young and foolish? I fell in love with an illusion, James, and it came close to breaking me. Tell me my judgement and instincts are right this time and you're truly my love and my hero, because right now I feel a hundred times a fool for loving you. This time it's no illusion and I know I'll be afflicted with it for life. Now walk away and leave me be, because if it's not going to be love you feel for me, I won't settle for less.'

'Yes,' he said about as enthusiastically as a man about to ascend the scaffold. He saw her flinch and stepped forward to grab her arms and hold her until he could get her to stop risking a hair on her head. 'I mean, yes, I love you, heaven help me. If I didn't, I'd be tempted to strangle you right now.'

'Sweet,' she said with an ironic smile he could hardly have outdone in his halcyon days as a supposedly carefree society buck.

'If you want pretty words and easy smiles, you've got the wrong man on the wrong day,' he told her grumpily.

'Now I've made you admit you love me, I can at least tell you I think you're the right man for me every day for the rest of our lives,' she informed him kindly and how come she looked more vivid and alive as he watched her with reluctant fascination, this woman he loved so deeply he couldn't keep her out of his life however hard he tried.

'I love,' he informed her out loud as if it was the eighth wonder of the world. 'I can love,' he added foolishly.

'Verbs *and* conjugations now?' she said with a laugh he realised he'd been waiting to hear sound carefree and light as an autumn leaf for so long.

'I love you,' he confirmed as if it was a huge revelation to both of them, then blinked as she smiled at him openly and fully for the first time. None of the wariness that once shadowed her bluest of blue eyes held that smile back now. All the Rowena Finch a man could ever dream of shone out of her. How could he have been such a damned fool as not to know he wanted this woman to truly shine only for him?

'Excellent, I've caught you two alone at last.' Bowood's smooth and precise voice interrupted this moment of revelation and discovery. 'I've been wanting to congratulate you on your engagement since I read about it in the *Morning Post*,' he added genially.

'Thank you—' James started to say, though he wished the man at Jericho.

'It was you in the wood that day,' Rowena interrupted and so many things he'd wondered about seemed to fall into place, even as James almost dismissed them as impossible. Except he trusted her judgement and an instinct he'd been ignoring far too long whispered it wasn't as outlandish an idea as it sounded.

'What wood?' the man asked, looking as if searching for the quickest way to escape a pair of lunatics.

'That one,' she said steadily, waving at Lord Laughraine's arboretum.

'Why would I be in the same wood as you and not make myself known?' he replied, but there was a blank wariness in his eyes that made James shiver.

'Maybe you were taking your best shot at a man you call friend, but use without a second thought whenever it suits you?' Rowena cut across his excuses.

'You fool, what have you been telling her?'

'The truth,' James said steadily. 'Although I don't think you're that familiar with it.'

'How much does she know, then?'

'*She* knows all she needs to,' Rowena said implacably. 'You used James, played on his guilt and deliberately widened the cracks between him and his family. You stayed home and reaped the benefits of his success in the dirty trade your father introduced him to when he was too young and alone to resist the idea he was needed, if only by leeches like you.'

'You loose-mouthed fool, Winterley.'

'At least I'm not a murderer,' James said slowly, as so much he should have made himself think about long ago finally fell into place.

'No, you're too damned honourable. You collect strays and you ruined a perfectly good mission for the sake of a woman who couldn't say no to a man if her life depended on it. Now you're fool enough to want to marry the latest in line. At least Hebe la Courte was an aristocrat, before her country turned on their betters, not a country nobody like this one.'

'How do you know about Hebe? I never told you she was my contact in Paris.'

'I'm the spymaster, not the pawn. I know far more

about you than you will ever dare tell her,' Bowood blustered with a contemptuous wave at Rowena that made James wish he'd kept a pistol in his pocket, never mind the danger with six enterprising boys on the look-out for a likely plaything and one or two of them that could pick his pocket.

'I know all I need to,' Rowena said calmly. 'You killed her, didn't you? That's what this is all about.'

'I have no idea what you mean. I didn't know the woman.'

'Yet Amélie has your eyes, Mr Bowood.'

'Good Gad, so she has.' James gasped in shock as the lie that Bowood never met Amélie's mother sank without a trace. 'And you must have felt something for Hebe to make a child with her, so how could you kill her and leave your own daughter motherless?'

'I didn't, Bonaparte's police killed her.'

'You know, I don't think they did.' James said, wondering why he'd been such a simpleton about this man for so long. 'And you lied about my cover being compromised as well, didn't you? I have every ear I can call on to the ground and not a single one has heard so much as a whisper about me being a spy under any of my aliases.'

'My masters were beginning to look to the dog and not his handler, so I thought I'd give your bitch a try at the same time as I made a few contacts of my own and got hold of some money my father couldn't control into the bargain.'

'So you went to Paris to sell your father's lesser contacts and see if you could track down the woman I risked so much for when I was young?'

'She was an untied end for years, then my father fell

ill and it was my turn to have fun. So, yes, I tupped her, then she let herself get with child and refused to be rid of it. Father recovered more rapidly than I thought and nearly found out where I'd been, so I had to run back to Ireland with my tail between my legs. I had my fun, though, and who'd believe a French whore when everyone knew I spent the summer in Ireland with you, Winterley? I wasted enough time on the myth you were at some remote house party with your latest houri over the years for you to owe me that much at the very least.'

'So all those months we thought you were in Ireland you were with Hebe? No wonder she refused to tell me who the father of her child was. She must have worked out where the holes in your father's web lay and been too ashamed to admit she was ever fooled by a rat like you. I should have known it wasn't Amélie she was ashamed of, but the man who fathered her. You sold Fouché the little fish, didn't you? He must have been turning the screws tighter and tighter to make you sell him bigger ones ever since. I wonder how many brave men and women are dead because of you, but you still didn't dare tell him about me, did you? You and your father were the only ones who knew who I really was. Impossible to hide your treachery from him and his masters if you gave me up.'

'You have no proof of any of this.'

'Well, yes I do. It needs no more than Amélie's, luckily slight, resemblance to her father, does it? We found out enough to know an Englishman betrayed his country and our allies that summer. Now we know where you really were, you're the only one in the right place at the right time with access to enough of your country's secrets to have all that blood on your hands, Bowood.'

'I was in Ireland. You can't prove otherwise, because that would give away the fact you weren't there either.'

'I'll take a chance on my secrets coming out if that's the only way to unmask yours.'

'And have society turn up its nose at the brother of a viscount dirtying his hands as a spy? I doubt even Farenze's influence could gild your grubby trade with glory once that nasty little detail is out.'

'I don't much care for society or its skewed opinions any more, Bowood. Being a social outcast is nowhere near as bad as being hung for a traitor and a lot less permanent.'

'Why did you kill Amélie's mother?' Rowena asked implacably.

'Because she let out to her mother that her child was an English milord's grandchild. The stupid female wrote and asked my father to find out if any lord had mislaid a son that summer and could be persuaded to take her grandchild out of France to somewhere she might be safe from her mother's enemies. I had to stop Hebe's mouth before she came out and actually told him something that gave away the fact the brat was mine and ruined me.'

'That would have been a disaster both here and in Paris, wouldn't it?' James said scornfully, fear heavy in his gut because the man was telling them as if it didn't matter. 'If your own country didn't hunt you down and put a stop to your evil trade, then the French would see you as a loose knot they needed to snap in order to protect their own agents. So you have been hunting your own child like a quarry lest anyone drew the same conclusion Mrs Westhope has just come to, I suppose? What did you intend doing if you managed to get her out of my hands, Bowood? I suppose you killed the dam, so disposing of your own flesh and blood is simply one more step along your road to hell.'

Bowood shrugged, then seemed to feel he had to justify himself for some reason. 'There are still convents that will take a love child and keep her immured for life if a dowry is paid. Yes, if it came out I was in Paris that summer suspicion would fall on me for those leaks I pretended to plug. Fouché keeps pushing for information and offering money with one hand, then he threatens to let the British know who his source inside the Aliens Office really is with the other. I did my best not to tell him too much and at the same time keep as many of you safe as I could.'

'It that's your best, I hate to think what your worst must be like,' Rowena goaded him recklessly. Couldn't she see this man was looking for the best way to kill them?

'You're about to find out,' Bowood said almost casually and produced the two deadly little pistols he'd been concealing in his coat-tails.

'I suppose the servants directed you out here? Before that one must have taken charge of your horse and another will have carried your bags. At this very moment they are doubtless consulting our list of wedding guests and discovering you're not on it,' Rowena pointed out and how had he ever missed the fact his supposed friend was rather stupid under all that *I know everything about you* pretence? James wondered.

'Obviously I shall be eager to find you as soon as I have changed out of my dirt, but sadly I will arrive too late to stop your assailants shooting you. Luckily I'm here to organise a manhunt and nobody will think I could possibly be involved in such a tragedy. We were boyhood friends and I've been at Raigne two or three times this year, so obviously I stumbled on this attack only moments too late to prevent it. I shall have to remember to be distraught about that when there's time.'

'Friends don't shoot one another, particularly from behind a bush,' Rowena said implacably and how could James ever have doubted he loved the loyal, brave, reckless idiot?

'I'm beyond your family's reach, Winterley, and you'll be too dead to care,' the man said coolly. It would feel better to think him mad, but there wasn't a trace of manic purpose in the light-brown eyes that held his so stonily.

James was really intent on Rowena in what might be his last moments. Her hand was steady as she held it out to him and he took it for maybe the last time. Still she gave nothing away, but startled him with a quick demand.

'Down!' she ordered and yanked on his hand so hard he went without even thinking.

For the second time since they met James felt a bullet whoosh past his ear and embed itself in a tree. He waited for the next one to slam into him as he tried to roll over Rowena and block the second shot with his body. Nothing happened, so he risked a sidelong glance at the cur and discovered him lying on the ground nowhere near far enough away for comfort. The man's neatly booted legs twitched so he seemed to be alive.

'Excellent staff work, Laughraine,' he heard Tom say in his old casual drawl as he emerged from the nearest stand of brushwood.

'My thanks, Mantaigne,' Gideon said modestly, straightening up with a neat slingshot in his hand. 'Jago has a steady arm and good timing. He'll make a very fine lawyer one day,' he added as he strolled over to kick the semi-conscious Harry Bowood, then bound him with the fine cord he pulled from a pocket of his greatcoat as if a gentleman never knew when he might need to tie up an enemy and ought to be prepared.

'Don't tell Lady Wakebourne or Miss Polly, will you?' Jago said gruffly and ran off to join his friends as if felling a turncoat spy was something he did every day.

'Best if we keep it to ourselves for now, if you ask me,' Tom said calmly, then held out his hand to James, who was still sitting on the ground. He was tugged to his feet, then held out his hand to Rowena.

'You sat on me,' she complained as soon as she was upright again.

'With good reason,' he told her with a frown.

'Ah, young love, hey?' Gideon said blithely and Tom laughed.

'Come on, then, you two, Luke will be wondering what's going on and he and Lady Wakebourne have been in sole charge of the mob for long enough,' he said jovially.

'Are we going to leave him there, then?' James said as any feeling of being in charge of his own destiny seemed about to seep away.

'Well, I don't want his company, do you?' Tom asked as if it was a social problem nobody else wanted to take by the scruff of its neck and admit to.

'Certainly not, but he's a murderer and a traitor.'

'Hmm, what do you think, Sir Gideon?' Tom asked his lawyer.

'I believe we should consult my uncle, who is sure to know the right grandees to arrange a nice little passage to the Colonies for the felon we've discovered is smuggling guineas into the country and spies out, as well as selling our agents to the French. I don't think he'll have a comfortable journey, do you? I doubt he'll survive it for very long.'

'My father is a bigger grandee than any that old fool knows,' Bowood mumbled groggily as he tried to gather his scattered senses after Jago's missile hit him square on the forehead.

'Fellow's obviously deranged,' Tom said jovially, hauling the man to his feet and prodding him into motion. 'I'll take care of him if you tell me where your nearest dungeon is, Laughraine.'

'Gladly, Mantaigne, but perhaps I'd best show you myself. You two can cope with the barbarian invasion whilst I see this piece of carrion locked up, I dare say?'

'I think we can manage that, as long as you hurry back,' James said with a rueful grin at his love that said *How did this tragedy turn into a farce?* 'Together we can do almost anything,' he declared rashly.

'You haven't seen my brothers-in-law and Lady Wakebourne's hooligans in full battle cry yet,' Tom warned half-seriously as he marched his captive away and left them to it.

'No, James, we can't,' Rowena said half-heartedly

as he seized her as if he never wanted to let her go and kissed her as if his life depended on it.

'Yes, Rowena, we can.' He raised his head long enough to breathe and proved it until they were both breathless. 'Oh, we definitely can.'

'Well, maybe we can, but we really should go and rescue your brother and Lady Wakebourne first.'

'It'll be good practice for him and she must love those three rogues for some reason best known to herself, or she would never have rescued them in the first place.'

'However wayward the next generation of Winterleys proves to be they will probably only come one at a time and even Lady Wakebourne needs a helping hand now and again.'

'Don't you love me any more, then, lovely Rowena?' he joked, let her go reluctantly, then grabbed her hand because there was only so much restraint a man could endure in one go.

'I will always love you, James, but there's far too much to do for me to bed you right now, however much I might want to.'

'I know I told you to come out of your shell and assert yourself more, but there are limits, you know?' he said tenderly as he leaned his forehead against hers and stared into her eyes and never wanted to stop. 'I was so terrified I learnt all about fear in one sharp and very permanent lesson. Don't ever do that to me again, will you, love?'

'Stop making enemies, then,' she replied breathily.

He wanted to find the nearest private hollow and lay her down and make love to her until they both forgot it was November and their families were far too close for comfort and they had the rest of their lives for that. At least that part of being them hadn't changed and if it ever did he'd probably be dead.

'How did you know Gideon and his unlikely David were out there, love?' he asked as they slowly walked back towards Luke and the sound of mischief and mayhem.

'I didn't, but Polly and I agreed it was best to bring the whole thing into the open before you did something noble and dangerous and got yourself killed.'

'Instead of you?'

'No, we agreed I would lead you into the woods and when she saw that man follow us she would go and get Tom and they could think about how to disarm him when he got here.'

'That was reckless and impulsive of you, then.'

'No, it was trusting them to come up with the right plan to make sure nobody who mattered was hurt. And it worked, didn't it?'

'I suppose so, but I think it took a decade off my life even so.'

'Mine, too, since you're already one in front of me and I can't spare you.'

'Do you think I'm too old for you after all?' he asked in a sudden panic.

'Idiot,' she said rather fondly, then snuggled in under his arm so unselfconsciously he could have cheered, but didn't, in case she noticed how easy she was with him now and forgot to be so all of a sudden.

'I never thought I'd have this, you know,' he told her with a quick, tight hug of sheer joy as he snatched a look at the troop of loud and unruly children, the helplessly enthralled adults and his own particular lady warm and laughing and so loved at his side. 'For a decade and a half I convinced myself I didn't deserve this.'

'When all the time you were simply waiting to be my beloved Mr Winterley,' she said pertly and kissed him in front of anyone who wasn't part of the noise and dirt and chaos that was the family Lady Virginia Winterley had set out to build when she sat down to write letters to the four men and one woman she loved most in the world over a twelvemonth ago.

'Of course I was,' James admitted quite solemnly, then scooped up his eldest daughter as Amélie came trotting towards him with a proprietary glare at Rowena and a sharp elbow in the gut for her new brother and sister. 'James the family man,' he admitted as he submitted to rolling on the ground and being sat on by all three of them.

Your quest from me is to learn how to love with all the strength and humour and power in that great heart of yours... Virginia's words to him echoed in his head. *Mission accomplished, my love*, he silently told the woman who'd insisted on loving him when he still thought nobody should.

'I love you, Rowena Winterley,' he said as he pulled her to the ground with the rest of his ready-made family with a huge grin and a big sloppy kiss for the woman who had finally managed to crack open the hard shell he kept round his heart and march right into it with a sniff and a Rowena-type glare at the cobwebs.

'I know,' she said smugly.

* * *

It was such a fine, clear day Rowena was reminded of the one in the woods when Hes made sure she couldn't ignore James Winterley any longer. She twitched the skirts of her dark-red velvet pelisse and checked her finely twilled cream-silk wedding gown was lying straight underneath it. Eve Winterley ordered her almost-aunt to wait while she adjusted the veil on the bride's cream straw bonnet and twitched the ribbons to match her smart coat into a more perfect bow. Hes solemnly handed Rowena the neat posy of very late roses and evergreens the Raigne House gardeners had fashioned for her so beautifully.

'Ready?' Polly Banburgh asked as she and the rest of Rowena's matrons of honour gathered to greet the bride.

Three married ladies, two of them almost visibly with child, might make unusual attendants for a widowed bride, but it had felt right to push and pull and badger Chloe, Callie and Polly to walk up the aisle with her for the finale of Lady Virginia Winterley's year of wonders. If not for that lady, would any of them have met their fate this year? Rowena shivered at the thought of missing James. She would only have half a life stretching in front of her instead of this wondrous adventure if not for Lady Virginia's mission to help four men she loved perhaps more than she would the sons she couldn't have herself. *Thank you*, she whispered to a woman she'd never met.

'I'm going to marry James Winterley,' she announced, somewhere between smug and incredulous.

'Good,' Polly said briskly, 'my toes are cold and the

boys won't keep still much longer. And you do deserve one another,' she added with an impulsive hug.

'They all said it couldn't be done, Rowena,' Chloe whispered with a conspiratorial smile as they moved towards the lovely old church where James was waiting impatiently to be her last husband.

'Ah, love, I wish you so happy,' Callie chimed in.

'I shall be, Callie, trust my soon-to-be-husband for that.'

'This time I believe I can,' she replied and Rowena spared a moment out of her happiest wedding day to pity Nate, buried on a dusty battlefield so far away.

'This time I *know* you can,' Rowena said, sure and strong and blissfully in love. 'I don't quite know how it happened, but I'll settle for being grateful it has.

'Do I owe your Lady Virginia all this, do you think?' Rowena whispered to Gideon as he held out his arm to accompany her to the altar and give her away, since Reverend Finch would be conducting the wedding and Luke was James's groomsman.

'Partly—my so-called great-uncle tells me he saw James in your room very late one night and knew all Virginia's wildest dreams would come true sooner rather than later.'

'So it was him who saw us?' She only just managed not to gasp in surprise and relief that Lord Laughraine was the one down in the Old Lord's Courtyard that night and he'd never said a word.

'He was a very good friend of Virgil and Virginia's, you know? He may have learnt when to push and when to leave things be from them, don't you think?'

'Yes, but with those three busy about your affairs it's a wonder you four weren't wed years ago.'

'Even they couldn't work miracles and Virginia wanted James to be truly happy and that means he had to wait for you, love. If she was here, she'd glory in her last triumph.'

'She must have loved you all so much. She'd be dancing for joy for all her boys today if she could see you now.'

'Who says she can't?' he said as they reached the church door and the village band started a fine serenade.

Rowena caught her first glimpse of James standing tall and immaculate and, yes, nervous, at the chancel steps. 'I love that man so much,' she murmured almost to herself.

As if he'd heard, which was clearly impossible, James turned his dark head and let her and the whole world see how he felt about her. Cool and sophisticated Beau Winterley was gone and openly adoring, strong, true and passionate James Winterley, husband, brother, uncle and father stood in his place.

'Dearly beloved…' Rowena's father began the rolling, reverent words of the marriage service and his eldest daughter stepped up to start her new life as the beloved wife of the finest man she'd ever met.

'I love you quite ridiculously, James,' she whispered as soon as he'd eagerly accepted his new father-in-law's invitation to kiss the bride and they began to lead the congregation out.

'And I love you with every last unworthy bit of me, Rowena Winterley.'

'Good, because I mean to be a very happy and enthusiastic wife and I believe I shall like being Mrs Winterley quite immoderately.'

'I never did approve of moderation,' he whispered as they emerged into the clear beauty of the fine November day as husband and wife.

* * * * *